Was it possible that this had something to do with the spell we'd thought had failed?

I didn't see how a simple cosmetic charm could possibly warp itself into whatever this was, but perhaps if Grimm had miscast it, in addition to the amplification of blood...

I took my hands off my ears and began to sift through my pockets. My quill and ink were still fine. Most of the paper was damp, but I managed to find a piece from an inner pocket that had been protected by the spells woven into my coat. Tools in hand, I sat down on the stone floor and rolled my wet sleeves up so I could write without dripping over everything.

"What are you doing?" Grimm asked.

"Testing out a theory." I finished the last word of my spell with a flourish. "We're going to cast the spell we thought did nothing, same as before. Except this time, I want to hear you cast it out loud."

SORCERY *and* SMALL MAGICS

The Wildersongs: Book One

MAIGA DOOCY

orbit

orbitbooks.net

Copyright © 2024 by Maiga Doocy
Excerpt from *The Honey Witch* copyright © 2024 by Sydney Shields

Cover design by Lisa Marie Pompilio
Cover images by Shutterstock
Cover copyright © 2024 by Hachette Book Group, Inc.
Author photograph by Maiga Doocy

Orbit
Hachette Book Group
1290 Avenue of the Americas
New York, NY 10104
orbitbooks.net

First Edition: October 2024
Simultaneously published in Great Britain by Orbit.

Orbit is an imprint of Hachette Book Group.
The Orbit name and logo are registered trademarks of Little, Brown Book Group Limited.

The publisher is not responsible for websites (or their content) that are not owned by the publisher.

The Hachette Speakers Bureau provides a wide range of authors for speaking events. To find out more, go to hachettespeakersbureau.com or email HachetteSpeakers@hbgusa.com.

Orbit books may be purchased in bulk for business, educational, or promotional use. For information, please contact your local bookseller or the Hachette Book Group Special Markets Department at special.markets@hbgusa.com.

Print book interior design by Bart Dawson

Library of Congress Cataloging-in-Publication Data
Names: Doocy, Maiga, author.
Title: Sorcery and small magics / Maiga Doocy.
Description: First edition. | New York, NY : Orbit, 2024. | Series: The Wildersongs
Identifiers: LCCN 2024010680 | ISBN 9780316576758 (trade paperback) | ISBN 9780316576765 (ebook)
Subjects: LCGFT: Fantasy fiction. | Romance fiction. | Queer fiction. | Novels.
Classification: LCC PS3604.O56747 S67 2024 | DDC 813/.6—dc23/eng/20240326
LC record available at https://lccn.loc.gov/2024010680

ISBNs: 9780316576758 (trade paperback), 9780316576765 (ebook)

Printed in the United States of America

LSC-C

Printing 2, 2024

for my mom, who taught me to see magic everywhere

CHAPTER ONE

It was not my intention to cause mischief immediately upon arriving back at the Fount, despite what anyone else may tell you. And yet, by the time the night was over, I was drunk, my nose was bleeding, and Sebastian Grimm was furious with me.

It should be noted that only one of these things was unusual.

In order to understand these happenings, you must first understand the circumstances of my return to the Fount. Chiefly, that I was lucky to be there at all. My previous year of study had come to a close with an unfortunate incident involving a spell that caused one of my instructors to think she was a duck for a full hour, and no matter how much I argued that this was how the spell was *supposed to work*, no one seemed to agree that explanation made things better. I'd been allowed to come back, but it had involved quite a lot of hand-wringing and promises of good behavior (on my part), as well as some stern lectures and threats of immediate expulsion if I did not meet certain standards (on the part of the Fount's academic board).

In short: I was on thin ice before even stepping foot on the Fount grounds.

The sun was setting as I passed through the city gates, and I delayed further by grabbing my violin case and hopping out of the carriage, directing the driver to deliver the rest of my belongings without me. ("Care of Agnes Quest, if you please. She'll know where to put them.")

The Fount was situated in the city of Luxe's southern quarter, with towers of pale stone that rose high above the surrounding buildings and paper-choked depths that sank far below the city streets. Inside those walls existed a separate world that revolved entirely around magic and discipline. Not being in the mood to subject myself to either of those things a moment sooner than necessary, I veered off course and made my way to the boisterous streets of the northern quarter, where I proceeded to distract myself with music and cards and good company.

The night air was mild when I stumbled out onto the street hours later, summer still clinging to it. I decided to take the long way back in order to enjoy both the breeze and my last few moments of freedom. Despite that, I'm certain I would have reached the Fount gates before the midnight bell struck were it not for two factors:

One: I was slightly tipsy. Only slightly, but that was enough for me to be distracted by the moon, peeking out from between the building spires above me, and I took a wrong turn.

Two: I was followed by two of my companions from that night's card table.

Perhaps they were upset by the amount of their coin I'd managed to walk away with, or perhaps the celebratory winner's song I'd played whilst perched on top of the bar had rubbed them the wrong way. Who's to say? Usually, I was better at spotting sore losers, but I'd entered the game already inebriated, which improved my opinion of most people.

I had just enough presence of mind to make a few quick turns and then scramble up a drainpipe before my followers could match my pace. Perhaps if I was a caster a more direct approach would have been possible, but there are two kinds of sorcerers: those who cast spells and those who write them. I was the latter—and not even an impressive scriver at that.

I held my breath as my two erstwhile gaming companions rounded the corner and looked around wildly.

"Lost him," the man with the deep voice said.

"Well, we know where he's going," the woman replied. She wore tall red boots that I had complimented her on, back when we'd been friends an hour ago. "The Fount is back in session tomorrow, and only a sorcerer would be seen about town in one of those hideous coats."

I bristled at this. My coat was midlength and black, with many pockets both on the outside and running along the inner lining. A sorcerer's coat is a wonderful thing to have, with spells on the pockets so you could carry far more than the space should have allowed for and more magic woven into the fabric to keep the wearer cool in summer and warm in winter. I also thought it happened to be an unquestionably stylish piece of clothing and that I looked quite dashing in it.

My would-be robbers, unaware of my outrage, continued on in the direction of the Fount. Once their footsteps had faded, I pulled myself from the gutter and onto the roof proper. It wasn't the first time I had avoided attention by scrambling over Luxe's rooftops, and it was a faster (if more dangerous) route.

The journey went mostly without incident, though I did lose several minutes untangling my boot from a wash-line full of someone's clothing. Nevertheless, when I finally caught sight of the Fount's grand front gate, my followers were still nowhere in sight.

I shimmied down another drainpipe with more haste than grace, clutching my violin case awkwardly, then darted across the road. It wasn't until I slid to a stop in front of the gate that I realized something that should have been clear to me from first glance—it was shut.

This was a fairly new development. Until recently, the Fount's doors had been open all hours of the day, but the previous year a troop of Coterie members had gone rogue and broken into one of the library's locked vaults, stealing an undisclosed number of extremely rare spells. Needless to say, security measures had been heightened in the wake of the robbery. These measures included closing the gates at midnight, as I now belatedly recalled.

I swore softly and looked over my shoulder.

"You missed the midnight bell by twenty minutes at least."

The voice was flat, remarkable only for its deep tenor and the unmistakable disapproval lacing each word. I flinched in surprise and looked back toward the door just as a figure stepped forward from the collected gloom of the gate's arch.

"Oh. Hello, Grimm," I said with little enthusiasm.

Sebastian Grimm lived up to his name in every way imaginable, like a thundercloud in human form. His hair was a shockingly pale gray and had been that way even when we first met at seventeen. A permanent line of displeasure was etched between his dark brows, and his mouth had a habit of settling into a thin line, turning his expression sour. Or at least, that was the expression he wore whenever he caught sight of me.

Grimm's usually immaculate sorcerer's coat was covered in a thin layer of dust, and the indigo caster's sash wrapped around his waist was creased. A bag hung from his shoulder, packed so tightly the seams were straining. It looked heavy. Grimm looked tired.

Grimm was always easiest to annoy when he was tired, and I have always been unable to resist low-hanging fruit.

I shook my head and made a tutting sound with my tongue. "Sebastian Grimm, out cavorting the night before our final tier commences. What is the world coming to?"

Grimm's lips tugged down at the corners. "My return was delayed when a stream decided to forge itself a new path directly across one of the main roads. It took the Coterie nearly two hours to spell it back in place." He gave me a once-over, making note of my rumpled clothes and flushed face. "What's your excuse?"

"Lost track of time," I said, and winked for good measure. "What are you waiting here for?"

Grimm looked down his nose at me like I was a particularly stupid bug he was thinking about stepping on. "No one answered when I knocked."

I laughed. "Do you mean to say, in nearly five years of attending the Fount, you've never bothered to find another way in besides the front gate?"

Grimm, tellingly, said nothing. It was not so surprising, considering what I knew of his habits. No reveling with friends in the streets of Luxe for Sebastian Grimm. I could not imagine he had ever found himself in a situation that demanded sneaking back into the Fount after hours.

It was tempting, very tempting, to turn around and leave him there without another word. It's undoubtedly what Grimm would have done to me, had our positions been reversed. But I couldn't help but think what would happen if my pursuers arrived and found Grimm outside the gate instead of me. I wasn't concerned for his safety, understand, but the last thing I needed was for Grimm to discover I'd been gambling. I was sure he'd be only too eager to share my transgressions with the Fount's board of sorcerers, and I'd already received a very clearly worded letter from them detailing exactly what would happen if I so much as thought about breaking a rule this year.

I sighed heavily. "Come along, then. Or do you intend to sleep in the dust of the street tonight, simply to avoid following me?"

Then I turned on my heel and started walking, not bothering to wait for an answer.

After a moment I was rewarded by the sound of Grimm's footsteps, leaving the gate to trail reluctantly after me down the road.

Around the eastern side of the Fount, there is a particularly pretty stretch of wall where trees border the walkway and their branches stretch up and outward, leaning over to kiss leaves with the trees overflowing from the Fount's garden within. By day, this area is a popular place to stroll because of the shade and the view. By night, it's the perfect place to sneak over the wall, making use of the natural handholds provided by greenery.

There were, of course, spells in place to prevent outsiders from doing this, but Grimm and I were not outsiders; we were simply residents resorting to inconvenient measures. I'd climbed these trees many times on my own since the midnight bell's implementation, when I'd been unwilling to let the Fount's rules deprive me of a full night of fun.

"There's no need to climb with me here," Grimm said impatiently, once I'd explained this. "A lightfoot charm will see us over the wall easily." He looked at me expectantly.

"Oh," I said, surprised. "You want me to write it?"

"It's only a charm, Loveage," Grimm said. "You should be capable of that much, yes?"

Yes, I could write charms. Cantrips too. I could even transcribe other scrivers' Grandmagic spells without issue. It was when I wrote my own that things went wrong—that was what Grimm was hinting at. Grandmagic had a habit of turning out so poorly for me that I avoided writing it altogether. My last brush with it had been an accident in second tier, when I'd unintentionally written a wind spell with a bit too much power built into it. The demonstration of said spell had destroyed an entire classroom, knocked one person out a first-story window (Grimm), and resulted in the cracking of three ribs (my own). This had earned me a bit of a reputation, as well as a fair amount of laughter and whispers behind my back. A Fount-trained scriver who couldn't write Grandmagic? What was the point?

I had said something very similar to my father when he insisted I enroll. In fact, I believe my exact words were "Why would I want to spend five years as a laughingstock?" I'd been considered a scriving prodigy when I was young, but that talent had withered on the vine. I'd held more promise as a child than I ever would again, but my father had yet to accept this.

"You've had a place at the Fount since you were born," he'd said.

"Well, I don't want it," I told him, which had led to a week of heated arguments and ended with him making it clear that, if I didn't attend the Fount and become a fifth-tier sorcerer like my older brother had, I could kiss my portion of the inheritance goodbye. The money, the title, the land holdings, all of it.

I didn't much like to think about that confrontation, but sometimes my father's parting words still echoed in my ears.

You will learn to control your magic and your attitude and become a fully trained sorcerer, or you will become nothing at all.

After four years at the Fount, I rather thought my father had overlooked the possibility that I could become a fully trained sorcerer and *still* amount to nothing at all. But Grimm was right; I could write charms, at least.

I reached into my pocket to retrieve paper and quill. The words of the lightfoot charm Grimm mentioned were lost to me—I was shit at memorization—but it was the work of a moment to come up with my own version of the spell, combining what words in the old language I remembered with a few more I found fitting. When it was done, I blew the ink dry and handed the spell to Grimm.

"Your penmanship is awful" was the first thing he said. There was plenty of light from the street for him to read by, so I thought the show he made of squinting and frowning down at the paper was a bit much. "This is incorrect."

"It's not," I said. "I just couldn't remember the words to the lightfoot spell so I wrote my own. It should work the same. Mostly."

Grimm stared at me. "Surely you've memorized something as basic as that by now?"

I shrugged. "Didn't stick."

Grimm looked horrified by this admission. He took ages reading over the spell again, probably searching it for traps. This was insulting but perhaps not entirely unwarranted. Grimm and I had been collecting grievances against each other since first tier, like honey catches flies. I'd once tricked him into casting a charm that turned his pale hair a delightful shade of pink. I'd thought it rather fetching, but he vehemently disagreed. That incident had been the launching point for the enmity that had stuck like a thorn between us ever since.

Once he'd assured himself the spell was as I said, Grimm motioned me closer and gingerly grabbed my left arm with one hand. With the other, he held the spell paper between thumb and forefinger and began to cast. His brow furrowed in concentration. Smoke gathered in his hand and rose up into the air as magic ate the words I'd written, burning away the paper as it went. He didn't even have to speak the words of the spell aloud.

I will passionately deny admitting this if asked, but Grimm is a brilliant caster. Most sorcerers can't cast silently, but he did it as a matter of course. If he'd been even a little bit better-natured, this kind of careless display of power might have been attractive. As it was, I found Grimm about as appealing as the austere marble statues that graced the Fount's hallways—just as haughty and twice as cold. Most of our tiermates disagreed with me on that front. Grimm had plenty of admirers who were willing to overlook his personality in favor of his talent. Little good it did them. Grimm had just given more attention to studying my spell than I'd seen him devote to any of his followers over the years.

The paper wasn't even completely finished burning when Grimm tugged me forward and our feet left the ground. This spell was undoubtedly more exciting than a lightfoot charm, which floated you upward with all the urgency of dandelion fluff drifting on a light breeze. *My* version hit with the same adrenaline as a gutless drop, only in reverse. A sort of falling upward, if you like. We had nearly cleared the wall when Grimm's free hand shot out and grabbed the nearest tree limb, halting our progress before we could descend on the other side. I was hardly tipsy anymore, but our landing was awkward enough that only Grimm's unsteady grip on my arm kept me from tumbling down. I wobbled on top of the wall like a toddler, laughing and giddy, buzzing from the rush.

"That was brilliant. Why did you stop us?"

"We were going too fast," Grimm said, scowling. "Your spell likely would have catapulted us headfirst into the ground had I let it continue."

A little of my rush faded, replaced by annoyance. It was one thing to have everyone turn their noses up at me for something I was admittedly bad at, but my charms worked just fine. I wouldn't have dared let anyone use them otherwise.

"Climb down on your own then, if you don't trust my scriving." I pulled my arm away with a quick tug, intending to move toward the nearest tree and away from Grimm. But *hardly tipsy* is not quite the same thing as absolutely sober, especially when one is standing on a narrow bit of stone ten feet above the ground.

I leaned.

First one way, then the other. My balance was further thrown off by my violin case, heavier than usual thanks to the winnings I'd stashed there. My free arm flailed for something, anything, to hold on to, and the only thing within reach was Grimm.

My fingers caught on the sash at his waist, causing Grimm to cling even tighter to the branch he held, rather than offering me any assistance.

"Let go," he snarled, but I clutched that sash like a lifeline, silk twisting in my grasp. Briefly, I thought it would hold, but the fabric was too delicate. It gave way under my fingers with a hushed *riiip*, and I tumbled over the wall.

It was fortunate that there was grass beneath me, rather than stone, but the impact still rattled my bones and sent the case in my grasp bouncing forward to connect with my face, hard enough to leave me seeing stars. I lay there, dazed, as something wet trickled down from my nose and the metallic tang of blood bloomed at the back of my throat.

By the time I managed to sit up, Grimm was just finishing making his way down one of the trees, landing with an elegant hop. He slowly leaned over to pick up the pieces of his sash. It had been torn neatly in two.

Sorcerers decorate their sashes, you know, or at least most of us do. I'd never bothered, but Grimm's sash was covered in careful stitches that depicted droplets of water and waves. Now the threads trailed through the air, ripped down the middle of the design.

Grimm folded the pieces carefully and put them in his pocket. Then he looked down at me, coldly furious, and said, "I don't know how you manage to keep your place here. You're useless, Loveage."

There were many things I had argued with Grimm about over the years, but this was not one of them. I didn't say anything now, either, as he walked away. My own uselessness was something I'd spent years perfecting. Not all sorcerers could be like Grimm. Some of us had powers best left untouched.

CHAPTER TWO

Beginning my last year at the Fount with a blackened eye wasn't ideal, but at least it gave me an air of mystery. Though I caught several people looking at me curiously the next day, it wasn't until I was eating lunch in the refectory, book propped open in front of me, that anyone asked me about it outright.

"Your face looks like shit. Did you walk into a door?" This question was accompanied by Agnes Quest plopping herself down onto the bench beside me and stealing a piece of fruit from my plate.

"No," I said, lowering my book. "I walked into Sebastian Grimm."

Agnes's eyes widened comically behind her gold-rimmed spectacles. "You fought? *Already*, Leo?"

I told her the story of my evening, not bothering to hold back the details of my less-than-legal activities. Agnes didn't exactly support my lack of regard for rules, but she never condemned me for it either. Our lives had been intertwined since long before the Fount, through both the friendship and the politics of our parents. The number of people with a seat in the Citadel, Miendor's department of magical governance, formed a very small circle, and their children an even smaller one, which meant Agnes and I had shared near identical childhoods full of high expectations

SORCERY and SMALL MAGICS

and too many fancy parties. We had emerged from the experience bonded. This bond was cemented during the time after my mother's death, when I lived at her family estate for several months. We knew each other's best and worst qualities, and in general supported or forgave them, but this time Agnes's forehead creased in a frown.

"I thought you were going to keep your head down this year."

"I wasn't even back on Fount grounds yet!" I protested. "It was a last hurrah. A parting kiss with revelry before I commit myself to turning over a new leaf. You really needn't scold me." I prodded gingerly at the sore skin underneath my eye. "Not when I've already paid for it."

Her dark braids bounced as she shook her head at me. "Well, it serves you right. Do you know how long it took me to haul your luggage inside last night? The least you could have done was send along a charm to make the chest weigh less. Now hurry up. I'll give you worse problems than a black eye if you make us late to Duality."

I closed my book without further prompting. The passage I'd been reading had focused on obscure words anyway, and I did my best to avoid those in my spells. Anything too obscure and the magic might think I was actually trying to write something complicated, and that was a problem.

The first time such a problem had occurred was when I was eleven and set fire to my tutor's beard.

It would have been amusing if I'd intended for it to happen (it was a small fire, and he was an odious man), but that wasn't the case. And facial hair wasn't the only victim of my warped compositions. I wrote a spell meant to help my brother practice his sword forms, and he ended up with a broken collarbone. Agnes still has a tiny scar on her cheek from where one of my spells had exploded in her face. I nearly killed my cat trying to use magic to get him down from a tree. The list went on. Any time I attempted to write Grandmagic, it twisted to something wrong in my hands.

Depending on who you asked, I was either a menace or a waste of space. Neither option made casters particularly eager to test out my spells. Fortunately, Agnes had no such compunctions, and she was who I'd been paired up with for Duality class.

The seats were mostly taken by the time we got there. Grimm was stationed at a table on the far side of the room, impossible to miss thanks to his pale hair and height. He had a clear view of the doorway, and I watched his eyes narrow and lips grow pinched as he noticed my arrival.

"Don't start," Agnes muttered, and pulled me past Grimm's table, farther into the high-ceilinged room.

Like everything at the Fount, the lecture halls were beautiful in an austere sort of way, marbled floors and dark wood-paneled walls offset by tall windows that lined one side of the room. Beyond the glass lay sprawling, sunny gardens, still flourishing in the last few weeks of summer.

Agnes and I had just found our seats when, from the front of the room, there came the sound of a throat being cleared.

Silence fell immediately. The few sorcerers not yet seated scurried to find their places as Sorcerer Phade rose from their desk, cane in hand. Phade had been at the Fount longest out of all the instructors, and it showed in the wrinkles creasing their dark skin and the stark white of their hair. Phade was not the type of old that grew feeble. Instead, they had gathered their years around them like the assembled rings of a tree and used them to become formidable.

The cane they carried was a souvenir from the same library break-in that had left the Fount's security so heightened. Supposedly, Phade had arrived first on the scene and taken on the thieves single-handed. During our fourth tier, they had barely been able to walk at all, but now they simply moved with a pronounced limp.

"Scrivers, please rise," Phade said in a carrying voice.

Chairs scraped and feet shuffled as we complied. There were fewer scrivers than casters in the room, which was not uncommon. It's easy to test whether someone can cast magic, harder to tell if someone is capable of writing it. You needed a scriver to imbue the words of a spell with magic, otherwise it was just ink on paper. But even someone who *did* have the gift for scriving still needed to use the old language to write spells, and not everyone learned it as children. Gentry families, like my own, usually passed the language on, or hired tutors to do so, but if you weren't born into a family of sorcerers, your chances of learning it were small. As a result, plenty of scrivers went unnoticed and untrained.

To make up the difference, some of the tables in the room housed groups of multiple casters working with a single scriver, while a few of us remained in pairs. This was similar to how the disparity was dealt with in the Coterie, where sorcerers usually worked together in troops but occasionally operated as a duo.

Phade's eyes flickered over us, face stern and remote in a way that reminded me of Grimm.

Rumor had it Phade was the one who had nominated Grimm for admittance into the Fount when he was discovered as a child. I'd often wondered if this early association was to blame for Grimm's character. Perhaps he'd imprinted on Phade like a baby duckling and decided to emulate their forbidding nature.

Phade began to walk down the line of tables, cane tapping lightly, and as they walked, they spoke.

"For the past four years I've endeavored to teach you how to work with a specific partner, or partners, learning what you can of their skills as a means to hone your own. Partnerships such as this are useful and essential to much of magic. But the situations that arise outside this room are not nearly so neat and controlled. The Coterie will have its eye on many of you this year, and they want sorcerers who are versatile and cooperative. Sorcerers who can work well with everyone in their troop. It is my job to make sure you are ready to meet this challenge. Which is why I will be assigning all scrivers to new tables for the rest of this tier."

A murmur of surprise rose and then subsided just as quickly when Phade brought their cane down on the floor with a bang. "The new partnerships will be chosen at random and will not be reconsidered. When I call your name, please come to the front of the room."

I looked at Agnes. She shot me a sympathetic look back but shrugged slightly. *There's nothing to be done*, that shrug seemed to say.

Someone was about to be very disappointed by hearing my name called. No fifth-tier caster would be satisfied practicing charms and cantrips.

"Cassius Bethe," Phade said, and the sorcerer who had been seated next to Grimm stepped forward.

Cassius was short and slender, with mousy brown hair that flopped forward to cover nalf his face. He had the sort of soft voice and wide eyes that made people underestimate both his age and his skill, but he'd already had two of his own spells added to the Fount's library, a fact I was heartily tired of being reminded of. Cassius was too inoffensive for me to truly resent him, but the way our instructors fawned over him made it a near thing.

He paused in front of Phade's desk and picked a slip of paper from the basket they held out. Unfolding it carefully, he read aloud, "Agnes Quest."

Agnes let out a little sigh of relief, which I tried not to take personally. With Coterie recruitment beginning soon, Cassius was a good match for her. I stepped aside to let him take my place at our table and stood awkwardly in the middle of the aisle as I waited for my name to be called. I hoped that I would at least end up at a table with only one caster, so as not to dash the hopes of too many people.

"Leovander Loveage," Phade said.

I don't think I imagined the little pause that ran around the room when my name was spoken. Like all the casters who had not been matched up yet were suddenly bracing themselves.

Ignoring this, I walked up to Phade's desk and plucked a piece of paper from the top of the pile.

While I had many acquaintances in the crowd, there were none in particular I would have picked to work with besides Agnes. There was one person, however, who I definitely would not have chosen.

"Sebastian Grimm," I read aloud.

This time the hush that fell over the room was of a different variety, crackling with a certain level of amusement.

It was no secret Grimm and I did not work well together. In fact, we'd been actively banned from interacting in most class-rooms, the results having been deemed "too disruptive" by our instructors. Now every eye in the room fixed upon me, waiting to see if I would drop the piece of paper with Grimm's name on it right back into the basket.

I nearly did just that, thinking that the same rules that normally applied to Grimm and myself must apply here as well, but then I caught Phade watching me, keen-eyed with interest. They had not said a word of protest when I drew Grimm's name. Abruptly, I remembered their promise that no new pairing would be reconsidered, as well as the letter of warning from the Fount board that I was under strict orders to heed.

Not one toe out of line. That's what I had committed to, or else the past four years would be for naught. I just hadn't expected that commitment to be so soundly tested, and so soon.

I met Phade's eyes squarely over the scrap of paper. Then, after the briefest hesitation, I crossed to my new seat.

The atmosphere in the room seemed to lighten as everyone realized all at once that they no longer had to worry I would end up at *their* table.

Grimm said nothing as I placed my bag down and slid onto the bench next to him, only sat there, straight-backed, looking deeply displeased. This close, I noticed Grimm's sash was held together by a neat line of stitches. He had obviously gone to great effort to make the stitches as careful and small as possible, but the repair still stood out, like a stain on a white shirt. Perhaps I should have felt a glimmer of remorse. Instead, all I felt was a savage sort of glee at witnessing the blemish in his otherwise perfect image, knowing I put it there.

Once partners had been assigned, the scrivers were instructed to choose one of the spells we'd written over break for our new partner to cast. My offerings were slightly more intricate than usual, given that I'd had all summer to devote to their making, but they were still only charms and cantrips. Nothing that would be a stretch for any caster in the room. Yet, similar to the night before, Grimm spent an inordinate amount of time studying the spell I handed him. In fact, he took so long looking at it that many of the other sorcerers finished casting before we had even begun.

I watched the woman at the table in front of us flicker in and out of sight as her partner recited a lackluster invisibility spell. Across the room, a spell meant to freeze someone in place went wrong and left broken bits of ice melting on the floor. The scriver of that spell swore as Phade pursed their lips at the mess. Many different Grandmagic spells were being tested, with varying levels of success, but the most ambitious one by far was cast by Agnes. I looked over at her table just as the spell in her hand finished burning away and Cassius's form shimmered and began to wiggle and shake like jelly. It was both uncomfortable and fascinating to watch, but after only a few seconds of this display Cassius disappeared altogether, replaced by a small brown sparrow.

The spell lasted less than a minute, but this was still very impressive. Successful transformation spells were rare.

A petty part of me couldn't help but notice that Cassius didn't quite dare test out his wings. He simply sat on the chair for the duration of his birdhood, occasionally letting out an excited chirp.

My spells may have been small, but they were fully functional.

Grimm cleared his throat pointedly, and I turned back round to face him as he began casting. Gray tendrils of smoke drifted up from his hands. The windows in the room were all cracked open, but I knew my hair would smell like fire for the rest of the day.

Once the paper was gone, Grimm brushed the ash from his hands, unfazed. Not for the first time, I wondered what it would be like to have that kind of power at your disposal.

Scrivers can't cast. Or at least, we can't cast anything that requires more than a thimbleful of magic. It was dangerous to try for anything more than that. Bite your cheek. Feel the softness against your teeth as you bear down. Press to the point of skin breaking. You could keep going, but why would you? There's a line there, between pressure and pain. No one needs to tell you where it is; you can feel it for yourself.

That's casting a spell.

I don't know exactly what Grimm felt, but wherever that point lay for him, it was far past anything I could even imagine.

Grimm frowned. "Your spell didn't work."

"Oh, it did," I told him. "Maybe too well."

He looked me over, clearly confused. "What is it meant to do?"

"It warms your clothes. So that you never have to put on cold socks, or cold anything, really. I probably should have just taken something off for you to cast it on, though." I was already sweating.

Grimm looked around the room, at Cassius, who was marveling with Agnes over the fact that his bird form had left behind a downy feather on the bench, and the woman who appeared to be holding a very tiny lightning bolt in her hand, and even the partners who were busy cleaning up the puddles on the floor. Then he looked back at me.

"I see," he said.

Those two little words, spoken with such cold formality, managed to convey far more than if Grimm had said twice as much. It was the verbal equivalent of someone looking down their nose at you. Phade had been keeping an especially close watch on our table for the duration of the class, so I could not respond as I wished to, but I resolved then and there to only give Grimm spells I knew he would hate for the remainder of our partnership. I would smother him in cosmetic charms and prank

SORCERY and SMALL MAGICS   21

cantrips. I would give him exactly what he expected of me, and nothing more.

I didn't linger over this choice at the time, but in hindsight, I think it's what sealed our fate. This one simple, petty decision, not so different from others I had made before. All because I couldn't stand the way Grimm looked at me.

I did it to spite him, but really, I have always been my own worst enemy.

CHAPTER THREE

Not even a full week back at the Fount and I already had three new spells to write, and more to memorize than I had fingers on my hands to count with. I was certain that for every new bit of magic I managed to make stick, something else would slip from my head like water from a duck's back, but I had to at least try. New leaf and all that.

Even so, I had not forgotten Grimm's derision, nor my resolve to vex him thoroughly the next time we met.

It was in this frame of mind—frazzled, slightly sleep-deprived, head stuffed full of other people's words and resentful of each one of them, and even *more* resentful of Sebastian Grimm—that I ran into Cassius Bethe.

I mean that quite literally. I was making my escape from the library after six hours of study when Cassius rounded a corner and walked straight into me, sending my books and spell folder tumbling to the floor. This wasn't so bad, but Cassius had been carrying a stack of unbound spell papers, and the collision sent them flying in every direction until the floor between us was carpeted in white.

There's a game that's very popular in Luxe, played in bars and on street corners, or any place where people can stop and stare for a while. It uses shells and a stone, or sometimes cups and a marble, shuffled among one another fast enough to make your head spin.

They have a version of this game everywhere. It never goes out of style because people never tire of the idea that they can win. The key is to not get distracted. Don't look away. Don't fall for the trick.

I'm really, *really* bad at this game. I fall for it every time.

Cassius's face was a study in agony. "Oh no," he whispered, taking in the scattered spells. Then he looked up and recognized me. "I'm so sorry, Leo. I was in a hurry and, well…" He gestured helplessly at the mess.

"No harm done," I said. It was hard to be ungracious to Cassius. There was too much about him that seemed inherently apologetic. His demeanor was as mousy as his brown hair. We'd never spent much time together before, and I'd never cared to change that, assuming that anyone who was friends with Grimm would not be interested in my company, but I knelt down and began to help him anyway. He was Agnes's partner now, after all.

"Do you like him better than me?" I'd asked her, just the night before.

"He's quite nice," Agnes said, distracted. She'd spent the past half hour trying to cast a disorientation spell silently, but the paper wasn't catching. Unlike Grimm, she did better when she could shout the spell at something. "I think he'll be a good partner."

"You *do* like him better," I said, aggrieved.

Agnes let out a grunt of frustration and lowered the unconsumed spell before facing me. "I do not like him better; I just think he's a good scriver. So are you, no matter how you insist otherwise. Cassius just…tries harder."

I was fairly certain Cassius and I tried equal amounts, only in different directions, but the comparison had stuck in my mind. It returned anew as I helped Cassius gather a truly staggering number of spells off the floor.

"Are these all yours?" I asked.

"Goodness, no," Cassius said, laughing softly. "I'm not so prolific as all that. These are for the library. They're sent so many spells for admittance that they have trouble keeping on top of the backlog. I'm helping sort through and pick out the ones worth reviewing."

This only made my eyebrows raise higher. "You must have pissed someone off spectacularly. Even I haven't been assigned any extra work yet."

No one at the Fount would have trusted me to sort through incoming spells even if I had, but that was beside the point.

Cassius shook his head. "It's not punishment; I volunteered. I find the task interesting. Most of the spells the library receives are too derivative to be worth adding to the shelves, but some of the structures I've seen are quite creative. Inspiring, even. And, well, this sort of thing looks good to the Coterie when it comes time for recruitment."

I handed over a messy stack of spell papers and said, "Recruitment. Right."

Almost everyone who attended the Fount did so with an eye for being recruited by the Coterie after graduation. Ostensibly, this was so they could use their training to protect Miendor's citizens from the monsters that liked to creep over our borders from the strange and sprawling Wilderlands beyond, where magic flourished unhindered, producing all sorts of odd creatures and plant life. Sorcerers who served for the requisite amount of time were also automatically granted property, initiating them into the ranks of Miendor's gentry. And if you were already from a gentry family (as most sorcerers attending the Fount were), there was the prestige of having a Coterie title attached to your name to consider.

Gentry families are snobs about that sort of thing. I would know.

There are some other draws to the Coterie, besides property and bragging rights. During fourth tier, we'd spent one week out of every month assisting the Coterie on low-level missions in order to gain practical experience. They didn't send us to take care of anything high-stakes—the things we'd helped with wouldn't end up in any history books—but we'd gotten to roam all over Miendor, solving different problems every day. Those weeks had been...fun, as far as occupations went. Certainly more to my taste than sitting in the library for hours on end, getting zapped by quietude spells every time I spoke too loudly or began to whistle. Definitely a more interesting line of work than becoming a craft sorcerer and focusing on only one area of magic day in and day out.

But only the cleverest, most powerful sorcerers made it through recruitment.

"Oh, I think this one's yours," Cassius said, handing over a spell that had escaped from my folder in the collision. It was easy to spot as mine because no one would bother trying to get a tooth-whitening charm admitted into the Fount library. "Do you have a plan yet?" Cassius asked.

I busied myself with putting the spell away. "For what?"

"The first recruitment trial, of course!"

"Oh. Not really."

Every year, after the harvest, Coterie captains visited the Fount to recruit the most promising fifth-tier sorcerers early, before the final trials in the spring took place. It was a badge of honor to earn your place during the autumn trials, and everyone in fifth tier was even more tense than usual, falling all over themselves to learn new tricks like dogs hoping to earn a treat.

Cassius tapped a sheaf of paper against the floor neatly and then shot me a little smile that I thought was meant to be conspiratorial. "Come on, Leo, you must have something up your sleeve."

"Well." I made a point of looking around the corridor, as though making sure there was no one else listening. "There is one thing, if you promise not to tell anyone."

Interest kindled in Cassius's eyes. "Of course not."

"The trick is...I just don't care what happens." I laughed aloud as Cassius's face slackened in surprise. "Come on, there's nothing I could possibly do that would impress a captain. Charms and cantrips aren't going to help them fight monsters."

"Maybe not," Cassius said. "But troops are meant to be well balanced, not just powerful. You don't know what they'll be looking for."

But I did know. He was right in front of me. No wonder Cassius and Grimm got along; they were both picture-perfect versions of what a sorcerer should be. Grimm, with magic leaping to answer his very thoughts, and Cassius, eagerly studying the words of others so that he might write the sort of spells the library would never refuse from their shelves. Both of them wanted so badly to be noticed for their sorcery, and no doubt they would be.

The last thing I wanted was to be deemed remarkable for my scriving. I wanted people to look at me because I had picked up my violin and begun to play. I wanted attention for being clever or even for being outrageous. Not magic. Never magic. The only spells of mine worth anyone's notice were never noticeable for a good reason.

I looked at Cassius and said, "Any troop looking to round out their arsenal with a few cosmetic cantrips is simply going to have to contain their disappointment at my refusal. I have no interest in the Coterie."

"Of course," Cassius said. "My mistake." But he said it with the tiniest quirk to his lips and a slight bob of his head. I don't think he believed me.

It wasn't long before we'd finished collecting the spells off the floor and had them sorted back into their proper folders. I gathered my things and bid Cassius farewell, more than ready to escape further discussion of the Coterie.

Cassius called out my name when I was halfway down the corridor.

"Yes?" I said, turning back to face him.

"I hope there are no hard feelings over Duality class. About the partner switch, I mean. I know you and Agnes are close."

"It's not your fault," I said, surprised. "If your name hadn't been called, it just would have been someone else."

"I know. But I can't help but feel that you and Grimm have a harder task than the rest of us. It's no secret that the two of you don't get on." Cassius hesitated, biting his lip, then said, "Can I offer a word of advice?"

"Please," I said, interest piqued.

"Grimm likes straightforward wording to his spells. Nothing too long or overly complicated. Not that he's incapable of adapting, of course," Cassius hastened to add. "It's just that he prefers short and simple."

I smiled at Cassius, slow and sweet. "Thank you. I'll keep that in mind."

After that, I spent every spare moment leading up to the next Duality class writing the most unnecessarily long and elaborate charms I had ever composed. I also went out of my way to choose the most flowery, ridiculous words in the old language that I could think of.

Was this a good use of my limited time? No.

Was it at least a valuable exercise in the effect vocabulary can have on simple charms?

Also no.

But it was a form of stress relief. I had trouble falling asleep most nights, and thinking up convoluted spells to annoy Grimm with was nearly as soothing as playing my violin or getting drunk. I lay down after writing them and didn't remember my dreams come morning.

By the time our second class as partners came around, my spell folder was well padded. I took great joy in tossing it onto the table between us.

"Pick whatever you like," I told Grimm. "Doesn't matter to me."

Today, Phade had told us to practice physical means of making magic stronger. Most of what determined a spell's strength was due to how it was written, but there were other ways of boosting effectiveness, if you had the time. It mostly had to do with casting, so I leaned back in my chair and relaxed.

Grimm hesitated only a moment before opening my folder and flipping through the spells there. As before, he took far longer than was necessary looking them over, the furrow in his brow growing deeper and deeper before he eventually selected a piece of paper. Next, he retrieved his caster's kit from his bag.

Agnes kept her tools in a leather pouch with various compartments, but Grimm's kit was a small wooden box. From inside he withdrew a candle, which he lit with a fancy silver lighter before placing it on the table, wick still guttering slightly from the movement. Next, he drew out a slim silver knife and ran it through the flame.

"Hold out your hand," he said.

Apprehension tickled the back of my neck as I eyed the knife. Blood was commonly used as an amplifier, so it wasn't as though Grimm was suggesting anything shocking; I just didn't fancy the idea of letting him near me with a blade. But Phade was watching, and I hadn't done anything to Grimm today that warranted violence (yet), so after a moment I held out my hand.

Grimm steadied my palm, fingers light and warm on the back of my wrist, wielding the knife with clinical precision. The silver blade was thin. It bit into my thumb with scarcely more pain than I would have felt from a pinprick. Blood welled to form a scarlet bead, and Grimm briefly touched his thumb to mine, just long enough to smear the blood into the whorls on his own skin. Then he picked up his chosen spell and pressed a bloody fingerprint into the paper like a stamp.

As usual, Grimm didn't speak the spell aloud, but I could tell when he'd begun to cast by the swirling smoke and the sudden heat in my chest. It felt like I'd swallowed sunlight and was being warmed from the inside. The paper in Grimm's hand curled away to nothing and was gone, leaving the air between us smelling faintly of copper.

"Which one did you choose?" I asked, rubbing my chest. The heat there was unexpected, but sometimes amplifying certain spells could have side effects.

"The shortest," Grimm said.

It took me a moment to remember which spell that was, but once I had, I smiled and fluttered my eyes outrageously. "What color?"

"What?"

"My eyes. The spell is meant to change their color. With the extra boost, they should be something truly spectacular."

Grimm stared at me, looking utterly put out at the thought that he had just expended energy casting such a spell. Then he met my eyes and said, "Blue."

I frowned. "My eyes were blue already. Are you sure you don't mean turquoise? Cyan, perhaps?"

"No," Grimm said flatly. "They're the same as they were before. Vanities are unpredictable and a waste of paper."

"It's exactly because vanity spells are unpredictable that they're so expensive and coveted," I retorted. "They're complicated to pull off."

Grimm ran the silver blade through the flame again, then put it away. "That explains why yours didn't work, then."

"I didn't say they were too complicated for *me!*"

Grimm blew the candle out. "Results suggest otherwise."

I seethed over this for the remainder of our lesson.

Where other scrivers may have skipped over charms in favor of more impressive spells, I'd had no choice but to learn how to perfect them. They were my specialty. But much as I wanted to blame this failure on Grimm's casting, I couldn't. I had watched the magic consume the paper in his hand and I had felt *something* happen—the strange heat in my chest was proof of that. Yet when it came time to fill out our lesson report for Phade, Grimm wrote down *spell did not fulfill its given purpose*, and I couldn't even protest because my eyes were very much still their original color. This was confirmed by Agnes when I snuck across the room just to make sure that Grimm wasn't lying.

Considering how well the morning had gone so far, it was hardly a surprise when Phade called my name and beckoned me to approach their desk rather than file out of the classroom alongside everyone else. They held the piece of paper with Grimm's report in one hand but waited for the room to finish emptying before speaking.

"Mr. Loveage, I thought it was made clear that our standards for you would be higher this year."

"It was," I ground out. "Perhaps if someone else were to cast the spell—"

"Are you suggesting that Mr. Grimm's talents are lacking?"

"No. But maybe that's the problem. Pairing Grimm and me together is like asking a waterfall to flow out of a decorative fountain. We're not a good match."

Phade put the report down and looked at me, dark eyes unsympathetic. "I suggest you find a way to remedy that, at least inside this classroom. Or do I need to remind you of the consequences if the board finds your efforts lacking this year?"

"What about Grimm's efforts?" I asked mulishly. "Aren't we supposed to be partners? He's the one who cast the spell."

"Mr. Grimm is not on probation," Phade said simply. "His moves are not the ones in question. Yours are."

And that was the crux of the matter, wasn't it? Phade's words were a warning as much as an admonishment. A reminder that, if our partnership failed, the blame would rest squarely on my shoulders, and so it fell to me to find a way to make sure that didn't happen.

I just didn't know how, seeing as Grimm and I were apparently as incompatible in magic as we were in every other way.

CHAPTER FOUR

The warm feeling in my chest caused by the failed spell lingered for the rest of the day. It was not painful, exactly, it might have even been pleasant—like the afterglow of a strong drink—except that I didn't know *why it was happening.*

Even if I'd messed something up, the spell should have failed without causing any side effects. Unless I'd misjudged the potential of the amplification combined with Grimm's already considerable power. Perhaps I would wake up the following day with eyes that constantly shifted color, or the blue of my irises would stretch to cover the whites of my eyes and stick that way.

Like I'd told Grimm, cosmetic charms could be surprisingly tricky.

Sleep eluded me even more thoroughly than usual that night. When a bottle of wine and an hour of playing violently depressing songs on my violin wasn't enough to soothe me, I sighed and rearranged my fingers on the strings to play a lullaby cantrip.

I did this sometimes, setting words in the old language to music instead of writing them down. Usually magic consumed paper, but it seemed just as happy to eat the notes I played for it. I would never be a caster, but spellsongs made it possible for me to push the boundaries of what I was normally capable of. I'd tried it with a charm once and nearly passed out, but cantrips, when sung, only tired me slightly. I'd often wondered if other sorcerers would find it cost them less to cast this way as well, but never had a chance to find out. Agnes couldn't hold a tune, and the only time I'd mentioned it to one of my instructors, they'd been horrified.

"It's dangerous to leave magic unfed," they'd scolded, as though music itself could never be a proper meal. "You'll hurt yourself, experimenting with such things."

I nodded and let them think that their words would dissuade me, then kept right on tinkering with my spellsongs in private.

The lullaby tune was soothing, as all lullabies were meant to be. Simple, even. The melody was my paper, and my voice took the place of ink spreading over the page. By the time I let my bow fall, I was winded from pressing too close to the edge of my abilities, but I was also sleepy. So sleepy that it was all I could do to wipe down the strings and put my violin away properly before falling into bed.

The next morning, the warmth in my chest was gone. When I looked in the mirror, no ill effects seemed to have appeared overnight. My eyes were their usual blue, whites only slightly bloodshot. My hair, sleep-mussed and curling around my face, was its usual brown. In fact, all my features seemed to be in their usual place. I decided my anxiety had been unwarranted.

I did not forget about the failed spell, exactly, but it was shuffled to the back of my mind. Past failures mattered less at this point than ensuring such things didn't happen again. I needed to be more disciplined and focused than I had been before if I ever wanted to see my inheritance.

I met with Agnes to run through sword forms. Sat through a soul-suckingly boring lecture on the merits of using rhymes versus iambic pentameter in the old language. Went to the library and hastily memorized two spells before sprinting to my next class, where I proved my recall by regurgitating said spells word for word.

Despite my best efforts to focus, I was twitchy, bothered by the sense that I was forgetting something or that there was someplace I was meant to be. Given that every student at the Fount is plagued by such feelings at one point or another, I did not think anything of it.

That night I shuffled through all my impending assignments, in case my subconscious was trying to warn me of something I'd overlooked. But everything was in order (or at least as much order as I was ever capable of maintaining).

The feeling persisted the following day. And the next.

"It's the pressure," Agnes said when I couldn't stop pacing the length of her room. We were meant to be studying, but I couldn't sit still long enough to read more than a few words. "You've never had to work this hard before."

"I have, in fact, put in some amount of effort over the past four years," I said indignantly. "Otherwise it wouldn't have taken this long for them to threaten to kick me out."

"Some effort, sure, but you didn't *care* before. In fact, you acted like you were allergic to caring about your academic standing. Now you're just like the rest of us."

This was said with a certain amount of satisfaction. Agnes had always been brilliant, but it was a hard-won brilliance. She was used to sacrificing hours and days to maintain her reputation as a promising young sorcerer, while I had always proclaimed that too little freedom made my mind feel like it was shriveling up into something the size of a walnut.

With this in mind, I went out that night, trying to reclaim some of my previous nonchalance. But when I woke the next morning, hungover and bleary, that same itching sensation of unease was back, worse than ever.

I *wanted* something. I just didn't know what.

Normally I lazed in bed for as long as possible to make up for my late nights, but I couldn't stay still, not with that prickling, aimless hunger chasing itself across my skin. I dressed and stepped outside just as the sun rose high enough to wash the Fount's pale halls with blush-touched gold. It was far too early for breakfast to be served in the refectory, so I settled for slipping into the kitchens and stealing an apple. Then I went for a walk around the gardens, hoping that the combination of food and movement would quiet the gnawing sensation in the pit of my stomach.

The Fount grounds were lovingly maintained and absolutely massive. If you ignored the faint sounds of the city in the distance, and the Fount bell tower occasionally tolling out the time, it was possible to pretend you were someplace else entirely. The farther I walked, the more something inside me seemed to loosen, like a flower unfurling its petals to the warm sun. We were nearing the harvest, and it showed in the golden hues around me—nature's windfall.

I ate my apple and strolled toward the pond on the south side of the grounds. Fading water lilies dotted the water's surface, and on the far side was a stone pavilion with a dock running out from it. Upon walking closer, I realized I was not the only one up and about at this hour. A figure was just visible through the open, arched windows of the pavilion, running through the paces of a sword form. His coat and sash had been laid aside for freedom of movement, but the pale hair and upright posture were recognizable even from this distance.

It was Sebastian Grimm.

I should have left, but something in me rebelled against the idea. Agnes had accused me on more than one occasion of not knowing when to just let things be, and Grimm brought that tendency out in me more than anyone. Our animosity was like a scab, itching to be picked. I couldn't resist trying to draw blood.

I ducked inside the pavilion to watch Grimm run through his sword form.

It had been a long time since we had been in the same combat class (after a rather heated exchange in first tier, our instructor had wisely decided it was best we learned such skills separately), but I could still remember how haltingly he'd moved through the forms after first arriving at the Fount. Like many of the other sorcerers, I'd been tutored in the blade since childhood. Grimm obviously had not and had just as obviously been bothered by his own lack of skill. But he seemed to have put that frustration to good use. There was no hesitance in his movement now. Forms were designed to condition your body for fighting, but there was art to be found in the ritual as well. Grimm made it look effortless the same way a dancer would have. If I hadn't known he had once struggled, I would have thought the skill came naturally to him. It was beautiful to watch.

Seeing Grimm like that, alone and unbothered, completely in his element, made something reckless rise within me. Agnes was right, I could never let things be.

I drew back a step, half-hidden in the doorway. Then I sang a few words in the old language under my breath. It was just a tiny cantrip, but when I was finished, my hands trembled and my stomach felt hollow, even though I'd just eaten an apple. But the cost was worth it when I saw the spell begin to take effect.

A butterfly swooped into the pavilion and settled on Grimm's head. The bright blue of its wings stood out markedly against his pale hair. Next, a yellow butterfly drifted in and landed on Grimm's shoulder. Then a dragonfly settled on his back.

This continued for several moments without Grimm noticing anything was amiss, until a large orange butterfly landed on his hand. He paused mid lunge, the most delightful expression of confusion on his face as he realized he was inexplicably covered in tiny wings.

I chuckled, and Grimm immediately turned toward the sound, sword raised.

"Who's there?"

"Hullo, Grimm," I said, stepping into the light. "Lovely morning for a stroll, isn't it?"

Grimm's face reorganized itself at the sight of me, shifting from wariness to outright displeasure. "Did you *cast* something on me?" He sounded almost shocked, though I wasn't certain if it was me being capable of such a thing that surprised him, or just that I had dared cast something on *him*.

"It was only a passing fancy," I said, watching the butterflies on his shoulders flap their wings gently. They looked like dots of paint splattered on his dark coat. "No harm done."

Grimm's expression darkened further. "Get rid of them," he said.

It was the work of a moment to sing out a reversal, and I did so quickly. The winged things perched on Grimm rose up in a cloud and drifted away, back to the water lilies and meadow flowers outside. I frowned a little as they went. I hadn't intended to drop the spell so easily, but something in Grimm's tone had compelled my acquiescence.

"It's impolite to cast on someone without their knowledge," Grimm said. "And a bad idea to distract someone holding a blade."

"I'm not that worried. You were moving so slow I would have had plenty of time to defend myself." This wasn't actually true, but I was disgruntled by my own cooperation and found myself searching for sore spots to press against in retaliation.

"I was focusing on precision," Grimm said through gritted teeth.

"If you say so," I responded blithely. "Hey, we should spar sometime."

"We should not."

"Don't be that way." I smiled, as though I couldn't feel the hair's edge that Grimm's temper was balanced on. "You could use the practice."

Grimm's eyes flashed and his hand flexed—as though, for all his protests, he would have very much liked the chance to raise his blade against me. "Go jump in a lake, Loveage," he snapped. "I don't need your help."

The venom in Grimm's voice contrasting against the tameness of his words rendered the whole thing more amusing than threatening. But another, more insistent part of me seemed to say, *Well, if that's what you want.*

There was no lake, but there was another body of water conveniently close by.

I turned away from Grimm and walked out of the pavilion and onto the dock. The water stretched out before me, sun-dappled and serene in the cool morning air. It was a pretty sight, but I didn't pause to take it in. There was something I was meant to do.

I walked to the end of the dock and threw myself in.

CHAPTER FIVE

Jumping into the water felt right for about two seconds. Blissfully right in a bone-deep sort of way that I seldom felt about any of my own actions. Satisfaction with what I had done filled me up from the inside, leaving me floating in both the metaphorical and physical sense.

And then the feeling was gone, and I was thrashing in a cold pond with lilies wrapped around my limbs.

I surfaced, spluttering. My feet quickly touched down and I stood, boots sinking into the muck at the bottom. My coat was heavy with water and stringy bits of vegetation. A lily blossom clung to my shoulder.

Grimm had stepped out of the pavilion and was standing on the dock looking down at me, mouth slightly parted and eyebrows high.

I plucked the lily off my shoulder and threw it at him. It landed by his feet with a wet *splat*.

"What the fuck was that? What did you do to me?"

"I've done nothing," Grimm said. "You're the one who flung yourself into the water."

"You—you compelled me to!" I said, beginning to slog toward the shallows. "I felt it."

"I've done nothing of the sort."

Finally, I reached the place where the water lapped at the pavilion's edge and was able to awkwardly haul myself up. I stood there, dripping all over the stone floor as I glared at Grimm.

"I can recognize what a spell feels like. I write them, remember? Is this payback for the tricks I've played on you?"

Grimm had come back inside the pavilion as well and was watching me warily. He looked very warm and dry, and I wanted to push him into the water, just to level the playing field. I took a step forward, and as though sensing my half-formed intention, Grimm took one back.

"Don't come any closer," he said, turning his face away. "You smell of pond scum."

Any impulse I had to keep moving evaporated. I halted midstep, foot raised but with no place to put it. The thought of moving toward Grimm was suddenly inconceivable.

"I can't move," I whispered, but it was more an observance of a phenomenon than a complaint. In fact, I was quite content to hover there, awash with the same sense of fulfillment that had swept over me in the water.

"Don't be absurd," Grimm scoffed. "Of course you can."

Just like that, the invisible wall in my mind that kept me from moving forward was gone and my foot touched the ground. I was too stunned to actually keep walking.

Dread replaced all the ease I'd experienced while following Grimm's order. I covered my ears with my hands.

"You've made your point. Whatever spell this is, you can get rid of it now." Then, though it felt like the word was being dragged from me, I added, "Please."

Grimm's eyes narrowed, and he looked me over very carefully. Whatever he saw must have convinced him that my horror was genuine.

"If you're under a spell," he said slowly, "it was not cast by me. The only spells I've cast on you were the ones you gave me."

His voice was muffled due to my palms still being clamped down over my ears. I searched his face, trying to find some hint of smugness or deception there, but he mostly seemed perplexed.

Was it possible that this had something to do with the spell we'd thought had failed? I didn't see how a simple cosmetic charm could possibly warp itself into whatever this was, but perhaps if Grimm had miscast it, in addition to the amplification of blood...

I took my hands off my ears and began to sift through my pockets. My quill and ink were still fine. Most of the paper was damp, but I managed to find a piece from an inner pocket that had been protected by the spells woven into my coat. Tools in hand, I sat down on the stone floor and rolled my wet sleeves up so I could write without dripping over everything.

"What are you doing?" Grimm asked.

"Testing out a theory." I finished the last word of my spell with a flourish. "We're going to cast the spell we thought did nothing, same as before. Except this time, I want to hear you cast it out loud."

Grimm frowned but took the spell from me when it was offered. "What will that prove?"

"Possibly nothing. We might get exactly the same result as last time." If we didn't though, if everything else was the same but the spell *worked*, that meant Grimm had done something different last time. Either by accident, or he'd purposefully cast silently to conceal that he was using a different spell.

Grimm hesitated, still staring down at the spell in his hands, brow knotted in concentration. "I can already tell you that the result will be different," he said at last.

"Why is that?"

"Because this isn't the same spell I took out of your folder that day."

I blinked back at him, nonplussed. "You said you chose the shortest spell."

Grimm nodded. "I did, but this isn't it. There must have been one you forgot about."

"Don't be ridiculous. I wouldn't forget the contents of my own spell folder."

"And I wouldn't forget a spell I cast," Grimm said firmly. "I can tell you what it said, if you don't believe me."

"You remember all the words?" I asked, surprised. Casters usually didn't. They could read the old language, and recite it in order to cast, but remembering it was a scriver's job.

Grimm nodded. "I spent time looking at it beforehand. To make sure—" He seemed to think better of finishing the sentence, but I could guess what he'd been going to say: To make sure it wasn't a trick. That I wasn't about to turn his hair some garish color, or make him look foolish in some other way.

Grimm crouched down on the floor, careful not to rest his knee in the puddle accumulating around me. Then he turned the spell over and used my quill to write on the paper's blank back side. Grimm wrote neatly but slowly. By the time he was done I was twitching with impatience. I snatched the paper from his hand before the ink was dry and began to read.

It was short and sweet, exactly the sort of spell Cassius had told me Grimm was drawn to.

Translations from the old language are an inexact science, since those words could encompass so much more than the everyday tongue spoken in Miendor, but the essence of the spell was simple enough.

> *Will you look for me?*
> *Each glimpse a beckon*
> *Calling from within*
> *Listen for me*
> *Until the ringing of my voice*
> *Becomes your only song*
> *Hold my name in your bones*
> *Until every wish*
> *Need not be spoken*

I hadn't written it. For all that the spell was short, there was power packed into these words. Enough that I did not think it could be called a cantrip or even a charm. It was Grandmagic, pure and simple.

"You cast this on me?" I whispered.

"Yes," Grimm said.

It was the readiness of his answer that saved him. If he had hesitated, if he had been less willing to write the words down in the first place, I would have stormed out of the pavilion and condemned Grimm then and there. As it was, I sat silently for a moment, thinking it over. Weighing my options.

"Do you know what this spell does?" I asked.

"You said it was a cosmetic charm." A hint of uncertainty had crept into Grimm's voice. He seemed to understand that something was wrong but not yet the extent of it.

"I didn't write this spell," I said flatly, waving the paper at him. "This is a control spell."

I watched Grimm's face closely, but since he always looked varying degrees of displeased, there wasn't much to be read from his expression. He did go very still though. Almost as still as I had been when he'd ordered me not to move.

"That's illegal magic, Grimm," I continued. "I could have you thrown out of the Fount for casting something like this on me."

That got Grimm moving. He rose to standing again and scowled down at me.

"You gave it to me. I could just as easily have you thrown out for writing such magic."

"I just told you I didn't write it." Being glowered at from such a height felt belittling, so I scrambled to my feet as well. "What *I* wrote was a simple cosmetic charm, and it's absolutely beyond me how you could ever confuse the two."

"I'm not a scriver!" Grimm said, exasperated. "Knowing a spell's intention is your job, not mine."

"You spent ages staring at it. Do you really expect me to believe you didn't realize what you were casting? It's right there in the words!"

Grimm had gone very pale, lips pressed together in a bloodless line. He took a short breath in, steeling himself, then said, "I read very slowly, especially in the old language. I try to memorize as many spells as possible in order to cast them quickly, otherwise . . . *That's* why I spent so long looking at the words first. The magic doesn't usually catch when I try to read and cast at the same time."

I remembered watching Grimm read all my spells, frowning in concentration. I'd thought he was suspicious because they were mine, and perhaps that had been part of it. But it had also been this. *Grimm likes straightforward wording to his spells*, Cassius had said, trying to help us both without giving anything away. And upon hearing that, I had added the most convoluted spells I could muster into my folder, practically ensuring that Grimm would reach for the one he was least likely to stumble over.

"Oh," I said. There was no need to ask why Grimm hadn't shared this with me, even though his former partner obviously knew. He'd kept quiet about it for the same reason I hadn't wanted him to know I was being chased that first night back in Luxe—neither of us wanted to give the other anything they could use as ammunition.

"If you didn't write this spell, where did it come from?" Grimm asked, apparently eager to move back to more pressing and less personal matters. "How did it get in your folder?" There was a hint of accusation in his tone. Clearly Grimm was about as certain I could be trusted as ever, which was to say, not at all.

But he asked a fair question: Where had the spell come from? No answers came to me at first. Then, with stunning clarity, I recalled what else had happened the afternoon Cassius had tried to give me advice. In the confusion of collecting the scattered paper it would have been easy, so easy, for one of the spells bound for library review to have been mixed in with my own with neither Cassius nor myself noticing.

"Ah. I may have an inkling of what happened," I said. "And I think I know someone who can tell us for sure."

Cassius looked very surprised to see the two of us together on his doorstep, but he was far too polite to say anything about that, or about my state of dishevelment. He ushered us inside and listened, wide-eyed, to my explanation of the morning's events. As soon as I was finished, he fetched an overflowing spell folder and began to sift through its contents.

"You're right," he said a few minutes later. "I'm short one submission. It wasn't sent in with a name attached, which is hardly surprising, considering the nature of the spell."

Control spells were nasty, complicated pieces of magic, all variations of which had been outlawed by the Coterie years ago. My threat of getting Grimm expelled for casting such a spell hadn't been an idle one. I vaguely recalled that a sorcerer in my brother's tier had been kicked out for practicing illegal magic, but that was years ago, before I had been at the Fount, and I couldn't remember what had become of her, only that her disgrace was thorough.

"Why would someone send something like this to the library?" I asked. "They must know it would never be accepted."

"Some people are very bitter when their spells are turned down," Cassius said. "I suppose this person might have been seeking revenge for a past rejection, hoping it would catch whoever was reviewing the spell off guard, or that someone hoping to cause mischief would snatch it for themselves." There was a long, uncomfortable pause, and then Cassius rushed to say, "Not that that's what happened here! I'm sure Leo didn't realize what the spell was. Or that it was in his folder. And obviously Grimm wouldn't cast something of this nature even on—" Cassius cut himself off abruptly and then stood there, wringing his hands.

There was another awkward stretch of silence.

"Thank you, Cassius," I said. "You've given us a lot to think about. Now, if you'll excuse us, we have some things to take care of."

Cassius seemed extremely worried as he saw us out. Maybe he expected Grimm and me to leap for each other's throats as soon as he closed the door. That didn't happen though. Instead, we walked down the hall in complete silence, until we came to the high-ceilinged vestibule at the front of the building. There we paused.

I glanced over at Grimm. The floor of the vestibule was patterned in black-and-white marble. As the two of us stood facing each other, I couldn't help but be reminded of pieces resting on a game board.

His moves are not the ones in question, Phade had said. *Yours are.*

I squared my shoulders and met Grimm's eye. "So, we need to get rid of this thing. Obviously."

"Yes."

"We should start testing counterspells. I have time before my first class if you want to..." I trailed off as Grimm shook his head.

"I have a lecture to attend. It will have to wait until tonight."

I didn't want to wait five more minutes, never mind until evening. The magic under my skin made me feel slimier than the pond scum on top of it, and worse than that was the thought of what Grimm might do once out of my sight.

Grimm and I had a long and public history of getting in each other's way. Even Cassius seemed to have a hard time believing that our enmity was not in some way to blame for this, and he had been there when the mix-up happened! If Grimm went to the Fount's board, told them that I'd written the control spell and tricked him into casting it... Well, they were already looking for reasons to get rid of me. I'd be expelled faster than Grimm could cast a good-riddance charm.

Unless I accused him first.

I had more marks against me, but surely whoever reported the other first would have the upper hand? That, combined with the fact that Grimm was the one who had cast the spell, could work in my favor. And I could lean on my family name if I had to, whereas Grimm did not come from gentry stock. It was the smartest move. I knew that. But the thought of actually doing it made me feel a little nauseous.

The truth was, much as I disliked Grimm, I did not think he had cast the control spell knowingly. To realize this and still try to get him thrown out of the Fount would be an act of pure spite on my part, on a much greater level than any of our past squabbles.

A paragon of morality I was not, but I didn't have this in me. I'd been silent for too long. Grimm was turning away.

"I'll see you at the eighth bell, then," he said, walking toward the doors of the vestibule, like everything had been decided. Perhaps it was, in his mind, but that didn't mean I couldn't try to change it.

"I didn't know the spell was there," I called out after him, louder than I'd meant to. The words echoed a little off the walls.

Grimm paused to look back over his shoulder at me. "So you've said."

"It's true. If I were going to cause mischief, it would be the type I could laugh over. Not this. You have to believe me."

"Do I? Seeing my reputation tarnished has always seemed to bring you amusement before."

I rolled my eyes. "Pink hair does not a reputation tarnish, Grimm. You hate me because I'm a useless, petty bastard, fine. But this is far beyond any of the tricks I've ever played on you before. It doesn't match up, right? Besides, if this was all some devious plan on my part, I'd be reporting you already. But I'm not!" I added hastily, when Grimm's eyes narrowed. "I promise not a whisper of this will leave my lips."

"All right," he said.

I looked at him expectantly, but it appeared there were no more words forthcoming.

"What of you?" I prompted. "What assurance do I have that you'll keep this to yourself? Or that you didn't cast the spell intentionally, for that matter."

Grimm's left eyebrow raised. "If I had cast this spell knowingly, don't you think I would use it now to order your silence? The fact that I haven't should offer you some assurance that is not the case. At least as much assurance as your promise offers me. But if it makes you feel better, no, I didn't do this on purpose."

"And you won't tell anyone?" I asked, even though it felt terribly desperate to do so. Like a fish with its mouth caught in a hook, waiting to see if I would be released or left to hang here, wriggling.

Grimm let the silence stretch. I thought it pleased him, to see me wanting and be left waiting.

"No," he said at last. "Not yet."

Back in my room, I filled the bath and stripped off my soggy clothes, all the while checking myself for symptoms of the spell. My limbs moved normally. My body bore no strange marks. My mind was...well, it was not at its best, but the panicked thoughts seemed entirely my own. It was frustrating to find nothing physically wrong with me, when I knew that all was not as it should be.

I had experienced my fair share of consequences over the years, but only a few had taken me by surprise. I was not averse to making trouble, but I liked to know the parameters of its expense before I threw myself in, and who would end up paying. With this in mind, I scrubbed myself clean hastily and hurried to the library, hair still wet.

The stacks were crowded by the time I arrived, full of other students in their unmarked black coats. The aisles and worktables were also dotted with the brightly colored collars of craft sorcerers and the distinctive gold trim of Coterie members. There were even a few obvious tourists, wandering about with wide eyes. The library's most powerful spells were locked away in the lower levels, coiling deep underground like the whorls of a conch shell, but the upper levels were open to all and drew people from far and wide, for research purposes or just to admire the library itself. Visitors claim it's one of the most stunning examples of magical architecture in existence—a whole world of spellbooks and scrolls somehow stuffed inside a building that took up less space on the Fount grounds than the kitchens did.

It *is* pretty, I'll give you that. It's also deathly quiet and full of dust. Familiarity breeds contempt, they say, and after nearly five years, I was familiar with almost every hidden nook and cranny of the library.

There was nothing to be gained in researching control spells themselves, since the upper levels held no trace of materials that could be used to help someone write such an abomination. But there were public records of people who had used such magic—and their punishment.

It didn't take me long to discover an accounting of the sorcerer I remembered from my brother's tier. Once I had, I was able to find several articles detailing her crime and subsequent trial. The magic described there did not sound nearly so powerful as whatever I was infected with, but her sentence was severe enough to make my palms sweat. I'd been worried about being thrown out of the Fount (I still was), but it turned out that expulsion was only the first thing in a list of punishments bestowed upon sorcerers unlucky enough to get caught using illegal magic.

We needed that counterspell. The eighth bell seemed ages away.

I'd planned to go to class that day. To put the events of the morning aside as best I could and continue to play at being a good little sorcerer until I met with Grimm. But after reading the articles, I changed my mind.

Instead, once I had returned all the papers to their proper places myself (so that the contents of my reading would not be left on the library carts, for anyone to see), I proceeded to ignore my previous engagements in favor of disappearing into the city and getting astoundingly drunk.

CHAPTER SIX

It was well after dark when I got back to the Fount, and Sebastian Grimm was waiting at my door.

He did not wait leaning against the wall or slouching against the nearest hallway pillar, as I would have. Instead, he stood directly in the center of the corridor, arms crossed and posture immaculately straight, one finger tapping insistently against the fold of his arm lest anyone doubt his impatience.

"You're late," he said.

I pushed past him to open the door. "I had things to do in the city."

The *things* I had done still sloshed a little in my stomach and made me fumble the key, but Grimm was too busy glaring at the back of my head to notice my unsteady hands. Once we were both inside, I clapped my hands to bring the charmed lamps sputtering to life, illuminating the piles of paper and books on the room's only table, as well as the various instrument cases and sheet music that littered the floor. Clothes were draped everywhere in a manner I considered *lavish* and Agnes had once referred to as *slovenly*. Grimm looked entirely out of place standing in the midst of it all, with his perfectly pressed coat.

Does he cast a spell to stay so neat all the time? I wondered. By contrast, my hair was slipping from its tie, and I'd definitely dragged my sleeve through someone's drink earlier (it may have been my own).

Grimm cleared his throat. "Where should we begin?"

"With generic counterspells, I guess. Here, I'll write down the books I want, and you can fetch them from the library while I look over the spell again. By the time you get back I should have a better idea which counterspells might actually do the trick."

I derived petty satisfaction from having an excuse to order Grimm around (see how *he* liked it!) and took full advantage of the situation, adding a few titles to the list that had nothing to do with counterspells at all.

Once I'd finished scribbling, I laid the paper flat on my palm and sang a few words over it. This cantrip was stronger than what I would usually attempt, but my senses were still dulled by the drinking I'd done. It made it easier to ignore the discomfort and keep casting until the paper in my hand folded itself into the shape of a bird.

"Ha!" I said, a little breathlessly. I pinched the paper bird's wings shut before it could escape and held it out to Grimm.

"Release this and follow it. The books it lands on are the ones I want."

Grimm didn't move to take it. He stared at the paper in my hand with grave suspicion.

"It's a piece of paper. It's not going to bite you."

"You made it. Will it not?"

"Careful, Grimm," I said. "That was almost a joke. Think of your reputation. I promise the worst this can do is give you a paper cut."

I leaned farther over the table and waved the paper bird directly in Grimm's face until he finally took it, pinching the wings gingerly between thumb and forefinger.

Grimm's nose wrinkled. "You smell like a distillery."

I sat back down hastily and tucked my soiled sleeve under the table. "Do I? How strange."

"We are meant to be *working*."

"Yes, and that would be much easier for me to do with the proper reading material. So, hurry along." I made a little shooing motion with my hand and, in the process, nearly knocked my quill and inkpot over.

Grimm's lip curled in disgust. "Can you even read in this state?"

"Better than you can, certainly," I snapped.

It was crueler than I'd meant to be. That was always how my worst mistakes happened: carelessly. The fact that I didn't want to hurt anyone rarely stopped it from happening.

"Grimm," I began, but he turned away with a flourish of his black coat and marched across the room, letting go of the spell as he went. I briefly saw the flutter of paper wings before the door slammed shut.

He was gone a long while. Long enough for the squirming feeling in my stomach to settle into a leaden sense of remorse. I splashed some cold water on my face and did my best to shrug off my guilty conscience in order to study the curse before he came back. The copy Grimm had written out earlier was a little wrinkled and still had my cosmetic charm on the other side, so I wrote it onto a new piece of paper with plenty of room for me to make notes in the margins. By the time Grimm returned almost an hour later, I had read the thing so many times I was certain I would fall asleep with those words running endlessly through my head.

Grimm placed the stack of books at my elbow, pushed his chair to the opposite side of the table from me, and then sat. He didn't ask if I'd discovered anything. He barely looked at me.

I pushed the curse across the table toward him. "You may as well take a look while I start scriving out counterspells. Perhaps there's something a caster might notice that I would not."

"I am unlikely to notice anything. As you pointed out earlier," Grimm said coldly.

I winced. "That was...uncalled for. You should have just told me to shut up," I joked weakly, though the very idea made me want to run from the room.

The effort was lost on Grimm. "This is not a laughing matter," he said, stern as an instructor admonishing an errant pupil. "Are you so inebriated that the danger of this spell has escaped your attention?"

"Oh, fuck off, Grimm. I don't need a lecture about what this means from you. *I'm* the one who's had the spell cast on him, aren't I?" I jabbed myself in the chest with my pointer finger to illustrate. "Excuse me if I needed to take the edge off before spending a few hours with someone who could easily order me to go jump off a cliff. I feel on the verge of a heart attack every time you open your mouth!"

We glared across the table at each other. The room seemed to grow palpably colder, though it was probably just the night air.

"I wouldn't," Grimm said.

"What?"

"I don't like you, but I dislike this magic more. I used it accidentally, before. I will be more mindful from now on. You have my word."

That took the wind out of my sails a bit. It was hard to maintain my righteous anger when Grimm insisted on being decent, in his own holier-than-thou sort of way.

"In the interest of helping you keep that promise, I will, er, also attempt to curb my tongue. As much as I am able. Silence doesn't come naturally to me."

"I've noticed," he said emphatically.

We settled into an uneasy sort of peace. One of the books Grimm had brought back contained a counterspell that called itself *all-purpose* so I scrived it onto a blank piece of paper while Grimm took out his casting kit. Everything else was an echo of what we'd done to cast the spell in the first place: a pinprick of blood from my fingertip, smeared onto Grimm's and then pressed to the paper I'd handed him. The only difference was that this time each of us hesitated right before it was cast.

"Would it be helpful if I read it aloud first?" I asked, then immediately wondered if the offer was insulting.

"Unnecessary," Grimm said shortly. "I'm familiar with this spell. I've used it before."

"Oh?" Casters didn't often have cause to undo their work. "Whatever for?"

Grimm hesitated. "To change my hair back to its normal color."

I pictured him, seventeen and pink-haired and too proud to just wait out the duration of my simple charm, and had to bite the inside of my cheek to keep the laughter from spilling out in a delighted burst.

"Lucky, really, that you've had some practice," I said, once I was certain I could do so with a straight face.

"Indeed," Grimm said, voice clipped. "Are you ready?"

"Yes," I said. "Wait, no! Cast it out loud. The first time you cast silently; this time should be the opposite. Reverse verbal components and all that." This was true, but it was also true that the idea of just standing there and waiting in the quiet made me feel even more helpless than I already was. If I

could hear the spell being cast, at least I would know when it
was over.

Grimm raised his eyebrow at the request but complied.

As he began the casting, I closed my eyes and directed my
attention inward, hoping to feel a shift. My gut told me a curse
as devious as this one would not be undone on the first try, but
a small tendril of hope unfurled within me all the same. We
had been so unlucky already, perhaps we were owed this one
reprieve.

I should have known better. Magic has no concept of debt.
There is no payment it does not either take or refuse immediately. It holds nothing back for later.

Smoke from the burning parchment filled my nostrils.
Grimm's voice rumbled over the words in the old language
before coming to a stop. I opened my eyes.

The paper in Grimm's hand was gone, smeared to ash on his
fingertips.

We stared at each other uncertainly.

"We have to test it," I said. "Tell me to do something,"

Grimm pursed his lips, looking deeply reluctant. After a
moment he said, "Sit down, Loveage."

Gladly. I would gladly sit. Such a simple request, so easy to
fulfill that it made my heart sing. If that's what Grimm wanted,
I would—

When the haze of contentment cleared, I found myself sitting in my chair, fists clenched tightly enough to leave half-moon
imprints of each nail across my palms. I remembered moving,
but the recollection was vague, overwhelmed by how much I had
wanted to move.

I stood. The chair that a moment before had seemed perfectly
comfortable was now the last place I wanted to be.

"The chances of getting it right on the first try were slim," I said. "It doesn't mean anything. Let's try the next one."

By the time we'd worked our way through all the basic counterspells I could think of, my nerves were jangling with repressed panic. Each time I told myself the answer was simply to resist, and each time I found myself incapable of doing so. Every time Grimm ordered me to sit, I obeyed with the same happy eagerness of a dog. By the time the eleventh bell rang, I was worn down by our lack of success, and even Grimm was beginning to show signs of fatigue.

"That was the last one."

Grimm removed a handkerchief from his pocket to wipe the ash from his hands as he frowned down at the library books. "You said a custom counterspell was the most likely solution. Perhaps we should refocus our efforts?"

"Probably," I said reluctantly. "But that poses another set of problems." Grimm raised one brow, and I sighed. "Control magic is strong stuff. It will require a counterspell of equal measure. I'm not sure if you've noticed, but that's not really my area of expertise."

A look of confusion briefly passed over Grimm's face, then his expression cleared. "Right. I'd forgotten." Of course he had. For someone like Grimm, who handled Grandmagic with the same ease most people handled cutlery, avoiding such a tool was inconceivable. "You're saying we need help."

"Yes."

"If we go to the Fount's board and explain what happened, that it truly was an accident—"

"No," I said quickly. "That's not a good idea. I'm on thin ice with the board already. Phade as good as told me I'd be kicked out the next time I put so much as a toe out of line, and control magic is so far outside that line I don't see how this could end well for me. Even if they don't think I did it on purpose, they'll say it shows a pattern of careless behavior, or something like that."

Grimm's eyes flickered down to meet mine. I knew what he was going to say before he even opened his mouth. I hated him for it, and myself for giving him the opening.

"Would they be wrong?" he asked. "Allowing that spell to get mixed in with your own *was* careless. If trouble finds you so easily, perhaps you should accept your fate. You're unlikely to make it through the entire year without causing another upset anyway."

From anyone else, this would have sounded like a taunt, but Grimm's voice was flat, emotionless. This was simply how he saw the world, shades of black and white, good and bad, practical or senseless. It was how he saw *me*. Talking with him was like talking to a wall. It made me want to throw something just to watch it smash against him.

Four years of experience had taught me that such theatrics would have very little lasting effect on Grimm—but I knew what would. I couldn't remember a lightfoot charm, or write the sort of spells that would impress our peers in Duality class, but I had always had a knack for worrying away at Grimm's composure.

"Fine." I settled back in my chair and steepled my fingers together. "Let's follow this thought through. Say we do go to the board, what then? Maybe they'll help us. Maybe I get kicked out in the process, huzzah for you, but what about after that? Do you know what happened to the last caster who was caught using control magic, Grimm? Because I do. I looked it up in the library over lunch today. Dreadful story. She was thrown out of the Fount, of course, but she also had to face a Coterie tribunal. They sentenced her to wear magic-dampening bracelets for ten years. Ten years! And that was just for casting a persuasion charm, not even something so strong as the curse you put on me. Even if they blame me for writing the spell, you have to admit that casting it doesn't look good for you."

Grimm's face paled several shades as I spoke, and his mouth settled itself into a flat, unhappy line. I leaned forward and tilted my head to ask, "Do you think the Coterie will jump to recruit a caster whose name is associated with such a mistake? My father has a seat in the Citadel, you know. Should I ask him what your chances are?"

"Enough, Loveage," Grimm said, turning his face away. "You've made your point. We will seek aid elsewhere."

"Excellent!" I said brightly. "Cassius seems like the best option, since he knows already. Agnes can help as well. Not with the scriving, obviously, but she has access to some of the locked vaults for her studies. She might be able to rustle up some more information on control spells."

"No," Grimm said sharply. "There's no need to involve Quest."

I frowned. "This whole thing started because we're obviously terrible at working together. Doesn't it make sense that, to fix it, we would ask for help from the people we actually know how to collaborate with?"

"Cassius is the natural choice. He already knows, and he can scrive what you cannot. I see no use in bringing someone else into this mess."

"Cassius may be skilled, but it's no small thing to scrive a counterspell for something you have no knowledge of. Any information Agnes can get from the vaults would make his job easier. And she's hardly going to turn us in." I looked Grimm over thoughtfully. "But maybe that's not what you're concerned with. Maybe you just don't want anyone else to know that the great Sebastian Grimm actually made a mistake."

With that, the fragile peace we'd been operating under shattered with an almost audible crash. Grimm snatched his casting kit off the table and fixed his cold, dark eyes on me.

"I am no stranger to error," he said, "but in this case, the only mistake I made was believing you were capable of at least a modicum of skill. You're right, Agnes and Cassius should be informed. It's best you and I work together as little as possible."

Then he turned and stormed out of the room. Or at least, he did his best to storm. In reality he had to jerkily navigate around all the items scattered across the floor, which rather ruined the effect.

"What do you know, Grimm," I called out cheerfully, just before he slammed my door shut for the second time. "We've found something to agree upon!"

I dreamed about Grandmagic that night.

I could feel it coming on after Grimm left. There was a secret stash of liquor hidden under my bed for just this sort of occasion, but even drinking myself into a stupor didn't help this time. The control spell was running through my head in an endless loop when I finally fell asleep, so it was hardly surprising that I woke with words I didn't dare put to paper burning my fingertips.

You see, it's one thing to avoid writing Grandmagic, but it's quite another thing to stop thinking about it.

I never did, really.

It was like being placed in an empty room with an elephant and being told, *Do not think about the elephant.* I could write all the elaborate charms and clever cantrips I wanted, but Grandmagic was still *there*, and sometimes the urge to reach out and touch it was so strong it overflowed into my dreams to keep my other nightmares company.

The funny thing was, nothing bad ever happened in these dreams. I always woke up just before the spells I created in sleep could be cast. I never had to watch them go wrong. And every time, there was a part of me that was certain that this time, *this time*, it would have worked.

These particular nightmares didn't frighten me because of anything that happened inside them—they were terrifying because of how dangerous they made me feel upon waking.

CHAPTER SEVEN

You are both idiots" was Agnes's pronouncement upon hearing of the control spell. "It would serve you right if Cassius and I refused to get involved and the two of you had to sort this mess out yourselves."

But neither of them did refuse. Cassius promised he would begin researching counterspells immediately, and Agnes agreed to look through the vaults she had access to for any information about control spells. "In the meantime," Agnes said, "be careful. If Grimm slips up and gives you an order in public, people are bound to notice. You two should stay far away from each other whenever possible."

"Gladly," Grimm said, and I heartily concurred. So I was surprised when Agnes made a point of repeating this instruction to me once Grimm had left.

"I don't know why you're so concerned," I complained. "Grimm and I already avoid each other. This will hardly alter my daily schedule."

"No, you don't," Agnes said.

"What?"

She pushed her spectacles farther up her nose and sighed. "You're usually kept apart because anything else is more trouble than it's worth for the rest of us, but that's not the same thing as avoiding each other. Those restrictions were put in place *because* you both seem incapable of doing just that. So be careful, Leo."

I wanted to protest the need for such a warning, but under Agnes's shrewd gaze, I could not. The fact that we were in this situation at all spoke to my tendency to abandon common sense the second Grimm walked into the room.

"I will be," I said, and meant it.

It did not seem like such a difficult promise to keep, at first. The only place Grimm and I were required to interact was Duality, where I had not ceased my campaign of charms designed to annoy (though I had made certain concessions as to their length and word choice). Grimm seemed determined to speak to me as little as possible during class, but his continued frustration with our partnership was made clear by the marked clench of his jaw as he was forced to cast spells of increasing frivolity: a cantrip that captured your favorite smell to be used as a perfume, another that could move freckles around on a person's body, and a charm I was particularly proud of that made hair grow nearly a whole inch in one minute.

Days turned into a week. Then two. By the third, I was feeling impatient enough to corner Cassius in the library and ask how the counterspell was coming along.

"It's going very well," he assured me. But when I asked to see what he'd come up with so far, Cassius just smiled his blandest, most impersonal smile and told me firmly that he did not like sharing his spells with anyone until they were finished.

"I bet he hasn't even started yet," I complained to Agnes later that day, during what was meant to be our sparring session on the practice grounds. Agnes was taking it very seriously, but I was too distracted to be bothered. "At this rate he won't have anything for us to cast before the harvest break."

"Cassius is meticulous," Agnes pointed out. "He's probably still researching." She darted forward, and I only just managed to block her blow.

"Maybe," I said darkly. "Or maybe Grimm likes having me under his thumb and told Cassius to stall."

"Oh, please." Agnes snorted. "If Grimm wanted to take advantage of the spell, he would have done it last week when you taught the first tiers that rude song about him."

"It was good for his image!" I protested. "Besides, I don't think he realized I wrote it."

"Everyone realized you wrote it." Agnes flicked her braid over her shoulder in irritation. "Can we please focus on fighting instead of Grimm? The trials are coming up, and I need the practice. It's important."

"So is getting rid of the curse!" I said, annoyed now too. "Anyway, you're Agnesia Quest, do you really think you'll have any trouble during the trials?"

Agnes dropped her stance and lowered her practice sword. "If you're too impatient to let Cassius finish the counterspell," she snapped, "then why don't you spend your time writing one yourself, instead of wasting mine?"

I gaped at her, stung. Agnes was one of the few people I could usually count on not to push that particular button. But then, I usually steered well clear of her boundaries too. I knew Agnes hated the way her family name seemed to dictate how others saw her.

"Sorry," I muttered. Grimm was the only person I actually enjoyed having mad at me. Fighting with Agnes always made my heart shrivel up.

"Me too," she said. "Let's just forget about it."

It was easy enough to forget about our tiff, less so the reason for it. But she was right, short of writing the counterspell myself (which would only lead to further disaster), there was little I could do to hasten its completion. Besides, now that it seemed unlikely Grimm would decide to go back on his word and frame me for writing illegal magic, I was worried about being expelled for more mundane reasons.

I was falling short in my studies.

Restlessness plagued me. I tried every trick that had helped me in the past and even spent a few days adopting Agnes's rigid study schedule in hopes that a change of pace would help, but to no avail. My tiermates were settling into a state of determined focus, trying to achieve as much as possible before the harvest break came, followed by the trials. But *my* attention, never steady even at the best of times, now drifted to the point that sometimes I would abruptly realize I'd been walking in the opposite direction of where I'd meant to, with no clear idea of where I'd been going. I was late to several lectures because I'd gone into the wrong building before recognizing my mistake.

"Where have you been?" Agnes hissed at me when I arrived, nearly a quarter bell late to our shared combat training.

"Got lost," I whispered back.

She looked me over suspiciously. "Are you drunk?"

"No," I answered. "But I sure would like to be."

But even drinking didn't soothe my agitation. I took to playing my violin later and later into the night—frantic songs that caused many of the hairs on my bow to break and made my neighbor across the hall come bang on my door, until I had Agnes renew the silencing charms on my room. I woke in the morning restless, feeling like there was something I wanted, or was meant to do, but I couldn't pin down what it was.

It wasn't until our next Duality practice that I had my answer.

Grimm wasn't there yet when I arrived, so I took a seat at our table and tapped my fingers idly across its surface while I waited. I felt full to the brim with nervous energy, and it made it hard to sit still. I had to *go* somewhere but had no destination in mind.

And then Grimm walked through the door, and the feeling vanished.

There was no subtlety to it. One moment, I was being driven to distraction by a hollow sort of wanting, and the next, Grimm came into sight and the feeling was gone. I sat there, reeling with confusion and relief, while Grimm crossed the room and sat down beside me. He began laying out his casting supplies without a word, unaware that anything had changed, while I sat frozen in horror.

It was the curse.

Quickly, I counted back in my head to when the restlessness had first overtaken me. And of course, *of course*, it was not until after the curse had been cast. Perhaps if this symptom had not so addled my brain, I would have put it together sooner. This was magic, tugging me into Grimm's presence so that it could better do its work.

From a scriver's perspective, I couldn't help but admire the mechanics: If a spell worked only when its subject was close enough to hear what the caster said, didn't it follow that you would want to keep them close? My opinion of the person who scrived this spell went down another notch, even as my assessment of their skill went up.

I must have let out some small noise of distress, because Grimm finally glanced my way. "Is something wrong?"

I opened my mouth and then closed it again promptly. The only thing that could make this new development worse was having Grimm *know* that I was being compelled to follow him around like some sort of doting lackey, waiting to jump at his command.

"Not at all," I said. "I just had an idea for an absolutely *inspired* enhancement charm." Which was enough to make Grimm huff and turn his attention from me.

He didn't need to know. No one did. This part of the curse was not so overpowering I couldn't handle it on my own. I would simply resist for as long as it took Cassius to write a counterspell that worked.

This seemed a fine plan when I was face-to-face with Grimm, with the restless ache caused by the curse soothed, but my assurance had worn off somewhat by the time I woke the next morning and the itchy, ants-under-my-skin feeling had returned worse than before, accompanied by an angry ache that sat underneath my ribs. I had classes to attend. Charms to write. Instructors to impress with said charms, in hopes they would ignore my abysmal memorization of spells they'd been trying to teach me for the past five years. All of this was very hard to do when I was being driven to distraction by the need to seek out Sebastian Grimm.

So, I cheated.

I began to linger in places I knew Grimm would have to pass through. This was surprisingly easy to do. As Agnes had so acidly pointed out, Grimm and I had a history of being drawn into each other's orbit, so I already knew a frankly concerning amount about his habits.

The only thing I worried about was that Grimm would notice my presence. Scrivers and casters shared very few classes together, the nature of our training being quite different. And Grimm seemed to have a sixth sense for whenever I was nearby; if I walked into a room, he looked up. If I sat down three tables behind him in the refectory to eat breakfast, the meal would undoubtedly end with Grimm glaring at me. If he noticed me on those occasions, he would certainly notice my lurking outside one of his classrooms. Or someone else would.

Embarrassing.

Eventually I resorted to humming a little cantrip under my breath to help me blend into my surroundings, just enough that I could escape attention so long as no one looked at me directly. It left me tired all the time, but that was better than the prickly discomfort of ignoring the curse, or having to explain myself to anyone.

My relief when Cassius finally called on us to meet was profound. He'd had weeks to study the wording of the curse by now, plenty of time for him to have come up with a working counterspell.

All four of us gathered in Agnes's room. It was a better place for such a meeting than my own room, since Agnes actually took some care with her surroundings and did not currently have a multitude of empty bottles rolling around on the floor, but the space was still not really designed to entertain guests. Agnes and I perched on the bed, allowing Grimm and Cassius the honor of sitting in the two creaky chairs we'd pulled away from the table and into the center of the room, allowing us all to face one another.

Cassius, true to form, began by apologizing.

"I'm sorry this took so long, but I wanted to be thorough in my approach." As he spoke, Cassius reached into his pocket and withdrew three separate pieces of paper, which he handed to Grimm.

Having made the mistake of allowing something I'd not read be cast on me so recently, I was not about to do so again.

I waggled my fingers under Grimm's nose until he handed over two of the spells for me to read while he studied the first, then we swapped.

Cassius hadn't lied about being thorough. Each counterspell approached untangling the curse from a different angle. His word choice was a little plodding, and the structure a tad predictable, but I could hardly fault Cassius for not writing the spells the same way *I* would have. Not when my own efforts doubtless would have ended up making things worse instead of better.

Please, please, please, I begged in my head as the first counterspell was cast. I would never roll my eyes at Cassius again if this worked. I would never roll my eyes at *Grimm* again if this worked.

"Go on," I told Grimm once the casting was finished, and braced myself. The weight of expectation was heavier with Agnes and Cassius watching. I wasn't the only one holding my breath as Grimm said, "Stand up, Loveage."

I did so. Immediately.

"Oh," Cassius said in a voice that was as small as my sinking hopes.

"There are still two more," Agnes reminded. But the same thing happened with the second spell. And the third. We tried having Agnes cast them too, just in case, but the effect was the same.

"I was afraid this might happen," Cassius confessed. "It's just so tricky, trying to unravel another scriver's work. It's like having someone else describe a scene to you and then being asked to paint it; the details are never going to look right."

Agnes opened a second window to help clear the room of spell smoke. "Well," she said with a sigh, "at least knowing what doesn't work will help us narrow down our approach going forward. I've heard that the third time's the charm."

"About that," Cassius said with some hesitancy. "I likely won't have any more counterspells for you until after the trials are done."

"What?" I said, more sharply than I'd meant to. Everyone stared at me, and Cassius's face fell.

"It's just that—I mean—that is to say, I'm a little busy," he stuttered, looking half-ready to keel over from remorse. "But maybe I can find a few spare moments—"

"We *all* have plenty to do getting ready for the trials," Agnes broke in, shooting a pointed glare in my direction.

"But we'll lose momentum!" I said desperately. Unlike everyone else, I didn't care a whit about prepping for the trials, but I still had the everyday expectations of the Fount to worry about, and it was getting harder and harder to meet those expectations while keeping the curse satisfied. "I really think we're so close. If we just give it another—"

"Quest is right," Grimm said. He began to pack away his caster's kit. "We can't risk dividing our attention; the trials are too important. Waiting to solve this will make little difference."

Of course it wouldn't—for *him*. The only person this made a difference to was *me*. Just that morning I'd been late to my first lecture because I had to track Grimm to the far side of the grounds in order to ensure I wasn't too distracted to actually sit still for said lecture. But there was no way to explain why waiting was a problem without, well, explaining. And I was still firmly of the opinion that occasional tardiness was better than telling everyone I'd been spying on Grimm from the bushes like some kind of stalker.

"I suppose waiting a little longer won't make anything worse," I said. Like an idiot.

CHAPTER EIGHT

Before the trials came the harvest, when all six provinces put aside their normal routines for two weeks to celebrate the bounty of summer and welcome the change of season. Of course, celebration meant something very different, depending on who you were. For the Loveage family, it took the form of a lavish party, held at my father's estate just outside the city.

I didn't want to go.

Activity at the Fount was suspended, and I would much rather have spent the free time attending any of the parties happening around Luxe, or venturing out to a smaller celebration in one of the six provinces... Sahnt, for instance. That's where I'd spent all my harvests as a child, at my mother's home. I could still remember her standing between my brother and me, clasping our hands in her own larger ones while we watched the crackling flames of a bonfire. I remembered feeling warm.

The Sahnt estate was meant to be part of my inheritance. My older brother had inherited the lavish apartments in Luxe that had belonged to our maternal grandmother, but the rambling old country house where we had grown up, that had been left to me. My father knew I loved that place, curse him.

"You have to go to the party," Agnes told me. "There will be Coterie captains there. The same ones who will be at the trials.

You know how these things work. Impressions made in a ball-room hold weight."

"It doesn't matter," I said. "I don't care what they think of me."

"Well, *I* care," Agnes said. "The only edge I have over Grimm in these trials is that I'm actually pleasant to speak to, and the harvest party circuit is my chance to prove it. If you won't attend for your own sake, you can at least help me make a good impression."

I snorted. "Because that's what I'm known for at these types of events."

"I'll look good in comparison, at least," Agnes said. Then, more seriously, she added, "You know your father will want you there."

It was an inescapable truth. There was never any real chance of dodging this obligation. My father expected to see me, and until I'd secured my inheritance, I was under his thumb.

I woke the morning of the party with what was by now a familiar ache in my chest, compelling me to get up far earlier than I would have normally. I attempted to ignore it, but I'd stayed up late the night before drinking, and the mild hangover combined with the spell's symptoms made my bed feel like a moving vessel.

I cursed Grimm softly under my breath. Then I went to look for him.

I barely even had to think about where to go anymore; the curse drew me to Grimm without effort. Like I was a compass whose true north just so happened to be a person. Whenever my symptoms grew particularly bad, I gave in and let myself be pulled just long enough to spot a flash of pale hair or dour expression before returning to my own business, curse momentarily satisfied. It had become routine, like drinking water when you're thirsty or reaching for a coat to stave off the cold. As a result of this, I'd grown more familiar than ever with Grimm's favorite haunts in recent weeks. When he wasn't attending class, I most often found him in the gardens, which was convenient for me since it was easy to pass by unnoticed amid the trees and winding hedges. His second favorite place was (unsurprisingly) the casting hall, where he practiced with such focus that my being seen wasn't usually a concern. The one time he *had* turned round suddenly, I'd just pretended to be looking for Agnes. He practiced swordplay in the mornings, and studied at the library in the evenings, and was always back in his room before the tenth bell rang, which I found deeply embarrassing, both for Grimm and myself.

Rivals were meant to be more exciting than this.

Grimm was such a creature of habit that I didn't expect his routine to vary much for the holiday, but instead of being drawn toward any of the places I was used to, the insistent pull of the spell led me to the Fount's main entrance. I paused there, staring out at the city street before me, discomfort fluttering in my chest like a trapped bird.

Grimm was not in the Fount.

I began the walk back to my room. The spell weighed a little heavier with each step I took, but it was not so distressing yet that I was about to go searching for him in the city; I did have *some* pride. I would just have to hope he returned before I left later that day.

Back in my room I began to pack. I was traveling to the estate with Agnes but would be expected to stay there for the remainder of the harvest break without her. I wasn't looking forward to spending my days rattling around the giant house, or my evenings being dragged along to whatever celebrations my father decided we should attend, holding stilted conversations with the gentry elite over dinner. I'd gotten my fill of all that during the week I'd spent there during the summer.

I threw clothes in a bag without really looking at them. The only thing I took care with was my outfit for the party— tailored black trousers and a silk jacket with a lamentable lack of pockets, cut for fashion rather than practical wear. I'd used the jacket for a charm experiment a while back, and now the dark blue color shifted in incremental shades when worn, so that it appeared I had draped myself in water rather than fabric. I sang a little dewrinkling cantrip over my clothes before laying them out on my bed. The spell was at the edge of my limits and left me so tired that I had to take a nap. When I woke, the urgency of the curse was such that I immediately went looking for Grimm again.

I found myself back at the front gate.

"Where the fuck are you?" I muttered, peering out at the bustling street.

When had I last seen him? I had never tested how long it took before the urge to go searching for Grimm caught up with me, or what happened if I resisted the call. Now, with the restless skitter of magic dancing underneath my skin worse than it ever had before, and an ache beginning to grow in my chest, I was beginning to think I had made a mistake in not tracking the curse's requirements.

I made my way back to my room, fuming over Grimm's sudden development of a social life.

A figure stood waiting at my door when I returned. At first, I thought it was Agnes, come to make sure I would be ready on time, but as I drew close enough to make out more than the black coat, I recognized Cassius's slighter frame and dull brown hair. He smiled as I approached, raising one hand in greeting while the other clutched a book at his side.

"What brings you here?" I asked, opening my door and gesturing for him to follow me inside.

"I found something that might interest you." Cassius seemed distracted for a moment by the cozy clutter of the room, taking it all in. He gestured to the bags piled on my bed. "Off to join in the celebrations somewhere?"

My father's harvest party was well known in Coterie circles, but no one in the Bethe family had been invited for years. They were middling sorcerers. Cassius was the only one who seemed likely to make a name for himself, and until he did so, there would be no invitations sent by my father.

"Nothing that I'm looking forward to," I said hastily. "What is it you wanted to show me?"

Cassius looked slightly crestfallen but recovered enough to smile and hold out the book in his hand.

"I discovered this while looking for counterspells. There's nothing in here that can be used on the curse, I'm afraid, but I thought you might be interested all the same."

"Why's that?"

"In the course of my research these last few weeks, I've noticed that many of the counterspells housed in the library were written by the same person. They only used their initials, but I kept seeing them again and again: S. L. And then I found this book." Cassius tapped the book in question with his index finger. "It's more of a research journal, really. Full of stories of people like you, who found themselves under a spell that they didn't know how to undo, and the sorcerer who helped them. The same one whose initials I kept seeing everywhere. I was thinking... maybe they could help you too."

I took the book and flipped through the pages briefly. Like Cassius said, it was more of a journal than anything else, written by hand and covered in preservation spells that made my finger-tips tingle slightly upon contact.

I squinted at the flowing script. "Does it say where this sor-cerer lives?"

"Ah," said Cassius, hesitating slightly. "According to the tales in this book, she operates outside of Miendor. In the Unquiet Wood."

I gaped at Cassius. Then I began to laugh. The laughter had a slightly hysterical note to it, brought on by the agitation of the curse.

"You must be joking. Are you suggesting I just nip over the border into the Wilderlands on our off day? Fight my way through the Unquiet Wood in search of some unnamed person, then be back in time for my next lecture with no one the wiser?"

"Of course not! But it's harvest break right now. If this is something you and Grimm want to pursue, now would be the time."

I scoffed. "Grimm would think this idea is even more ridicu-lous than I do. What if we were delayed and missed getting back in time for the trials?"

"I'm sure that wouldn't happen," Cassius said soothingly. Contrary to his intent, this only made the prickle of unease run-ning down my spine worse.

Nothing about the Wilderlands invited surety. They were everywhere; all the uninhabited places where people did not belong. The Wilderlands were so vast they did not just shape our continent, they *were* our continent. From Miendor to the three water-bound city-states of the lake country, to the mountain-ous region of Granvoir, and beyond. People had found ways of making their settlements a little less dangerous—a little less wild—but it was all right there, just beyond our carefully constructed barriers, forests teeming with unbidden magic, open fields growing thick with it, and monsters roaming everywhere. There were ways to travel through the Wilderlands in relative safety, but none of those ways included the Unquiet Wood.

Frustrated, I tossed the book away from me onto the bed and said bitterly, "If you didn't want to help us write a counterspell, you could have just said so, rather than trying to send us on a wild-goose chase."

Cassius took a faltering step back, eyes wide.

"Grimm is my friend," he said, voice wavering. "I have only ever wanted to help him. And you. I'm very sorry if anything I've said has led you to feel differently. I'll try again—really, I will—but you seemed so upset at the thought of waiting, and I don't know how long it will take me to come up with a counterspell that actually works, even once the trials are over. If you want to get rid of the curse quickly, it might be time to consult an expert. And unless you can think of someone from the Fount or Coterie you trust enough—"

"No," I said hastily. "No, I still don't think that's a good idea."

Cassius tilted his head and looked at me, expression cannier than I was altogether comfortable with. "Is everything all right, Leo? You've seemed . . . not yourself ever since I got here. Is something bothering you?"

The itch underneath my skin intensified, and so did the anxious churning in my gut. I needed to get ahold of myself. I needed to find Grimm and make the curse go back to sleep so that I could think.

"Sorry. That was—I'm sorry." I ran a shaky hand through

my hair. "I know you're trying to help. I'm just...overtired." This was technically a lie since I'd only recently woken from a nap, but it didn't *feel* like a lie. My limbs were heavy with fatigue.

"Think nothing of it," Cassius said, seemingly mollified. "The book is in your hands now. What you choose to do with it is entirely up to you. It makes no difference to me, though I do think Grimm should at least be told about it."

"Yes, yes," I said. Then in as casual a voice as I could manage, "Have you seen him, by chance? I had a question for him earlier, but I think he's already found some sort of revelry in the city to escape to."

"Oh, he's not in the city," Cassius said. "He's gone home."

"Home?" I repeated, wits made dull with surprise. The small glimmer of hope I'd held for Grimm returning before I left was instantly snuffed out.

"Yes, to Dwull."

My heart sank even further, landing somewhere around my boots. Dwull was hours away from the Fount. No wonder the curse was making me want to jump out of my own skin.

Cassius was still talking, unaware of my distress. "I understand his family has a small farm there, and he goes to help with the harvest every year. I always forget Sebastian doesn't come from gentry. I find it hard to imagine him in a field, don't you?" Cassius spoke the words smilingly, as though asking me to join in on the absurdity of the image.

It was true that I had a hard time picturing Grimm, with his neatly pressed sash and pristine coat, getting his hands dirty in any sense of the word, but I didn't smile back. The offhand snobbishness of the remark was a little too close to something my father might have said.

Cassius seemed to mistake my silence for something other than disapproval, because his own face turned serious again.

"Are you looking for him because of…that is to say, has something changed?"

Yes, something had fucking changed. Grimm had decided to put miles between us, and now I would have to spend the next few days feeling like an entire anthill had taken up residence beneath my skin.

"No. Like I said, I just had a question for him. Nothing important."

"Well, I can write his address down for you, in case you want to contact him before break is over."

It took a moment for me to find a blank piece of paper in the mess on my table, but then Cassius quickly scratched out a few lines that I folded and stuffed in one of my pockets.

"Happy harvest to you," I said, nodding as he made his way to the door.

"Same to you." Then, with a little nod of his own and a rueful smile, Cassius said, "Please give my best to your father this evening."

CHAPTER NINE

The journey to my father's estate took us only about an hour outside of Luxe, but it felt longer. I attempted to distract myself with the book Cassius had given me, but instead just gave myself a headache—little sparks of pain that burst at the base of my skull before migrating up to my temples.

The book was, as he'd said, full of desperate people who had sought out this sorcerer in the woods based on rumor or on other spells she'd written. It was intriguing, but the whole thing had the ring of a folktale to it. The stories themselves were spread out over a period of time that suggested the sorcerer in question was not even the same person, despite the initials. I wondered at Cassius, that he would judge this a straw worth grasping at.

Did he really think I was so far gone as the people in this book? Surely my curse was not so bad as all that.

I tucked the book away and did my best to rub the tension out of my neck, but the pain persisted.

Agnes sat beside me in the carriage, resplendent in a gown the color of ripe wheat that fell off her shoulders in just such a way as to highlight their strength. Gold jewelry clasped each of her wrists and wove through the braids in her dark hair. She looked as elegant and powerful as any of the sorcerer portraits that lined the halls of the Citadel, but the effect was somewhat ruined by the way she kept nervously biting her lip and smoothing her skirt.

"Do you know which Coterie captains will be there?" she asked.

"My father doesn't send me the guest list."

"I should have asked my mother if she knew." Agnes paused in her fretting to look at me, forehead wrinkling slightly. "You're quieter than usual."

"Headache," I grunted, though it wasn't as simple as that. We were moving away from Dwull, not toward it, and the spell liked it not one bit. I felt worse than ever, sick from the rocking of the carriage and the dull ache under my ribs, and too hot from the magic angrily buzzing underneath my skin. The curse was always unpleasant, but now it actually *hurt*.

I considered breaking my silence to explain what was happening to Agnes—she wasn't easy to fool, and I really was feeling poorly—but in the end I decided against it. I may not have been looking forward to the party, but she was. I could worry her later, after she'd had a chance to impress the Coterie elite.

"I think I might be coming down with something," I said, and then coughed a little into my hand.

Agnes looked me over, expression more suspicious than sympathetic. "I hope you're not plotting anything."

"Are you suggesting that I would intentionally cause a scene?" I clutched my chest. "I'm wounded."

In fact, I did have a history of attempting to enliven these sorts of events. The year before, I'd gotten my hands on a fire works spell and tricked an extremely drunk caster into setting them off. The harvest before that, I'd dragged an anatomically impressive straw effigy into my father's courtyard and set it alight, and the year before that, well... I'd gotten drunk and fallen off a balcony. Humiliating, but also entertaining, in its own way. People loved having something to gossip about.

"This year is different," Agnes reminded, a note of pleading in her voice.

"I know, I know." I patted her hand comfortingly. "I don't have any mischief planned, I promise."

"That makes it sound like you planned it the other times," Agnes muttered, but she appeared mollified. When I rested my head on her shoulder, she didn't push me off but adjusted her arm in order to run her fingers soothingly through the hair at my temples and continued to do so until we had passed through the gates of the estate.

There was still a hint of light in the sky as we exited the carriage and walked arm in arm up the many stone steps to the open front doors. The windows glowed warm and bright with the reflection of the setting sun, but it did little to soften my impression of the place—I'd always found my father's house to be unwelcoming, and no amount of decoration was likely to change that.

As though summoned by this thought, the man himself appeared, walking toward us from the arched doorway leading into the main parlor.

"Agnesia," he said, smiling and extending his hand. "It's lovely to see you."

Agnes, ever the diplomat, dropped my arm to let him clasp her fingers briefly. "The pleasure is mine, I'm sure," she said. "Thank you for the invitation."

My father turned to me next. The smile on his face didn't drop, but it flickered. A nearly imperceptible stutter, like the guttering of a candle. I was taller than him, and it wasn't a recent development, but it always felt like a surprise. The fact that he had to tilt his chin up slightly to look at me was enjoyable in theory but, in reality, just made me inclined to slouch.

"Leo." He spoke my name like it was too small to contain the feeling he wished it to carry. An imperfect vessel.

"Hello, Father."

"You look well," he said smoothly. "It's good you're here early. Your brother will be glad to have a chance to catch up with you."

"Rainer's here?" He hadn't been free to attend last year's party. Or the one before that. I'd assumed this year would be the same, but Father nodded.

"You should seek him out," he said. As though Rainer was just another party guest whose company was to be acquired. "But I'd like a word with you first."

"I think I see my mother over there," Agnes said, the traitor. "I'll give you both a moment to talk while I go say hello." She withdrew, and I was left to follow my father away from the open doorway and toward a corner unoccupied by guests. A servant carrying a carefully balanced tray of fluted glasses passed by, and I snatched one. My father followed the movement with his eyes.

"How is the Fount?" he asked.

"Dull as ever," I said, taking a sip of my drink. The combination of my father's presence and the magic simmering in my blood made it hard to stand in one place. My headache, which had lessened slightly without the jostling of the carriage, began to make a comeback.

"You have an active mind." The delicacy with which he spoke made me nervous. Like he was hoping to ease me into a conversation I might have otherwise struggled against. "You should put it to work, especially now. You'll have an easier time finding a Coterie troop to your liking if you make a name for yourself in fifth tier."

"Was this what you wanted to talk about?" I asked, hoping to steer the conversation away from my future plans with the Coterie, or lack thereof.

"In a way. I know you have a taste for...revelry." His eyes lingered over the glass in my hands. "And that you like to add your own flair to these gatherings. But I would ask you to remember that a party and a stage are not the same thing. Nor are entertainment and spectacle. There are representatives from the lake country and Granvoir here tonight, not to mention captains looking to recruit. These are people you would do well to impress."

"Am I to take this to mean you didn't appreciate last year's fireworks?" I asked dryly.

"You disgrace yourself with such displays," my father said. He didn't say it cruelly. As far as he was concerned, this was simply a fact. "It's a mistake to dally over the sort of magic a child could write when you could be working to fix your Grandmagic instead. *That's* what you should be showing off."

I froze, fingers clenched around my glass.

There had been a time when he'd felt quite differently. A time when I'd tearfully shown him my most ambitious, most doomed spellwork, and he'd wrapped his hand tight around my wrist until the bones ground together and said, "Never, *never* practice magic like this again."

"Children write all sorts of spells," I said. "Or have you forgotten?"

My tone was bland, but the words caused my father to grow very still. He looked at me sharply. The tops of his cheeks turned a blotchy red. I could practically see the thoughts unspooling in his mind. That I would hint at something like that *here*, of all places. But there was nothing he could say, unless he wanted to acknowledge the truth. And avoiding that at all costs was one of the few things we agreed upon.

"Control is important for a scriver," he said gruffly. "I'm simply asking you to exhibit some tonight. Make yourself memorable for something other than pyrotechnics. Now, if you'll excuse me, I must go and greet the other guests."

Once he was gone, I took another sip of my drink, hardly tasting it.

"Well," I said to myself. "At least that part's done with."

Party guests began to arrive in earnest, congregating in the rooms and softly lit hallways—little clusters of sorcerers dressed up in their very best clothes. The main parlor was dressed up as well, with garlands of late-season flowers and spelled lights hanging high in the air, reflecting off the gilt-edged designs on the wallpaper. The furniture had been pushed aside to make space for dancing, and there was a dais for the musicians set up in the center of the floor. I vaguely recognized the violinist as someone I had either played music with before or slept with before, but they were busy warming up, so I didn't drift closer to confirm either way.

Agnes caught my eye from one room over and beckoned, but I shook my head. She was standing in a circle of important-looking people and I knew if I went over there now, I would be tempted to behave badly purely to spite my father.

Instead, I made my way upstairs to the library. The doors had been left open as a refuge for those who wished to retreat from the noise and bright lights, but it was early in the evening yet for anyone to be searching for a secluded corner. I walked over to one of the windows and pulled it open a crack, then closed my eyes.

My entire chest hurt from resisting the tugging in my sternum, telling me, *Go back, find him.*

I sucked in a deep breath and braced my arms on either side of the window frame, steadying myself against the pull.

"Leo!" someone said, low and pleased.

I turned just in time to see a backlit shape in the doorway step into the room. For a moment I felt a stab of irritation at my hiding place being found so quickly, then I recognized my brother's face.

You could be twins, someone had told us once. It had been at a gala and it was possible the person in question was inclined toward seeing double at that point, but we did look alike. We were of a height, with the same blue eyes and dark hair, though Rainer had shorn his close where I let mine grow long. He wore the Coterie dress uniform, golden collar bright against the black coat. His indigo caster's sash was embroidered with scarlet thread, depicting crossing swords and musical notes alike. The overall effect was very dashing, though lessened slightly by the sling holding his left arm close to his chest.

Rainer smiled widely at me, and some of the swirling discomfort I felt faded into the background. "It's good to see you." He clasped my hand with his good one and shook it. The sort of gesture I supposed he exchanged with his friends and comrades in the Coterie. It was not unfriendly. Not unwarm.

There was a period of time when we were young (after our

mother's death), when I'd acted as though every hurt I received
in Rainer's presence was a mortal injury, just so he would put his
arm around me in concern. Until our father noticed and snapped,
"You're not an infant." And, to Rainer, "Don't encourage him."
"It's good to see you too," I said. Rainer's hand was warm
and sword-calloused under my own. I let go when he drew back,
glancing pointedly toward the sling. "I suppose whatever heroics
caused this are also what we have to thank for your presence here
tonight?"

He laughed a little. "I'm not sure how heroic it was, but yes, I
was ordered to take some time to recover."

I followed him over to the low chaise arranged in front of the
unlit hearth, then sat down beside him when he gestured to the
open place. I'd forgotten how easy Rainer always made things.
The graciousness of his voice and movements.

I nodded to his arm. "What happened?"

"Lucky arrow. Well"—he smiled again, ruefully this time—
"not lucky for me. But it could have been worse."

"You were shot?" I leaned toward him automatically, alarmed.
"By whom? I thought you were stationed by the barrier." The
Wilderlands teemed with magic, and the beasts that lived there
steeped in it—but beasts didn't shoot arrows.

"We were," Rainer said. "This happened when we were
refreshing the spells on a section of the barrier in Dwull. It should
have been a standard mission, but we crossed some outlaws who
were using that section to pass into the Wilderlands and got into
a skirmish. Only two of them, but they took us by surprise and
got away."

Rainer's hand drifted to his arm, pressing briefly against his
shoulder before drifting back down to his lap. "We're used to
dealing with monsters, not Coterie members gone rogue."

My eyes widened. Outlaw Coterie members were hardly common. In fact, I could think of only one group that had ever gone rogue.

"The library thieves!" I said. "You're sure?" They had managed to neatly evade capture thus far, despite the troops sent out to search for them following the break-in, and the sizable reward the Citadel was offering for any information on their whereabouts. It wasn't easy to find a sorcerer who was determined to stay hidden. Especially ones who had been Coterie members themselves.

"I'm sure," Rainer said grimly. "I used to be in the same troop as two of them. Only briefly," he hurried to say, noting my surprise. "They both moved on shortly after I joined, but I remember their faces well enough. Siblings, as it happens. Even if I hadn't recognized them, the spells they fended us off with identified them clearly enough. One of the vaults they snuck into held a collection of paralysis spells." Rainer grimaced. "We could only watch them leave."

"What else did they take during the break-in?" I asked, curious.

"Whatever they could get their hands on," Rainer said, mouth still twisted in disapproval. "I heard one member of the troop had been granted special access to the vaults for research purposes; that's how they got in so easily, before Phade sounded the alarm. There were a bunch of monster wards missing. Memory and invisibility spells too. But we think they were there for something in particular. One of Titus's last works."

The name sent a little frisson of shock up the back of my neck. "Titus?"

"Yes. My understanding is that the break-in was prompted by one of their troop members getting injured on a Coterie mission.

They were desperate, I suppose, although that's no excuse. That was the only functional healing spell the library had available for study."

I sat very still, digesting this. Very few sorcerers had ever managed to craft a successful healing spell, but Alexander Titus was one of them. He'd composed a spell strong enough to heal almost any injury but had never managed a version that could be replicated by another scriver's hand. After his death, the number of remaining spells had dwindled away until there was only one, which the Fount had secured in their vaults. Not to be used, but to be studied, in hopes of one day re-creating it.

"Did you ever get a look at it?" Rainer asked.

"What would be the point?" I'd been obsessed with Titus and his works when I was young—but by the time I was actually at the Fount, I had long abandoned my dream of being the person to crack that particular code. Now the thought of seeing his words made me feel vaguely ill.

Rainer glanced sideways at me, noting my discomfort. He quirked his lips and gracefully changed the subject. "I probably shouldn't be talking about any of this. It's not common knowledge that they were able to make off with a Titus original. But you'll know all about it soon enough anyway."

"What do you mean?"

"Once you join, of course. It's not a secret among Coterie members." Rainer made a face. "Little is, to be honest. If you think gossip at the Fount is bad, just wait until you're part of the Coterie rumor mill."

I didn't say anything. This was a technique that worked perfectly well on our father, who would either keep talking about whatever future he envisioned or move on to the next subject, assuming that we were in perfect agreement. It didn't work so well on Rainer. He paused, then leaned in to look at me more closely.

"Oh," he said softly. "Still, Leo?"

"I never planned to join," I said. "The only reason I went to the Fount was because I had to, you know that."

"I thought you might change your mind once you were there. I thought you *had*. Last time I saw you, you said you'd enjoyed working with the Coterie in fourth tier."

"I did. That doesn't mean I've changed my mind."

"You'd be well suited to it, Leo," Rainer said, his earnestness sharp as a knife. "It's not like what you're doing now, all memorization and rules. Quick thinking and innovation are highly prized skills. The Coterie always needs more scrivers, especially ones with a knack for composing, and I've seen you write spells in the blink of an eye. Do you know how useful that would be to the right captain? Or the Citadel, even?"

"Charms meant to call a breeze closer in summer or invite a bird to perch on my hand are hardly the sort of magic they're looking for," I pointed out. "My spells are too small to be of any help."

"You're more capable than you give yourself credit for."

I looked away, wishing I had chosen someplace else to hide so that I might have avoided this conversation. Where was my drink? I must have set it down somewhere on the way to the library. I wished for something to hold. Something to do with my mouth besides speak. I quelled the urge to flee and then smiled at Rainer. "Familiarity is clouding your judgment. I don't lack creativity, that much is true, but I'm afraid I don't have your motivation to channel it into anything better." I clapped him lightly on his good shoulder. "One success per family is enough. Let me finish this bargain with Father and then waste my days with music and the occasional amusing cantrip. That's all I want."

"Are you certain?"

"That we have better things to do right now than discussing my five-year plan? Absolutely positive. There *is* a party happening, brother mine."

I ignored the disappointed tilt to Rainer's mouth and kept my voice firm. He'd never enjoyed confrontation, and I was the more stubborn of the two of us.

Eventually he sighed. "I'm still going to show you off tonight, you know. Father made me promise to introduce you to all sorts of people. I hope you'll keep an open mind."

"You can show me off to whomever you like," I said. "Just don't expect it to change anything."

True to his word, Rainer steered me through the party with a silver tongue and an easy smile. Only the most powerful Coterie members were invited to my father's parties—or if they weren't powerful, they were beautiful, or if they weren't either of those things, they wanted to be, with the sort of desperation that nearly makes something true. It meant that the crowd assembled in his house that night practically glittered, each of them a jewel and very few of them unpolished.

Rainer introduced me to people whose names I did not know and had no intention of remembering, and guided me toward others I knew from their long association with our family. The only good thing about all of this was that I was able to collect Agnes and thus divide some of the attention. Even Agnes wasn't enough to save me from my aunt Delilah. She shared all my father's directness with none of his ability to ration words, and she cornered me with a flurry of questions before finally looking at me cannily over the rim of her wineglass and saying, "I'm glad to see you've made it to fifth tier. Some of us in the family were worried you might abandon your responsibilities and run off with an unseemly musician." She let out a little titter. "Can you imagine?"

I let my lips stretch across my teeth in a smile. "Don't be silly, Aunt Delilah, there was never any chance of that. You see, I want to *be* the unseemly musician that someone runs off with, not the other way around." And then, while her mouth was still open in a perfect O of surprise, I excused myself to the dance floor.

I had no shortage of partners; Rainer had seen to that. I danced with a woman from his troop, then with a captain from the lake country's Coterie branch, and with a man who smugly informed me he was the Citadel's chief overseer of spellwork (as though I kept track of boring Citadel job titles and their meanings). After that, the faces blurred together until I was dizzy with them. The heat of the room crawled up my spine and settled under my collar, stifling around my throat.

I did not feel well. My stomach churned even though I'd barely had anything to eat or drink. The music was enjoyable, but everything else in the room felt like too much all at once, an assault on my senses. During the next pause between songs, I bowed to my partner and quickly made my retreat from the dance floor to escape out onto the balcony.

A bench sat pressed up against the side of the house in the shadow of the open door. That was where I settled, tilting my head back to breathe the cool air in gulps. It soothed my flushed cheeks but did nothing to dispel the sensation that I might burst out of my own skin at any moment. The curse pounded against my rib cage like a second heartbeat, and the thought of trying to ignore it while I stood around trading bland witticisms made me want to gouge my own eye out with a caviar spoon.

I wished (mortifyingly) that Grimm was there. Not so close that I would have to bear the weight of his presence, just... nearby, like he usually was. It was possible I had underestimated the effects of distance. Perhaps if I didn't stay at my father's estate, if I returned to the Fount, the miles between us would be lessened enough for the spell to go back to its low-grade level of annoyance.

As I was considering this, two people stepped through the door and onto the balcony, walking forward to lean against the railing. The newcomers didn't see me, tucked away as I was. Thinking themselves alone, they did not lower their voices.

"I saw you dancing with Warde," the man said. "Are you considering him for next year?"

"He's a possibility," the woman replied. I recognized her—a troop captain my brother had introduced me to earlier. The man looked familiar as well, but he was facing away from me, making it difficult to place him. "I'm more impressed by Quest. If it's between the two of them, she's by far the better choice."

I hadn't been trying to eavesdrop, but at the sound of Agnes's name I pulled myself farther back in the shadows, so that I could listen and carry any praise back to her.

"You'll have competition there," the man said.

I caught a glimpse of the woman's smile before her face turned away from me. "I'm willing to fight you for her, if it comes to that."

The man dismissed this with a wave of his hand. "You won't have to. I have enough casters in my crew."

"There's no one here to tempt you?"

"I didn't say that. I said I don't need any more *casters*. Loveage, though, I have my eye on him."

Shock swept over me, leaving me cold in its wake. I didn't want to hear any more, but I couldn't move without attracting attention.

The woman chuckled. "Betting on the dark horse, are you? His spellwork hardly extends beyond cantrips. And he has a reputation."

The man shook his head a little. "He doesn't look good on paper, I'll grant you that. But I oversaw some of the work he did last year, when the Coterie sent fourth-tier sorcerers to help us. He's inventive."

Even in the dim light, I could see the skeptical arch of his companion's eyebrow. "Inventive enough for you to make a claim during the trials? That's quite the statement."

"My troop is big enough to make good use of a support scriver," the man said. Then he lowered his voice and added, "Besides, his brother and I started off in the same troop, and Rainer put in a good word for him with me."

"Ahhh, I see," the woman said, voice turning thoughtful. "It's not a bad idea to have the Loveage name on your side."

"Don't get any ideas," he warned. "I spotted him first."

"If you didn't want me getting ideas, you shouldn't have given them to me."

"Maybe another drink will make you forget," the man said, and pulled her back inside, the two of them laughing.

I stayed where I was, frozen.

This whole time, I had thought no one would give me a second glance during the trials. That they would see my meager charms and collected letters of warning from the Fount and simply steer clear. But it was just as Rainer had said: Scrivers were always in demand. Apparently, there were too few of us for captains to turn their noses up at even the most lackluster candidate... provided they came with the right gentry qualifications.

It was one thing for me to tell my brother, or Agnes, or even my father I wanted nothing to do with that life, but if a Coterie captain had looked beyond my puny abilities and seen someone inventive and promising, I might not have been able to resist saying yes.

But that wasn't what this was.

This had nothing to do with me, beyond the name shared between my father, my brother, and myself. I wasn't really wanted. My skills, such as they were, were an afterthought. For years I'd lived in fear of slipping up and overextending myself, causing mayhem and hurt by simply trying to do what came so naturally to everyone else.

But, apparently, no one even thought me capable enough to cause trouble.

In my flustered, curse-stricken state, only one thing was clear to me: Someone needed to disabuse them of that notion.

CHAPTER TEN

Head and heart pounding, I stood up from my hiding spot and made my way back inside. I snatched a glass off a tray and threw my head back to down the wine quickly, so that the sickly sweet taste of it had less time to linger. Then I wiped my mouth with the back of my hand and looked around the room.

I hadn't lied to Agnes about having no plan for any sort of disruptive event this year, which made it harder now that I suddenly found myself in need of one. *These are people you would do well to impress,* my father had said, but I wanted to do the opposite. I wanted them all to see me at my worst. *Then* let them decide if I was worth their time at the trials.

Dancing had ceased while the musicians took a break to tune. My eyes settled on the violinist I'd noticed earlier. With effort, I was able to recall going toe-to-toe with her in some sort of musical battle late one night at my favorite bar, though the memory was blurry. I looked now at the violin, resting softly under her chin as she tuned it.

Swaying slightly, I began to walk across the room. My mind was hazier than the one drink could explain. The spell, probably. The fucking curse. That would have been the perfect reveal to warn everyone off me, but I couldn't do that without ruining Grimm's reputation as well.

The violinist looked up as I approached, eyeing me curiously.

"Hello," I said, fixing my most charming smile in place. "Do you remember me?"

She looked me over, taking in my fine clothes and scarlet scriver's sash. "You look a little different, but yes, I remember."

I smiled at her, fingers already toying with the rings on my fingers. "Lovely to see you again. I have an odd request."

The woman's expression turned wary. I could only imagine the sort of "odd requests" she usually received from stumbling party guests. "What is it?"

"I want to borrow your violin."

Her fingers tightened around the instrument reflexively. "What?"

"Only briefly." I had my own, but it either was still in the carriage or had been brought to my room, several floors above. If I took the time to get it, I worried the moment would pass and I'd lose my nerve.

The woman clutched her violin a little closer. "I don't think—"

"I'll be careful with it, I promise. And I'll give you this!" I pulled the largest ring off my hand and held it out to her. It was gold, with a ruby set in the middle. Expensive, probably. It had been given to me as a gift when I entered the Fount.

One of the nearby musicians let out a gasp, quickly muffled.

"It's yours," I said, holding the ring out farther when the violinist didn't take it right away. "Just let me play something."

The violinist still looked confused, but after a moment she took the ring. "I'm not sure what you're getting out of this, but sure." She presented the violin and bow to me. "Have at it."

"Thank you," I said.

Then it was back across the floor to the empty dais, which I climbed onto with more determination than grace. The people standing nearest watched with inquiring eyes, but most of the room's attention was still elsewhere. That simply would not do.

I cleared my throat.

"Esteemed guests!" At the sound of my voice heads began to turn, and even like this, with a bitter taste in my mouth and my temples pounding, I still felt the flutter of excitement that being on a stage always brought. "A night such as this calls for a special kind of entertainment. And I am here to provide!" I allowed my words to slur more than strictly necessary. Let them think my wits were dimmed by drink rather than by magic.

Across the room there was a sudden burst of movement as my father pushed his way to the front of the crowd. He halted there and stared at me, eyes full of warning.

I cradled the violin beneath my chin and sent out a silent prayer that the musician I'd borrowed it from had done a thorough job tuning. Then I raised my bow.

The music that poured from me was different from the pleasant melodies that had filtered through the room all evening. It was a storm of a song, and for a brief stretch of time it swept me up wholly. I threw my body into the playing of it, letting everything except my purpose melt away.

As I played, I began to weave a bit of magic into the notes, improvising a spellsong. I wasn't in a fit state to be casting cantrips, and the magic dragged at me like gravity. The notes didn't want to be played, almost like the unfamiliar violin was fighting me, but I gritted my teeth and ignored the discomfort, just as I'd been doing all evening.

Little sparks began to leap from where my bow touched string, turning into shining winged things that soared over everyone's heads. Not fireworks, but explosive in their own way.

For a moment the only sound in the parlor was the music and the hushed *ahhhh* of the crowd, as they lifted their faces toward the light. Then the sparks drifted downward, delicate as snowflakes, and the room erupted in chaos.

It was not my intent to cause harm, but I wanted to remind everyone (myself most of all) what they risked by thinking me harmless.

The sparks that drifted low enough to settle in the crowd were immediately put out, but the ones that settled in the curtains and decorative swaths of fabric hanging from the ceiling began to smoke. There was shouting and a few screams as the party guests noticed the beginnings of fire.

Through it all I kept playing, unconcerned. I would not have risked this stunt if I wasn't in a room full of the people most capable of making sure this didn't go terribly wrong.

Sure enough, it didn't take long for the first spell to be cast. The assembled Coterie members had dealt with far worse than this, although I think they were slowed down by not wanting to destroy my father's beautiful parlor in the process of putting out the fire. In the end no one made rain fall from the ceiling, which I felt was a missed opportunity, but the flames were quickly smothered nonetheless.

I waited until their attention was unoccupied to finish my song, sending my bow gliding along the strings with a flourish, then I stood on the dais, panting slightly.

The remains of my audience looked back at me, murmurs already rising like the wind.

He's drunk, he must be.

What a display.

Careless.

The far reaches of the room appeared oddly blurry to me.

Had someone turned the lights down? I couldn't make out my father among the crowd, or Agnes, or my brother. The only face close enough for me to recognize was that of the Coterie captain whom I'd heard on the balcony. He was looking up at me, a frown reminiscent of Grimm creasing his brow.

With great solemnity, I bowed in his direction.

As soon as I straightened, the adrenaline that had carried me this far vanished. I nearly dropped the violin as the room spun. I stumbled getting off the dais, and the only reason I didn't fall was because someone caught my elbow in a bruising grip.

I blinked down at my father, whose face was set in a mask of fury.

With some effort, I managed to speak. "You said to make myself memorable. Did I not?"

Then—in the grand finale of the evening—I listed to the side, arm slipping out of his grasp as I crashed into one of the closest gawkers. Someone swore and a glass broke, shattering on the floor with a merry chime.

"Catch him!" someone shouted, but I wasn't awake to discover if anyone listened.

I came to flat on my back, with pain lancing through the left side of my face. Moving very slowly, I lifted a hand and found that the skin around my eye was tender and puffy. Before I could feel more, my fingers were slapped away.

"Don't," Agnes said sharply. Fluttering my eyes open, I discovered her seated beside me wearing a glum expression. She reached for something just beyond the scope of my still blurry vision, and her hands returned with a cool cloth, which she laid over my aching face.

"Ow," I said weakly. "What happened?"

"You fainted," Agnes said.

I sat up, slowly, holding the cloth so the blessed coolness stayed in place. "I figured that part out, thank you. But why does my face feel like it's been brawling without me?"

"You hit it on the way down. On someone's elbow, I think. You're lucky they caught you before your head hit the floor."

"How chivalrous of them," I said, willing my head to stop spinning. Now that I was upright, I realized we were in the same library where I'd spoken to Rainer earlier. The door had been closed and a fire had been lit in the hearth. I was laid out on the chaise in front of it, with Agnes perched beside me. The comfort of my surroundings suggested that my brother or Agnes had been in charge of my removal from the party. If it had been my father's choice, I might have woken outside the main gate.

Agnes looked down at me, face still very solemn.

"Am I bleeding?" I asked, removing the cloth from over my eye.

"No," she said, after the briefest glance.

"Hm. How ungratifying."

Agnes let out a faint, unamused snort. Then she said, in a sharp-edged sort of voice, "Tell me, Leo, is it your intent to make yourself the center of attention in every room you walk into, or does it just happen by chance?"

An added layer of discomfort settled over me, twisting my insides just as surely as the spell did. Agnes should have been back at the party, collecting admirers and speaking with the same people I'd just done my best to repel—Coterie members she'd be working alongside next year.

Instead, she was here, sitting beside me in an otherwise empty room.

"M'sorry," I mumbled, and reached forward to pat her knee. But the movement caused the room to tilt around me. Leaping from the chaise, I grabbed a vase from the nearby end table, tossed the flowers onto the floor, and then was violently sick into the prettily patterned ceramic.

I crouched on the floor after, sweaty and shaking. The room was dimly lit, but everything looked too bright. My senses felt like glassy, fragile things.

"Exactly how much did you have to drink?" Agnes asked, sounding resigned.

I hugged the vase closer and shot her a shaky grin over its rim. "Would you believe me if I said not very much at all?"

By the time I finished my second round of retching, Agnes was kneeling next to me.

"You can see why that would be hard for me to believe, can't you?" She reached to gather my hair back, and as she did so her fingers brushed against my cheek. She frowned, then laid the back of her hand against my forehead. "Leo, are you ill?"

I hiccuped out a pathetic laugh. "In a manner of speaking."

"You should have said. You're burning up!"

"Am I? That explains a lot."

"Can you stand to make it to your room? You need to be in bed."

She started to rise, but I caught her hand. "Don't," I said. "My bed won't cure this."

Agnes rolled her eyes, obviously assuming I was just feverish and stubborn, but she let herself be pulled back down next to me and tucked a loose curl back from my sweaty face. "What will, then?"

I tilted my head back to rest against the wall rather than look at her. There were no distractions left. All the fight had gone out of me, and there was nothing to do but face the inevitable.

"I need you to take me to Sebastian Grimm," I said.

CHAPTER ELEVEN

Agnes let out a short laugh. "Your fever must be worse than I thought."

I shook my head, then stopped quickly when it made my stomach lurch. "I'm not delirious. It's the spell."

"Oh," Agnes said. Then she collapsed down onto the floor beside me all at once, limbs gone heavy. "Oh, shit."

"Yes," I agreed. "I'm sorry to report that the inconvenience level has been updated to moderate."

"But Grimm's not even here!" Agnes said, at a loss.

I winced. "That's the problem, actually. The magic, it acts up if Grimm isn't around. I barely noticed when we were at the Fount because he wasn't far away and because, well, I could easily sneak a glimpse of him if it started bothering me too much. But he went home for the harvest, and since then it's been getting worse."

Beside me Agnes was very still. "You knew," she said quietly. "You knew something was changing and you didn't say anything to any of us. Not even me."

"I thought I could manage it on my own. At least until the trials were over and Cassius could write another counter-spell."

Agnes shook her head. "You're such an idiot, Leo," she said

sadly, and the disappointment in her voice was worse than any amount of anger would have been. "Tell me what's changed. And I mean everything."

I described the gradual, creeping need. The stolen glimpses I'd employed to keep the symptoms at bay. The way that my heart's very function seemed tied to the spell now, beating out a frantic rhythm in my chest. How, without Grimm there, each breath felt like it was leaving a bruise.

By the time I was finished, Agnes's frown was deep enough to give Grimm competition. The last time she'd looked at me with such concern we were twelve and I'd just gotten the wind knocked out of me falling from a horse. The discomfort that had racked me then wasn't so different from now—as though a knife slipped under my skin with each breath.

"Leo," Agnes said. "We're right next to a whole room of people who could help us solve this. Your father is a powerful scriver, even if we told just him—"

"No!" I grabbed Agnes's arm. "He has a seat in the Citadel. He'd feel obliged to handle this fairly, and Grimm and I would be kicked out of the Fount."

"Better than you winding up dead," Agnes said bluntly.

"I'm not sure that's true." Agnes looked horrified, but I continued on. "I have no idea how far punishment for something like this would go, Agnes. Maybe they'd be satisfied by kicking us out, maybe not. All I know is that I don't want to be locked up in the Citadel because I *accidentally* cursed *myself.* Just help me get to Grimm. Then I'll be able to think clearly enough to decide what comes next."

"I don't even know where he lives."

"He's from Dwull," I said, remembering what Cassius had told me earlier. Was it really just that morning we had spoken? It

felt longer. The day had aged me. I was a different person from
the man who had looked upon the prospect of living with the
spell and felt only mild annoyance.

"Dwull is a big province," Agnes said doubtfully. "How are
we supposed to find him?"

"I have his address in the pocket of my coat, packed away
with the rest of my things."

Agnes chewed on her lip, indecision plain on her face. I
waited, hoping. I was getting to Dwull no matter what, but I
wanted her help badly. The only thing worse than showing up
on Grimm's doorstep to explain what was happening would be if
I had to crawl there.

"All right," Agnes said. She drew in a deep breath, and by
the time she let it out, her expression had morphed into one of
steely-eyed determination. "Let's get you to Dwull."

Within fifteen minutes we were making our way down one of
the hallways that led to a side door. My arm was slung across
Agnes's back, and she was very kindly not commenting on how
much I needed to lean on her in order to walk.

"My things—" I said weakly.

"I already got them from your room," Agnes informed me
as we shuffled forward. "They're in the carriage I bribed one of
your father's stable hands into letting us borrow. You owe me
three gold coins, by the way."

"Pretty sure I'm going to owe you more than that by the time
this is through." I laughed a little under my breath. "Imagine my

father's face when he realizes I've run away, rather than sticking around to hear the rant he's got brewing for me."

"I'd rather not," Agnes said. "I'm already imagining my mother's face when she realizes I've left without so much as a goodbye. I was supposed to ride back with her to Luxe tonight." I patted her left cheek with the hand slung across her shoulder. "You're a good friend."

"I'm the *best* friend."

"Mm-hmm," I agreed, then lurched away from her abruptly to lean against the wall. "Excuse me," I said, before expelling what little remained in my stomach onto the floor.

"Magic preserve us," Agnes muttered.

We made it the rest of the way without stopping, but each step cost me. I'd hoped that the spell would somehow sense my compliance and lessen its effects, but it didn't seem to care that I was doing my best. The tugging against my insides did not cease. I *wanted* so badly that my skin felt like it was on fire.

"How are you doing?" Agnes asked once we were situated in the carriage.

I whimpered. If anyone asked later, I would have denied it, but at that moment I couldn't help myself. At least Agnes was the only one there to hear.

"Just hold on, Leo," she said, in her most soothing voice.

Why couldn't it have been her? I thought blearily. If I was to be saddled with this curse, why couldn't it have been cast by someone I was already bound to? Someone who cared for me.

Agnes flicked the reins across the horse's back with a sure hand, and the carriage pulled away from the stable and toward the front gate, leaving my father's estate behind us as we struck out into the night.

My memories of that journey are hazy at best. Brief moments

of lucidity were interspersed with fever dreams, and when I awoke, I noticed only fragments of our surroundings: The lantern at the front of the carriage cast weak light onto the road, and everything beyond that dim glow was just a suggestion of landscape in the dark. A shadowed mass of trees here, a hill there. I tried to let the rocking motion of the carriage lull me to sleep, but the curse drummed a ceaseless command against every tender part of me, until it was all I could do not to lean my head back and sob.

Hours passed that way.

We were going down what appeared to be a straight road with no variance in sight when I let out a sharp gasp and clutched at my chest, struck all at once by a strong need to move sideways. To turn, *now*.

"Here," I said. "Something's here."

The road, when Agnes found it, was really more of a path. Easy to miss in the dark. Agnes slowly guided the horse along the path until it ended in front of the looming, dark shape of a building—a barn, I thought.

As soon as we came to a stop, I scrambled out of the carriage on legs that shook.

"Leo, wait," Agnes said.

"We're close. I can tell."

Around the corner of the barn, I found rocky steps winding up a hill. I began to climb.

"Wait!" Agnes called out again, hurrying to secure the horse to the hitching post in front of the barn. I didn't listen to her. I couldn't. The curse propelled me onward, and the thought of not obeying made my chest feel like something was about to crack open within it.

A dark shape at the top of the hill turned out to be a tall fence covered in growing things. In daytime I thought it might have been a pleasant sight, but it was too dark and I was too feverish to appreciate it now. I followed the fence around, until I found a gate. A lantern hung next to it, the flame low. Pushing against the gate's door, I found it unlocked, which was surprising but suited me just fine. As the door swung open under my hand, I caught a shadowy glimpse of the courtyard and house beyond, details indistinct in the night.

Before I could step through the gate, something sharp traced the ridge of my spine, right between my shoulder blades.

"Don't move," a low voice warned.

I stopped, every muscle locking in place. The order quieted something within me at once. I barely had time to feel relieved by this before another came, fast on the heels of the first.

"Tell me what you're doing here."

When I spoke, my voice was wiped clean of its familiar cadence and inflections. "I came to find you." There was nothing else I could say. The first command was still in place, locking my lips tight against further explanation.

The steel against my back disappeared. "Loveage?" Grimm stepped round to look at me, eyes wide with surprise in the dim light thrown by the lantern. "What are you *doing here?*" he asked again, in an entirely different manner than he had the first time.

I glared back at him, unable to do anything else.

"You can move," he said, realizing. "You can do as you like."

My muscles relaxed all at once, legs folding underneath me in a sort of controlled descent. I was shaking, not from pain this time, but the absence of it.

Grimm stared down at me. He was frowning, but it seemed to be from confusion rather than exasperation, for once.

I sprawled on the ground and grinned up at him tiredly. "I never thought I would say this, Grimm, but I'm actually quite glad to see you."

My exhaustion broke like a cresting wave, catching me up and carrying me along. I did not swoon (I refused to swoon twice in the span of one evening), but I did slump over sideways. And I did allow my head to be cushioned by the cool grass. And I did close my eyes.

CHAPTER TWELVE

I woke up in an unfamiliar room, and not in the fun way. Which is to say, I was quite alone in the narrow bed I lay in, and while my memories of the previous night were a little blurry in places, I recalled most of it better than I would have liked.

Upon sitting up, I saw that the room was small and relatively plain, furnished with only the bed, a chest of drawers, and a chair in the corner upon which my violin case and bag had been placed. Agnes was sleeping in a mess of blankets on the floor beside me.

Moving quietly, I rose and sorted through my belongings until I found a clean shirt and my sorcerer's coat, which I swapped for the creased and sweat-stained formal jacket I'd worn the night before. The room's only door was covered by a simple cloth curtain. After one last look to confirm that Agnes was still deeply asleep, I pushed the curtain aside and left the bedroom behind.

The curtained doorway led to a kitchen, with a well-worn table and chairs at its center and dried herbs hanging from the rafters over the sink. Everyday items lay scattered atop the table and counters, but none of them were presently in use, and when I called out a soft "Hello?" no one answered.

I decided to investigate further. An uncharitable person might have called it snooping.

To my right was a ladder that led up to a loft bedroom. The two pairs of slippers that had been left at the foot of the bed led me to believe this room belonged to Grimm's parents, which meant that the bare little room given to me and Agnes must have been his.

Off the kitchen was a sitting room full of books (fiction, I realized upon closer inspection—not a spellbook in sight) and threadbare chairs. Sweetly fading watercolors decorated the walls, along with a floral brocade wallpaper that reminded me of something I might have seen in my father's parlor—though his walls would have been covered in the stuff, and here there was only a scrap that someone had cut and framed. It was hung in a spot where the rich pattern caught the light from the window.

There is a particular thrill to exploring someone else's home for the first time. It's like peeling a curtain back from all your notions about who that person is, and instead seeing them as both who they are and who they want to be. My father's house, for example, is a magnificent building, full of beautiful things. But look closer and you'll find that all of that loveliness was manufactured. I doubt he picked out a single item in that house for himself; he just paid for everything to be arranged for him. What did that mean, you might ask? Well, I thought it meant this: Deep down, my father enjoyed being there about as much as I did. It was a home in name only.

This house, by contrast, was a comfortable space—lived-in. I liked it.

It held none of the austerity I had come to associate with Grimm, which made me suspect he spent little time here. I did find evidence of him, though, in a portrait hanging above the sitting room fireplace, centered between an illustration of peonies and another of forget-me-nots. It was obviously Grimm, for all that he could not have been much older than twelve when the portrait was painted. His hair was the same shockingly pale shade of gray, and the miniature furrow between his brows made it clear that he had spent a good portion of the sitting glaring at the artist.

It made me chuckle, to see that Grimm's grumpiness was apparently long-standing. It also made something inside my chest turn over restlessly.

With some trepidation, I closed my eyes and sought after the spell's guiding influence. Grimm wasn't far; I could tell that much immediately. The invisible thread connecting us was an almost palpable presence now, much more so than it had been at the Fount.

I followed the sensation out the kitchen door and onto a stone porch overlooking a courtyard full of half-broken flagstones with grass sprouting through the cracks, past the trellised fruit trees lining the fence around the house, and through the gate, toward the barn we'd stopped in front of the night before. By day, the surrounding landscape was all gentle slopes and open fields. Some of them were already laid bare, empty until next year's planting.

Inside the barn, I found more signs of the harvest—golden sheaves of wheat hanging from the ceiling, with more stacked waiting on the floor. Crates full of apples lined one wall, and another was given over to baskets of potatoes. Amid all of that stood Grimm, back to me and hands busy with a spell.

I was trying to be quiet, but my boot scuffed against the rough barn floor as I entered. Not enough of a distraction to disrupt anything, but enough that Grimm's shoulders stiffened. He waited until the paper in his hand was burned away before turning to face me.

"Good morning," I said, trying to sound casual and not at all like I was feeling slightly embarrassed about showing up on Grimm's doorstep with no warning in the middle of the night, only to collapse upon said doorstep. Who would be embarrassed by such a display? Not me, certainly.

"You're awake, I see." Grimm looked and sounded as he always did, voice clipped and face remote, coat neatly pressed. There was something strange about seeing him here, in the softened countryside setting, his bearing just as proper as it was at the Fount. The incongruity of it struck me as hilarious, and I laughed.

"Ah, Grimm," I said, "it's too much. You're a farmer. A farmer, *you!*"

Grimm scowled. "Your snobbery does you no credit."

"*My* snobbery! You're the haughtiest person I know; that's why this is so funny. You're so good at looking down your nose at everyone that you might as well be gentry already."

"I am not snobbish," he said primly. "I am simply mindful of who I associate with."

"Oh, my mistake," I said, with exaggerated sarcasm.

Grimm opened his mouth, shut it, and then appeared to physically bite his tongue. Which was disappointing. He was more fun when he spoke without thinking. "I'm glad to see you've recovered enough to find this humorous," he said at last, not sounding glad at all.

"Yes, yes. Quite recovered. Er, did Agnes happen to explain the circumstances of our arrival?"

Grimm's scowl deepened. "She said the spell worsened and you chose to make yourself ill rather than tell anyone about it. And that you've been following me secretly as a form of…curse management."

I turned away and began to inspect the worktable next to me, covered with tools and dirt and dust. There were neat little stacks of spells there too. Food preservation charms—that's what Grimm had been casting. I looked down at them rather than meet his eyes as I said, "Sorry about that. And about this. Probably should have waited until morning before I came snooping around your house. Don't know what we were thinking."

"Agnes thought you were dying."

"Absurd," I scoffed, even though I wasn't sure it was. I'd felt untethered toward the end there. Like parts of myself were beginning to drift away.

Grimm shook his head slightly, a condemnation. "It was foolish of you to try to bear it alone."

That this was true did nothing to stop the flash of annoyance I felt at him for saying so.

"What would telling anyone have changed? We all agreed to take a break until after the trials, so what can I do besides bear it and try to resist? I don't think trying to fight it was so foolish. I certainly can't haunt your footsteps the rest of our lives."

Referring to the curse as anything but temporary left me with a bitter taste in my mouth. I had never much enjoyed being constrained by anything (another reason the deal with my father chafed so), and everyone knew Grimm was Coterie-bound. I'd be in quite the predicament if we couldn't find a way to undo this.

This was the same trap, coming to catch me in a new and unexpected way.

Agnes was awake when we got back to the house. The three of us gathered on the little stone porch, seated around the rough wooden table there, and Grimm brought out a tray with a dented silver teapot and mismatched cups, as well as breakfast for Agnes and myself—cold leftovers from the morning, two hastily boiled eggs, and some sliced-up late-season peaches. The fruit made me wrinkle my nose, and I pushed it toward Agnes, trying not to shudder at the mere sight of the furry peach skin, but I ate everything else. I was so hungry that it didn't matter that Grimm's skills as a cook were obviously nonexistent.

"What did you tell your family about why we're here?" I asked him curiously.

"That you are a tiermate from the Fount who fell ill while traveling nearby. They do not know the particulars of your illness." Grimm paused, hands suspended in the action of pouring tea. "I would prefer to keep it that way."

His meaning was clear: No one in his family knew of our blunder, and we were not meant to tell them.

"Easy enough to explain this time," Agnes said, "but what about the next? What if it gets worse? Perhaps Cassius could be persuaded to have another stab at the counterspell before the trials begin, given how things have changed."

"I'm not so sure it's a matter of his willingness." I took a sip of tea, then winced and set my cup aside. It was a dark and bitter brew, nothing like what was usually served at the Fount. "I ran into Cassius before we left for the party. He didn't seem confident that he would be able to find a solution easily, even after the trials are over. He did have another idea, though."

I explained the book that Cassius had given me and his suggestion that Grimm and I might seek out the sorcerer in the woods. As I spoke, Grimm's natural stillness seemed to intensify.

"You can't seriously be considering this as a viable option," he said, in the flat sort of voice I'd begun to recognize he used when I'd done or said something he found particularly ridiculous.

"Why not?" I asked, even though I had said something very similar to Cassius the day before. "Whoever this sorcerer is, she's far enough outside the influence of the Coterie that I doubt we have to worry about her turning us in. And the library is full of her counterspells—working ones. Surely someone with that amount of experience would make short work of this curse?"

"The quickest solutions are rarely the best," Grimm said. This sounded almost exactly like something one of our instructors would have told me, and it was delivered with the same all-knowing air. I'd never enjoyed getting such advice, and I appreciated it even less coming from Grimm.

We argued back and forth, with me pointing out every benefit that would come from having the curse gone by the time the Fount was back in session, while Grimm methodically went through all the reasons why such a thing should not be attempted. It was too dangerous, he insisted, and the stories in the book sounded like something you would read aloud to a child, based on more fiction than fact.

"I won't go," he said firmly. "Even if I thought this plan was sensible, which I do not, we have less than two weeks before the trials start. That's not enough time to search an entire forest."

"It's plenty of time to at least try! We could spend a week searching and still make it back to Luxe long before we're expected."

"And what if we stumble upon a monster instead of your sorcerer? What if one or both of us are injured and we *don't* make it back in time? What then?"

"I don't know why everyone acts like the trials are the be-all and end-all," I grumbled. "Any sorcerer worth their salt could find placement without parading themselves around like some sort of prize stallion to be bought."

"The trials are not the only issue here," said Grimm. "Your quest offers too many problems and only the faintest hope of a solution."

"Well, what would *you* have us do?" I asked.

"Cassius is the best scriver in our tier," Grimm said simply. "We should give him more time, before we begin grasping at straws that will likely only get us in deeper trouble."

I rolled my eyes. "I'm well aware that everyone thinks the sun shines out of Cassius's ass because he managed to get a spell admitted to the library, but we've already given him loads of time, and it did nothing. Do you really trust that giving him more will change anything?"

Grimm took a sip of tea. He didn't wince at the taste, accustomed, perhaps, to its bitterness. He lowered his cup to the table and said, with great deliberation, "More than I'd trust a nameless sorcerer in the woods."

I turned to Agnes, hoping to gain some support, but in this, I was disappointed.

"He's right," she said, adding, "Oh, don't look at me like that," when I let out a small gasp, betrayed. "Crossing the barrier in search of some sort of—of *mythical woman* to solve all your problems is a terrible idea. The Unquiet Wood is full of monsters, Leo. There's a reason people don't go there."

I slumped back in my chair, outnumbered and unhappy about it. Grimm's refusal to venture into the Wilderlands wasn't surprising, but I was frustrated all the same. At the heart of this disagreement was the fact that there was simply no way for me to share with him the sensation of something foreign and wrong taking up residency in my bones, and the powerlessness that followed. I could describe it, but that wasn't at all the same. I could not help but think that, were *Grimm* to find himself at the mercy of such a feeling, he too would be willing to face down monsters and the unknown to see it gone.

But Grimm could not feel what I felt.

"What now, then?" Agnes said, breaking the tense silence that had fallen. "Leo can't return to his father's estate without falling ill again, and I doubt he'd fare much better trying to go back to the Fount before you do. That's still hours away from here."

Grimm's and my eyes met in a sort of mutual dismay as Agnes's words sank in. To his credit, Grimm hesitated for only an instant before saying, "You may stay here until it's time for us to return to the Fount. I will be busy helping with the harvest, but you are both free to make yourselves comfortable."

He spoke too stiffly for the offer to be entirely gracious, but I doubt I could have done much better were the circumstances reversed. He made his excuses shortly afterward and disappeared back to the barn to resume casting the preservation spells I had interrupted.

I imagined I could feel the invisible leash between us stretching with every step he took, but that was likely just a result of my overtaxed nerves. I hoped.

Agnes poured us each another cup of the dark tea. Its flavor was not improved by being cold. We sat there, looking out over the colorful courtyard.

"Well, it's not the worst place for us to have a vacation," I said. "A little provincial, but very pretty."

Agnes said in a low voice, "I'm not staying."

I spun round in my seat to face her, certain I had misheard, but Agnes remained looking stubbornly into her teacup.

"My mother has arranged an invitation for me at a Coterie party tonight, and there will be other harvest celebrations around the city for the rest of this week. She'll have my head if I disappear into the countryside with you instead of attending them. And, if I'm being truthful, I don't *want* to miss them." She finally looked up, eyes gravely serious behind her spectacles. "Don't ask me to, Leo."

This was a taste of what the coming year had in store for us, I realized, bitter as the tea we drank. Agnes and I had always done everything together, through choice or circumstance. The one good thing about being forced to attend the Fount was that it had prolonged our effortless closeness. But once Agnes joined the Coterie, she would be launched into a different world. At some point, she would likely have more in common with Sebastian Grimm than she did with me.

I did not know what upset me more: the thought of Agnes leaving me here so she could step further into that future, or that I could not join her.

I selfishly, desperately wanted to beg her to stay, but I could read the set of her jaw and knew that doing so would only push her away faster. So instead, I said, "Of course! It's harvest time, and you have Coterie captains to charm. Of course, you must go."

Agnes's shoulders slumped slightly in relief. "You're sure?" she asked.

"You've already delivered me safely here, that's more than enough."

"But you and Grimm—"

"What about us?"

"I know you two have history," Agnes said haltingly.

"Ugh, can you not say it like that?"

"Fine. I know you have a strange obsession with Grimm, is that better?"

"It is not," I said tartly, "but go on."

"I worry about leaving you two alone. This habit you have of getting on each other's nerves as though it's a sport, it won't serve you well here."

I rolled my eyes. "I think we can manage unsupervised for a couple of weeks. Besides, you heard Grimm, his days here are full. We won't have to interact that much, and I'll be on my best behavior."

Agnes didn't appear entirely convinced (perhaps because my previous promise of good behavior had been followed up by nearly burning my father's house to the ground), but there was no time to argue with me if she wanted to make it back to Luxe in time for whatever festivities the Coterie elite had planned for the evening. And yet, still she hesitated, biting her lip as she looked at me, eyes solemn.

"Leo," she said, and leaned across the table to catch my hand in hers. There was an urgency in her voice that put me on guard. "Promise me you won't go to the forest."

"You heard Grimm; he thinks it's just a story, not worth his time."

"Yes, but I know you. You're still enamored with the idea of running off to the woods to solve this. Some sort of grand quest that will cure all your ills. But that's hardly ever how these things work."

"Grimm must be rubbing off on you," I joked. "Have you so little imagination after only a few hours in his presence?"

"Promise me, Leo. If I could stay, it wouldn't matter. But I'm worried you're going to bite off more than you can chew trying to solve this thing, and I won't be there to stand at your back. I'm not leaving until you tell me you won't go beyond the barrier alone."

Agnes's hand was tight around mine. Once again, I found myself wishing that it was her I could not stand to be parted from. It would have made all of this so much easier. Yet, when I thought of Agnes driving away, it did not make my insides squirm with discomfort. I would feel lonely without her, yes, but I could survive it.

I lifted her hand and kissed the back of it quickly. "You have my word I will not go to the Unquiet Wood alone," I said.

Agnes let out a sigh of relief and settled back into her seat, loosening her grasp.

What I did not say was this: The woods were far too vast for me to search by myself—I would last only a day, maybe two, before the curse left me incapacitated—but the towns in Dwull nearest the barrier were not so difficult to reach, and who knew what information might be found there?

Grimm and Agnes had their plans for the next two weeks, and I had mine.

CHAPTER THIRTEEN

The temptation to sneak away to Dwull's border immediately after Agnes left was great. But it would take more time than there was daylight left to walk there, and I was still worn out from our drive through the night.

"Think this through, Loveage," I said to myself. "Don't bite off more than you can chew."

Pretending to follow this advice, I decided to delay my departure until the next morning. Instead, I went for a walk, wandering outside the fence and down the hill until I found a patch of soft grass to lie down on. The day was warm, the curse was quiet for the moment, and I had a plan. For once, that was enough to lull me into a dreamless sleep.

It wasn't until hours later that Grimm's looming shadow woke me.

"It's time for dinner," he informed me, once I'd blinked my eyes open, and then waited impatiently for me to yawn and stretch before leading the way back to the house.

As we walked, I observed the fields around us, cast in the softened shadows of evening. Wheat was the most common crop in Dwull, and there was certainly plenty of that swaying gold to be seen, but a surprising number of fields had been given over to growing flowers. There were rows upon rows of them, some clearly past their season, but others still put forth blooms in a rainbow of colors. A cheerful sight.

I gestured toward the nearest field. "I was expecting your crops to be more practical. Aren't flowers a frivolous thing to grow?"

"The bouquets that fill the homes of the gentry have to come from somewhere," Grimm answered. "Or did you think they grew them themselves?"

"I suppose not." Certainly, my father had never gotten his hands dirty with such a thing.

"It's my mother's trade. She's well-known for it, in fact. She grows rare varieties that many seek out."

"And will you follow in her footsteps, learning the family trade?" I was only joking—it was laughable to think of Grimm on any path that didn't lead to the Coterie—but to my surprise, he nodded.

"That was my intention. Before we discovered how strong my casting abilities were. After, it made more sense for me to pursue a place at the Fount." He paused. "And a gentry title, someday."

"Of course." I shoved my hands in my pockets as my mouth twisted in something like a smile. "That much-coveted title."

"Coveted for a reason," Grimm said, faintly reproving. "Land and a title for ten years of Coterie service is a generous trade. Not to mention the wealth that comes with those things."

I gazed out over the sea of scarlet blossoms and the golden fields beyond. All this space made something in my heart sing. "I don't know," I said. "If I had to choose between money and all of this, I don't think the coin would win."

Grimm stopped walking and looked over at me. I nearly flinched back at the clear enmity in his eyes.

"How lucky for you," he said in a low voice, "that is a choice you don't have to make."

It only took one startled moment for me to realize I'd made an ass out of myself. My fondness for criticizing the gentry's snobbery did not mean I was innocent of it. I opened my mouth, unsure of what I would say, only that this was not the way I preferred to upset Grimm, but he spoke first.

"Dinner is waiting," he said, and lengthened his stride so that we arrived back at the house with me still a few steps behind.

The courtyard was a flurry of activity, full of friends and neighbors who had shared the work of threshing wheat in the fields that day and were now setting up for a meal. A long table had been placed on the flagstones, with two benches on either side. Grimm was apparently too annoyed with me to carry out introductions—he left me by the open gate and disappeared amid the bustle of strangers without a word.

Unlike Grimm, I was in possession of a working set of manners, and so sought out my hosts to thank them for their hospitality. Both of Grimm's parents were dark-haired, with only a few threads of gray gathered at his father's temples. His mother asked warmly after my health, which I assured her had much improved since my arrival, but she fussed over me anyway. Her face was as bright as the flowers she grew, and I was utterly won over. I'm predisposed to like anyone who tries to take care of me. It's a failing, as Agnes had informed me on many occasions.

Both of his parents were so pleasant I could only assume Grimm had never spoken a word of me to them. Grimm's mother even took me by the elbow, steering me toward the table where she pointedly gestured at the seat closest to the brazier burning in the center of the courtyard.

"You looked halfway to a ghost when you arrived last night," she said. "It wouldn't do for you to catch cold once the light fades. Move down, Sebastian. What sort of friend would you be if you allowed our guest to take ill again?"

It took me a moment to realize she was talking to Grimm, sitting on the end of the bench. I was shocked when he actually complied, moving to a spot farther down the table without a word.

I took the seat without protest. Not because I was actually cold, but because telling Grimm's mother *I'm not sure your son knows the meaning of the word* friend*, and if he did, it certainly wouldn't apply to me* didn't seem like the right thing to do.

Before eating, everyone joined hands round the table in a ritual I vaguely remembered from my childhood. Grimm's mother stood up and said, "Let this harvest be bountiful, but not so bountiful as the next. Let our fields never lie fallow, and let our hands always be busy. Magic preserve us, magic keep us, magic hear us." The table rattled as everyone stamped their feet, before reaching for the plates running down the table's center.

There were greens that had been blanched and dressed in tangy sauce, bread stuffed with olives and peppers, and sweet corn that had been cut from the cob and mixed with a variety of other vegetables and spices. A whole chicken had been roasted and dressed with fresh herbs and chutney.

Everyone was so distracted by filling their plates that it was easy for me to tuck two of the stuffed breads into my pockets— provisions for my journey the following day.

As we ate, I tried to make sense of Grimm in this environment and found it impossible. He spoke with his parents easily and addressed the people around him as plates were passed from hand to hand. But though he sat at the very center of them all, he seemed somehow removed, the same way he did at the

Fount. I caught a few of the guests casting furtive glances at him every now and again. At first, I thought this was due to having a trained sorcerer in their midst, but the same people treated me with much more ease, even though I wore my coat and had my scarlet sash tied firmly at my waist. It wasn't Grimm's status but something about the man himself that seemed to cause everyone around him to lean back. The warmth of their company stopped short at the edges of him.

Meanwhile, I was having the opposite problem.

"And what of your family?" the woman sitting across the table from me asked. She was either a cousin or a neighbor, but I'd only been half paying attention when she'd introduced herself and had forgotten which. "Are they sorcerers as well?"

"Yes," I answered, resigned to the inevitable small talk about family, and its just as inevitable conclusion. "They both served in the Coterie, and now my father has a seat in the Citadel."

"Oh, how impressive! And your mother? Does she still serve?"

In situations such as this, I often found that sharing too much rather than a few tantalizing details led to the end of conversation much sooner. So I said, "Oh, no. She died when I was eleven. A masquerade flower crept over the border from the Wilderlands and hid itself in her garden. Nasty plant. Very poisonous, you know. Dreadful way to go."

The woman's expression fell. "That's awful."

"Yes," I said blandly, "it was," and the topic was quickly changed after that.

As the last of the daylight slowly faded from the sky, lanterns hanging from the porch were lit. The benches were rearranged so everyone could sit closer to the brazier. Acting on impulse, I retrieved my violin from inside and struck up a tune

I remembered my mother playing during the harvest years and years ago. The words had slipped from my memory, as words so often did, but some of the people around the fire knew the song and began to sing along. They called out a few requests after that, and then, once everyone's voices had grown tired, I played a less dramatic version of the spell that had unleashed chaos in my father's parlor.

This time the burning shapes danced off my bow and floated up into the open air of the night sky, accompanied by sparks and soft murmurs of appreciation from those watching. The sound soothed something inside of me that had been left rumpled and aching since leaving my father's house.

"What was that?"

I was startled to find Grimm standing next to me in the dark. His eyes were fixed on the glowing remains of my spell as they winked out, one by one.

"It doesn't have a name."

"Not the song, the spell." Grimm looked me over and frowned. "You did something similar before, when you brought that piece of paper to life in order to guide me around the library. You hummed something over it."

"I call them spellsongs," I said, loosening my bow before tucking it back in its case. "They're just little fancies. Things I make to amuse myself."

"Casting such things is costly for scrivers. You should be more cautious, lest you overextend yourself."

I chuckled. "I'm touched by your concern, Grimm, but I know my limits. Besides, casting always costs me less when I do it through music."

"I did not know you played so well," he said.

"Surprised?"

"Yes," Grimm answered. "I thought such a skill would require more…"

I raised an eyebrow at him. "More what?"

"Discipline. More than you possess, at least."

"Ouch," I said. "Fucking *ouch*, Grimm. I'll have you know that I can be very disciplined when I want to be. Or did you think I survived our first four tiers at the Fount simply because of my charming personality?"

"No," Grimm said. "I did not think it was because of *that*."

Judging by his tone, there was more he could have said on the subject. But before I could provoke a more thorough explanation, Grimm withdrew to the other side of the fire. His mother, passing by, said something to him that I could not hear, and Grimm looked at her and smiled.

It seemed practically unnatural to watch Grimm's mouth curve in a direction that wasn't down, but it was there. It happened. And then, in response, his mother laid a hand on his shoulder.

A wave of longing swept over me, breathtaking in its severity. I had to look away.

Nothing here fit neatly with the image I had of Grimm. I wished I could unsee it. Better I had not learned of where he came from, or realized I was jealous of it.

I stayed on my own side of the brazier for the rest of the night. It would be much easier to keep my promise of good behavior to Agnes if I spent as little time speaking to Sebastian Grimm as possible.

The next morning, I lay in bed, listening to the sounds of the house emptying as Grimm and his family returned to work in the fields. Once I was certain they were gone, I rose and wrote a note explaining where I was going and placed it on Grimm's pillow. Then I got dressed, gathered my things, and left, giving the barn a wide berth in case Grimm was inside.

As I walked, the early-morning fog began to burn off and the blue sky revealed itself—a perfect day for traveling, sunny but with just enough bite to the air to make walking pleasant. I had spent enough time in Dwull to have a general understanding of the geography, and Grimm's home was no more than a day's walk from the southernmost edge of Miendor, with the Unquiet Wood beyond. My plan was to follow the road south until I found the dwellings or town nearest the wood and start asking questions. If the sorcerer actually existed, perhaps she was known there. I thought the curse would be uncomfortable by that point, but not unbearable, so I would spend that evening listening to what tales the people there could tell me, and then return to Grimm's property the following day.

That was my plan, but I had not gone very far down the path before my heels began to drag with tiredness.

I cursed the third cup of wine I'd had to drink last night and continued.

My stomach began to churn unpleasantly at the half-mile point. The air was cool, but I was sweating. Fields stretched out on either side of me, and I had a powerful urge to lie down in one of them and close my eyes. Or better yet, to turn and make my way back to the house.

With a growing sense of trepidation, I paused in the middle of the road. The moment I stopped moving, something inside me heaved a sigh of relief. I was still too warm, but all the other unpleasantness was suspended.

One step back down the road the way I had come, and my queasiness receded even further. Then I darted three steps forward and had to pause, gasping, as it all came crashing back. My stomach leapt and my heart pounded. My legs trembled, threatening to give out entirely.

There was no mistaking the signs of the curse. *Go back*, the magic in my blood seemed to whisper. *You are not where you should be.*

I clenched my fists tight, determined not to listen. This was much, much sooner than I'd expected the curse to make its presence known. I was not even a mile down the road. Grimm had been gone from the Fount for at least a full day before I'd even noticed his absence last time. It seemed impossible that the leash binding me to him could have grown so much shorter so quickly.

I pushed onward. If anyone had been there to see my progress, they would surely have thought me drunk. I stumbled forward, weaving from side to side as I fought against the urge to move backward. It was a slow, painful process, and within a dishearteningly short period of time, I was nearly in the same state that had prompted Agnes to bundle me into a carriage and drive me all the way to Dwull.

The turnoff for the main road was in sight, but I couldn't make it there. Neither could I bring myself to concede defeat by turning back, so instead I collapsed in a spot of shade by the side of the path and sat in my discomfort, waiting to see if it would lessen enough for me to take a few more steps.

I'm not sure why I thought reaching the road was so important (by this point it was clear I would not be traveling anywhere alone). I suppose it came from a need to prove to myself that my world had not really shrunk so alarmingly. That I was the same person I had been yesterday, capable of the same things.

But I wasn't. This was worse, even, than being bound by my father's wishes. At least I had carved some freedom for myself out of the Fount's hallowed walls, and I could have walked away at any time, though it would have meant losing something dear to me. But here, now, I literally could not walk away from Grimm. I carried the curse with me. There was no trick I could pull to leave it behind, even for a moment, and the inescapable weight made me feel very small.

The discomfort didn't lessen and neither did my stubborn urge to resist it, and so I was left at an impasse, feeling just as terrible at the thought of going back as I did about moving forward.

This was the state in which Grimm found me.

I knew he was coming by the way my nausea began to lessen, along with the terrible, feverish ache in my limbs. But there was also something else that I recognized from my time surreptitiously following Grimm at the Fount—a prickling sort of awareness that overcame me in degrees, as each step of distance between us was eaten up. It reminded me of the tide coming in or a piece of yarn being gathered into a neat ball—something being drawn inexorably closer. The sensation was odd and carried with it far more familiarity than I'd ever hoped or wanted to hold for Sebastian Grimm.

It was quite clear that this bond did not extend both ways, because Grimm passed by me entirely, hidden as I was by the long grass at the side of the road. He walked with a sense of brisk purpose and held a scrap of paper clutched tightly in one hand. I was fairly certain it was the note I'd left on his bed.

That, and the clear annoyance on Grimm's face, made me reasonably certain he was looking for me, rather than just out for an afternoon stroll.

I sat up with a rustle of grass. "Over here."

Grimm stopped and spun round. He looked me over, first with thin-lipped disapproval and then, as he noticed my wilting form and the sweat-soaked tendrils of hair plastered to my face, with an air of puzzlement.

He held up the crumpled piece of paper. "Did you actually intend to visit the border, or was the idea of making me take time out of my day to come looking for you simply amusing?"

"I was going to go," I answered sullenly.

"Then why are you here?"

He would not have gone much farther in search of me, I realized. If I had made it just a little farther down the road, Grimm probably would have let me go and welcomed the reprieve. It was possible he was just as annoyed about finding me as he was about being made to look in the first place.

Well, there would be no reprieve for either of us now.

"It's gotten worse," I said. In as stark terms as possible, I outlined the new parameters of the curse for him, leaving nothing out. If I was going to be made to feel all of it, I thought it only fair that Grimm should at least suffer the weight of knowing how dire this had become.

Indeed, he looked more and more alarmed as I spoke.

"Well, this changes things," he said, once I was finished.

I was surprised Grimm had come to the same conclusion I had so quickly, but also relieved. "It certainly does," I said. "Now we both need to go."

Grimm, who had been directing a concentrated sort of frown down at the ground, looked up at me and said, "Go where?"

"To look for the sorcerer, of course. We can't wait this out, not anymore. Isn't that what you meant?"

"No," Grimm said. "I meant that we will have to be

more careful than ever to keep this hidden until we find a counterspell."

At first, I was stunned. Then, beneath that numb surprise, I realized that I was angry. Very angry, actually. If I hadn't by this point spent hours stewing in my own misery by the roadside, I might have been able to recognize that Grimm was only one of many things I was angry about, but I *had* sat there stewing, and now Grimm was standing in front of me, the perfect receptacle for my frustration.

I got to my feet.

"Until we find a counterspell? Do you suppose there's one that will just be left lying around somewhere for us, Grimm? Or are you still placing all your faith in Cassius to cough one up, because I can tell you right now that my patience on that front is running quite thin. The curse is tightening its hold every day. Do you really think we'll be able to keep it hidden once we're back at the Fount? Do you think no one will ask questions once the curse has me on a leash so short I'm forced to sleep outside your door like a dog?" I sneered. "And as for the trials, I'd like to see what it does to your chances when you have to complete them with me shadowing your every step."

Grimm blinked at me. "You're upset," he said. "I understand that. But the risk of discovery is lesser than the risk of going to the Unquiet—"

"What about the risk to me!" I shouted. "You're so good at memorizing spells, don't you remember the words of the curse?" This was one of the things that had been running through my head again and again over the past few hours. There was no word without meaning given over to a spell—I was a scriver, I knew—and the words of the curse were harrowing indeed.

"*Until every wish need not be spoken,*" I quoted. "That's how it ends. Maybe you're willing to let the curse progress until I'm a mindless puppet, but I'm not. If you won't agree to find the sorcerer, I'll just have to ask someone else for help."

"Who?" Grimm asked, eyes turning sharp.

"There's a long list of powerful scrivers I could go to. My father, for instance. He's a bit of a stickler for rules, but I confess I don't much care anymore what trouble we get into if it means getting rid of this."

In fact, my father was the last person I would have gone to. Putting aside the fact that he held the Sahnt estate hostage against my good behavior, my father's involvement would alert not only the Coterie but also the Citadel council who governed it. I wasn't actually desperate enough to invite that kind of scrutiny. But Grimm didn't know that, and I thought the idea would provoke him.

When he did not immediately react, I added, "I could write him a letter and have this solved by tomorrow. I'm sure his arrival would be a little confusing for your family, so perhaps we had better tell them what's happened now."

I turned and began to walk back in the direction of the house, but made it only two steps before Grimm said, "Stop."

The command locked my limbs in place. With great difficulty I was able to turn my head to look at Grimm where he stood in the road. I'd wanted to provoke him and now I had. It showed in the clenched fists hanging at his sides, and the way that he still hadn't revoked his order, even though the effect of his words was clear.

This, I supposed, was what Agnes had been afraid of, leaving the two of us alone together, but in a twisted way, it felt right. Being at odds with Grimm was part of the natural order of things, like thunder followed lightning and night gave way to dawn.

"Are you enjoying this?" I asked him, coldly furious. So long as the fury was there, I didn't have to think what might happen next, or wonder what it would feel like if Grimm simply turned on his heel and left me standing frozen in the road. Being angry with Grimm was easier than being afraid of him.

Grimm drew in a short breath. There was a war fought in the span of that one inhalation. "Never mind," he said, and the tension in my limbs released.

The first time Grimm had ordered me to do something, I'd wanted to run, but this time I knew that the curse wouldn't let me go far, even if I tried. I gave in to it instead, taking a few steps toward him. Finding that line where everyone else seemed to pause when approaching Grimm, and then deliberately crossing it.

This close, I could see the way Grimm's whole body trembled with how tightly he held himself in check. It had been a long time since we'd actually come to blows, but we weren't bound by the rules of the Fount here, and part of me relished the idea of pushing Grimm until he snapped. There were some things even I could not say with words. Some emotions that could only be expressed through contact.

And I so badly wanted to ruin that finely kept control.

"You didn't answer my question," I said. "Shall I answer it for you? You act so perfect. So noble. But admit it, you'd love to just give in and use the curse to tell me what to do."

"Maybe someone should!" Grimm shouted, and finally, finally exploded into motion.

I braced myself, nerve endings already alight with the impulse to strike back, but all he did was grasp the collar of my coat and jerk me forward. Fabric pulled tight against my throat, causing me to choke a little, even as sparks of exhilaration skittered down my spine.

"Maybe if someone else were making your decisions, we wouldn't be in this position in the first place. And what about you? You accuse me of wanting to abuse my power, but you're the one who's fond of issuing threats." Grimm scoffed. "You're just like every other gentry-born sorcerer. Worse, because you're not even making anything of yourself. You're spoiled with privilege, yet put none of it to good use. So, no, to answer your question, Loveage, I am not enjoying myself. How could I, when I'm stuck with you?"

He released me all at once and I stumbled back. Blood roared in my ears, and my skin stung with heat. I wished Grimm had just punched me. That would have been cleaner, somehow. But if this was the fight he wanted, I knew how to respond.

I did not know how to win Grimm over by being pleasant, but I could work with him like this, when we were both at our worst.

I reached up and made a show of brushing the creases from my coat, as though my own hands weren't trembling now too. Then I said, "Well, Grimm. Since you're so keen on deciding what's right for the both of us, let me lay out your options, as they stand. The first option is that we go on a little jaunt to the Unquiet Wood and see what we can find there. I even promise we'll be back in time for the trials. The second option is that I seek help elsewhere and this whole thing is blown wide open. What would happen after, I don't know." I paused. "And then there's the third option. Where we do things your way. Not because I agree to it, but because you make me."

The challenge hung in the air between us. It was an ugly

suggestion, and we both knew it. Spoken like this, it could not be shrugged off as a mistake or a provocation. I did not think Grimm would actually want to be so tainted, but there was always the chance I'd misjudged him. Or that the curse was changing him in less perceptible ways than it was me.

I raised my chin and met Grimm's unhappy gaze with my own. "The choice is yours."

CHAPTER FOURTEEN

We left for the Unquiet Wood the following day. On foot, since Grimm's family owned no horse or carriage. The sun rose hot and stayed that way—not as suitable for walking as the previous day had been, but at least Grimm was there to cast the charm I wrote to shield us from the worst of the heat.

It was a pity I could think of no spell to make Grimm's presence tolerable in the same way.

He had hardly spoken to me since our dispute, except to inform me he would allow a week to look for the sorcerer, after which we would return to civilization no matter what we found. There were the trials to think of, after all. Then he stormed off to explain to his family he would not be available to help for the rest of the harvest. What excuses he gave, I did not know, only that they must have borne seeds of the truth, for his mother saw us off with an earnest wish that I would "find the cure I was looking for."

I sensed Grimm did not like to lie to her and resented me all the more for forcing him to do so.

For the first hour of our journey, I mimicked his sullen quiet, until I realized this was more punishment for me than Grimm, to whom silence was the natural and preferable option. After that, I decided to amuse myself by the only means available: the sound of my own voice.

"How long until we reach the border town, do you think?" I asked.

Grimm answered without looking at me. "Late in the day, if we walk quickly."

"Is there an inn there?"

"Not that I know of."

I groaned. I'd had to sleep out under the stars a time or two, but I'd hoped to spend at least one more night in a soft bed before we crossed the barrier and left such comforts behind.

We walked a little farther. The sun rose higher in the sky. Sweat trickled down the back of my neck and caused my collar to stick there. The heels of my boots began to rub.

"We should have seen about renting a carriage," I said.

Grimm didn't answer. He stared pointedly ahead and lengthened his stride, as though hoping to leave the sound of my voice swirling behind him like dust in the road.

I quickened my own steps to keep pace.

"Do people use this road often? Maybe we could hitch a ride with someone to save our strength. I'll have a much better chance of convincing this sorcerer to help us if I'm not exhausted and covered in dust."

Grimm finally looked over to glance pointedly at the violin case in my hand. I was beginning to wish I'd found a way to strap it to my back instead of carrying it. It had an unfortunate way of bouncing off my leg every other step.

"You would be less tired if you'd brought less with you," Grimm said.

"I couldn't leave my violin behind. What if I have to sing for our supper?" I took another step and winced. "I swear I've already got at least two blisters on each heel. They sting awfully. Do you think a wagon will come? You never answered, before."

"You have the endurance of a child," Grimm snapped. "I have no idea if a wagon will come, but perhaps you should consider this practice for the Coterie. They demand a level of competence you are sorely lacking."

"That won't matter for me," I said.

A muscle twitched in Grimm's jaw, but he refrained from answering.

I kept up a steady stream of mostly one-sided conversation as the day wore on, commenting on everything from the scenery, to our instructors at the Fount, to the weather. It was revenge of a sort, for the long moments I'd spent locked in place the day before, and I continued for far longer than I would have otherwise. But eventually the aches and pains I'd exaggerated early in the day began to take a real toll, and my words dried up. Occasionally we passed by a stretch of fields with people working, but the only wagons I saw were full to bursting with sheaves of wheat, with no room for extra passengers.

By late afternoon the heat began to fade. The shadows turned lavender and stretched out long over the road.

"How much farther?" I asked again. My stoicism had limits and my feet had long passed from pain to numbness. I thought longingly of writing a basic cushioning charm for the inside of my boots but balked at asking Grimm to cast it.

"Another hour at least," Grimm said. "If we're lucky, we'll reach the last town before dark."

Just as he spoke, the wind shifted, bringing with it an acrid tang that lingered in the back of my throat. Looking around for the source of the smell, I saw the road ahead was darkened by a billowing cloud of smoke hanging low in the sky.

Both Grimm and I paused to stare.

"That looks rather ominous," I said.

The smoke worsened as we got closer, and little licks of flame lit up the gloom. I was afraid we would arrive to find the house or barn of an outlying property in ruins. But when we finally drew near enough to see the source of the smoke, there were no buildings in sight. It was a field that burned.

The destruction of the crop was controlled, systematic, not the raging blaze I'd feared. Most of the wheat had already turned to ash, but at the far corner of the field I could make out a few figures overseeing the burning of what was left.

More people stood in the road, watching.

"What happened here?" I asked the woman standing closest to us.

"Silver rot in the crop," she said. Her eyes were bloodshot from the smoke, and she held a cloth over her face, muffling her voice.

I held my sleeve over my mouth as my own lungs tickled, a cough brewing. "What's silver rot?" I murmured to Grimm. I thought he might know, for his frown had deepened significantly.

"It's a spore," he said. "It drifts in from the Wilderlands and settles in the dirt, withering whatever grows there."

"Fire kills it?"

Grimm and the woman who had spoken exchanged a heavy glance. "No," Grimm answered. "It can sometimes stop it from spreading, if burned in time, but the rot hides too deep in the soil for fire to kill it completely. The only thing that can truly get rid of it is magic."

I nodded, understanding. Monsters weren't the only thing that tried to creep over the border into Miendor; they were just the simplest to stop. It was easy to be on guard for three-headed creatures, less so a lone flower growing in a hedge, though both could kill you.

If you ask me, the flower is the more terrifying of the two. At least with monsters, you know what you're getting.

I frowned out over the ruined field. "Shouldn't the Coterie be here to deal with it?"

The woman eyed the red sash at my waist and spat out a scornful little "ha" under her breath. It was second nature for me to wear both coat and sash, but I wondered if it had been a mistake to don them for this journey. I felt out of place standing there in my silk. A dressed-up, useless sorcerer.

"The Coterie will show up eventually," the woman said, "but not in time to save these fields. All we can do is set the fires and hope that it hasn't spread." She nodded to us and walked back to join the rest of the crowd, who folded in around her, forming a contained unit while Grimm and I stood to the side.

The fire was mesmerizing to watch. It ate away the remaining wheat in neat segments, gold stalks turning red and then black before collapsing. The people in charge of burning cast the fire ahead of them in orderly lines, following an unseen grid pattern. Watching them work absorbed my attention so completely I almost didn't notice when Grimm began to walk again.

I hurried to catch up. "Where are you going?"

"This is people's livelihood going up in smoke," he said brusquely. "We needn't watch as though it's entertainment."

"I'm not entertained," I protested. "I'm horrified. Isn't there anything we can do?"

Grimm looked surprised by the question, or perhaps just that I was the one asking it, which was vaguely insulting. He gave it some thought before answering. "I've seen the spell that's used to remove silver rot. I might even be able to recall it. But it requires a group to cast, many sorcerers surrounding the field and weaving a magical net to catch the rot and draw it from the soil and roots. When the Coterie comes, they will make use of it."

I looked past the burning to where another field lay. And another beyond that. Perhaps it was my imagination, but I thought the wheat there looked less golden—grayish in a way that had nothing to do with the smoke in the air.

"But not before the rest of this burns," I said. "Right?"

Grimm, following my gaze, said nothing.

There seemed little choice but to keep walking and let the evening breeze wash our hair and clothes free of the scent of burning. But it didn't sit right. The spell Grimm had described did not seem an ideal solution to me at all.

The Coterie was always stretched thin, sending troops to all corners of Miendor to deal with monster breakthroughs, or flooding when one of the rivers that originated in the Wilderlands suddenly diverted to run through a town, or roads too near the border mysteriously deciding to rearrange themselves. It left them with precious little time to deal with things like diseased crops. It had always seemed strange to me that so many of the spells that fixed problems like this still required a full Coterie party to cast them—inefficient. But then, I'd heard my father complain often enough of the shortage of scrivers working to replace such antiquated magic. Perhaps if there were more of us writing new spells, there would have been magic these people could have called upon to save their land without the Coterie.

We had walked another two minutes or so when I noticed that the field we currently were passing was full of flowers, rather than wheat. Not the neatly planted rows of blooms I had seen back on Grimm's property, but stuffed full to bursting with sun-flowers, their heads angled toward the sky.

I stepped off the road to get a closer look, ignoring Grimm's frustrated call of "Loveage!"

The scrub I waded through was thick, and burrs stuck to the legs of my trousers by the time I reached the nearest flower. Acting on instinct, I reached out and flipped over one of the leaves. The back of it was shot through with silver veins that should have been green. The iridescent lines could have been described as pretty, if you didn't know what they meant.

"The plants drink the rot from the dirt," Grimm said, appearing at my shoulder. "If it reaches the leaves, the roots are completely infested." He looked around the field of bright flowers, beautiful but doomed. "Pity that it wasn't contained to this field, where no one would feel the loss."

I was about to chide Grimm for saying such a thing (he was the son of a flower farmer, after all), but then I paused, struck by his words. "That's a very interesting idea, Grimm."

Setting my violin case at my feet, I began to rifle through my coat pockets for quill and paper. "Can you explain to me again how the spell the Coterie uses works?"

Grimm looked mystified by my sudden interest, but told me what he knew. It didn't take long (like many of the Coterie's favorite spells, it relied more on power than intricacy), and by the time he'd finished, I was crouched on the ground, using my instrument case as a makeshift desk. The paper I'd found was wrinkled from being in my pocket, but I smoothed it out as best I could.

"What are you doing?" Grimm asked.

"I have an idea. For a charm that might...do something." I hesitated to say *help*, since helpful spells were not my specialty.

However, by necessity, I was rather good at composing spells that made use of what little I had to work with, and that seemed to fit this situation perfectly.

Grimm glanced up at the smoke cloud hanging in the sky. "You won't be able to fix this with a charm."

I waggled my brows and shook my quill at him. "Not with that attitude, we won't. Have a little faith, Grimm."

"This is about facts, not faith. The spell I described uses Grandmagic and the strength of ten sorcerers. Do you really think you can write a charm that does the same thing?"

"I'm not trying to do the same thing," I said. "That spell works by force. I just want to *ask* the rot to go someplace different, rather than ripping it from the ground. You don't need ten casters for that, you just need one."

"You want me to ask the rot to move."

"Invite? Perhaps *invite* is more accurate. And more polite."

Now Grimm looked truly flummoxed. "You think something like that could work?"

"Well, it won't make it worse. These flowers are already dying, poor things. A failed charm won't hurt anything except my pride, which I assure you has taken harsher blows."

I expected Grimm to keep arguing simply because *I* was the one who'd suggested it. That was how this sort of thing usually went. However, after casting one more look at the darkened skyline, Grimm turned to me and said, "Very well. Write your song."

I was so surprised that I nearly dropped my quill. "My *song*?"

"You said putting spells to music gave you more power when casting them. If I am to do this alone, would it not be useful for me to benefit from that?"

"Well, yes, in theory," I said. "But I've never had much luck writing them for anyone else." Admittedly, one of the only people who'd been willing to try was Agnes, and she couldn't carry a tune to save her life. But my brother had been the other, and he'd had the same musical education as I had growing up. Our mother had taught us both how to read music and play the violin, but the spellsongs I'd given to him never caught. I thought this failure was similar to the way many spells couldn't be re-created by another scriver. Just as no other person's hand was capable of writing Titus's healing spells, it seemed that no other voice or instrument could cast using my spellsongs. Or so it had always been.

Grimm made an imperious motion with his fingers as though brushing away the thought of failure. "If you teach me the words and tune, I will cast it."

I put the parchment back in my pocket. Then, because it felt right, I grabbed Grimm's wrist. He startled slightly and perhaps would have shaken me off, but I took advantage of his surprise and firmly towed him toward the center of the field. Once we were surrounded by golden petals and silver-threaded leaves on all sides I let go of Grimm's arm and opened my violin case.

I took my time with tuning, and then ran through a few scales and arpeggios in order to organize my thoughts. Composing music came more naturally to me than scriving onto paper, but I wasn't used to creating spellsongs for another person, least of all Grimm.

I settled on a simple melody, one that evoked the sense of invitation I had spoken of earlier. This was a request for the thing living in the ground to move—backed up by magic, but still a request. A transfer, rather than the eviction the Coterie's net spell would have been. Next, I added lyrics, choosing words from the old language and laying them over the music the same way I would have scratched ink across paper.

"Listen," I told Grimm, and played the song once all the way through. Then I looked at him and said, "Now you sing along. Don't cast yet, just sing."

Grimm's eyes flickered toward the road where a small crowd of people had gathered, drawn away from the burning field by the sound of music. I happily angled myself so they would have a better view. Grimm, on the other hand, hunched his shoulders and tried to hide behind one of the taller sunflowers.

"I did not realize there would be an audience," he grumbled.

"Come now, Grimm," I said. "What is magic if not a performance?"

I launched into the song for a third time. My fingertips began to tingle and the words felt heavy on my tongue, even without the weight of casting behind them. I sang and stared at Grimm until he straightened his shoulders and joined in. He had no difficulty remembering the words, but sang them so quietly I could not tell if he was even in tune.

"Louder, Grimm," I complained, starting the song again.

Grimm was an unpracticed singer, but not a bad one. He was more of a true baritone than I was, voice turning slightly raspy on the high notes in a way that was nearly charming.

"Good," I said, surprised to find that I meant it. There was a held-breath quality to the air around us, as though magic were waiting to taste the words I'd written. That had never happened before when my brother or Agnes had sung. "Do you want to run through it again?"

"No," Grimm said. "We can begin."

He waited for the melody to come round again and then, between one breath and the next, he began to cast.

The quality of the music changed. The resonance grew greater, until I felt the hum of it in my bones. This didn't happen when I was the one casting a spellsong. I shivered and focused on not fumbling my bow, keeping the tune steady for Grimm to sing over.

Grimm's voice was still slightly hesitant but no longer quiet. It rang out over the field and beyond, amplified by the spell. It was a little strange, to watch him be so wholly absorbed in a casting built entirely of sound, when he was known for being able to cast without speaking a word.

I would not be so impressed by his silence after this, I thought. Not now that I'd heard him call magic with a song. The listening of it hollowed something inside my chest and filled it back up with bittersweet longing.

Grimm was casting my spellsong the way I'd always wanted to and could not.

In his mouth, the words took on new meaning, and the melody gained urgency. The song was alive. It made me feel alive too, in a different way than I had a moment before. I was not casting the spell, but my playing made me a part of it, and I wanted it to last forever.

It couldn't, of course. The moment ended and the spell broke. It was only a charm, after all.

With the last note lingering, Grimm and I stood staring at each other. Even when the magic ate that last bit of sound, something seemed to hang in the air between us.

I tucked my violin under one arm and asked, "Do you think it worked?"

Grimm finally looked away. "Yes," he said after a moment. "I think it did."

I turned my head to follow his gaze.

Where before there had been a sea of golden flowers, now there was only silver everywhere I looked. The petals around us glowed, each flower head a shining, shriveled version of its former self, home to the rot that had made its way up from the dirt and could now be cut away like a rotten limb.

CHAPTER FIFTEEN

We were heroes, of a sort, that evening. And it turned out that heroes were not expected to sleep under the stars, but were instead offered a ride into town and a bed in the loft above the local pub.

"A wagon, Grimm!" I said. "We're saved!"

"We were almost there anyway," Grimm pointed out, but I refused to let him dampen my spirits.

The pub was a one-roomed building, with dark wood walls and floors worn smooth by the passing of countless feet. A two-headed wolf hung above the fireplace, and something resembling a long branch hung in a place of honor above the bar, only when you got close enough it resembled an arm too much to be mistaken for an ordinary branch. Other bits of grisly decor spotted the room, preserved with spells strong enough that they could almost be felt, a low-level awareness that made my fingers itch.

It was a little macabre, but I knew that all of these remnants had likely been found already dead or earned their deaths through violence. People of Miendor didn't kill monsters for sport; it was considered bad luck. There was an entire abandoned city to the north where the last dragon killer had supposedly lived. He had gotten it into his head to go monster hunting, and in return, magic had forsaken not only him and his family but his entire place of residence. A whole city of sorcerers, suddenly cut off, bereft of power. Or at least, that's how the story went.

Even the Coterie, whose entire purpose was to defend against monsters, spent far more time herding the creatures that broke through Miendor's barrier back to the other side than it did killing them outright.

The pub was full to bursting with people who wanted to thank us for what we'd done in the field. Grimm seemed determined to sidestep the attention like a dog escaping a bath, which left me the recipient of their gratitude and the free drinks that came with it.

I listened to so many iterations of "may magic always find you" followed by the clinking of glass that it wasn't long before my senses began to feel pleasantly blurred. From there, it took very little coaxing for me to get up on the bar with my violin and begin taking requests. And then, when I was quite certain that I had won them over, I clambered down and began asking questions.

If there were stories to be heard about the sorcerer, I thought there was as good a chance of hearing them in this place as any other. And my theory turned out to be correct, though not quite in the way I'd hoped.

"The sorcerer from the Unquiet Wood, you mean?" one man said, raising a bushy eyebrow. "Sure, my nan's half brother's cousin's son by marriage bought a charm from her once."

"Really?" I asked, ready to haul him over to Grimm and make him repeat what he'd said.

The man chuckled. "Friend, everyone around here's got a story like that. People buy one spell from a stranger and it gets added to the list of tales. There're plenty of scrivers that pass through, you're proof of that. Five years from now, maybe people will say it was the sorcerer in the woods who saved our fields. That's how stories work." He winked at me and went back to his beer.

It was much the same with everyone I spoke with. Those who didn't laugh at me outright shook their heads in a bemused manner, like I was asking how to find the moon in daytime. I was almost ready to drop the matter entirely, lest Grimm overhear and use this as reason why we should turn back, when someone new sidled up to me—a tall woman, with white skin and a face half-hidden by a deep green hood. The eyes peering out from beneath were so intent I wanted to lean away, the same way I would have flinched from a match held too long. Then the woman blinked and the feeling was gone.

"So, you're the hero of the hour," she said, voice low and amused.

I winked at her. "Are you here to buy me a drink? Almost everyone else has."

The stranger shook her head. "I had a different offer in mind."

For a moment my imagination took flight (I can't be blamed for having a weakness for dark-eyed strangers in cloaks), but she continued in a brisk, businesslike tone. "I couldn't help but overhear that you're looking for someone in the Unquiet Wood."

"The sorcerer. You know of her?" I asked eagerly.

"I know the wood. And I know of someone living there who is certainly a sorcerer. I cannot say for certain she is the one you seek, but given the—"

"Never mind," I said, pushing away from the bar. "Come with me and say all that again."

Grimm had claimed a table in the far corner of the room and

sat there the entire evening, a forbidding expression acting as a wall between himself and the crowd. People passed his table but came no closer. It was almost like magic.

"Good news!" I announced, settling into the chair across from Grimm. "I've found someone who can take us to the sorcerer. A guide."

The woman hadn't said as much, but it had been implied in her phrasing, and she didn't correct me now or back away when Grimm turned to her and said, in his chilliest voice, "How convenient."

"*Fortuitous* is the word I would use," the woman said, pushing back her hood. Free of the shadows, her face was sun-freckled and pleasant, though slightly lean. When she smiled, faint lines creased the corners of her eyes. "I'm returning to the Unquiet Wood myself. Perhaps we can be of help to each other."

Her name was Jayne, she said, and she was a forager. I knew, of course, that there were people who braved the Wilderlands to seek out various materials, but I'd never met one before. There weren't many who were interested in taking on such a risky job. Too much interference with the natural world beyond Miendor's border was dangerous, for the same reason it was dangerous to hunt monsters without just cause (magic didn't like when you messed with the things that belonged to it), but it was possible to collect some items without attracting ire, many of which were highly useful to craftspeople. Spider silk was woven into sorcerers' coats alongside spells to help hold the magic in place, and apothecaries worked closely with foragers to help source herbs that couldn't be found anywhere else. There were other, rarer items to be found in the Wilderlands—scales, teeth, and claws, or any other treasures shed by particularly powerful monsters—but those types of things were hard to find and cost so much coin that usually the only people who could afford them were wealthy collectors.

"I'm new to the trade," Jayne explained, "but the Unquiet Wood is a forager's dream, if you know how to keep your wits about you."

As she spoke, I looked Jayne over with renewed interest, noting the daggers strapped to each leg and the small leather case strung over her chest. It looked like the cases I'd seen Coterie members use to hold prepared spells. If ever anyone had a need to hold magic at the ready, rather than fumbling through pockets for the right spell, I supposed it would be foragers.

"Are you saying you've actually met this sorcerer?" Grimm asked, obviously skeptical.

"Not exactly." Jayne's lip quirked upward, a little ruefully. "She lives in a tower with a barrier around it. Much like the one around Miendor, only it keeps out people as well as monsters. I've never been inside, but I could take you there."

"What would you get out of it?" Grimm asked.

"Compensation, naturally. You look like you can afford it." Jayne's eyes lingered on the rings I wore. I'd donned them for my father's party and hadn't bothered taking them off, save the one I'd given to the violinist. To look at Jayne, sitting relaxed at the table between us, she did not seem like a desperate person. But the gleam in her eyes said differently.

This woman wanted something. I could work with that.

"Your proposal sounds reasonable to me," I said, and held out a hand. "Guide us to this tower, and we will pay you for your time."

Jayne clasped my hand and shook it. "It's a deal." Her palm was covered in calluses similar to my own. As though she wielded a blade regularly. Unsurprising, considering her line of work.

We planned a time to meet in the morning, a little before the
ride I'd arranged to the barrier was supposed to pick us up, then
Jayne stood and bid us good night. I wondered if she had other
accommodations or just hadn't the money to afford one of the
rickety cots we'd been shown in the loft above.

"Do you trust her?" Grimm asked as soon as she was out of
sight.

I shrugged. "I trust that she can get us where we want to go.
That's the most important thing, isn't it?"

"She could be lying."

"If she wanted to trick us out of our money, she would have
demanded payment ahead of time," I pointed out. "She's the
closest thing to a map we've got, so I think it's worth the risk."

Grimm, whose idea of risk was probably having a second
glass of wine with dinner, didn't seem convinced. He insisted we
prepare some spells before setting foot in the woods.

"You might be willing to place our fate entirely in the hands
of a stranger, but I am not. I would feel better going into this if
my pockets weren't empty. We really should have stocked up on a
few basic survival spells before we left. Heating spells and protective bubbles at the very least. Maybe a few repulsion charms, in
case something gets the jump on us."

"All right, all right," I said, though I was not feeling nearly
the same level of practicality after all the drinks I'd had pressed
upon me. "I suppose a protective bubble would be a good thing
to have on hand, so that no monsters come sniffing after our delicate flesh in the night." I rummaged through my pockets until
I found a few pieces of paper, then held my quill at the ready and
looked at Grimm expectantly.

"You'll have to recite them," I explained. "I haven't had to
scrive a protective bubble since third tier, and I don't remember

a word of the standard repulsion spell. Not sure if I remember anything but the first line of the heating charm either, now that I think of it."

Grimm took in a deep breath and then let it out slowly through his nose. "Hopeless," he murmured, before reciting each spell unfalteringly. He looked pained at having to do so and seemed out of sorts even after the spells were copied down.

"I don't understand how you can write something like the song you came up with today, yet still not remember a basic heating charm," he grumbled.

"Perhaps I'm able to write spellsongs *because* I don't have a bunch of other stuff taking up space in my brain," I retorted, tapping a finger against my temple. "Did you ever think of that?"

"No," Grimm said. "Because it sounds like nonsense."

He'd carefully sorted and stacked the spells I'd written, and now he distributed them among his coat pockets. I could never remember which one I'd left my quill in, but I had a feeling that Grimm always remembered which pocket to reach for, the same way he remembered the words to each spell hidden safely inside. I expected him to leave now that we were finished, withdrawing to the relative quiet of the loft above, but he stayed seated and fixed his eyes on me.

"That spellsong," he said. "Do you think it could work for anyone? If we taught it to one of the untrained sorcerers in town or told the Coterie about it, do you think they could sing it too?"

"I don't know. I don't really think so. They've never worked for anyone else before. And there was something about it that felt... particular."

"Particular to what?"

To us. To standing in that field, and the unexpected harmony of Grimm's voice and my playing. But I couldn't make sense of why this would be, so I didn't say anything, just shook my head and shrugged. Grimm probably just would have sniffed and called it nonsense again, and this time I would have agreed with him.

"It's a pity," Grimm said. "It was well done. The spell, I mean. Unconventional but effective."

I leaned forward over the table and cupped one hand around my ear. "Was that a compliment I heard? You'd best be careful what you say or I'll begin to think this forced proximity is improving your opinion of me."

Grimm huffed and looked away, nostrils flaring slightly. "My opinion of you personally is unchanged. But," he added, with great reluctance, "it's possible my assessment of your abilities was lacking."

"Stop," I said dryly. "I'm blushing."

"You'll do well in the Coterie," he said with an air of grudging acceptance.

Up until that moment I'd been flushed full of warmth from the drinks I'd received, and the overcrowded room, and yes, maybe a little bit from the unexpected thrill of hearing Grimm admit that I had done something well. But mention of the Coterie chased all that away.

"I won't, actually. I'm not joining."

Grimm stared at me in clear astonishment. "But you've nearly finished your fifth tier. Why would you even bother attending the Fount if you don't intend to do anything with your education?"

"My father wanted me to attend." I ran a finger idly along the rim of my glass as I spoke, until it hummed faintly. "In fact, he wanted me there so badly he made reaching fifth tier a condition of my inheritance. Not just the money my mother left me when she died, but her estate as well—the property in Sahnt where I spent most of my childhood. I couldn't bear the thought of the place belonging to anyone else, so I enrolled at the Fount." I must have had more to drink than I'd realized, to be sharing this much with Grimm. I kept going. "I believe my father thought I would emerge from the experience... transformed. But that hasn't been the case. I've known for a long time that I don't belong anywhere near the Coterie. Once we're done with fifth tier, I'll be a free man."

"That's what you meant earlier," Grimm said slowly. "When you said the Coterie's requirements wouldn't matter for you."

It took me a moment to organize my spinning thoughts enough to recall our conversation that morning, when Grimm suggested I treat our journey as a training exercise. I remembered the way his jaw had tightened and the sour look he'd given me.

"Thought I meant to buy my way in, did you?" I spoke the words jokingly, but in truth they turned my stomach a little, remembering the conversation I'd overheard on the balcony. I was certain no money had passed hands between my brother and that Coterie captain, but an exchange had taken place all the same.

Grimm said, "What will you do instead?"

That was the question, wasn't it? Any time I tried to settle on an answer, my mind skipped away like a stone on water, bouncing from idea to idea and discarding all of them in the end. I looked away from Grimm and into the black eyes of the wolf's heads over the fire. The deadened gaze was strangely piercing.

"Anything I like," I told Grimm airily, tucking my hands behind my head and tilting my chair back a little. "I haven't given the matter much thought, beyond rejoicing over the idea of not having to memorize any more dusty old spellbooks. I'm tired of sitting inside all day, surrounded by other people's words. Maybe I'll become a farmer instead of a sorcerer. Maybe I'll return to Dwull and ask your mother to teach me to grow flowers. I could be her assistant or apprentice or something."

I said it partially to annoy Grimm, and indeed, the corners of his mouth immediately flattened. But surprisingly I found myself warming to the idea. I imagined what it would be like to don a wide-brimmed hat and spend my days surrounded by blossoms, writing charms that introduced outlandish colors to their petals. Nurturing something that would bring others joy. I thought I could feel useful, doing something like that, even if it wasn't providing the same service the Coterie did. Even if it didn't provide the same thrill as I'd gotten earlier, hearing Grimm cast my spellsong.

Grimm let out a sound that came perilously close to being a snort. "You could never do that type of work."

"Why not?" I asked, offended. I'd put on a show all day of being weak and lazy, but I was perfectly capable of working hard when properly motivated.

"Farming requires effort without notice, day after day, year after year. You'd wither like a plant during drought without a steady stream of attention."

Well.

The feeling of being *seen* was not an enjoyable one. Not in this context. And not when the insight was delivered in Grimm's most scornful tone. It left me squirming in my chair.

"You don't know that. Maybe I would surprise you. I did today, after all, with the spellsong."

"What's the point of rising above expectation for only a moment? Once you finish fifth tier, you'll have the advantage of your inheritance, and you will continue to be capable of magic like the kind you wrote today...but it will benefit no one. You will keep wasting yourself on silly tricks and cosmetic charms, if you bother with magic at all. I may have been briefly surprised by you, today, Loveage, but don't think it means anything. Everything else you said is nothing more than I expected."

That was the thing about Grimm. Most of the time he used a single word to every one of my ten, but when he *did* speak, everything he said hit like a sledgehammer. Back at the Fount people fell all over themselves trying to win Grimm's approval, and I'd always rolled my eyes watching it happen. But apparently all it took was a few minutes of harmony in a field and I was ready to do some falling of my own. As though I didn't know better. As though I hadn't spent years cultivating the belief that I would never be able to please anyone but myself and there was no use trying. For an instant, with Grimm staring down his nose at me, I wanted to throw all that away and...

And do what?

There was nothing I could say. Grimm may have thought the way I used magic was selfish, but I had my reasons, and they were good ones. He could go on thinking what he liked of me.

I smiled blandly across the table. "Here's to managing expectations," I said, then raised my drink in Grimm's direction and downed the rest of its contents in one long swallow, trying not to wince when I found the beer had gone lukewarm.

By the time I slammed the empty glass down, Grimm had left.

CHAPTER SIXTEEN

To say that I emerged from the pub the following morning in a state of gentle dishevelment would be a gross understatement. I'd stayed up far too late the night before, only stumbling up to the loft once I was certain Grimm would be asleep, and paid for it by waking up with a dry mouth and a pounding headache. My clothes were rumpled from being slept in, and every time my pulse beat, my temples felt like my whole head would cave in.

Both Jayne and the driver were waiting for us, so there was nothing to do except step out into the too-bright morning, take my place on the back of the wagon, and try not to heave my breakfast over the side.

When the wagon began moving with a clatter, I let out a quiet moan. Grimm gave me a long glance that managed to be both disapproving and self-satisfied. It made me want to muss his hair or tug at the perfectly smooth line of his coat—anything to put us on more even footing—but I was certain if I tried to move so much as a pinkie finger, I would embarrass myself in front of Jayne, so I simply closed my eyes to block out his smug face.

By midmorning my stomach had settled and my head was well enough for me to look ahead and see the spelled flags waving at the top of the barrier posts. The fabric was unworn by the elements, suggesting that the Coterie had been by to refresh the spells on this section recently. Trees grew close against the other side of the tall wooden poles, but not past them. As though the magic discouraged new growth as well as monsters.

Other places had different ways of deterring magical beasts: The lake country used twisting, deadly waterways built like mazes, and sorcerers in the mountains had ways of making their paths and roadways precarious to uninvited guests. Miendor was low and mostly flat, with little protection in the natural landscape, so we had these posts with spells strung delicately between them—like a massive loom weaving a pattern designed to keep the monsters out. A handful still managed to sneak through, every now and then, but it kept the influx manageable.

I'd heard of places beyond the sea that had tamed their surroundings somehow, so they did not need barriers at all. But they had turned themselves into dead zones doing so. No magic answered to them anymore. That was the price of breaking the balance.

Jayne signaled to the driver, and the wagon slowed to a halt. The man watched us climb down with a worried expression.

"You're sure you don't want me to come back for you?" he asked. "I don't recommend being out past the barrier when night falls."

"I appreciate the offer," I said, "but what we're looking for won't be found in a day. Besides, we've hired an expert. You'll keep us in one piece, won't you, Jayne?"

Jayne had shown up that morning with a sword belted to her waist and a crossbow slung across her back. When she'd caught me staring at it, she told me, "There are things in the forest I'd rather not get within blade's reach of."

"I'll do my best," she said now.

Not exactly a ringing endorsement, but it was enough for the driver to wash his hands of us with a clear conscience. He turned the wagon around and disappeared back the way we'd come, leaving us standing on a small rise that dropped away on one side, providing an unhindered view of the Unquiet Wood, rolling out beyond the barrier in a blanket of green.

The forests I'd grown up with in Sahnt were full of tall, thin trees whose delicate branches allowed sunlight to trickle down through their leaves. It was unlikely you could find a patch large enough to truly lose yourself in.

These trees were nothing like that.

They were enormous, growing so close together that the space beneath their branches seemed a different world—gloomier and stranger. From our vantage point, the forest stretched on forever. It reminded me of standing on the edge of the ocean as a child, wondering what was hidden in those depths.

"I recommend you have your swords ready from here on out," Jayne said. She waited while Grimm and I retrieved our blades from our packs and belted them to our waists. I also took a moment to untie my sash and wrangle it into a halter of sorts, so that I could carry my violin case slung over my back. Grimm looked horror-struck at the rough treatment of the silk, but it left my hands free and that was more important.

"Any advice before we go in?" I asked Jayne. "Words of wisdom?" I wasn't frightened exactly, but I had a sudden visceral awareness that we were about to step beyond the bounds of what was considered *ours*.

"Follow me," Jayne said. "Watch where you step. Don't touch anything without asking me first. And stay quiet."

Grimm looked at me. "We're doomed."

It was said softly, almost to himself, and with such wryness that I couldn't help but chuckle—forgetting for a moment that we had not shared more than two words since our tense conversation the night before. I raised an eyebrow at Grimm and mimed sealing my lips, then I followed Jayne down the hill. I had never set foot beyond Miendor's barrier before, or even been close to doing so. A low throb of power emanated from the spaces between flagpoles, but Jayne didn't visibly react when she walked through the weave of magic strung between them. I held my breath when it was my turn to step through, expecting *something*. But I was disappointed. There was no ripple of sensation, no change in my vision or surroundings. The world on the other side of the barrier was unchanged and so was I—still hungover, still stuck with Grimm, still cursed.

Jayne's worth as a guide became apparent almost immediately. It was difficult to make out details under the trees with so little sunlight trickling through the branches, but she never faltered, moving over the root-buckled earth with an assurance that Grimm and I both lacked, used as we were to Luxe's smooth streets. Her eyes were always watchful. Her hand barely left the hilt of her sword.

"How far is the tower?" I asked, shortly after we passed through the barrier.

"About a day's journey," Jayne answered. "Provided we move quickly and the forest cooperates."

Mindful of this time frame, I didn't complain nearly as much as I had on our walk the day before, even when my blisters began to rub and break.

The farther into the trees we went, the more I noticed a prickling, raised-hair awareness. It made me want to glance over my shoulder after every other step, half-afraid and half-eager for what I might see lurking there. Once, I caught sight of Grimm out of the corner of my eye and nearly jumped, for the dim, uncanny light under the trees had washed his pale skin in a ghostly cast and made his hair look unworldly.

The air smelled green. Not in the fresh, bright way of spring, but heavy, oppressive almost. It was the green of a hothouse, everything growing in profusion and in the same space.

This was all undoubtedly eerie, yet the forest did not at first seem to be the roiling pit of monsters I'd been led to expect. By late afternoon the only other sign of life was the bugs. They resembled furry dragonflies and hovered around our faces in a swarm, darting forward to leave little bites that didn't itch but *burned*. Jayne assured us the bites would cause no lasting damage, so while the bugs were monstrously annoying, they were not an especially impressive representative of their kind.

Supposedly more than half of all the monsters that managed to slip past Miendor's barrier came from these trees. Yet it was so quiet that morning I couldn't help but wonder if such reports were an exaggeration. A tall tale to discourage reckless adventurers and frighten children.

At midday we stopped to eat, and Jayne instructed Grimm to cast a protective bubble around us. It seemed a pity to waste the spell, since we were all awake and watchful, but I said nothing. The water from Grimm's enchanted canteen tasted stale, but I said nothing of that either. Lunch was cold because Jayne said lighting a fire would attract the wrong sort of attention. All in all, it was a rather bleak affair.

I was starting to suspect this was all an act and that Jayne had overstated the forest's danger just to collect an easy paycheck by convincing us her protection was necessary.

"So, Jayne," I said, wearing my most engaging smile. "What's the most exciting thing you've foraged here?" If she said something boring like *singing frogs' tongues*, that would be a bad sign. Or a good sign, depending on if you were more concerned with being eaten or being wrong about someone's character.

Jayne thought about it for a moment and said, "A griffin feather."

I let out a low whistle, impressed. "That must have fetched you a pretty penny."

"It will. Someday. But it's hard to find buyers for more expensive items in the border towns, and we haven't had an opportunity to visit Luxe in some time."

I was just about to ask if she'd actually seen the griffin the feather had come from when Jayne held up a hand and said, "Hush."

She moved in a crouch to the edge of the bubble and stayed there for many minutes, looking intently out into the darkest part of the trees around us. Just when I was certain that this too was for show, that the griffin feather was a lie and we'd been tip-toeing through the woods for no reason at all, something stepped out of the trees.

It resembled a stag, but with fur so white it appeared ghostly and antlers that shone like a star. They weren't rounded, as an ordinary stag's antlers would have been, but instead had edges that gleamed as sharp as a sword. This was alarming, but what made me shiver were the teeth growing on the outer edge of the creature's jaw, like a mouth turned inside out.

All three of us stared at the thing that was not a stag. It stared back.

"Can it get through the bubble?" I asked softly, looking at the honed tips of the beast's antlers.

"No," Jayne answered just as quietly. "Your friend is a strong caster. Be glad of it."

After another moment or so, the monster tossed its head and walked away.

"I'm going to do a quick look around before we leave," Jayne said. "Just to check... just to check that it's really gone."

You could not have paid me to step outside the comforting iridescence of our bubble so soon, but Jayne was made of sterner stuff. She wasn't gone long and assured us everything was clear when she returned.

The Unquiet Wood seemed determined to clear up any doubts I'd had about its reputation during the second half of the day. We'd barely gone two miles after lunch before Grimm nearly stepped on a snake hidden in the ferns. It rose up in front of him, hissing, and Grimm reeled back so quickly that he almost bumped into me. The snake's scales were as green as the ferns it hid beneath, its eyes a stunningly putrid shade of yellow. I reached for my sword, but before I could draw it, there was a *thunk* and the snake's head dropped, pinned to the ground by one of Jayne's daggers. Drops of venom dribbled from its ruined mouth. When they hit the ground, the dirt sizzled and hardened, forming gemstones the same shade of yellow as the snake's now glassy eyes.

We paused our journey so that Jayne could bury the snake and gemstones, careful not to let either touch the bare skin of her hands.

Both Grimm and I were more careful of where we stepped after that. So much so that we almost didn't notice the birds perched in the trees a little while later. There were five of them, with feathers black as night, sitting in a row on a branch. In place of talons, they had long-fingered hands that curled around their perch. Jayne steered us to the left, so as not to pass directly beneath them, but otherwise didn't seem overly concerned.

"It's the ones with regular talons you need to watch out for," she said, once we were well past.

"Why's that?" I asked.

Jayne looked very pointedly down at my hands. "Because they're still searching."

The day was full of little encounters like that, strange and unmistakably dangerous. And it wasn't only the animals that were weird inside the wood. I didn't have a good sense of time passing under the trees, but I guessed it was well into the afternoon when Jayne suddenly paused and sniffed the air, looking for all the world like a dog that had caught a scent.

"Something wrong?" Grimm asked, hand already on his sword. The forest had that effect on you.

Jayne shook her head. "The opposite, actually."

We'd been traveling along a faint path, worn into the dirt by the passing of monsters and foragers both, but now Jayne stepped off it and pushed a little way into the undergrowth, stopping in front of a thick tree trunk covered with blooming vines. It was the flowers Jayne must have smelled, and now I could too—a warm, sweet scent unlike anything I was familiar with. I eyed the blossoms warily, thinking of other growing things from the Wilderlands that had crossed the border in the past, only to wreak havoc.

"Is this something you forage?" I asked.

"Not the flowers," Jayne said. "They don't do anything except smell nice. It's what grows near them that's valuable." She pushed back the vines at the bottom of the trunk to reveal a cluster of blue mushrooms.

"What are they used for?" Grimm asked, leaning forward to get a better look at the sky-colored fungi.

I fought an urge to pull him back to a safer distance. Mushrooms had spores, didn't they? Surely a farmer's son should know better than to get too near unfamiliar flora.

"They have strong sedative properties," Jayne said. "Dangerous to eat, but we make them into an elixir to coat our weapons with. It's never our aim to fight monsters, only gather their leavings, but it's useful to have the added protection if we find ourselves in a tight corner." She reached for the ties of her cloak and undid them to lay the fabric on the ground at the tree's base. "Take a moment to rest while I gather these."

While Jayne began to harvest the mushrooms, laying them gently in her hood for safekeeping, Grimm and I settled in to wait. Grimm sat down on a mossy patch of ground after inspecting it closely, still wary after the snake incident, while I leaned against a slender tree. I was afraid that if I sat down, my feet might refuse to carry me again when the time came to get up. The bugs were much worse standing still, and so I improvised a cantrip to sing under my breath—just a little something to keep the buzzing creatures from setting fire to my face with their bites. It worked, and for a moment I was miraculously free of the feeling of tiny, furry bodies bumping into me.

Grimm looked up at the sound of my voice, frowning. I thought he would scold me for making too much noise, but he only said, "Just because you *can* cast small magics doesn't mean you should. I thought all scrivers knew the dangers of overreaching."

"This? This is barely anything," I said. As soon as I stopped singing, all the bugs rushed close again.

"All magic is something," Grimm insisted.

"If you're so concerned, why don't you cast the song, then?" It would probably keep the bugs away better anyway, Grimm being who he was. But Grimm shook his head.

"It's not worth wasting energy on something so trivial."

I rolled my eyes and picked up the tune again, but it *was* a bit much for me to keep going with for long. Such a small spell likely wouldn't have caused Grimm any strain at all, but fatigue prickled at the edges of my awareness, along with that same hollow-stomach feeling that always accompanied my castings. Once I fell silent, the bugs pressed back in again, and I looked around for something to distract me from their sting.

"Have you ever been beyond the barrier before now?" I asked Grimm.

"No."

"Neither have I." I leaned a little farther back against the tree trunk, lifting my face to try to catch the weak rays of light filtering down through the branches. "Makes me wonder what the rest of the world beyond Miendor looks like. Maybe that's what I'll do after the Fount. Become a traveler and climb the mountains to the north, or sail across the sea. I can picture myself as an intrepid explorer." I tilted my chin down toward Grimm. "What do you think? Is that not a noble calling?"

Grimm, who had been intently studying the surrounding trees this whole time, finally turned to look at me. "I think that, without Jayne, you probably would have been throttled by a bird or stabbed by a deer by now. Likely because you *couldn't keep quiet.*"

"I'm not the one who nearly got bitten by a snake earlier. You should really watch where you step."

"Loveage!" Grimm's voice was so sharp that for a moment

I thought I'd actually managed to hit a nerve. But he gestured toward the ground and said, "Your foot."

I blinked and looked down. There were tendrils of *something* wrapped around my right boot, twining up and around my ankle. My first impulse was to shake them off the same way you would a bug, but watching how Jayne moved through the forest had granted me an unusual degree of caution, so I fought the urge and leaned over to inspect the problem more closely.

Silly, really. I'd just been so concerned by Grimm doing the same thing.

The tendrils resembled roots. Slender, moving roots that had grown up around me so delicately and so quickly that I hadn't even noticed. I tried to gently pull one of them away, but they were quite stubborn and couldn't be loosened.

"Jayne," I called out, and our guide looked up from her task. "What is it?"

"There's something—" I began, and then my words became a strangled shout as the tendrils tightened around my ankle and I was swept off my feet and into the air.

As I hung there, dangling, blood rushing to my head, I became aware of two things:

One: The tree that I'd been leaning against had moved. I could see the trunk of it above me, strangely crooked.

Two: It wasn't a tree; it was a leg.

Craning my neck, I saw other crooked joints coming to life, causing the leaves of the real trees around us to quiver. I tried to count how many legs the monster had, but my vantage point wasn't very good, and they kept moving. Many. There were many legs. They all straightened to their full height, and I was lifted higher. At the same time, a huge, bulbous body appeared above me, no longer hidden by branches.

Somewhere on the ground, I heard Jayne swear.

The beast was spiderlike, and yet there was something about it that stopped me from firmly placing it in the arachnid family. For one thing, it did not move with the frightening speed of a spider, but with a ponderous inelegance in keeping with its size. For another, there were no eyes on the body of the monster, only more tendrils like the ones that had caught hold of me. They waved through the air with the same weightless delicacy of hair floating in water. Even though it was only my leg that was trapped, I imagined I could feel their touch over my entire body.

I reached for my sword, thinking to cut myself free, but this was easier said than done. My arms tangled in the bunched-up fabric of my own coat, as well as the straps of my bag, and I had to fumble around for what felt like an eternity to draw my blade. Then, just when it came free, the monster let out a piercing, inhuman screech.

Its mouth was a cavernous black space. When it opened, the scent of blood and rotten leaves rolled over me in a putrid wave.

"Oh, please, no," I whimpered. I had never wanted anything in my life as much as I wanted to be far, far away from that mouth.

The monster screamed again. Looking down, I caught sight of the source of its anger—Grimm, standing next to one of the creature's legs, was using his sword like an axe to hack away at it. Blood thick as sap coated the blade, and on the next blow, the leg holding me spasmed and flailed.

The world blurred as I was flung this way and that like a rag doll. A voice was shouting something in the old language, but I was too distracted to decipher what sort of spell was being cast. It was all I could do not to vomit, and I thought I might lose that battle if the monster didn't stop shaking me soon. And then, abruptly, it *did* stop.

I swung gently over the ground like a human pendulum. The grip on my leg hadn't loosened, and that terrible mouth was still a wide-open thing of nightmares, but it wasn't moving or making a sound. It was, in fact, frozen.

Below me, Jayne dropped her hands, fingers still coated in ash from the spell she'd cast. "It won't remain paralyzed for long," she said in a tight voice. "We need to hurry."

It was a mark of Jayne's skill as a caster that she was able to halt the movement of a creature this size. Paralysis spells were difficult, both to write and to cast. The thought made something in the back of my mind chime like a bell, but there was no time to ponder it further. I swung my sword, but the angle was very bad, and it seemed just as likely I would cut my own foot as whatever held me. Fortunately, Grimm arrived before I was able to do any damage. After two strikes, the tendrils holding my leg parted and I fell to the ground in a heap.

"You should really watch where you step, Loveage," Grimm said.

"Oh, fuck you," I groaned, scrambling upright. As I did so, I thought I saw one of the tendrils still attached to the monster's leg twitch—a jerky, aborted movement.

Jayne saw it too. "Let's go."

She abandoned her usual caution in favor of speed as she swept her cloak off the ground and headed back the way we had come, toward that slim path that cut through the trees, Grimm on her heels.

I followed last. There was a part of me that dreaded looking away from the monster, because as long as I was watching, at least I would know when it moved. If I looked away, the spell might be broken and it would be free to come after us without me even being aware. That unknowing was somehow even more terrible than the promise of danger. But being left to stare at it alone was the worst thing of all, so I gathered my frayed nerves about me and ran.

In the end, there was no uncertainty at all. After only a few minutes of the three of us crashing down the path at top speed, we all heard a scream, piercing in its rage, and then the sound of groaning trees as the monster threw the spell off and began to follow.

CHAPTER SEVENTEEN

There is a particular flavor to the terror of being chased. It is overwhelming, but it also strains the bounds of credulity. Much like the monster, our situation was too big to comprehend, happening too fast. Reality felt fragile, like something that would be shattered either by a spindled limb reaching out to grab my shoulder or by waking up in my own bed.

Perhaps we weren't there at all. Perhaps the forest was only another of my nightmares. After all, it would hardly be the first time I had dreamed of being pursued.

A scream cut through the air, closer than before.

"Here," Jayne said, sudden and urgent. She veered to the left, down a little rise that ended in a cluster of thick roots. They formed a cave of sorts, and we dove for it, scrambling to find openings large enough to slip through. Once inside, Grimm hastily cast a protective bubble around us, and then we crouched there, looking out through the crisscrossing wood.

It was easy to track the monster's progress, for it was too large to move without disrupting everything around it. The trees swayed, as though in the wake of a strong breeze. I held my breath as the shaking leaves grew closer and closer, and then, gradually, farther away. The monster had not noticed us beneath it. The searching tendrils of its mouth did not seem to taste our presence within the bubble.

"What was that thing?" I whispered.

"It's called a wood kraken," Jayne said. "They're not usually a danger in the daytime as they sleep very heavily. Something must have woken this one up. We should not move just yet."

I was happy to follow this advice, letting my trembling legs finally fold so I could sit in the dirt of our hidey-hole as we listened for the monster.

We waited, and waited, but the only sounds we heard were the birds in the trees, picking up their songs again now that the threat had passed. As the adrenaline began to fade, my mind settled on Jayne and the surprising contents of her spell case.

The thing was, paralysis spells were rare. Or at least, it was rare to find one that could lock the limbs of anything in front of you. If I had wanted to freeze Grimm in place, I could have written a spell that did so, but it would have to be a spell written *specifically* for Grimm. I couldn't expect the same words to work on Jayne, and I certainly couldn't expect they would work on whatever monster stumbled by. There were a few scrivers who had managed to write paralysis spells with broader reach, but they'd never been replicated. Existing copies were kept in the Fount library for study, along with other rare spells.

Or at least they had been.

One of the vaults they snuck into held a collection of paralysis spells, Rainer had told me.

I looked at Jayne, and my pulse, which had finally begun to steady, sped up again.

The thieves who had broken into the Fount's library had never been caught.

Don't be silly, I told myself. But the thought, once had, would not allow itself to be banished.

It made an awful sort of sense. The thieves weren't common thugs; they had been Coterie members, and here was Jayne, with her sword-calloused hands, and her skill as a caster, her easy calm when facing monsters, as though she'd been trained to do so. Jayne, whose hood had been drawn close around her face when I first met her. Because she'd feared being recognized. I was willing to bet my inheritance that whatever other spells she carried in that case around her neck would match neatly up against the list of spells taken from the library. The only thing I couldn't make sense of was why she was playing tour guide for us. What did she actually want?

I sat in our nest of roots, furiously mulling over all the possibilities and reaching no definitive answers. Jayne had protected us from the monsters, so her intentions didn't seem entirely nefarious, but I couldn't figure out why she would risk being recognized simply to earn a little coin from two Fount students. It didn't seem wise to just come out with it and ask, so instead I sat scant feet from the person I was now certain was a sought-after outlaw, wondering how to convey this information to Grimm.

I got lucky on that front. After a little while, Jayne shifted next to me and spoke.

"I think it's gone, but I'd like to go out and have a quick look around before we leave the bubble." She got to her feet and slipped out past the roots, leaving me and Grimm alone.

I forced myself to wait until Jayne was out of sight, and then a little bit longer, just to be sure she was out of earshot. Then I turned to Grimm.

"We have a problem."

Grimm's face turned thunderous as I explained.

"We need to leave," he said. "Now. Before she gets back."

I hesitated, remembering the terror of staring straight into the wood kraken's mouth. *I* didn't have any spells that could have stopped that thing. "Is that wise? She may be an outlaw, but she's kept us alive. There are things more dangerous than Jayne living in this forest, and we don't know where we're going."

"What do you mean?" Grimm asked. "We're going back to Miendor."

We blinked at each other, both surprised.

"But we have to find the sorcerer," I said. It had never, not once, occurred to me that this might mean we should abandon our quest. The thought of returning to Miendor with the curse still living under my skin was almost as horrifying to me as the monster's gaping maw had been. "Jayne's identity is a stumbling block, sure, but it's no reason to throw aside the progress we've made! We must be close to the tower by now."

Grimm was shaking his head. "Do you really think that's where she's taking us? No, this was likely a trap all along. She's dangerous."

"She could have left us to the wood kraken," I pointed out. "But she didn't. Jayne may be a thief, but she's also a Coterie member."

Grimm set his jaw stubbornly. "*Former* Coterie member. And I don't care who she used to be. She and her troop nearly killed Phade, or have you forgotten? They're obviously not sorcerers to be trusted."

I *had* forgotten that bit, actually. It was hard to associate the quiet, steady woman we'd been following with what had happened to Phade, or my brother's injured arm for that matter. Grimm's words elicited a rare flicker of guilt, as well as a stab of genuine worry. Thievery was one thing, but violence was another. Suddenly our little bubble of protection didn't feel so safe, knowing that Jayne could return at any moment.

"All right," I said. "Let's go before she comes back." I had every intention of convincing Grimm that we should continue to look for the sorcerer on our own, but that could wait until we were away.

Grimm narrowed his eyes at me, as though suspecting I had given in a bit too easily, but he must have also decided now was not the time for that particular argument. Instead, he quietly beckoned for me to follow as he led the way out of our shelter and back into the open forest. We went as quickly as we could while still watching for all the little signs of danger Jayne had taught us to be aware of, as well as watching out for Jayne herself.

"I heard the sound of moving water while we were running," Grimm said, keeping his voice low. "We should retrace our steps and look for it. If it's the River Noire, we can follow it all the way back without getting lost."

This was a sound plan of escape from the forest, since the River Noire flowed straight out of the trees and into Dwull. We would end up much nearer to the coast than where we'd started, but still firmly back in Miendor. Of course, I wasn't interested in escaping the wood just yet and was therefore disappointed when Grimm was right and we found the river after only ten minutes of walking.

We both stopped on the bank. The ground fell away sharply in front of us, and the water below was wide and deep. Swirling currents formed little patterns of foam on its dark surface.

"You know," I said, taking advantage of this pause, "if it wasn't for the wood kraken, we probably would have reached the sorcerer's tower by now. If we walk upstream, deeper into the woods, maybe we could find—"

"The sorcerer likely doesn't exist," Grimm said, cutting me

off firmly. "These outlaws are liars and oath breakers. Jayne fed you a story she knew would get you to follow her, and it worked. We need to leave this forest now before she can connect with the other members of her troop."

"A little late for that."

The voice carried over the sound of the water crashing below us, faintly amused in a way that held little real mirth. Grimm and I both spun round in time to watch the speaker step out from the shadow of the trees.

Jayne, I thought, even though the voice was too deep and the shoulders too broad. The man's face, however, was strikingly similar to that of our guide—same fair, narrow brows and freckled skin, same slightly overlarge nose. He had a crossbow like Jayne's as well. But where Jayne exuded a practiced sort of calm, this man simmered with resentful energy.

Oh, I thought, *here is someone I can imagine leaving Phade for dead.* My palms began to sweat.

Grimm reached for his sword, and the man made a soft *tsk*ing sound.

"Don't tempt me," he said, and shifted the crossbow so it pointed directly at Grimm's heart. "Leave your blade where it is and drop whatever scrap is in your other hand while you're at it."

Grimm reluctantly lowered his hands, and a piece of paper fell to the ground. It was one of the repulsion charms Grimm had stocked his pockets with. Now the spell lay at our feet for a moment before a breeze caught it up and sent it twirling a few feet away.

I could taste my heartbeat in my throat. The man seemed a breath away from releasing an arrow at Grimm, and I had the strangest urge to say something that would make him take notice of me instead.

"Who are you?" I blurted.

The bolt didn't waver, but his gaze shifted to me. "Didn't you hear? I'm a liar and an oath breaker. Best do as I say. Who knows what other sins I'm willing to commit?"

Before I could begin to formulate an answer to this, the leaves behind the outlaw rustled and Jayne appeared. She looked at Grimm and me, standing frozen on the edge of the bank, then to the man with his crossbow, and sighed. It was a weary sort of sound. The sound of someone whose day was not going at all how she would have liked.

"I see you've met my brother, Mathias," she said.

The man—Mathias—didn't lower the crossbow but shifted so that he could stand a little closer to Jayne and murmured, "They know who you are."

"I inferred that much, thank you." Jayne turned to me. "Something must have given us away for you to run. What was it?"

"The paralysis spell," I answered, seeing no reason to lie. "You couldn't have bought anything so rare from a vendor. They're all locked up in the library vaults." I tilted my head to one side, and then amended with "Or at least, they were."

Jayne nodded, fingers playing idly with the strap her spell case hung from. "Clever reasoning. I knew using that spell was a gamble, but it seemed worth it, at the time."

"You should be thanking her," Mathias said. "I wouldn't have wasted that spell on you, considering you're the one who probably woke the kraken up in the first place, with your little song."

I was so shocked by this accusation that it took me a moment to process its second meaning: Mathias hadn't just appeared now; he'd been following us from the start. Trailing behind and watching our progress through the trees. Jayne hadn't come to us alone.

"I know what you must be thinking," Jayne began.

"I'm thinking that Grimm was right about you. Which is upsetting for me on a number of levels." I took a very small step toward her that also, coincidentally, moved me closer to the spell on the ground, and said plaintively, "Did you ever even see the sorcerer's tower?"

"Believe it or not, I did. Once. But... I don't actually know how to find my way back there. I think there's a spell on the tower that disorients anyone trying to seek her out. I'm sorry." Jayne really did sound apologetic, but her brother was still aiming a crossbow at us, so I didn't feel particularly inclined to forgive anything.

"What was all this about, then?" Grimm asked, voice cold. "What do you want from us?"

Jayne and Mathias exchanged a loaded glance.

"*I'm* not going to explain," he muttered. "I thought this idea was more trouble than it was worth from the beginning."

Jayne sighed again, then looked to me. "I wanted your help, Leo. Not everything I told you was a lie; we really are trying to make our way as foragers here. But surviving in this forest requires magic, and our spells are dwindling. We have neither enough money to purchase more, nor anyone in our troop left who can scrive them. When I spotted you at the pub, I saw an opportunity and I took it. I'm sorry I lured you here under false pretenses, but I couldn't think of any other way to get what we needed."

I stared. "You brought me out here because you want a scriver?"

Jayne nodded. "We need someone who can restock our

pockets, and you're Fount trained…" She trailed off as I began to laugh.

"I'm sorry," I said, dabbing at my eyes a little. "It's just terribly funny. You see, I'm an awful scriver. Absolutely the worst person you could have kidnapped for this purpose. Ask Grimm!"

Jayne's brow furrowed. "I heard what you did for that town. It wasn't the work of an amateur."

I waved my hand dismissively, using the gesture to distract from my inching a little bit closer to the paper in the grass. "A stroke of luck. Most of the time I can't even remember the words to a basic heating spell. And don't get me started on what happens when I'm asked to compose anything more powerful than a charm. Disastrous! Isn't that right, Grimm?"

Grimm gave a stiff nod.

Jayne looked back and forth between us, doubt written clearly across her face. I was close enough to reach out and nudge the paper with my toe now. I held off, hoping that Jayne would reconsider. Give the whole job up as a bad idea and let us go. I thought she wanted to.

But in the end, the same desperation that had prompted her to bring us here in the first place won out.

She let out a short, frustrated breath and said, "Your skill might be limited, but it's more than we have currently. I'm going to approach you now to bind your hands. If you struggle, I have methods that will make it easier for me, but I'd prefer not to use them. I'd like to keep this as civil as possible."

It was my turn to hesitate. I didn't *want* to play along nicely while my hands were tied up, but I had only one idea to prevent that from happening and it wasn't a particularly good one. And then there was Mathias, who still had his crossbow pointed at

Grimm, giving me heart palpitations. Surely it was not such a bad thing to cooperate with outlaws if they asked you very politely and it meant not getting shot?

But on this matter, as on so many others, Grimm and I did not seem to be in agreement.

He tilted his head to look down his long nose at Jayne as she took her first step toward us and said, in a voice dripping with scorn, "You're thieves and liars. You have earned no civility from me."

This seemed like an ill-advised declaration, all things considered, but it was just like Grimm to be unwilling to compromise, even with a bolt pointed at him.

"The high and mighty have spoken," Mathias said with a sneer that I didn't care for at all. Without lowering the crossbow, he leaned in his sister's direction and whispered, not quite so quietly that we wouldn't overhear, "We don't need both of them. It will be easier with just the scriver."

"Hang on," I said, voice jumping a few octaves, but neither of them paid me any mind. Jayne was looking at Grimm with consideration.

Before anything else could be said or done, she reached into the spell case around her neck. It was a practiced motion, fingers easily retrieving the strip of paper they sought. "This will not hurt," Jayne told Grimm soothingly as the edges of the paper began to smoke. "It's for the best."

I panicked, plain and simple. It came over me all at once, sweeping aside any scrap of reason. They'd drilled us on defensive measures during combat training at the Fount, but much like the words to a hundred spells I'd once memorized, every one of them flew from my head. All I could think about was that she was going to kill Grimm and I would be left alone with these people and (more importantly) Grimm would be *dead*. The desolation I felt at that thought was profound and overwhelming and not entirely my own. But I had no time to recognize the maneuverings of the curse; all I had time to do was step forward so my boot settled over the repulsion spell on the ground and speak the few short words needed to cast it.

My only thought toward self-preservation was to sing the words, hoping that would be enough to lessen the cost of a spell I had no business casting. I picked three notes and sang my intention into them.

Away. I want to be away from these people. I want them away from us.

Mathias's brow furrowed at the sound, but he did not shoot. I was the one they had a use for, after all, and I don't think he'd yet realized what was burning up under my foot. Grimm made a half-surprised, half-outraged noise behind me, but by then it was already done. The last word hung in the air, trembling, before the magic consumed both it and the paper beneath my boot and the casting was complete.

Several things happened all at once. Most of them bad.

Mathias and Jayne were lifted unceremoniously off their feet and blown backward.

Unfortunately, the spell, being inexpertly cast, also blasted Grimm and myself backward with the same force.

There was a clicking sound, followed by the soft hiss of displaced air as the bolt in Mathias's crossbow released. Whether this was in retaliation or by accident was hard to say (though I have my suspicions). Grimm was who he'd been aiming for, but all of us now being in the air changed things, and I yelped as the arrow grazed my right arm, pain blooming in its wake.

There was no time to reckon with that, or mourn the tear in my coat, because I was falling. Not back to earth as Mathias and Jayne were, but down and down, over the steep riverbank. I had a brief glimpse of Grimm falling beside me, all tangled limbs and a flash of pale hair. Then we both hit the water.

CHAPTER EIGHTEEN

The river was in my eyes. It filled my mouth and flooded my nose. It was everywhere, sending me spinning and tumbling until I wasn't sure which way was up.

When I was a child, I'd spent most of my summers at Agnes's family home on the coast. I was no stranger to swimming in strong currents, but the repulsion spell had left me weak as a kitten. The river cared not which way I moved my limbs, and every time I broke the surface it plunged me back underwater just as quickly.

My lungs began to ache.

Just when I was certain that, this time, I would not reach air before my breath gave out, I collided with something solid. Something that reached out to grasp my arm.

I flailed, certain I was about to be eaten by a river monster, before realizing it was only Grimm. The current had thrown us back together. He pulled us to the surface, and together we inched toward the river's edge, finding one rock to cling to, then another. Finally, a bend in the river slowed the water enough that we could haul ourselves dripping onto the bank.

The earth there was muddy, but I collapsed onto it, uncaring. I wanted to fall asleep in the muck and never move again.

"We need to keep going," Grimm said.

I let out a muffled groan of protest, but he was right. We had come out on the other side of the river but were still in full view of the opposite bank. I was certain a crossbow bolt could make the leap, and I had no desire to be shot again. The wound on my arm already hurt enough. I wrapped my tattered coat sleeve around it, so I would not leave behind a trail of blood.

Grimm led the way through the trees while I did my best to walk without stumbling. It wasn't just my arm that hurt; my whole body felt bruised and my throat ached from the spellsong. When Grimm finally steered us toward the weeping branches of a tree, I crawled beneath the leaves and curled up on the roots there as though they were a feather bed. My eyes were already closed when I heard Grimm say, "Loveage, the protective bubble..."

I opened my eyes. Grimm sat across from me, hunched so that his head didn't brush the low branches of our shelter. In the dim light, I saw the mangled remains of a bubble spell in his hand, ink seeping from the sodden mass of paper.

Sorcerers' coats were made to resist water, but being plunged into a raging river was apparently beyond their capabilities. When I checked my own pockets, I found the paper there in a similar state—just sopping clumps of mush. I stared at the mess blankly for a moment before brushing it off my fingers and beginning to pick at the knot in my sash holding my violin case strapped to my back. It had stayed in place in the river, which was more than could be said of my bag, but the water had made the knot grow tighter and my fingers were shaking. Eventually, Grimm made an impatient sound and brushed my hands away to untie the knot himself.

Once it was undone and the case lay before me, I opened the lid slowly, afraid of what I would find. The case had been a gift from my brother several years ago, and he must have spent a pretty penny because the enchantments on it had held stronger than those on my coat. The inside was bone-dry, and my violin unharmed. I dug into the compartment where I kept rosin and spare strings and found a piece of paper. Only one, but that was a worry for later. The inkwell in my pocket was slightly diluted but still plenty dark enough to scratch out the words in the old language. It hurt to write, but everything hurt, so I didn't think much of it until Grimm said, "You're bleeding," and gestured to my arm.

The bolt had torn through the flesh of my forearm in an ugly line. In my muddled state, the first concern that floated to the top of my mind was *That will make playing uncomfortable.*

"It will keep," I said, and set about finding a better position to hold my arm in so I could finish scriving. Once the bubble spell was written, I shoved it in Grimm's direction and fell promptly asleep.

It was not a restful sleep, more like a drifting of consciousness. I had bitten off more than I could chew with the repulsion charm, and this was the result: tiredness that winnowed into my bones to such a degree that even the remedy was not an escape.

I came back to myself with a start when Grimm shook my shoulder and informed me sternly that he would not be carrying me back to Miendor if I fell ill from ignoring my wound.

The first aid spells we had prepared were nothing but pulp, but I used water from Grimm's canteen to wash the gash out as best I could. My bag had had bandages in it, but those were lost to the river. Grimm had one blanket that he'd taken out of his bag and hung over a tree branch to dry, but I didn't fancy ripping up our only source of heat, so I reached for my sash instead. It was already ruined and had dried while I slept.

"At least it will match if I bleed through," I quipped, wrapping the scarlet fabric around my arm. It was awkward to do one-handed, unraveling even as I worked.

Grimm watched me struggle for a moment, then held out a hand. "Let me, please," he said crisply, the *please* at the end tacked on just in time to avoid becoming an order. I held out my arm and let him work.

Grimm wrapped the makeshift bandage round and round with gentle fingers, before tucking the ragged ends of the sash away. It was neatly done—Grimm was always careful, so careful, with everything he touched. The only surprise was that such care would extend to me.

It was not our usual way of interacting. I sat very still once it was done, oddly warm despite the gooseflesh covering my arms, wondering if I should thank him. Before I could, Grimm ruined the gesture by saying, "You shouldn't have cast that spell. It was foolish of you."

Any trace of goodwill I felt immediately vanished.

"I think a little gratitude is in order," I said, pulling my arm back. "Since *you* were the one they were about to bespell. Or would you rather I had just stood there and let it happen?"

Grimm tilted his head to one side in a doubtful manner, as though questioning whether being vaulted into a river really counted as being rescued.

"It got us away at least," I added sulkily.

"At what cost?" Grimm reached out again, as though now that he had touched me without violence once, it was easier to keep doing so. I watched, bemused, as he lifted my hand and held it out to catch the fading light, too distracted by the contact to question the reason for it. His fingers were warm.

"Your nail, Loveage," Grimm prompted, when he saw me

blinking at him, and I quickly redirected my focus toward my hand instead of the person holding it.

One of my thumbnails was partially black.

I shook free of Grimm to inspect it more closely. The white half-moon that normally lived at the base of my nail had been replaced by a rising darkness. It looked for all the world like I'd hit myself there with a hammer. It was possible I had bashed my hand against something in the river, but I didn't really think that was the case.

Grimm clearly didn't think so either.

"You're lucky the magic didn't demand more of you," he said. "It's a mistake to underestimate the price of casting. The consequences of doing so are dire."

"I wouldn't call this dire," I said. The nail would likely grow out. Even if it didn't, one blackened nail seemed a fair exchange for getting away with our lives. I was still very much clinging to the idea that what I had done had been right and necessary, and not simply the result of a moment of sheer panic. And over Grimm, of all people.

Grimm's frown deepened. "Loveage—"

"Enough. I'm not in the mood for a lecture on how magic should or should not be used, and by whom. This was a one-off, and I feel poorly enough to have learned my lesson." My muscles felt like someone had stretched and wrung them out, and my voice was rough from where the spell had singed my throat. "You casters are lucky," I grumbled, "not having to worry about what you can afford."

"We do," Grimm said unexpectedly. "Though only when casting exceptionally powerful spells, or when we're young enough not to have learned how to channel it yet."

I looked at him curiously. I'd heard of plenty of scrivers who hadn't learned how to use their gift from birth (our skills usually developed later in childhood, after learning to speak and write in the old language), but casters were much easier to spot. All you had to do was hand your child a simple spell and see if they could cast it. Unlike scrivers, they didn't need to understand the meaning and cadence of the words, so long as they could sound them out.

But that might not have been possible for Grimm, I realized. Oh, he could read perfectly well *now*, as he'd reminded me on several occasions, but not without effort. It was very possible that it had been even more difficult for him as a child, and you couldn't cast a spell when the words were lost to you.

"Did something like this happen to you?" I asked, waggling my thumb.

Grimm looked at me, expression unreadable. "Yes."

"How?"

"I made a mistake."

It was shocking to hear it stated like that, so simply. *I made a mistake*, as though that was something that could just be admitted to. The concept was so startling that I had to press down hard on my ruined nail. The pain grounded me enough to focus on what he said next.

"When I was young," Grimm continued, "no one thought I had enough talent to be worth training. Then, the year I turned eleven, Dwull experienced a drought. The Coterie was occupied on the northern border that year. Rock giants, you remember?" I nodded, even though I didn't, really. Rock giants would not have been remarkable enough to penetrate the miserable blur of my own eleventh year. "The Citadel sent along weather spells for us to cast until someone from the Coterie could be spared, but no one in Dwull was powerful enough to call anything more than a few clouds."

My mouth twitched. "Let me guess, no one was powerful enough until *you* tried."

Grimm nodded. "I'd heard my mother reciting the spell often enough that I was certain of the words. I took one of the spells out into the field and cast it. And it began to rain."

I was hard-pressed not to roll my eyes. "That makes for a good story, but I don't see how you causing Dwull to bloom again can be called a mistake." If anything, the tale seemed designed to celebrate Grimm's origins. *Didn't you hear? The first spell he ever cast saved an entire province.*

Grimm shook his head, frustrated. "You don't understand. It didn't stop. I had the power, but not the skill to protect myself, or anyone else. I poured too much of myself into the spell and then I woke up a week later with my hair turned gray and it was *still raining.* The fields flooded and crops were lost just as they would have been from drought. Streams overflowed into people's homes. Even when the rain stopped everywhere else, a patch of it kept going over the place I was standing when I cast the spell. It's a pond now. I didn't pay attention to what cost the magic demanded, and the result was devastating."

It came back to me now, how Grimm had been set apart from the people who had gathered in his family home for the harvest. I'd thought it was awe that kept them at a distance, but perhaps it had been fear. Or resentment.

"What happened afterward?" I asked.

"The Coterie sent someone to reassess my abilities, since I could clearly cast. Phade was the one who came. They arranged for a scholarship that allowed me to study with a tutor in the city until I was old enough to begin at the Fount."

I could not imagine willingly leaving my home at that age in order to give myself over to such cold custody, but it wasn't difficult to picture a tinier, equally serious version of Grimm, dutifully studying. He'd likely had exactly the kind of tutor I'd always done my best to drive away. Maybe even one of the very same. It did help explain why Grimm always acted like there was someone constantly hovering over his shoulder, ready to rap his knuckles if he so much as thought of breaking a rule.

"I know you think I'm...unyielding," Grimm said, "but magic has guidelines for a reason. It is not always worth testing the limits of what you can do."

"Don't you think I know that?" I snapped. "Why else do you suppose I avoid Grandmagic? Anyway, the only one hurt was me, so I don't see why you're worried. A blackened nail is nothing to fuss over."

Grimm looked rather pointedly at my bandaged arm but let the subject drop before it could turn into a true argument.

It was fully dark by then, so we prepared for sleep as best we could. There was only the one (still slightly damp) blanket, and even huddling back-to-back, it wasn't quite enough to cover both of us fully. Added to the discomfort of the too-small blanket and the hard ground was the knobby line of Grimm's spine, pressing into my own back, warm and too close.

To distract from the awkwardness, I pointed up at the ceiling of the bubble, to where a large moth was throwing itself at the faintly iridescent barrier.

"Are moths carnivorous?" The thing was nearly the size of my own head, and it was batting its dusty wings with a worrying degree of determination.

"I don't think they have teeth," Grimm said, but he didn't sound certain.

The muffled *thump, thump* of the moth and the steady ache of my arm kept sleep at bay. I wished Grimm's canteen was filled with something other than water so I could dull the sharp edges of my thoughts.

"Have you ever slept under the stars before, Grimm?" I asked.

"Can't see any stars."

"You know what I meant."

He was quiet for a long while. Then, just when I was sure he'd decided to ignore me and feign sleep, he said, "In summer, when it was very hot, we sometimes slept out in the courtyard."

"Oh."

"Not all houses are built with magic in their bones," he added stiffly.

It hadn't been confusion that dried up my words, but memory.

"We did the same when I was small," I said.

On heavy summer nights, my mother had laid pallets in the stone courtyard so we could taste the faint breeze as it moved through the trees. It was such a long time ago that I'd nearly forgotten. My father's manor was built with just the sorts of spells that Grimm referred to, keeping it blissfully cool in summer and holding heat from the fires in winter. And yet I was never as comfortable there as I had been in my childhood home.

"Grimm," I said a while later, mind whirling with the prickling unease that so often accompanied my memories.

"What?" He was obviously closer to sleep than I was. His voice was rough with it. Maybe that's what made it easier for me to ask.

"Were you afraid to cast again, after?"

I felt the movement as Grimm turned his head slightly to look over his shoulder at me. "Phade said mistakes could be educational. If I chose to run from mine rather than choosing to improve, it would have felt like I was ignoring the lesson. I didn't want to do that. What would have been the point of it all?"

It didn't take long after that for Grimm to fall asleep. I lay awake as his breath grew even and deep, hating him a little for how easy he made it seem.

Everything always looks better in daylight was something Rainer used to whisper after waking me from my nightmares. These words had soothed me as a child, but now I knew them for what they were: a lie.

In the weak light of morning, we were still lost in the middle of the Unquiet Wood with no guide and no paper with which to replace our spells. My arm felt worse than it had the previous night, and the same persistent, furry dragonflies that had followed us since stepping into the forest hovered outside the barrier, waiting.

At least the moth was gone.

"Do you think you could compose a spellsong that would help us?" Grimm asked as we were preparing to leave the bubble.

I'd already spent time thinking about this. "Maybe, but I'm just as incapable of using Grandmagic in a song as I am putting it to paper. That means no more protective barriers, no more repulsion spells, and certainly nothing that will protect us from monsters."

Grimm let out a heavy breath but seemed to have expected this answer. "Limited resources are better than none."

"Actually," I said casually, "there is one spellsong I thought we could try."

"What's that?"

"I want to send a message. To the sorcerer."

Grimm paused in folding the blanket. "Messages don't work. The only people who say differently are charlatans on street corners trying to sell you something. Besides, if they *did* work, Agnes is the one we should be messaging, not some made-up sorcerer."

It was true that message spells were incredibly unreliable. Magic had a way of rearranging the letters of whatever you tried to send, as though it resented any words and paper not given to it to be eaten. But—

"This wouldn't be an ordinary message!" I'd given the matter a great deal of thought the night before when I should have been sleeping. "It's a song, not a letter. We can hide the meaning of our message in the words of the spell and then the recipient would only have to listen and translate that, rather than unscrambling a jumble of letters. And Jayne said the sorcerer is real, she just didn't know how to find her."

"Oh, well, if *Jayne* says it, it must be true," Grimm said, with what I thought was an unnecessary amount of sarcasm.

"Consider this a test," I said. "We've only cast one spellsong together before, and I'm not entirely convinced that wasn't just luck. Wouldn't it be better to know if we can get another to work before we set off?"

Appealing to Grimm's sensible nature was apparently the right approach.

"Fine," he said brusquely. "But we'll have to be quick. We have a lot of ground to cover today."

I'd already composed most of the song in my head the night before, careful to keep it within the bounds of a charm. Just as I'd feared, the hardest part of bringing it to life was playing with my injured arm. I tried to ignore the pain in favor of crafting a melody to catch the sorcerer's attention. I didn't just want to find her, I wanted to *impress* her. Entice her with something so unusual that she would seek us out, so that I didn't have to leave the forest with my figurative tail between my legs and the curse still round my neck like a yoke.

We only had to run through the song twice before it sounded close to what I'd imagined in my head, each word in the old language ringing with power un-cast.

"Do you want me to accompany you?" It wasn't strictly necessary. I could have rested my arm and let Grimm sing alone and the spell would have worked or failed just the same; it wasn't as though he *needed* my help. But the truth was I wanted to feel a part of the casting, not just privy to it. I wanted another taste of what had happened with the sunflowers, when my playing and Grimm's voice had combined in unexpected harmony.

"All right," Grimm said, so I pushed the sharp aching of my arm aside and raised my bow again.

I really had worried our experience in the field was a fluke, not to be repeated, but if anything, the spell flowed even more easily this time. Magic thrummed through the air as soon as Grimm began to sing, voice turning richer with the casting. After a moment he tilted his head back and shut his eyes in concentration, face stripped of self-consciousness as all his focus bent on performing the intricacies of the spell. The crinkle of Grimm's brow said that this was a challenge, but the way his voice soared said that it was a worthy one. And wasn't that a heady feeling—knowing something I had created, however simple, was deserving of that kind of power.

Grimm opened his eyes to look at me, and I grinned fiercely

back. Amazingly, the corners of his own lips lifted in a small half smile. This was unheard of. I had earned more scowls than I could count, but never a smile. The expression transformed Grimm's face into something I hardly recognized. With my words on his tongue, and the hum of the spellsong hanging thick in the air between us, I nearly found him beautiful.

I recoiled from the thought as soon as I had it. This was Grimm, after all—cold as winter and bitter as a lemon. It was only the spell we were casting that caused his eyes to be briefly clear of enmity, and for me to feel some sort of way about it.

I threw all my attention back to the spell: how it made my fingers tingle where they touched the strings; how sweet each note sounded; how it felt like I was part of the casting, even though I had given nothing to it. Nothing arcane, at least, just ordinary music. When we finally brought the spell to a close, the air inside our bubble hummed for a moment even after Grimm stopped singing. The sensation was like a pre-shiver or an almost-yawn, something about to take hold. Then Grimm spoke and the feeling vanished before I could give it a name.

"Did it work?" he asked.

I lowered my violin and busied myself with putting it away, grateful to have something to do with my hands, which were slightly unsteady. "How should I know?"

"You said this was a test!"

"Yes, but I'm not the intended audience of the message. I guess we'll know it worked if the sorcerer shows up to save us."

Grimm's eyebrows drew together. "You're—"

"Ingenious? Yes, I'm aware. But there's really no time to dwell on it; we have a lot of ground to cover today. Do hurry up, Grimm!"

I expected this to elicit a full-on scowl, but instead, when I glanced at him, the expression on Grimm's face was one I'd never seen before. A sort of wondrous horror lit up his eyes. He raised a hand and pointed at something over my shoulder. "Loveage," he said, voice hushed.

Turning my head, I discovered our song *had* attracted an audience, just not the one I'd intended.

Outside the barrier sat two small catlike creatures with round, owlish faces and another creature that resembled a black rabbit with two tiny mouths where its eyes should have been.

Monsters. Little monsters, gathered in close and with their heads all cocked to one side as they listened to us.

I froze, any lingering thoughts of Grimm now firmly banished in the face of this more pressing danger, but these creatures did not launch themselves at the barrier as the moths had; instead they seemed to be waiting for something. Their anticipation was one I recognized. That sense of breathlessness as you waited for a curtain to rise. It was this sense of familiarity that prompted me to crouch down in front of the creatures.

Grimm's hand shot out, clasping my shoulder tight. But I had no intention of moving beyond our bubble of safety. All I did was inhale somewhat shakily before I began to hum the same melody Grimm and I had just finished casting, running through the whole thing once more.

For a moment, nothing happened. I stayed where I was, with Grimm's fingers digging into my shoulder. Then the black rabbit threw back its head, opened its mouths, and sang out the last three notes of the spellsong in answer. Its pitch was eerily perfect.

After that, all three monsters turned and disappeared into the undergrowth.

"Well," I said, once I could say anything at all.

"Mm," Grimm hummed, in what sounded like agreement.

"Mathias said that I woke the wood kraken. I thought he meant I was too loud, but Grimm, do you think...Is it possible the monsters *liked* my spellsongs?"

I looked up at him and, for an instant, caught Grimm watching me in much the same manner he had the monsters, with equal parts wonder and wariness. His hand dropped from my shoulder, leaving it cold, and he looked away, into the trees.

"I don't know," he said. "But I think it's best we don't use one again until we're out of the woods, just in case."

CHAPTER NINETEEN

We retraced our steps from the previous night, intending to find the river and follow it back to Miendor. Every stretch of forest floor seemed suspicious without Jayne there to follow. Because we did not know which things in particular to be careful of, we were careful of everything, and it left us tense and moving far slower than we ought to have been. Still, as time wore on, one thing became clear: We should have reached the river already.

Neither of us said anything about this. Putting the realization to words would have only made the situation feel bleaker than it was already.

My arm itched and throbbed in turns. I didn't mention this either. Or the chills that swept over me periodically. Though perhaps the chills could be attributed to the fact that it had begun to rain—a cold sort of drizzle that seeped down through the branches above and soaked both our clothes.

If the forest was sinister on a pleasant day, I'll leave it to your imagination what the addition of thunder and the occasional flash of lightning added to the ambience.

Around midday Grimm surprised me by asking, "Is something wrong?"

I let out a short laugh. "Our woes are so many that I'm afraid to list them would take a while."

"I meant is there something wrong with *you*. You've been very quiet. It's…strange."

"Do you miss the sound of my voice? How touching."

Grimm looked at me with narrowed eyes. "On the contrary. I would find it relaxing were I not suspicious of the cause."

Even here, in this place of monsters, I was the thing that Grimm couldn't quite trust.

"I'm tired, Grimm. Not plotting anything, just tired."

Tired and sort of…murky. I couldn't hold as many thoughts as usual in my head, too occupied with where to put my feet and how to hold my arm so that it hurt less. Jayne had admitted the outlaws coated their blades in the mushroom elixir; had Mathias's arrow been coated with something as well? I had very little understanding of how such things worked (herbalism was not magic and therefore not taught at the Fount), but the idea of being exposed to any plant parts of unknown origin made my stomach swoop in unpleasant panic.

I was so busy weighing the strength of this new worry I did not realize Grimm had stopped walking until I stumbled into him, jostling my arm in such a way that I couldn't help but let out a swear and curl protectively over it.

"Why did you stop?" I asked, pain making the words accusatory.

"I thought I heard something." Grimm drew his sword in one smooth motion. "A sort of popping sound."

"Probably thunder," I said, glancing toward the obscured sky.

"No, I don't think so."

This section of forest was even darker than what we had traveled through previously. It was impossible to see farther than twenty yards ahead of us, and everything to either side disappeared into gloom as well. We both stood still for a moment, listening, but the sound didn't repeat itself. Eventually Grimm looked away from the trees and back at me.

"Your arm is bothering you," he said with the satisfied air of someone who had just fit a puzzle piece into its correct place.

"It's not so bad," I said, even though I'd just been contemplating whether the fact that my arm felt like it was burning meant I'd been poisoned or just infected with some flesh-eating river disease. "I'm not the type to complain about a little cut."

"Two days ago, you spent hours complaining about a blister," Grimm pointed out. "Literal hours."

"It was a very large blister."

Grimm sighed and sheathed his sword again. "Let me—I can take a look at it, if you want."

I raised an eyebrow. "At the blister? It's much better, thank you for asking."

"Your *wound*, Loveage," Grimm snapped, but I had encountered his exasperation far too often and was thus immune.

"It's a waste of time," I said, dancing backward to keep out of reach. "If we look now and it's bad, I'll only be distracted by wondering if my arm will fall off before we make it back to Miendor. I think we've got enough things to worry about without adding that to the list, don't you?"

"You're being dramatic. I doubt it would fall off that quickly."

This was said with such a straight face that I wasn't entirely sure if Grimm was in earnest or just in possession of a far drier wit than I'd given him credit for. Perhaps it was my fever, causing me to imagine Grimm with a sense of humor. I was saved the trouble of deciding when a sudden and distinct *pop* sounded from the trees off to our right. It was not like the crack of a stick breaking, or any other natural sound you might expect to hear in a forest. This was the delicate, half-imagined sound of a soap bubble breaking, amplified many times over until it was shocking and strange.

Grimm and I spun round to face the direction the sound came from. A pair of enormous silver eyes blinked back at us from the shadows. They blinked twice more, and then a wolf stepped out from the trees.

I call it a wolf because that is the closest example I can think to give, but it was clearly a monster. The creature's eyes were pure swirling silver, and its coat was true black, with no hint of sable or brown. It was far larger than an ordinary wolf, to the point where I thought that, if I were foolish enough to fling myself over its back, I would be taken for a ride.

The wolf monster looked at us cannily, head cocked to one side. It let out a low whine that caused all the hairs on the back of my neck to stand up.

Grimm, who had been reaching to draw his sword again, paused, clearly worried that movement would trigger an attack. I understood the impulse, but standing still made me feel like a mouse frozen in the eye of a cat. I looked at its long legs and thought that one leap would bring it nearly down on top of us. Every nerve ending in my body began to sing that we should move and move *now*. That to stand still was akin to offering ourselves up on a platter.

The wolf took another step toward us, and something within me snapped.

"Run," I said, and pushed Grimm toward the trees.

There was not much Grimm could do after that except follow my order, cursing under his breath. This was not a coordinated retreat. I did not have any plan in mind except for *away*.

But it didn't matter how fast we ran. A moment later, that same strange *pop* sounded and now the wolf was ahead of us, blocking our way forward and forcing us to skid to an abrupt stop. Its mouth was open in a lazy smile, red tongue lolling. This creature saw the chase as a sort of game. It had none of the dark malevolence of the wood kraken, tearing the forest apart to find us; nonetheless, its goal was the same and it was even more well equipped to catch us.

The wolf gathered its long limbs underneath itself and sprang. Grimm and I were not far apart, but he was just that little bit in the lead. It was clear that the beast would land on him. I could see it happening in my mind's eye, just as I had when we'd stood across from Jayne and Mathias on the riverbank—visions of Grimm being torn apart by arrow or spell or tooth. Once again, I felt called to act without thought, darting forward to place myself between Grimm and the monster.

This senseless bit of sacrifice was entirely discordant with my character, and I was just beginning to feel puzzled by it when the wolf landed on top of me.

I was bowled over backward in a tangle of limbs and fur. A blanket of moss cushioned my fall, but the weight of the monster pushed the air from my chest, leaving me gasping. The heavy scent of dog and something wilder overwhelmed my senses—a wet woolen blanket sort of smell, mixed with the bright ozone scent of lightning.

The wolf's teeth were very close, flashing white as my lungs strained for breath. My arm hurt terribly, but I couldn't do anything about it. Everything had happened so quickly that my body and mind seemed disconnected, unable to communicate well enough to put up a fight.

The wolf placed one paw firmly on my chest, holding me still. Its silver eyes swirled, faster and faster, until there was a *pop* and the world around us dissolved.

I was still where I was, and the wolf was still there too, but the colors of our surroundings bled together, green running into blue into red into brown, and on and on. It was like being inside a painting, watching all the brushstrokes melt away like butter on a hot pan. The chaos was beautiful, but no matter how much I wanted to look, my eyes couldn't quite comprehend what they saw. Eventually I had to blink, and in the instant I wasn't looking, the world turned solid again.

The wolf's cold nose pressed against my neck and I yelped. This was it. I had been taken to its lair and would be eaten for lunch. And all because I'd seen fit to leap in front of Grimm (*Grimm!*), who never in a million years would have understood or returned the gesture.

The worst part was, I was still glad I'd done it.

The wolf's head drew back slightly, and I braced myself. Then its tail thumped once against my legs, and it popped out of existence again, leaving me alone.

I didn't move right away, thinking that it would surely come back. But a minute passed and then another. I sat up slowly. My body still didn't feel quite like my own, limbs wobblier and spine more bendable.

My surroundings had shifted. Now I was in a grass-filled clearing, marked by birch trees around its edge. The trees grew in a near perfect circle, and beyond their pale and graceful trunks, the rest of the forest pressed in close.

At the center of the clearing, dark and tall, stood a tower.

My breath caught a little at the sight, and I scrambled to my feet.

The description in the book Cassius had given me had been quite clear: *The sorcerer lives in a tower built of black stone, unlined and organic, appearing to have grown fully formed from the earth rather than being built by human hands. It stands much taller than an ordinary house, looking like nothing so much as a lonely watchtower. Though what it watches for, I cannot say. The only view in that place was of trees, trees, trees, and more trees.*

This description was so apt that I felt a strange sense of déjà vu as I stood in front of the tower, marveling at its smooth sides and ebony height.

As I was doing this, there came a now-familiar popping sound, and I turned in time to see the wolf stepping off Grimm's prone form. Like me, he had arrived unharmed, though he'd clearly put up more of a fight. His sword was drawn, but he seemed disoriented, managing only one half-hearted swing at the monster as it retreated.

"All right, Grimm?" I called out, to let him know I was there and had not had my face bitten off (yet). When his eyes found me, they were glassy and unfocused. I had never seen Grimm drunk, but I imagined it might look a little like this.

"Loveage?" he said, and then dropped his sword to roll over and be sick in the grass. He remained kneeling even after it was over, head bent and eyes closed. Traveling by monster did not seem to agree with him.

I took a few steps closer and paused. The instinct was there to reach out and pat his back, as I would have done for Agnes. But this was Grimm. I did not think such a gesture would be appreciated.

"All right?" I asked again, this time cautiously.

"Fine," he croaked. "Where are we?"

I looked back at the tower. "Surprisingly, I think we're exactly where we want to be. Look, this must be where the sorcerer lives. I can't imagine there's that many towers like this in the Unquiet Wood. I think our message spell worked!"

"So she sent a monster to retrieve us?" Grimm hauled himself to his feet, frowning at the tower. "Some invitation."

The monster in question had been sitting on its haunches a few feet away, watching us. Now it got to its feet and trotted toward the tower, pausing once or twice to look back over its shoulder in an expectant manner. At the base of the tower was a door, left open as though in welcome. The wolf trotted easily inside.

I began to follow.

"We shouldn't just go inside," Grimm said.

"Why not?" I asked. "I don't think the door would have been left open unless we were meant to."

"This could be a trap, some trick of the forest, or another of Jayne's maneuverings. I don't trust it."

"You don't trust anything."

Grimm's mouth took on a decidedly stubborn tilt. "Whereas you have all the caution of an inebriated toddler! We know nothing about this person, and that puts us at a serious disadvantage. I have no spells in my pockets, and you've no paper to write more. I don't think we should go inside."

I gaped at him. "You can't mean for us to turn around and leave? Not when the person we've been looking for this whole time is likely just past that doorway. Be reasonable, Grimm!"

"I am reasonable," he said hotly. "Not wanting to be murdered by a mysterious wood dweller or her pet monster is a reasonable concern."

"And what about my concerns?" I asked, crossing my arms and glaring. "This curse isn't going away by itself, and I, for one, think that getting rid of it is worth a little risk."

"You have yet to meet a risk you didn't think was worth taking," Grimm said bitterly. "That's the problem."

The tower was at my back; I could feel it looming. So close. Close enough that I could walk away from Grimm and through that door without it even hurting. For all he wanted to be rid of me, there was no way Grimm could possibly understand how much I needed the curse gone. The desperation was all-consuming, like being drunk, or on stage, or in love. Maybe Grimm was right, maybe I was reckless with it, but I was afraid that if I let it linger, I would grow used to living with it, and that terrified me.

I looked Grimm square in the eyes and said, "Well, nothing ventured, nothing gained." Then I turned around and began to walk toward the tower.

I thought one of two things would happen next. The first was that Grimm would grudgingly concede and follow me inside. The second (and more likely) outcome was that he would stubbornly hold his ground while I went in to face the sorcerer alone. I would not have minded this outcome very much. I *wanted* to meet her, after all. Indeed, it felt like everything that had happened over the past few days had been leading up to this, events coiling tighter and tighter until there was no other result but that I should be spat out here to beg for her aid. I was certain I could do that without Grimm there. He would most likely only sulk and make a bad impression.

I had forgotten that there was, of course, a third option, which was Grimm letting me get a few steps away and then calling out, "Loveage, wait!"

Immediately, I froze and waited. There was nothing else I could do, nothing else I *wanted* to do. Behind the blissful haze of obedience, a frantic part of me wondered how long I would remain there, statue-still, if Grimm did not rescind his order. But that worry was distant, the part of my mind responsible for action vacant. I would wait for him, until all reason for the order was lost to time, and moss and lichen turned me into just another curiosity of the forest.

"Never mind," Grimm said, and just like that, the feeling was gone, leaving me hollow and vaguely nauseous instead.

Every time it happened like this was a little worse. Every time, I felt like I'd lost a little more when it was over. I stood very still and very straight, taking deep breaths until the panic receded and I could calmly turn around and face Grimm.

His face was still damp with sweat from being sick. A few pieces of pale hair were plastered across his forehead, nearly translucent. He looked thoroughly wretched, or as close to it as someone like Grimm could, anyway.

I found I didn't care.

Slowly, taking great care to enunciate each word so there would be no mistaking my meaning, I said, "I'm going to talk to that sorcerer."

"If you would just take a moment so we could at least—"

"No. I'm going inside now. You can do as you please."

I turned around again and pretended exposing my back didn't make me feel utterly vulnerable. Like this, I couldn't see if Grimm was about to speak, but I didn't think he would. Not in *that* way, at least.

"Curse you," Grimm said bitterly, and followed.

I didn't know if he wished me further cursed for making traveling together so fraught, or for making resisting the urge to order me around so difficult, or if it was simply my very presence that caused him grief. I suspected it was some combination of all three. But he followed anyway. Perhaps because he'd done something to be ashamed of and sticking with me was a type of penance.

That was the control *I* had over *him*, you see.

"Cheer up, Grimm," I called out with false gaiety. "If I'm right about this, you'll be rid of me soon."

With these words of encouragement filling the air between us, I stepped over the threshold and into the sorcerer's tower.

CHAPTER TWENTY

The tower was dim after the brightness of the clearing. I stood just inside the doorway until my eyes adjusted enough to make out the details before me. My first impression was one of space. The room I stood in was large and circular, unbroken by dividing walls. A staircase spiraled up the edge of the room and disappeared through an opening in the ceiling. The ceiling itself was covered in a mural of the sky, with painted clouds so realistic I suspected the artist had used a spell or two.

To my right was a stone hearth, and directly across from where I stood were bookshelves set into the curved wall. In the center of the room were two velvet sofas that sagged a little in the middle, aging but still doing their best. Overlapping rugs covered the floor, muffling my footsteps, and the air smelled faintly of beeswax and smoke. Not the smoke of fire or candles, but the unmistakable metallic tang of spell smoke.

After the imposing grandness of the tower's outside, I'd expected insides that matched. Instead, the tower's interior seemed to say, *Well, since you've made it this far, might as well stay awhile.*

Other than the wolf, who had flopped down on a pillow in front of the hearth, the room was empty of life. Grimm lingered awkwardly near the door, and even I felt a little hesitant to explore further. Snooping through a stranger's belongings was all well and good if you could be sure you weren't being watched, but who knew what sort of magic kept this place protected?

"Hello?" I called out.

As though waiting for this summons, there came the sound of footsteps, and a woman descended through the opening in the clouds where the stairs disappeared. She was small and round and dark-haired, with a generous mouth and an aquiline nose. She wore a dress made of shining purple silk, and over it a dark blue coat tailored to hug her curves. The coat had many pockets.

"Oh good," she said, smiling down at us. "You're here."

Being a performer myself, I knew when someone was making an entrance. This one was expertly done.

"I was worried it would take Beaugard longer to find you," the woman said as she came down the stairs, one hand trailing lazily along the metal railing. "I really should have known better. He has such a good nose for sniffing out anything strange in this forest."

"Are you the sorcerer?" I asked, uncertain. I had pictured someone more like Phade—older and stern, with stooped shoulders and eyes clouded by years of accumulated knowledge. Someone with an aura of gravitas, that sort of thing. This woman looked only a handful of years older than I was.

"I'm not sure I deserve to be referred to in the singular, but I am *a* sorcerer, yes." Her demeanor was as far from Phade's as I could imagine—playful rather than somber.

At the bottom of the stairs, she paused and looked both of us over thoroughly. Of the two of us, Grimm was clearly more remarkable, and yet her attention quickly settled on me alone, in a look of such stark appraisal that I quite forgot what I'd been going to say next.

I was overcome by the strangest sensation. Like I'd unexpectedly caught sight of myself in a mirror—that split second of surprised recognition. The sorcerer was a stranger, I was certain of that, and yet there was something about her that was as familiar as my own reflection.

"You must be the composer of my message," she said. "It was very nicely done. I've been humming it ever since."

"Have you really?" I asked, pleased.

"Oh yes. It was quite catching. I've never thought to try setting magic to music like that before. It's clever." She leaned forward on her toes a little, face alight with interest. "I tried to replicate it but couldn't get a feel for it, which is a little unusual for me. I suppose the trick lies in the composition of the tune itself, rather than just the words?"

"Probably. It was only my first time experimenting with messages. The spellsongs are something recent that I've been—"

Grimm cleared his throat pointedly, cutting me off. He'd taken a few steps away from the door to stand looming at my back like a dour guard dog. "Who are you?" he asked bluntly.

"Grimm!" I said. "There's no cause to be rude."

"She set a monster on us. I don't see what reason I have to be polite."

Grimm's suspicion wasn't entirely unwarranted. After all, the last person I'd asked to help us *had* turned out to be a wanted outlaw.

"Oh dear." The sorcerer looked to the wolf by the hearth, expression more indulgent than chagrined. "Beaugard *can* get a little enthusiastic sometimes. I'm very sorry if you were frightened, but he really wouldn't hurt a fly. Unless I asked him to."

This implied a degree of control that was more alarming than comforting. It was like the colorful display of some poisonous creature, warning that it was not nearly as innocuous as its stature implied. And the sorcerer *was* colorful, with her bright skirts, fine coat, and inquisitive eyes.

"I apologize." I flashed my most gracious smile, in hopes it would help balance out Grimm being so...himself. "We've had a trying time in the forest, you see, and it's made us forget our manners. This is Sebastian Grimm, and I'm Leovander Loveage, but you may call me Leo. We're very glad to have found you..."

"Sybilla," the sorcerer supplied, offering her hand. "My name is Sybilla Laurent."

S. L. The mysterious initials from the book Cassius had given me were transformed into a flesh-and-blood person.

"A pleasure, Sybilla."

Taking her hand, I swept my best version of a half bow over it. I managed to ignore the strangled, scoffing noise Grimm made, but the grand gesture was ruined anyway when my arm twinged so painfully that I was forced to lurch upright with a gasp, all elegance lost.

"Oh, but you're hurt!" Sybilla exclaimed, eyes widening.

"Just a scratch," I lied. "That's not actually why we're here. We wanted—"

But Sybilla cut me off, grabbing my good elbow firmly in one small, plump hand. "There will be time for explanations later," she said, steering me toward one of the velvet sofas.

In the end, the delay wasn't such a bad thing. The adrenaline from being chased by the wolf was wearing off, leaving me a little fuzzy from pain. I was happy enough to sink down into the cushions. Sybilla instructed, "Wait right there; I'll fetch my first aid box," before disappearing through a door I hadn't noticed before, tucked between two bookcases.

"That door is strange," I informed Grimm, somewhat woozily. I was nearly certain the tower had been perfectly round when viewed from the outside, which meant the door should have opened back out into the clearing. But the only door I'd seen on the building's exterior had been the one we'd come through, and the one Sybilla had just gone through offered a glimpse of a room behind, not grass and sunlight. "That door doesn't make *sense*," I said, gaining conviction.

Grimm first looked at me in concern, then at the door. His expression turned thoughtful.

"No, it doesn't," he said. Which was nice. It was nice when we agreed.

I may have said that last part out loud, because Grimm went back to frowning at me and continued to do so until Sybilla returned with a first aid kit.

The less said about what my arm looked like once Grimm cut away the stained sash, the better. I find it's best to forget painful things whenever possible. I do remember Grimm casting two rather strong anti-infection spells, and that they stung terribly but made my fever break almost immediately. Much to my amusement and his dismay, Sybilla insisted that Grimm also cast an anti-nausea charm from the kit for himself. Because, as she said, "Travel by ramble wolf really doesn't agree with everyone, and I'd rather not mop the floor today."

Once I was clearheaded and Grimm was less green, Sybilla went through the mysterious door again and returned with tea and a plate of cakes. She laid everything out on the little table between sofas and sat down across from us. And then finally, *finally* it was my chance to speak.

"You're a hard person to track down, you know."

"If you make your doorstep too easy to find, all sorts of

riffraff will show up on it asking for all sorts of things." The way Sybilla looked over her teacup at us made it quite clear that we weren't being excluded from the category of riffraff, and our relative interest to her was being weighed against the amount of bother she was willing to engage with. Which seemed fair, considering Grimm had already thrown up on her lawn and I had narrowly avoided bleeding on her sofa. "It's been a long time since I felt obliged to fix the problems of every errant sorcerer who decides to seek me out."

"And yet here we are," I said. "Not just on your doorstep but past it."

Sybilla smiled, cheeks dimpling. I was beginning to think she was the sort of person who smiled as often as Grimm frowned, and that each one held a different meaning.

"You're very sure of yourself, aren't you? I admit your message caught my attention, but sending Beau to find you was not a promise of aid, only of tea and some conversation. I find most of the problems people come to me with are too banal to waste my time unraveling these days." This said, she picked up one of the tiny cakes and calmly took a bite.

"You're not curious at all?" I asked, heart sinking.

"I didn't say that." Sybilla waved her cake-free hand at me encouragingly. "Go on, convince me. Tell me something interesting."

I could have launched into the whole story. It might have even impressed her, for I've been told I have a way with words. But a good storyteller knows how to set the scene, and there was nothing I could say that would have the same dramatic effect as actually seeing the curse in action.

My mouth went dry, but I didn't dare take another sip of tea. I was glad I had not sampled the cakes yet either. My skin crawled at the thought of what was to come.

"A demonstration will explain the problem better than I could." I nodded to Grimm. "Go ahead. Show her."

It was a little better when I knew what was coming. Not comfortable by any means, but when, after a long moment of hesitation, Grimm said, "Stand up on the sofa, Loveage," at least I expected to lose myself briefly in his words. I climbed onto the sofa and stood there, lost in a blissful haze. And then Grimm said, "That's enough," and the fuzziness went away, leaving me cold.

I looked down at Sybilla. "Do you see?"

"That your boots are on my sofa? Yes, I do see that." Her voice was light, but there was no hint of amusement on her face when Sybilla turned from me to Grimm.

Her eyes, which up until then I would have described as *twinkling*, went very dark.

"That's a nasty piece of spellwork to cast on someone."

"I know," Grimm said simply. "I wasn't aware what the spell would do at the time that I cast it."

"Neither of us were," I said, sitting down on the sofa once more. "It was a misunderstanding."

Sybilla wanted to be told something interesting, so I did my best to turn the whole sorry affair into something other than an absolute personal low. I did not lie, but I spun the truth into a tale that could have been seen on a stage or written in the pages of a book. It was better, looking at it like that.

Sybilla only interrupted once, to ask why I hadn't tried to write a counterspell myself.

"Grandmagic and I don't get along," I explained. "Charms and cantrips are fine, but I knew it would take more than that to unravel the curse."

"You didn't even try?"

I shook my head. "No. It would have only made things worse. It always does."

"Hm," Sybilla said. She took a dainty sip of her tea. "You may continue."

By the time I was done, the plate of cakes was half gone and my own teacup was empty. I reached for Grimm's cup and took a sip. The tea was long cold but still soothed my throat nicely after all the talking.

"That's mine," Grimm pointed out, but idly, like he wasn't actually bothered. He hadn't touched any of the food either, probably afraid it would come up again if Sybilla decided she'd had enough and told her wolf to whisk us away.

Sybilla rose to her feet, brushing crumbs off the front of her coat. She clasped her hands behind her back and walked over to the hearth, then spun on her heel and walked back toward us, head bent in thought.

"Do you have any questions?" I asked eventually, unable to contain myself.

"I do, actually." Sybilla looked up from studying the floor. At some point her eyes had gone bright again. "Has your magic always been like this, or were you once able to write Grandmagic without it going wrong?"

"Not always," I said, too surprised by the change of subject to be anything but truthful. "Though, it's been a very long time. But I meant do you have any questions about the curse."

"Oh, that." Sybilla thought for a moment, then said, "What would happen if he asked you to do something impossible?"

After brief deliberation on what was a suitably impossible order, Grimm asked me to fly up and touch the ceiling. I first tried to accomplish this by jumping as high as I could and then clambering up onto the sofa again and jumping from there, as though that would make a difference. This was rather embarrassing, but the truly concerning bit came next, when I calmly sat down and asked Sybilla to provide me with quill and paper so that I could write a spell that would grant me flight. This would have been no small bit of magic, but that did not seem to bother me in my altered state. Thankfully, Grimm took back his order before I could actually begin composing.

"And what did *that* tell you?" I muttered testily, to cover up how shaken I was.

"That this spell does not grant you any special abilities, only increased determination," Sybilla said. "Now, I'd like to see the spell as it was written."

This was one particular spell I wasn't in danger of forgetting anytime soon, but I still let Grimm do the honors. He took the quill Sybilla offered and wrote the whole thing down in his careful, precise hand while I watched over his shoulder, a sense of dread creeping further and further up my spine as each new word appeared.

Sybilla was quiet while she read, studying the whole thing intently. Afterward, she folded the paper up, smearing the ink irrevocably, and threw the spell into the hearth.

It curled and burned away immediately, going up in ordinary smoke. I felt relieved once it was gone.

"You spoke a great deal about the effects of the spell," Sybilla said. "But there's one rather significant symptom you did not mention. I find that curious. I wonder, do either of you know exactly what type of magic this is?"

"Control magic," I answered promptly.

Sybilla shook her head. "That's the effect, not the cause. The spell wants to control you, yes, but its method of doing so is quite ingenious. You see, most control spells are hard to maintain because the subject struggles against them so thoroughly. But whoever wrote this spell took that into consideration and came up with a more effective way of exerting control. It's something that many of us are influenced by, in one way or another. Would you like to share what that might be, Leo?"

Sybilla was looking at me, soft and searching, almost encouraging.

I blinked and looked to Grimm, not at all certain what I was being prompted to say or do. He appeared equally flummoxed.

"We really don't know. That's why we came to you."

Sybilla sighed, but with an air of great indulgence. "Very well, if you don't want to say it, I will. This is a love spell."

CHAPTER TWENTY-ONE

The room went completely silent as the words floated around and around my brain, refusing to make any sense. Even once their meaning was clear, I couldn't understand why Sybilla would say such a thing.

"I'm not in *love* with *Grimm*. I'd—I'd have noticed!"

Sybilla's eyebrows shot upward. "Oh, you really didn't know. I thought you were being coy about the whole thing. Goodness, how delightful." The corners of her mouth curved, and then, appallingly, Sybilla began to laugh, leaning one hand on the corner of the sofa for support as her whole body shook with mirth.

Grimm and I shared a brief horrified glance, then quickly looked away from each other.

"Sorry, sorry," Sybilla said, hiccuping slightly. "It's just that this is more entertainment than I've had in quite some time." She wiped the tears from her eyes and stood up straight again, seemingly getting ahold of herself. "All right, you've convinced me. I'll write your counterspell. Follow me."

Too dazed to do anything else, Grimm and I trailed along in Sybilla's wake. We followed her up the winding stairs to the place where they disappeared onto the second floor and emerged into a space that was empty of everything except the staircase we stood upon, the wall it clung to, and doors.

The doors were dotted along the stairs like beads on a necklace, set at regular intervals and just as impossible as the one I'd noticed down below, given that they should have opened into empty air. But nothing about this part of the tower seemed bound to the rules of possibility. When I looked back the way we had come, instead of floor or ceiling beams blocking my view of the first floor, there were only clouds, actual clouds, obscuring everything except the place where the stairs emerged. Above us the tower continued up far higher than the outside of the building would have suggested, until the spiraling stairs disappeared into shadow.

I could not see the top of the tower. Indeed, I was not sure there was one.

The whole place stank of Grandmagic. Not just the smoky scent of a spell recently cast, but the humming of active spellwork. If each individual work of magic had been set to music, it would have been enough to build a symphony.

"What is this place?" I wondered aloud.

Sybilla looked back over her shoulder and smiled. "This is the tower. What you saw down below, that was just the doorstep. Come along."

The first door we passed had a flower painted on the front of it, and the whole thing pulsed with magic, from the frame to the doorknob to the layers of blue paint. The second door was much the same, only the painting was of a tree. Sybilla led us up a little farther, until we came to a door with a book painted on it. The book lay open in profile, pages arcing to either side.

Sybilla opened this door and stepped over the threshold. The room beyond, when I paused to peer inside, was clearly a study. A large wooden table stood in the middle of the space, with more bookshelves like the ones below lining the walls, only these shelves were full of scrolls as well as books, and messy stacks of paper. Two shelves were given over entirely to pots of ink, while a different one displayed an impressive array of quills.

Curious, I reached out to touch the doorframe. It felt solid under my fingertips, but the buzz of magic was so strong that I had to wrench my hand back almost instantly. When I stepped into the room, the buzzing faded. The tower was still visible through the open door, stairs spiraling away to infinity, but I couldn't help but feel we were someplace else entirely. Like the magic at work here was a complex patchwork quilt, stitching together places that had no business existing alongside one another.

Once Grimm was inside, I closed the door and opened it again, just to see if everything stayed put. It did. Whatever spell held the room and the tower in place, it was a strong one. Far stronger than anything I would be able to write, though I thought I could sense the beginnings of how one might go about doing so.

"Fascinating," I muttered.

"You didn't think I just spent my time out here in the woods twiddling my thumbs, did you?" Sybilla called out. "I might be a little reclusive, but I have no desire to spend my days living in a simple one-room tower, I assure you. Now, stop staring at the door and come over here so I can start taking notes on your love spell."

The workings of the tower had distracted me, but Sybilla's words brought me back to the matter at hand.

"It's not a love spell!" I insisted, going to join her at the table. "I would have noticed."

"There've been no signs?" Sybilla asked. "Nothing out of the ordinary at all? Fits of passion, unexpected jealousies, protective urges?"

"Certainly not!" My feelings toward Grimm remained much as they always had been. Perhaps they had warmed slightly over the past few days, but that seemed a reasonable side effect of forced proximity. Facing down monsters and outlaws would have been a bonding experience for anyone; it didn't *mean* anything.

Except...

"You threw yourself in front of me," Grimm said, almost apologetically. "When you thought Jayne and Mathias were going to kill me. And again, when Beaugard leapt at me."

"That was—that was just me reacting in the moment. Instinct!"

Grimm didn't say anything, but I could practically hear what he was thinking. I was thinking it too: *Since when have either of us ever felt a protective instinct toward the other?*

I sagged weakly back in my chair, going over everything that had happened since the spell was cast. Reframing it. First had been the clear compulsion to do as Grimm bid, but then had been the creeping need to be near. What Sybilla was saying cast *that* particular urge in a very different light. I remembered the way I had shadowed Grimm's footsteps in those early days, just to catch a glimpse of him—like a shy teenager nursing a crush.

"*Oh,*" I said, and put my head down on the table. I couldn't look at Sybilla's smug face. I certainly couldn't look at Grimm.

"It's a very subtle piece of magic," Sybilla said, not unsympathetically. "You needn't feel badly for not noticing right away. In fact, I think it's likely designed to grow in strength over time for just that very reason, to stop you from understanding the true mechanics at work. It makes the whole thing doubly difficult to unravel." Sybilla's face darkened. "Whoever wrote this has a very devious mind."

How had I not known? I'd thought myself aware of every

effect the spell had on me, yet I had glimpsed only the tiniest part. It reminded me of when I'd fractured my ribs writing that overblown wind spell. Those bones had always been there, but their function had been silent, invisible. Then suddenly, with each painful breath, I was aware of them—their placement and their flaw.

Perhaps it was dramatic to compare love to an injury, but that's how this felt. Like something that needed to be mended.

Grimm was of a similar mind. He turned to Sybilla and asked, "Can you fix it?"

"I can certainly try. There are two ways I know of to remove a spell that doesn't want to be lifted. The first is a counterspell. Difficult to do if you're not the one who wrote the original magic, but as you know, that's a specialty of mine. Unraveling a stranger's words and meaning is no small task, especially with something as complex as your curse, but I do like a challenge!"

"What's the second way?" I asked.

Sybilla, distracted with sorting through one of the piles of paper on the table before us, didn't even look up. "What?"

"You said there were two ways to remove a stubborn spell. What's the second?" I'd never heard of anything but counterspells being used to break apart magic before.

"Ah," Sybilla said delicately. "That method is complicated in a different way. You wouldn't need me for it at all, as it doesn't rely on scriving."

"How can that be?"

Sybilla sighed. "It's difficult to explain, especially if you're only used to thinking about magic in straightforward terms, which is what the Fount likes to teach best, but I'll try." There was an overstuffed chair in the corner of the room that looked like a cousin to the sofas downstairs. Sybilla walked over to it and picked up a basket left perched on one of the chair's arms. From the basket, she withdrew a half-formed project still attached to a ball of yarn and needles. She held the whole thing up for us to see.

"Spells are conditional," she said. "They're rooted in the intention of the person who wrote them. That intent is like a seed that the spell grows from, watered with magic. But magic brings its own requirements into the mix, and if those requirements aren't met, there's no growth. Now, think of the spell's intent as these needles, and the magic as the yarn. Together they build something. But if something happens to divorce the two from each other?"

Sybilla slid the knitting off the needles in one smooth motion and pulled on the yarn until the whole thing began to unravel, stitch by stitch.

"That's very interesting," I said politely. "But so far the only thing I understand is that you've just ruined your sweater, or whatever that is."

Sybilla rolled her eyes and threw the whole tangled mess impatiently down onto the table. "The curse on you is built out of opposing forces. No one who felt true love or caring for the intended target would be able to cast it, and yet those are the feelings it incites. Now, a caster doesn't *set* the intention of a spell, but they do channel it during casting. They are part of a very delicate balance, and that balance is part of what the spell relies on to succeed. Yarn and needles. Intention and magic. If you want to unravel the curse without a counterspell, you would need to upset the balance."

Sybilla looked at us expectantly. Grimm and I stared back at her, utterly uncomprehending.

"Oh, come on," she said. "This is a very good analogy! It means that if the person who cast the spell were to return the feelings it provoked, the whole thing would likely dissolve on its own."

The room got very quiet. The sort of silence large enough to swallow a person whole.

Then I began to laugh. Not because I was amused, just because there really was nothing else to do *but* laugh. The only thing more ridiculous than me being in love with Grimm was the idea that he would return such feelings of his own volition.

"Guess the counterspell really *is* our only option, huh, Grimm?" I said, and for the first time since the love spell had been announced, I swayed into his space just long enough to jostle his shoulder with my own. Then I collapsed in another fit of giggles.

That night, we ate dinner in a dining room with velvet chairs and window hangings. The food was already laid out in covered dishes down the center of a long table when Sybilla opened the door, and the half-moon rising through the windows never moved the whole time we were there.

We'd seen several other rooms in the tower after leaving Sybilla's study: A bathing chamber so large it wouldn't have fit inside the ground floor of the tower. A solarium full of green and growing things in pots, oddly fragile seeming after the time we'd spent in the forest. A library that rivaled the one back at the Fount, in scope if not in size.

"They're memories," Sybilla explained. "Or at least, they're built from memories. Places I've been, filled with what I can recall of them. Some of them are more than memories now, like the study, or the other rooms I often spend time in. But some... some aren't meant to become anything new. They only hold their shape with someone inside them."

It was so far outside the realm of what I'd been taught to do with magic that for a moment I felt a stab of exquisite longing lance through me. To know that such a thing was possible, and know it wasn't possible for *me*.

After all, everything in the tower was inescapably Grandmagic.

I could tell that Sybilla didn't spend as much time in the dining room because it had a distinct air of unreality to it, the candles a little too bright, and that moon, hanging so still in the sky. But the food seemed real in my belly, and the wine Sybilla poured was real enough to leave my senses pleasantly softened.

"Is it always the same meal?" I asked curiously.

"Oh yes," Sybilla answered. She took another sip of her own wine, savoring it before she continued. "This was one of the best dinners I ever had, and the first room I created for something other than practical reasons."

"What happens when you get tired of this meal?" Grimm asked.

"Then I have the room that always serves afternoon tea, and the one that leaves me a breakfast tray," Sybilla said, in the tone of someone pointing out the obvious. "There's also the kitchen on the ground floor for when I want to actually cook something for myself, but nothing in the kitchen resets itself when I close the door. And I'm frightfully lazy, you see. I like it when the tower acts as my housekeeper. It leaves me more time to devote to my own interests."

"Like counterspells," I prompted.

"Counterspells are more of a business than a hobby," Sybilla said. "Speaking of which, we have yet to discuss payment."

"Of course." I had been distracted since arriving, first with fever, and then with the words *love spell*, and then with our tour of the tower. But now I rifled through my pockets until I found the rings I'd stored away there. They sparkled in the candlelight when I laid them out on the table before Sybilla. "This is what I had on me when we left. The gems in each ring are quite valuable, I assure you."

Sybilla looked at the assembled offering, then threw back her head and laughed. "I don't need gold or baubles, you silly thing! I need a caster."

She looked very pointedly across the table to Grimm, who went still as a prey animal.

"What do you need me for?" he asked.

"This tower didn't make itself," Sybilla said. "Nor did the protective barrier I put up around it. I wrote the spells, but they were cast by the people who came seeking my aid. It's been a long time since I wanted anything enough to seek out new clients, but I do have spells that are in need of updating, and a few new ones that I'd like to test out. You can go through the stack while you're here."

Grimm folded his napkin and set it back on the table. "How long will we be here for, exactly?"

"I've never unraveled a love spell before, so it's hard to say. A few days at least. Plenty of time for you to repay me with labor." Sybilla winked at him. "It's been a while since I had a Fount-trained sorcerer doing my bidding. I think I shall enjoy it."

Grimm scowled, clearly unused to the idea of being under anyone's thumb. *Let's see how he likes it*, I thought, amused and embittered all at once. Sybilla was unlikely to order him to do anything objectionable, but then, Grimm never told me to do anything awful either. The discomfort came from having to take orders at all, and it seemed only right that Grimm should experience at least a fraction of that.

I must not have been quick enough hiding my smile behind my glass, because Grimm's eyes settled on me and his expression grew even more severe.

"And what will you do?"

I looked back at him, uncomprehending. "Me?"

"Yes, you. She's writing the spell, I'm paying for it, or near enough. What are you doing?"

"Leo will be helping me, of course," Sybilla said smoothly. "The work will go ever so much faster with two scrivers picking away at it."

"I can't," I said, alarmed. "I'll ruin it."

"Oh yes, your Grandmagic predicament, I'd forgotten. Is this another curse laid over you, perhaps?"

"No. It's just the way I am. I have to be very careful to avoid composing anything too big; if I'm not, it goes terribly wrong. Grimm knows. Tell her what happened the last time I got too ambitious."

Grimm looked faintly embarrassed. "If I recall correctly, I was thrown out a window."

I nodded. "Exactly. It's really not a good idea for me to help write the counterspell."

Sybilla asked, "Has no one ever been able to tell you where the problem stems from? None of your tutors or instructors at the Fount, perhaps?"

"No," I said, ready to move on from the topic. "My father brought in a few people, when I was young, but they couldn't find any reason for it. I didn't think it was worth meddling with, beyond that."

Across the table, Grimm released a small punched-out breath, as though the idea that I would avoid meddling was laughable. Normally he would have been right, but not about this.

"You don't have an interest in knowing more?" Sybilla pressed. It was clear *she* was interested. She had put her fork down to rest her chin in her hand, focusing all her attention on every brusque answer I gave.

I took a long sip of wine before saying anything else, aware that Grimm was watching now too. "Not really. I'm well suited to my charms and cantrips. That's all I need."

"Is it?" Sybilla's eyebrows arched doubtfully. Even Grimm looked like he didn't believe this. But it was only because of who they were. Each of them lived and breathed Grandmagic, writing it, casting it, perfecting it. It was only natural that they would doubt my being satisfied with less.

"It is," I said firmly.

Sybilla looked at me a moment longer. Then she picked up her fork again. "If that's really how you feel, you can be an observer for the composing part. But that doesn't mean you can't help in other ways. It's rare that I get to bounce ideas off another scriver while working. You will be my assistant."

I didn't see any way I could keep objecting. Being an observer broke none of my rules, and I was curious to watch a master like Sybilla at work. I was even a little eager for it.

Once our plates were empty and the candles on the table had burned low, Sybilla led us back onto the staircase. It was properly night now, not just the forever evening that took place inside the dining room. Sconces in the wall lit up ahead of us as we ascended the stairs, lighting the way through the tower's shadows. Sybilla showed me to a door with a green glass doorknob, then pointed Grimm toward the next one, a few steps up.

"The sheets are fresh," she told us. "They always are, actually. Benefits of remembered guest rooms. You can leave your belongings in there safely, but I'm afraid that anything you unpack will go right back in your bags as soon as you leave the room. That's a snag I'm still working out." Sybilla clasped her hands over her chest and looked at us. "Oh, it's so nice to have guests again. Do sleep well!"

I intended to do just that. The day's events had caught up with me over dinner, and I'd drank enough wine that my senses felt pleasantly floaty. My room, once I stepped inside, revealed itself to be small but elegant, with dark green walls and bed hangings to match. There was a tiny hearth to keep me warm, and fluffy pillows, and a window that looked out over some sort of coastal scene. When I opened it, I swore I could hear waves crashing in the distance. It was all perfectly restful, but I had barely lain down before I started to feel it: an itching, restless sensation that crawled beneath my skin, urging me to get up again. To go somewhere. To find someone.

I groaned and rolled over, staring at the forest-green bed hangings above me and willing the feeling to subside. When it didn't, I got up and retrieved my violin, hoping that music would be enough to distract me. The first song nearly did. It had been too long since I'd played simply for pleasure, and there was comfort to be found there. But by the time I was halfway through the second song, I knew it would not be enough.

I set my bow down and looked longingly at the comfortable bed. Then I ripped the topmost blanket away, grabbed a pillow, and went back out onto the staircase.

My mood was black as I stomped up the stairs to Grimm's door. The persistent feeling of wrongness was much less now that I was no longer inside the memory room, but that didn't improve my temperament as I propped my pillow on the doorstep and wrapped the blanket around myself. The tower was much cooler than my cozy little chamber had been, but I was tired enough I thought it wouldn't matter. And then, when I'd finally gotten everything arranged just so, the door behind me swung open.

I yelped and spilled into the room, causing Grimm to step back hastily, staring down at me in shock.

"What are you doing?" I asked indignantly, because indignance was better than abject mortification.

"I was going to find you," Grimm said. "What are *you* doing?"

I sighed and began to untangle myself from the blanket. "I'm not precisely sure how these remembered spaces work, but I don't think we're actually as close together as rooms down the hall from each other would be in an ordinary house." I picked myself up with as much dignity as I could muster and met Grimm's eyes. "The curse doesn't like it. Felt like I was trying to sleep on top of an anthill."

"Oh," Grimm said. Then, "Why on earth didn't you just knock and say so?"

The truth was that I had thought it would be too awful to stand on Grimm's doorstep and explain that I apparently couldn't bear to be that far away from him. It would have been uncomfortable even before we knew what the spell was, and now there were several helpings of awkward layered on top. But being caught sleeping on his doorstep was decidedly worse, so perhaps he had a point about the knocking thing.

"Thought you'd be asleep already," I said airily, then busied myself with looking around the room.

Grimm's lodgings were slightly larger than mine, with wood paneling that matched all the furniture and deep red velvet bed hangings the same color as the wine we'd had at dinner. His bag sat (unpacked) at the foot of the bed, and his sword had been laid on top of the dresser.

"I was coming to see if you wanted me to do another casting over your arm before you went to sleep," Grimm said.

I turned around from inspecting a stack of books on top of the tiny writing desk. "It's feeling better, actually." I'd noticed a few twinges when I played, but the bandage was unstained, and the pain had turned to more of a dull ache. "Almost as good as new."

"Very well." Grimm was still standing awkwardly at the open door and, oh, this was awful. We hadn't actually been alone since the love spell had been spoken of, and he looked seconds away from fleeing.

I understood the impulse.

Steeling himself, Grimm turned and shut the door. "You can make up a spot on the floor," he said. "I think there are extra blankets in the chest over there."

There were, and I was able to make myself a nest that, while in no way as comfortable as the bed I'd been given, was also not the worst place I'd ever slept. Grimm blew out the candles and got underneath his own covers, and I'd just begun to think that maybe we were going to successfully ignore the elephant in the room with us when Grimm said, "Did you truly not know?"

I thought of pretending to be asleep. Or asking *Know what?* and hoping he would not have the courage to clarify. But

Grimm wasn't a coward, and perhaps it was better to get this conversation over now, in the dark, where we didn't have to face each other.

"I didn't. Truly, I had no idea." I stared up at the ceiling and sighed. "I blamed you for not realizing what the spell could do when you cast it, but in the end, I didn't recognize what it was either. At least, not entirely."

"Is there a chance Sybilla is wrong?"

"I think Sybilla is very good at what she does," I said carefully. "She's older than she looks, you know. She must be. The tales I read about her were in a book written twenty years ago. She must make use of cosmetic charms that put all of mine to shame. I think she's been doing this for a long time. So, no. I don't think she's wrong."

It was silent for a while, except for the sound of the fire crackling in the hearth.

"I just don't understand how you didn't notice," Grimm said quietly, sounding honestly perplexed. "This is so different from anything you would have felt before."

"You mean back when we were at each other's throats? I thought of that too. But you heard what Sybilla said, the spell works slowly. I suppose that I have enjoyed your company slightly more than usual lately, but I thought that was just a consequence of spending time together under unusual circumstances. Just the beginnings of a . . . friendship, of a sort."

The moment in the woods when I had become mesmerized by the sight of Grimm singing flashed through my mind, but I decided to forgive myself for not spotting that particular warning sign. It was totally normal to find your friends attractive, after all.

I continued doggedly on. "If there was anything else to it, I was oblivious. I have not loved many, to recognize the signs."

"Hm," Grimm said, openly skeptical. Everyone knew one another's business at the Fount. Everyone knew one another's reputations, and though my own was exaggerated, it was not entirely unearned.

I chuckled, amused for the first time since this conversation began. "I don't love everyone I fuck, Grimm. For that matter, I don't fuck everyone I love, which should comfort you. As far as I'm concerned, the spell has just tricked me into thinking you're a bit like Agnes—someone I care for."

Glancing up at Grimm, I thought I caught a glimmer of some dark emotion in his eyes, similar to what I'd seen after the spell had first been announced. I'd taken it for horror then, but now I almost thought it resembled disappointment. But that was ridiculous. Why would Grimm mind if my actions were only the result of the curse? He had never wanted my friendship in the first place.

"I promise that the only urges I've had to fling myself at you were of the protective variety," I joked, seeking to lighten his mood.

"I wasn't worried about *that*," Grimm said, but he sounded so affronted I was certain this was at least partially a lie.

That was all right. I was maybe lying too, a little bit.

My feelings for Grimm, both before and after the curse, had never resembled anything like what I felt for Agnes. Nor were they like anything I'd felt for lovers. Perhaps that was why I hadn't been able to recognize the spell for what it was. Whatever it made me feel for Grimm was something different. Something I wouldn't have known to look for.

There seemed nothing left to say, so I rolled over, pulling my blankets up to my chin. It had been a long day, and my pillow was very soft, even if the blankets between me and the floor were a little too thin for comfort. Grimm's breath evened out and grew deeper, and I measured my own against it until I felt the last traces of tension leave me. I knew now that any calm I felt because of his presence was likely caused by magic, but knowing did not lessen the effect.

I wondered if I would miss this feeling when it was gone.

CHAPTER TWENTY-TWO

We began work on the counterspell the following morning. In Sybilla's dressing room of all places, because that was where Grimm was casting, and I was only a useful assistant if we were in the same memory room.

We'd tested the limits of the curse further upon waking. I'd gone to the parlor where morning tea and toast were served, while Grimm lingered in his bedroom. The restless pull was not so bad on the stairs, but as soon as I stepped over the threshold into the quaint sitting room, the curse began to build itself up toward a tantrum. An absolute storm of turmoil in my chest that abated as soon as Grimm was back in sight.

"It makes a certain kind of sense," Sybilla said, tapping her chin thoughtfully. "The rooms in this tower don't exist in precisely the place they're meant to, and the memories they're built from belong all over the world. I've tethered them to the staircase but not one another, so I suppose that confuses your curse. It must think you're eating breakfast on one continent while he gets dressed in another."

This being the case, Sybilla and I gathered our supplies and prepared to follow Grimm around as he cast his way through the stack of spells Sybilla handed him over breakfast.

For once, I was the one eager to get to work, while Grimm

looked around at the profusion of silk and velvet overflowing from Sybilla's drawers with something like despair.

"Are you sure this is the most pressing issue?" he asked.

"Living alone in the woods is no excuse for not keeping up with fashion," Sybilla said, "and my wardrobe is dreadfully out of date."

Grimm took one last look around the dressing room, then squared his shoulders like a man about to go to war and began to read the first spell.

Meanwhile, Sybilla lifted her scriver's kit onto her cleared-off jewelry table. My own kit fit easily into one of the pockets of my coat (and was usually empty, since I hardly ever remembered to restock it), but Sybilla's was more like a chest. When opened, it unfolded like a flower, revealing drawer after drawer full of quills and paper and ink. In addition to this, she'd also brought enough books to build a small wall with.

"I need you to go through these and mark any pages you feel might provide insight into your curse, or love spells in general," Sybilla said. "The first step to writing any good piece of magic is arming yourself with knowledge."

I looked gloomily at the stack of books. "You sound like my instructors at the Fount."

"If you've changed your mind about the manner of help you're comfortable giving…"

"No, no," I said hastily. "Reading is fine."

In the end, it was not as much like my boring sessions of research at the Fount library as I'd feared. For one thing, anytime I found myself in need of cheering up, I had only to look over at Grimm, stoically sorting through what appeared to be twenty years' worth of silken underthings. For another, Sybilla was not the sort of work partner dedicated to silence. She liked to think out loud, and we often got swept away in conversation that had nothing to do with counterspells, prompting Grimm to repeatedly call out "One week, Loveage!" in order to steer us back toward more productive waters.

And so it went. After the dressing room, we followed Grimm to the bathing chamber so he could install a tap that spit out only bubbles. In the ballroom two doors down from where we slept, I got to participate, fetching my violin so that Grimm could cast a spell that ensured music would begin playing every time someone opened the door. Then we moved on to an empty greenhouse that was so much higher in the tower than any of the rooms we'd previously visited, it prompted Grimm to say, "If you can make rooms built of memories, surely you could open them all with the same door. I don't understand why you would bother with all these stairs."

"You have no sense of romance, do you?" Sybilla replied, somewhat sadly. "There's no point in building a giant, mysterious tower in the middle of the woods if you're going to ruin it by being sensible about interior design features. Of course I *could* have just one door, but that's not what I want. I want hundreds."

I thought about this in the bright light of the greenhouse, as Grimm cast spell after spell to add greenery to what had previously been an empty structure (empty, because Sybilla said the plants in the original building had been too boring, and she had needed to research ones worth adding).

"You could make a fortune," I noted idly, "if any of this could be replicated by another scriver's hand."

"Oh, it can be," Sybilla said. "Everything I write is that way. I do sell a few every now and again. But most of my ideas are either too big or too small for the general public."

"What do you mean?" I asked.

"Well, a tap that spits out bubbles is fine, I'm certain plenty of scrivers could come up with a version of that, if they cared to. But take the memory doors." Sybilla waved her quill at the greenhouse entrance. "The spell is solid, but the rooms themselves aren't always. They're a funny sort of in-between. I'm not sure everyone would know to be careful, and so I've kept them to myself. If I was capable of writing, oh, I don't know, spells that did away with hunger, or healed any wound, I wouldn't hoard them. But alas, I write either frivolities or magic so grand it comes attached to a host of pesky questions about how it should be *used*."

"I think I know what you mean," I said. "There's a weight to writing magic. A responsibility. Sometimes I almost wish I'd been born a caster."

Sybilla turned on me, dark eyes wide. "Don't say such things, Leo. Would you really rather be doing that?"

She pointed toward Grimm, who paused in the midst of extricating himself from an overly enthusiastic flowering vine to cast a baleful look our way.

"This is *not* what casters normally do."

"I know," Sybilla said placatingly, settling more firmly back into her patio lounger. "And yet you're doing *such* a good job. I think I'll have you cast the fountain next. Just over there."

I liked Sybilla, more and more as we spent time together. The only thing I didn't like was her persistent curiosity regarding my Grandmagic, or lack thereof.

The subject came up again after dinner. I had retrieved my violin at Sybilla's request, running through several ordinary songs before playing a melody that made the candles in the room spit out sparks that hung above me in a halo. Grimm's eyebrows furrowed, but it was a tiny casting, barely enough to leave me breathless. Beau stood up from where he'd been asleep under the table and sat at my feet until the song was finished, ears pricked forward and silver eyes swirling with interest.

Sybilla clapped and exclaimed at the trick.

"You're very skilled, Leo," she said. "I've never seen a scriver able to cast so well. Your methods are unique. Look, even Beau is impressed."

The wolf had gone to sit by Sybilla but was still watching me with an eerie intensity. "The monsters in the woods liked the music too," I admitted. "I'm not sure why."

Sybilla rested a palm lightly on Beau's head and began to scratch behind his ears, looking thoughtful. "Perhaps because your way of using magic shares something in common with them. They are creatures of the Wilderlands, and there is a hint of the wild in your spellsongs, I think. Or perhaps there is some other reason we will never know. Magic, like music, does not always need to be explained. It is enough that it exists. And the way you've combined the two is ever so lovely." Her attention on me was bright and warm as any flame, and I flushed with the praise. Then she said, "I'm very curious what Grandmagic might sound like written into one of your spellsongs, aren't you?"

I froze, then forced myself to smile disarmingly. "Little point in wondering. I'd rather spend my time writing the songs available to me than mourning the ones that are not."

"A fine sentiment," Sybilla agreed, but her eyes were glittering, and I was sure she could sense the lie in my words.

Because I *had* wondered. Of course I had. Especially now that I had Grimm there to sing my songs, it was impossible not to wonder what they might be capable of, if only there weren't this flaw in my making. But it was frightening to long for such things. When I dwelled in the wanting, it felt like an ocean, endlessly vast and moving just beneath the surface of my skin. If I stayed there, I would be swept away.

I did my best to shake the moment off, but it clung to me. I put my violin away without playing another song and was unusually quiet all through dessert, relieved when it was time for us to leave Sybilla and return to our room. Later that night, I awoke in the dark with Grimm's hand on my shoulder. Thoughtlessly, I reached for him, mind still thick with dreams of drowning in the things I disallowed during waking hours, and somehow Grimm and his hands were a part of that. My heart pounded hard enough that I could feel it in my mouth, underneath my tongue. For an instant the sensation was so overwhelming I thought I would choke on it.

And then I recalled myself and let go.

"What's wrong?" I asked, once I could speak.

Grimm was leaning half out of the bed to reach me. His hand fell away when I spoke. "You called out. I thought you might wish to be woken." He drew back under the covers, but I could still feel him watching me in the dark.

"Sorry I woke you," I whispered, unsure if I was grateful or mortified that I'd been loud enough for him to realize I needed saving.

"It's of no bother."

I waited for the rise and fall of his chest to turn steady before wiping at my cheeks. Then I crept out of the room and retrieved one of the endlessly full bottles of wine from the dining room. I drank half of it out on the stairs and brought the other half back to the room to keep under Grimm's bed, within easy reach in case the nightmare returned.

It didn't matter, in the end. I was still awake when the gray light of morning crept through the curtains.

The next day, instead of assigning him multiple projects to complete, Sybilla set Grimm the more arduous task of refreshing the barrier around her tower.

"Can one person do that?" Grimm asked doubtfully.

If it were any other task, I might have teased him about trying to get out of working, but I understood his concern. The barrier surrounding Miendor was notoriously strong—it had to be, in order to discourage monsters getting through. Refreshing the spell flags sometimes took as many as four or five casters from a troop, and it was a tiring process even then. Sybilla's barrier was smaller, and had trees instead of flags, but its purpose was the same. More complex even, since her barrier kept out humans as well. It seemed a tall order for one caster to complete, even when that caster was Grimm.

Sybilla's lip curled disdainfully. "The Coterie is good at many things, but efficiency is not one of them. Didn't you say you'd managed to do the job of ten casters in that field on your way here? This is the same. Every spell I write has to be useful to one person, because I rarely have more than one guest at a time. It will take you all of today and most of tomorrow, but you will feel no more tired at the end of it than you did yesterday."

She shooed him toward the door, at the last minute calling, "Take Beau. He'll have more fun out there with you."

Grimm eyed the wolf with some trepidation but waited for Beau to follow him outside.

Perhaps it was because I hadn't gotten enough sleep last night, but the shine of playing assistant wore off for me that day.

Sybilla and I set up on the ground level of the tower, the door-step, rather than following Grimm outside and risking our papers being blown away in the breeze. I had not thought this small amount of distance would bother me—this level of the tower's existence was perfectly ordinary, and Grimm wasn't far—but I felt the pinch of his absence in my chest.

It was getting worse again, I realized. The area in which I was allowed to exist independently was steadily growing smaller. At the Fount, I had been able to wander where I liked with ease so long as I was in Grimm's presence at some point during the day. Then, at Grimm's house, it had allowed me only a mile down the road before it acted up. Since arriving here, it hadn't even let me sleep alone, thanks to the tower's interference, and now it was making my skin crawl again without even that excuse. Grimm wasn't in a memory room, and neither was I; the curse just didn't like him being out of my sight. Grimm probably could have hidden behind the sofa and prompted the same reaction.

The worst part was that, instead of mourning my lack of autonomy, the thing I felt most keenly was the lack of Grimm's presence. I was bored and sullen without him there. Sybilla's companionship was suddenly too easy. I found myself missing the little quirks of Grimm's irritation when I talked too much, and the rarer glimpses of amusement. It left me frustrated with both myself and the work in front of me.

The smart thing to do would have been to calmly report this new symptom to Sybilla and then perhaps move our work outdoors, despite the inconvenience. Instead, I gritted my teeth and ignored the sensation. When Grimm had left the Fount for Dwull, it had taken me nearly a full day to realize he was even gone. Surely I could manage one afternoon of reading without him in my line of sight?

I could, but only just. My movements were slower as I sorted through the assembled books, and the words of each chapter swam before my eyes and took ages to understand. My notes for Sybilla were messy and lacked the consideration I'd given them the day before.

Most of all, the curse wore away at my patience.

"Surely we've collected enough information for a first draft to be written," I groaned, well into the afternoon. "You've been fiddling away at composition for ages."

"Counterspells take time," Sybilla said primly.

The words *One week, Loveage* rang out in my mind. Time was something we did not have an unlimited supply of, but I'd already told Sybilla this.

The ache at my center grew steadily worse, until I fidgeted in my chair and couldn't help looking hopefully toward the door.

"I wonder if this word might be a good choice for the opening line," Sybilla said, and pushed the page she'd been working on over the table for me to look at. She'd asked for my opinion before, always in a casual manner. Thus far I'd feigned ignorance or reminded her that such advice from me was unwise. But I was tired, the invisible string that connected me to Grimm drawn painfully tight, and so I answered without thinking.

"A word that mirrors the one used in the original poem would be better," I replied after a glance. "The reflection will provide a stronger countering effect." I spoke aloud the word in the old language that had been dancing at the back of my mind.

I didn't realize my mistake until Sybilla's lips curved into a satisfied smile.

"Just so," she said.

I pushed the paper away from myself, but the damage was done. Icy panic dripped down the back of my neck until I nearly shivered with it. "I shouldn't have said that. Don't use it. Think of something else."

Sybilla tutted at me. "I was already going to do just as you said. You speaking the word aloud doesn't change anything. I'm a very skilled scriver, Leo. Do you really think I wouldn't be able to spot an error in your work?"

"It's not the sort of error you can see," I insisted. "It's me. It's not safe for *me* to use Grandmagic, I told you."

"Oh, Leo," Sybilla said, and this time instead of exasperation, I heard only sadness in her voice. She reached out and laid her pointer finger lightly on my forehead, right between my eyes. "It's all terribly twisted up in here," she said softly, "isn't it?"

My mouth went dry. I'd gone about this all wrong. I should have laughed and changed the subject. Now I was stuck there, transfixed, as Sybilla stared into my eyes. I blinked and looked past her shoulder, lest she see everything.

"I don't know what you mean."

Sybilla sighed and her hand dropped away. "I'll tell you a secret. I said I would take your case because it intrigued me, and that much is true. But writing a counterspell doesn't interest me nearly as much as *you* do. Whatever has your magic so turned around that you can't so much as think about anything stronger than a charm without getting twitchy, *that's* a problem I'd like to solve."

"Are you trying to fix the curse, or me?"

Sybilla tilted her head a little, looking me over. Her eyes were bright and somehow faraway, like stars in the night sky. "Why can't it be both? I'm a good multitasker."

For a moment her age showed, and so did the power she held. Not in her face, but in her oh-so-careless interest. The way she wanted to lay me out to be dissected, just so she could see something new.

It was a strange way to be wanted.

I gave in to the impulse I'd been pushing aside for hours and stood, moving toward the door.

"I think I'll get some air and check on Grimm's progress."

Sybilla leaned back into the soft velvet of the sofa, and some of that strange intensity drained from her face. "A break sounds like a lovely idea. I think I'll have some tea. We can finish this later."

It was unclear if she meant our work or this horrible conversation. I didn't ask, too eager to flee the encounter. I was almost to the door when Sybilla spoke again.

"I'm not pushing you just to satisfy my own curiosity, no matter what you may think. This curse is highly personal. The more personal our counter to it is, the better. That might require you to give more of yourself into the making of this magic than you're comfortable with. Please think about it, at least."

"I will," I lied, immediately resolving to take this conversation, lock it up in a box, and hide it in the furthest reaches of my mind. Someplace where I would not be tempted to use Sybilla's reasoning as any sort of excuse for madness.

I found Grimm reclining in the dappled shade beneath the pale-barked birch trees that marked Sybilla's barrier, looking uncommonly relaxed. Drawing closer, I was startled by a loud and sudden *pop*, and then Beau appeared a few feet ahead of me with a stick in his mouth. He bounded the remaining distance toward Grimm and dropped the stick in front of him, tail wagging. Grimm, without hesitation, picked up the soggy piece of wood and threw it as far into the trees as he could. Beau went racing gleefully after it. Whatever protection Sybilla's barrier provided did not seem to apply to her pet monster.

"What's this?" I called out, delighted. "Are you *playing*, Grimm? Are you relaxing? How scandalous. Look what forest life has done to you."

I was only partially joking. Grimm's coat, normally so pristine, was wrinkled, he had not bothered tying his caster's sash in such a way as to hide the stitches holding it together, and now he'd clearly been caught playing fetch with a creature that only resembled a dog in the broadest sense. This was not quite the upright image of a Fount-trained sorcerer that everyone expected from Sebastian Grimm.

"He likes to bring it back," Grimm said simply. Sure enough, there was another *pop* and Beaugard reappeared. Grimm didn't throw the stick again, watching me instead as I flopped down onto the grass next to him. Beau dropped the stick near my feet and looked at me hopefully until I took my turn.

Grimm's sword lay in the grass between us. I nudged it with my knee and said, "Agnes will scold me for getting out of practice. Too bad the river ate my sword or we could spar."

"We fight enough as is."

"I suppose. Anyway, it's probably better for my dignity if we don't. I'd only end up on my ass in the dirt." Grimm, tactfully, said nothing. "Is this what you've been doing out here all day?" I asked, waving a hand in the direction Beau had gone. "Making friends with a monster of the wood?"

Grimm said, "Isn't that what we've both been doing?"

My first instinct was to protest that Sybilla wasn't monstrous at all. But the conversation I'd just fled from returned to me and I frowned.

"Did you and Sybilla argue?"

"Why would you ask that?"

"I can't imagine another reason why you would be out here with me."

Can't you? I nearly said, but even I was not so daring as all that. "We didn't argue, not really. Sybilla just has no sense of when to leave well enough alone."

Grimm shot me a sideways glance and said, in a flat sort of voice, "That must be very trying for you."

"*I* only bother people about trivial things," I said, raising one hand to my chest. Then hurriedly, before Grimm could ask what nontrivial matters Sybilla had been poking her nose into, I added, "You'd think someone who went to such lengths to escape being disturbed would extend the same courtesy to others, but I suppose living alone for as long as she has could warp anyone's social graces. It's wonderfully peaceful out here, though."

I waited for Grimm to respond by shooting a pointed glance to where my sprawled limbs overlapped into his space, or say something like *It was.* But all he did was look up at the leaves above us and say, "Yes, it is."

A warm shiver of pleasure swept over me. I leaned back in the grass, sprawling a little more thoroughly.

"Maybe I'll follow in Sybilla's footsteps after the Fount, build myself a tower somewhere remote. I'll only visit the nearest town on the day before the full moon, or something dramatic like that, and everyone will think me very mysterious."

"You could never be mysterious," Grimm said.

"Why not?" I said, offended by his decisiveness. "I'm rich, already considered strange by many, blindingly handsome, and I'm a sorcerer. All those things are perfectly mysterious."

"Mysterious people don't list off the traits that make them mysterious."

I spluttered a little but had no response that didn't further prove his point.

"Well, what are *your* plans?" I asked. "I've spilled all the secret yearnings of my heart at your feet on multiple occasions and you haven't reciprocated even once."

"I don't yearn for anything," Grimm said, looking uncomfortable at the very idea. "And you already know my plans. I'll join the Coterie once I'm done at the Fount. The path is already laid out for me."

"Yes, but where does it lead? Come on, play along for once."

Grimm studied his hands where they sat folded in his lap, then said haltingly, "Well...I suppose, eventually, it leads to the Citadel. A seat there. Someday."

"Oh." I shouldn't have been disappointed. Grimm was ambitious, this was no surprise. It was a good answer. My father would have liked this answer.

But Grimm wasn't finished speaking.

"The Coterie is flawed in some ways. Not in its purpose, but the ways of being that have sprung up around it. There is stagnancy there. People know it, bemoan it even, but doing something about it would mean disrupting the cycles that so many gentry families have grown used to. And gentry families make up the majority of the Coterie. So, nothing is done. I would like to be in a position to do something."

"You want to *disrupt* things?" I was scarcely able to believe my ears. "That's why you want a seat in the Citadel?"

Grimm looked up from his hands. "Yes," he said. "If I have a plan, I suppose it's that."

Oh, I thought, with an altogether different inflection this time.

Grimm's eyes were dark, and his face was set in familiar lines of determination. He also looked like he was bracing for some snide or teasing remark. But that wasn't at all the response his words had prompted in me.

I was suddenly wondering what it would be like to kiss Grimm.

I had once joked (meanly) to Agnes that kissing Grimm would be good only for bragging rights, since I was certain it would be akin to kissing a statue. But now I wasn't so sure. If I leaned across the grass and put my lips to his, would they really be so cold? I wanted to find out.

I'd already swayed forward slightly when I remembered: *This isn't real.*

The speed with which I scrambled to my feet made Grimm look up at me quizzically. Good, I thought. Better he be confused than have noticed how near I'd come to doing exactly what I'd promised him there was no danger of.

"I have to get back," I said, nervously ruffling my hair with one hand. "Counterspells to write and all that."

"All right," Grimm said. "I need to resume casting anyway."

I worried the curse would be upset I had done nothing to ease this new symptom, but it let me walk away without protest. I didn't have to act on my urge, but the thought was still there, impossible to leave alone, the same way your tongue would be drawn to a loose tooth.

I fled back to the relative safety of the tower, where the pain in my chest would be worse, but at least I would not be tempted to soothe it by kissing Sebastian Grimm.

CHAPTER TWENTY-THREE

I got spectacularly drunk that night, until Grimm turned away in disgust and Sybilla began to send me questioning glances over the table.

"Are you feeling all right, dearest?" she asked.

I hadn't told her what had (almost) happened. I wasn't quite sure why. I'd wanted to kiss many people before, and done so without shame. But there was something about wanting Grimm that made me feel like I was standing unclothed in front of a crowd, with no instrument or script to distract anyone from my nakedness.

Besides, Sybilla had annoyed me with her poking about Grandmagic.

"Everything is perfectly lovely, Sybilla, *dearest.* Perfectly lovely." I raised my wine in a toast to her and then spluttered indignantly when Grimm reached out and plucked the glass from my fingers.

"I think that's enough," he said sternly. "We should go, while you can still navigate the stairs between here and your pillow without tumbling down them." He pushed his chair back and stood, looking down at me expectantly.

I did not move. It had just occurred to me, far too late, that lowering all my inhibitions before spending the night alone in a room with Grimm was a terrible idea actually. Definitely up there in the top five worst ideas I'd ever had.

"It's early yet," I stalled. "How about some music?"

"I *have* been wanting another demonstration of some of your spellsongs," Sybilla said, and I decided at once to forgive her, so long as she continued to act as a barrier between me going anywhere alone with Grimm. "The ones you're able to cast yourself."

Grimm looked pointedly at the collection of wine bottles, scattered around the table. "Do you really think it's a good idea for him to cast in this state? Loveage barely has any restraint when sober."

Drinking usually makes me jovial—that's why I do it, to feel happy—but Grimm's words left me coldly furious. He had no right to judge my methods of distraction. *I* was the one who was cursed, not him.

"You don't have to join us," I said sharply. "We wouldn't have any fun with you there anyway. No one ever does. We'll go to the doorstep and you can go to your room, where you won't have to be bothered by witnessing my lack of restraint."

Grimm looked like there were several things he would have liked to say to that, but perhaps all of them were a little too close to being orders for him to speak aloud. He cast his eyes toward the ceiling, as though hoping to find some patience there, and then looked back down at me and spat out, "Fine." He glanced to where Sybilla sat at the head of the table and said, "See to it he doesn't injure himself, because I *won't* be waking up to cast any first aid spells." Then he stomped from the room wearing a very hostile expression.

I think he must have waited out of sight somewhere on the stairs for Sybilla and I to emerge before entering the bedroom, because I never felt the telltale agony that being in two separate memory rooms caused. The pulling in my chest grew no worse than what I'd been dealing with for most of the day.

I was *not* grateful for his consideration. Not at all.

My discomfort was somewhat more marked by the time we'd settled at the base of the tower, with Grimm sequestered away in his chamber. Each breath made my chest ache with warmth, like I'd swallowed a coal. Or had heartburn.

"Teach me the song you used on the candles," Sybilla said brightly. She was quite obviously trying to cheer me up. Perhaps she thought my mood was due in part to our uncomfortable conversation that afternoon.

We spent an hour or so trying to modify my candle trick to something Sybilla could sing, but no matter how many times I repeated the words for her, she couldn't seem to get them to work. She sang and sang, but every time the magic began to catch, she flinched from it.

"It tickles," she said, laughing. "But it also feels like it might burn me if I hold on too long."

"Maybe Grimm was right and I'm too drunk for this," I said, collapsing down onto the sofa beside Sybilla with a sigh. It was nice to sit next to her so casually. I'd forgotten that being close to someone didn't have to feel like trying to grasp a lit fuse. "I could try to teach you again tomorrow."

"There's no need," Sybilla said, waving the offer away. "I don't think one soul is really meant to do both. Or at least mine isn't. Who knows why music makes it more possible for you? Sorcerers like to pretend we have magic figured out, just because it allows us to use it sometimes. But the truth is, however many books we fill with spells and lore, there's an infinite amount yet to be discovered. Look at the lake country, and Granvoir. They're our nearest neighbors, but magic functions differently there. My theory is that there are as many different types of magic as there are people. It's a mystery that rewards us for believing in it, not understanding it."

"Poetic," I said solemnly, then had to duck when Sybilla threw a cushion at me.

"Oh, go on," she said. "Show me another of your tricks."

"I don't actually have that many," I admitted. "I'm still no caster." But after a moment of thought I got up and went to open the tower door. I stood there, looking out into the night. Then I sang the words to a spell I'd last cast on a sunlit morning, right before everything had changed.

It was late in the season for this to work, but eventually, a blinking light appeared. Then another. Then a handful of them, flashing closer in the dark—fireflies that had lingered through the cold long enough to be summoned by my song.

Sybilla had come to see what I was doing, and I beckoned the winged things closer to settle, flashing, against the dark wave of her hair and shoulders. A few settled like glowing jewels on her fingers. It was impossible not to remember how Grimm had looked that morning, covered in fluttering wings, but now the image was overlaid with Sybilla, raising her hands up and laughing.

I felt it again. That breathless recognition of someone cast from the same mold. Who moved like quicksilver and could flip like a coin at any moment. I *knew* her, and because of that it was so easy to make her happy. And right then all I wanted was for someone to look upon me with delight.

I leaned down and kissed her.

This close, Sybilla smelled of warm amber and something sweet like honey. I kept the kiss light, gentle like the misting of spring rain, in case she thought to pull away. Sybilla's lips may not have been the ones that had made me think of kissing to begin with, but they were very soft, and this was a choice *I* could make, not some compulsion pulling the strings of my heart.

At least that's what I thought, until we broke apart and Sybilla met my eyes and said, "I do not think that kiss was meant for me."

It was not said accusingly, only thoughtfully, with a little tilt to her head and a question in her eyes.

The magic of the evening dissipated all at once, and so too did my sense of ease. Instead, I felt abruptly and painfully sober.

"You're who I decided to give it to," I said. "I still have that much control over my actions."

The fireflies were leaving now, losing interest in Sybilla without my song to hold them there. Once her hands were bare of them, she raised one to my cheek.

"Poor Leo," she said. There was still warmth in her voice, but it was not the same warmth I had tasted against her mouth. "You really don't know how to escape the frying pan without flinging yourself into a fire. The spell has gotten worse again, hasn't it?"

I closed my eyes and nodded against her hand. "Yes."

"When did you notice?"

"This afternoon. I was outside with Grimm and I wanted to..." I opened my eyes and smiled tiredly down at Sybilla. "Well, I suppose you know what I wanted."

"Quite." She patted my cheek again, this time briskly. "That decides it. I'll write the counterspell tomorrow and we will cast it directly."

My heart gave a little jump of both surprise and hope. I was still only halfway through the books from Sybilla's library, and she'd made a great point that afternoon of waffling over what structure she wanted for the counterspell. She had not even written the first line yet.

"So fast?"

Sybilla cast me a pitying look. "Please. I've known what I would write since the first day you got here." She quickly checked her skirt for stray fireflies, then made her way back to the center of the room, leaving me gaping in the doorway.

"You villain!" I said, once I'd found my voice. I'd thought she'd been stalling, not outright lying about our progress. I was more impressed than angry at how thoroughly I'd been fooled. "You just wanted more time to have Grimm carry out all your little tasks, didn't you?"

Sybilla began to gather together the papers and books we'd left scattered throughout the room that day, looking pleased with herself. "The company was nice, too." Then her eyes turned sober. "More than that, I was hoping with enough time I could convince you to start dismantling the walls you've built up around your magic. I wasn't lying when I said something you compose would likely do a better job combating this curse than anything I come up with. You're the one who's experiencing it, after all. I don't suppose this latest progression has changed your mind?"

"It hasn't," I told her honestly. "I can't risk it. I don't want to hurt anyone, and that's all that happens every time I try to write Grandmagic."

"Keeping everyone safe is not your responsibility. It is not even an option. But I understand."

"Do you?" I asked, a little desperately.

"Of course. You've built a tower in your mind; I've built one in the woods. We're very much alike, Leo. Now, Grimm is probably asleep so you're safe to go back to your room. Tomorrow I will write the best counterspell I'm capable of and hope that it's enough."

"It will be," I said. How could it not? I was standing inside a tower constructed half of memory, all due to the skill of the woman standing before me. I had to believe she was wrong about my being better suited to write the counterspell. The alternative was too overwhelming to contemplate.

Sybilla doused the candles, and we walked up the stairs together in silence. I paused before opening the door to Grimm's room.

"I'm sorry," I said.

Sybilla paused on the stairs above me and looked back. "Don't apologize." She smiled crookedly. "Kisses are not so plentiful in this place for me to go around turning them down, even if they are stolen from somebody else."

It was a pity Sybilla was no longer pretending to need an assistant, because I could have used something to distract myself the following day. Each hour felt like honey dripping from a spoon as I waited for Sybilla to finish the counterspell.

Finally, she emerged from her study, and we gathered in the base of the tower.

"It's as good as I can make it," Sybilla said. She handed me the paper to read first, covered in her flowing script.

Just like the deceptively simple spell that had caused so much trouble, the counterspell was short. Its power lay in the meaning of the words chosen, not their quantity. Sybilla had crafted each line as an answer to directives of the curse and the result was beautiful. Elegant.

I read it and thought, *This is not how I would have written it.*

This was unquestionably a more artful, powerful counter than anything we'd tried thus far, and yet I was uneasy. There was something about the held-breath atmosphere in the tower that felt too much like every time Cassius had given us new paper to burn, each attempt going up in smoke and leaving me just the same.

"Any last-minute additions?" Sybilla asked, looking at me closely.

"No," I said, pushing my doubts aside. "No. Let's cast it."

Grimm insisted it would be best to cast the counterspell where there was no threat of other magic mingling with his work, so we stayed where we were instead of moving to one of the memory rooms. We pushed the furniture aside to stand at the center of the tower, because Sybilla insisted there was always more power at the center of things.

"Cast it aloud," I reminded Grimm.

We were, each in our own way, calling on anything we could think of to bring luck to this casting, be it superstition or sense. But eventually there was nothing to be done but stand facing Grimm and nod my readiness. He nodded back once before beginning to cast.

His voice was low and steady over the words. He'd spent a long time studying the spell after it was handed to him, and I knew it was now being recited from memory, even though his eyes were fixed on the page.

Before long, I felt an odd flicker across my skin. The sensation stung slightly, but rather than this bothering me, I smiled in relief. None of the other counterspells had felt like *anything*. The pain was a good sign.

Then Grimm reached the second line and the smile died on my lips.

There was pressure in my chest, sharp and unyielding. It was not the same as the tugging of the curse, which always felt as if it were pulling me in a specific direction. This felt like a hook had been latched to my insides and now all my internal organs were being reeled in.

My breath left my lips in a strangled gasp.

Grimm's voice did not falter, but he looked at me questioningly.

"It's fine," I said, gritting my teeth. "I think it's working."

Grimm didn't look back to the smoke-wreathed paper in his hands, instead keeping his eyes on me as he finished reciting the second line of the counterspell, watching my face closely. I wished he wouldn't because with each word he spoke the pain grew, and I was having a hard time not letting it show. Just as Grimm spoke the first word of the sixth line, so close to the end, a white-hot burst of agony bloomed at my center.

I cried out and crumpled to my knees.

"Leo!" Sybilla said, alarmed. She took a step closer but stopped short of touching me.

I couldn't look up. All I could focus on was Grimm's voice, which had slowed until each word dripped from his mouth with agonizing slowness. He dropped into a crouch beside me, and I could feel the effort it took to keep the spell going at this pace radiating off him.

"Just finish it," I ground out. It was all right that it hurt, I thought hazily. Shouldn't it hurt when your heart was being ripped from your body? Just a few more words. A few more words.

Something new wrenched within me. There was wetness on my face. Was I crying?

"Stop!" Sybilla ordered sharply.

Grimm's voice instantly cut out.

The pain disappeared and everything was blissfully quiet. For a moment my relief was so profound that I didn't fully understand what had happened. Then I realized it was quiet because Grimm had stopped casting. Hadn't *finished* casting, simply stopped. The magic still hung around us but was not being channeled.

"Don't," I protested weakly. "It was working."

"No," Grimm answered, voice somber. "I don't think it was." He reached out and swiped his thumb over my top lip. It came away red.

I stared dumbly at the blood on his hand.

"No more," Grimm told me firmly, then stood. He took in a deep breath, crumpled the mostly burnt piece of paper in his bloodied fingers, and raised both his arms. When he brought them down, the magic in the air around us evaporated like morning mist being chased by the sun. Gone.

I sat very still, mouth tasting of copper. My insides felt bruised, like when I'd cast the spell that tossed us into the river. I wanted to lie down on the floor and sleep for a year. I wanted a drink. I wanted Grimm to touch my lips again.

Power still crackled around Grimm, felt but unseen. He rounded on Sybilla and snapped, "What did you write? Why did it do that to him?"

Sybilla was visibly less composed than usual, face pale and eyes wide. Her hands were clasped together in front of her waist, fingers twisted tightly together. She appeared to gather herself with effort.

"I can only hazard a guess. Most spells either succeed or fail, but I think this one fell into a sort of in-between. My work was strong enough to destroy the curse, but..."

"But?" Grimm prompted.

"Not without hurting me," I finished. I didn't need Sybilla to spell it out, I'd felt it.

"Just so," Sybilla said, nodding. "The curse is too entrenched. Maybe if we'd done this the first week it would have worked, but now it's had time to reach into all the hidden corners of Leo's head and heart, making itself at home. The pain was a result of the counterspell's confusion."

I wiped idly at the blood still dripping sluggishly from my nose. "Well, it was certainly unpleasant, but at least we'll be prepared next time."

"There isn't going to be a next time, Loveage," Grimm said, aghast. "Don't be— That's absurd!"

"Grimm's right," Sybilla said, voice uncommonly stern. "This isn't a matter of bearing the pain while the spell is being cast. It hurt because my counterspell couldn't distinguish between what was the curse and what was *you*. It was destroying both."

"Then fix it," I said desperately. "You can write another one that knows the difference."

Sybilla shook her head. "No, I can't. That's what I've been trying to tell you. I can't write something into a spell that I don't know myself. You're the one who's cursed. You're the one who knows how it feels and can sort the edges of yourself out from what's false. It would be useless for me to attempt anything further." She hesitated, then pressed on. "But if *you* were to try—"

I no longer wanted to be on the floor. It made me too much of a sitting target. "We've been over this," I said, slowly unfolding my aching limbs. "I won't do it."

"You might not even have to compose a new spell," Sybilla said, coaxing. "If you were to set my words to music, turn it into one of your spellsongs, that might be enough for the counterspell to succeed. It's very close already. The fact that it did anything at all tells me that much. The missing component is you. Your feelings. Your magic."

"I'm not an ingredient," I told Sybilla hotly. "I'm a liability. It's too dangerous for me to compose Grandmagic."

"Are you certain it would be dangerous, even as a spellsong?" Grimm asked. "Have you ever tried?"

I turned to look at him in disbelief. "Not you too! How am I the only one in the room with a speck of caution?" The walls of the tower seemed somehow closer than they had been moments before. The whole building was shrinking around me. "You shouldn't be siding with her. You're the one most likely to get hurt, casting something of that nature with my fingerprints on it. It's not safe."

"Nothing we've done in pursuit of lifting the curse has been safe," Grimm argued. He took a step closer, looking at me with familiar suspicion, searching for the lie in my words, the trick, the joke. He hadn't looked at me in that way in a while, and it smarted a bit. "You're usually the first one to leap at a risky proposition. It doesn't make sense for you to back out now, unless there's something you're not telling us."

I took a step backward, but there was nowhere to go. Sybilla stood in front of the staircase and Grimm in front of the door. There was nothing but tower wall at my back. My limbs were shaky, and I wasn't sure if it was left over from the pain or caused by the look on Grimm's face.

"It's dangerous, what you're asking me to do," I whispered.

"I know that. I'm willing to try anyway. We can be alert, take precautions before casting," Grimm said.

I shook my head, not meeting Grimm's eyes. "You don't understand."

Grimm let out his breath in a huff of confused frustration.

"No, I don't. Why drag us all the way out here, past outlaws and monsters, only to dig your heels in now? Just tell me why you're being so stubborn about this!"

The sick feeling in the pit of my stomach vanished. It was replaced by a familiar calm. My limbs stopped shaking, suddenly light with purpose. Grimm wanted something, and of course I would give it to him. The thought made me happy, in a distant sort of way.

I said, "Because I wrote the Grandmagic that killed my mother, and I think it broke something inside of me, and I'm afraid I'll kill you too."

As soon as the order was obeyed, the blissful haze lifted, leaving me cold once more.

Grimm and Sybilla stood staring at me, twin expressions of horror frozen on their faces. The room was too small for my words to echo, but they lingered all the same.

"Well," I said. "Now you know."

Sybilla made no move to stop me when I tried to walk past, but Grimm reached out and caught my wrist.

"I'm sorry," he said, eyes agonized. "I didn't mean to—"

"Don't you dare touch me." The words were spoken with such venom that I barely recognized the voice as my own. Grimm let go instantly. As though my command had the weight of magic behind it.

Then I did what I should have done as soon as I'd felt the trap beginning to close and made my escape, stepping out of the tower and into the night.

CHAPTER TWENTY-FOUR

Everything had gone to shit. I should have known better than to be surprised by something blowing up in my face, but I was. The shock was so strong I felt sick with it.

I stumbled away from the tower as fast as I could, only pausing when Sybilla's birch tree barrier appeared in front of me. Their bark was a subtle glow in the dark, pale and moon soft, and beyond their slender trunks the rest of the forest loomed large.

The temptation to keep walking was strong. Doubtless there was some monster lurking nearby who would use tooth and claw to make all of me match—it had always seemed strange, how much agony could remain invisible—but in the end I didn't step beyond the circle's protection. Maybe it was some scrap of self-preservation kicking in, but more likely it was just the curse, making me reluctant to travel farther from Grimm. Even my misery was subject to his whims.

Sinking to the grass, I leaned forward and rested my head on my knees. My breath was shallow and quick, like my ribs couldn't fully expand. Every time I swallowed, I felt like I was holding something back. There was no music, or drink, or company to wash the panic away. There was only me and the memories flashing across the backs of my eyelids.

I wrote the Grandmagic that killed my mother.

The night was cold. I opened my eyes and tried to focus on the bite in the air, the discomfort of it. When that was not enough, I ran my hands through my hair and down to the back of my neck, pressing my nails in until I felt the sting. The pain gave me something to latch on to, like a drowning man might cling to a rope.

In the midst of this, the steady ache of the curse began to ebb. Then came footsteps, wandering this way and that—Grimm, looking for me in the dark.

He searched for some time, calling out my name in a hushed voice. I didn't answer. I wanted him a thousand miles away, even if it made me ill. But the circle around the tower was not large, and eventually the footsteps stopped short in front of me.

I did not look up. Doubtless it was too dark for me to read his face even if I had, but I was afraid that the horror I'd seen inside was still painted there.

Grimm let out a sigh. "Loveage," he began.

"Don't apologize again," I said sharply. "I swear if you do, I'll get up and walk into the woods and let myself get eaten by the first monster I find. And you may not miss me, and in fact it might solve many of your current problems, but I know you, and your conscience couldn't bear being responsible for something like that. So keep your apologies to yourself."

"All right," Grimm said. I'd hoped he would leave, but instead he sat down only an arm's length away. "Would you like to talk about it?"

"Why on earth would *i* want that?" I asked, astonished.

"Because a moment ago, all I said was your name and you spat back a whole monologue. You like to talk. And it can be helpful, sometimes. To speak things aloud. I don't know the details of what happened, but—"

"You're right. You don't."

"I would if you told me."

The nerve of him. To force a confession from me and then offer this. If I were going to lay my troubles at anyone's feet, it would not be Sebastian Grimm's, with his uncompromising morals and unsympathetic gaze.

And yet.

It was not sympathy I wanted. If this had been the case, I would have told Agnes, whose warmth and caring for me knew no bounds. This was Grimm, who already thought the worst of me anyway, most of the time. At least his opinion wouldn't have as far to sink. And, gallingly, he was right. The urge to explain myself was simmering under my skin. I'd never told this story. To anyone.

I found myself poised on a precipice, breath held and palms tingling. Then I began to speak.

"I was obsessed with Grandmagic as a child." I shot a sideways look at Grimm. "It might be hard for you to imagine now, but I was quite good at it back then. I wanted to be better, though. The best. I set my sights on healing spells, because those seemed the most likely to get me attention if I succeeded. I spent hours in the library, poring over every successful version of one. Why it worked, theories on why they were so hard to replicate. It was a puzzle, and I liked puzzles. I thought I was good at them. You think me insufferable now, but I was *shockingly* arrogant then. I'd never failed at anything, you see. I thought myself invincible. Then my mother was poisoned."

Rainer and I had been there when it happened, sparring in the garden. "Don't you dare trample my peonies," mother had shouted, but she'd been laughing. The next minute, she was falling, all her assembled blooms scattered around her. When Rainer and I came running, she made an agonized sound, one flower crushed close to her chest, as though she was trying to keep it hidden from us. It looked just like all the rest, an ordinary peony, save for the cut stem, which wept purple. That's what made masquerade flowers so dangerous—they were mimics, copying whatever plant they grew beside down to the tiniest outward detail, but the amethyst sap that ran through them was poison to the touch. Death disguised by beauty.

"We called for our father, and a doctor. Got her into the house." That part had been awful. Rainer was older and had taken most of the weight on himself, but I'd had to carry her legs so they wouldn't drag. Her eyes had been open but glassy, unseeing. "The doctor said her body would either fight the poison or succumb to it over the following days. That there was no cure except her own strength prevailing. Perhaps that would have been enough—my mother was very strong—but she never had a chance. I wrote a spell that night and got Rainer to cast it. He thought he was just humoring me, but the next morning our mother got out of bed like nothing had happened. I was so pleased. Not just that she was well, but that I'd been *right*. That *I* was the one who had cured her. She collapsed at the breakfast table later that morning. Gone."

A jar of peach jam had fallen from the table and smashed on the floor. There was so much about that morning that had become a blur, but I remembered that. The smell of it. I still couldn't look at a peach without feeling sick, never mind eating one. I started telling everyone I was allergic, and Rainer looked on knowingly but never said a word.

Grimm stirred beside me, calling me back to the present. "Failing to save someone is not the same thing as killing them."

I shook my head slowly. "My brother told me that too. He didn't understand. Neither did I, at first. But then I went back to look at the spell. I wanted to know why it hadn't worked. That's when I realized my mistake. I hadn't healed her at all. I'd only condensed the time she had left. The doctor said she needed to be strong, so I gathered all her strength and poured it into a handful of hours—not even a day's worth of time. Once it was used up, she had nothing left to fight with. The poison blazed through her and burned her up in an instant. My spell. My mistake. My fault, Grimm." I stretched my lips in a mockery of a smile. "Is this the part where I feel better, now that I've confessed? Or is this the part where you regret not turning me over to the Coterie when you had the chance?"

Grimm let out his breath in a huff. It was the same sound he made when annoyed, only much softer. "I don't know what will make you feel better. But you were a child who wanted to use your power to help and it went horribly, horribly wrong. You don't deserve to suffer for that."

This was edging uncomfortably close to pity for my taste. I wrapped the fingers of my right hand around my opposite wrist, clutching so tight I could feel where the bones ground together. Right over the spot where my father's hand had circled after I told him what I'd done.

"I know you feel guilty right now, Grimm, but you're wasting an opportunity to tell me I was wrong and careless and have me actually *agree with you*. The magic agrees with you too. It saw what I did and decided to punish me accordingly. That's why my scriving is the way it is. I've borne that judgment all these years, I think I can bear yours as well."

"Is that why you decided to tell me?" Grimm asked. "Because you thought I would condemn you?"

"I thought you would tell me the truth," I said. "Not give in to sympathy when it's undeserved."

Grimm leaned forward a little to study my face in the dark. He looked unhappy. Shadows gathered in the frown lines on his forehead, settling between his eyes.

"Fine," he said at last. "Here is the truth, though I don't think it's actually what you want to hear. You're wrong, Loveage. Magic thrives on intent, not judgment. You're punishing *yourself.* You're the one who believes you will cause harm. The magic is only listening to what you tell it."

If he had hit me, I don't think I could have been more shocked. "You think I'm doing it on *purpose?*"

Grimm shook his head impatiently. "No. I think you were afraid of hurting anyone with Grandmagic again, so you gave yourself a reason not to use it at all."

"That's ridiculous," I scoffed. "Utter garbage. You're not even a scriver; what do you know about it? You just turn on a faucet and let the magic flow through you."

Grimm raised one brow. "Shall we go ask Sybilla what she thinks about my theory?"

"No," I said quickly. Then, more quietly, "Not tonight. I'm tired."

I really was. A bone-deep sort of tiredness that would have made me want to curl up in the grass and fall asleep, if only I weren't so afraid of what I would see once my eyes were closed.

"Will you come inside?" Grimm asked. "It's very cold out here."

That was it, I realized. He had nothing more to say. I had laid bare the darkest, most wretched part of myself, and Grimm was still asking me to walk back to the tower with him in a matter-of-fact voice. As though there had never been any other possible conclusion.

My heart gave a painful thump.

I might have loved him for that, I thought, if I hadn't already loved him anyway. I did my best to tuck this thought away where it was safe from all the rest. This scrap of affection was mine. We got to our feet, brushing away grass and leaves. The ground floor of the tower was empty when we arrived, Sybilla having disappeared to one of the memory rooms. I was glad not to have to explain myself to her just now, though I was certain I would be forced to in the morning.

Grimm led the way up the stairs to our room. Opening the door, he glanced dismissively at my pile of blankets on the floor and told me to take the bed.

"It's your bed," I protested. "I'm sad, not an invalid."

Grimm's eyes narrowed. "I'm not giving it to you because you're sad, Loveage. I'm giving it to you because that spell we cast nearly knocked you out and you've been hobbling around ever since like you're one hundred years old."

The bed was obscenely comfortable. I wondered if it had been this soft in reality, or if it was Sybilla's memories that made the pillows fluffier and the blankets warmer. Despite all of this, and despite my exhaustion, I lay awake long after the candles had been extinguished, staring at the ceiling. I knew there was not enough wine or music in the world to stop bad dreams coming for me. It was all swirling around in my head, too close to the surface, just waiting for me to drift off.

I looked down at Grimm on the floor. His eyes were closed, but by now I was familiar with his sleeping face, and this was not it. When Grimm truly slept, his face went slack and oddly young, transformed by the lack of frown lines. It made me wonder what I looked like, when all my artifices were put to bed.

"Grimm," I whispered.

His eyes opened immediately. "What is it?"

"Will you do something for me?"

I watched him struggle over how to answer. He wanted to know what I was asking for before he agreed, but he had also upset the balance between us with his misstep earlier. I was shamelessly counting on that to earn me this favor.

Grimm was fair like that.

"All right," he said.

I licked my lips, full of both dread and desperate want.

"Tell me not to dream," I said. "I'm so tired, but I know the nightmares will come as soon as I fall asleep and I—I can't close my eyes. The only way I'll get any rest tonight is if I know I'm safe from them."

Grimm was quiet for a long time before answering. "Are you certain?"

"Yes."

"Wouldn't you rather I tell you to dream of happy things?"

"No," I said. "That's painful too."

Grimm shifted, blankets rustling as he rolled over so his whole body was facing me. We stayed that way for a moment, watching each other.

"Go to sleep, Leovander," he said at last. "Dream of nothing."

I shivered once at the sound of Grimm speaking my name, then the lull of obedience swept over me and I closed my eyes.

CHAPTER TWENTY-FIVE

The makeshift bed on the floor was gone when I woke the next morning, blankets folded and neatly placed on the chest they'd come from. When I shrugged my way out of the covers, I saw Grimm had his travel bag open, contents spread out on the rug.

"I'm compiling a list of things we should beg off of Sybilla," he said. "We'll need paper and ink, and a sword for you if she's got it. And food. We should also write out whatever spells we anticipate needing before we leave."

"Leave?" I echoed.

"There seems little point in staying now. Sybilla won't rewrite the counterspell unless..." I tensed, waiting for Grimm to suggest I write the counterspell as a song again, but he only shook his head slightly and said, "The trials are soon, anyway."

I flopped back onto the bed in despair and lay there while Grimm repacked his bag. His words from the night before worried at me.

Was it really possible the flaw in my scriving was as simple as he said? If that were the case, it made my refusal to cooperate seem silly. I should just do as Sybilla suggested and put her words to music. I could return to Miendor victorious, not only with the love spell lifted but as a transformed man. One whose magic wasn't fractured.

"I can't write the counterspell," I said, speaking to Grimm but addressing the ceiling above me. "I just can't."

Won't, a little voice inside my head whispered.

"I didn't ask you to," Grimm said. "We should go down for breakfast. I still have a few finishing touches to put on Sybilla's barrier spell before we go, and I'd like to get an early start."

I left off my sulking to follow Grimm to the morning parlor, since the alternative of waiting until he got far enough away that I was *compelled* to leave was not appealing.

That was another thing bothering me. Grimm knew to keep fairly close, but he didn't know how badly the curse had started to chafe even if he was just out of sight. He certainly didn't know about the other ways in which it had progressed. How would I survive back at the Fount, where we were always expected to be in different places? Worse, eventually he would notice the shift in my feelings toward him, and then we would have to have a terribly awkward conversation.

Or you could try to write the counterspell right now and be done with all of this, the little voice suggested.

My mood was very sour by the time we entered the morning parlor. Sybilla waited for us there, dressed in stunning blue velvet, teacup balanced on her lap. I froze halfway through the door, remembering that the last time she'd seen me, I had announced myself a killer and then fled the tower. That seemed the sort of thing that most people would want an explanation for.

Sybilla smiled at me. "You look chipper, Leo. Did you sleep well?"

I relaxed slightly and stepped fully into the room. "Well enough." I carefully avoided looking at Grimm. The sleep had been much needed, and I wasn't sorry I'd asked, but it made me shudder a little, to think of how thoroughly under Grimm's power I'd fallen.

The cozy parlor felt very at odds with both my mood and the state of things, with its soothing, soft green walls and the smell of tea and blackberry jam wafting appealingly through the air. I settled into one of the plush chairs, grabbed a piece of buttered toast, and then said to Sybilla, "So Grimm here thinks the reason my Grandmagic spells backfire is because I've got a guilty conscience that insists on my eternal suffering. What do *you* think?"

I took a bite of the toast and raised my eyebrows at her inquiringly as I chewed.

"I don't believe those were my exact words," Grimm said, after a long pause.

I waved my toast at him. "I'm paraphrasing your sentiment."

Sybilla sipped her tea calmly, then set the cup back in its saucer. "It's a good hypothesis."

"Can you fix it?"

She looked at me levelly. "My dear, you already know the answer. Only you can fix this, if indeed it's something that needs fixing at all. Weren't you just recently telling me how well suited you were to small magics? If that's what makes you happy..."

"None of this makes me happy." I flung my toast back on the plate. "How can I stop doing something that I don't even know I'm doing in the first place? It's not like I'm sabotaging myself on purpose. The feelings are just *there*."

They took up so much space inside of me that it was sometimes hard to find room for anything else. If I could have, I would have drawn them from my body, the same way Grimm had drawn silver rot from that field, and poured them into a stone or a piece of glass. Something I could pick up and hold when I had the strength, worrying away at the edges until they were worn down to something smooth and manageable.

But I couldn't. They were mine. Too tangled up in what I had become to ever be extricated. Feelings were a curse in that way.

I sat bolt upright in my chair. "I have an idea."

"For what?" Grimm asked, sounding deeply apprehensive.

There was no trick to removing the broken parts of myself. They could only be lived with, not dismantled. But the love spell was different. It was magic, other, just as the silver rot living in the soil had been.

"What if we don't need to destroy the curse? What if we just need to *move* it?"

Sybilla flat-out refused to let us try siphoning the curse from my body and into any of her possessions.

"You know how magic eats through too-small containers," she said reprovingly. "I don't have anything that could hold Grandmagic long enough for it to be useful to us. Whatever I gave you would be ruined, and for what?"

This was hard to argue with. If spells were easy to bottle up inside any old thing, everyone would have a cupboard at home full of them. To store a spell, you needed an object of equal magical weight: scales or claws, feathers and teeth, anything that came from a particularly powerful monster. Those were the sorts of things strong enough to hold a Grandmagic spell, but they were so hard to get your hands on that hardly anyone bothered. Once you released the bound spell, the object would go up in smoke just like a piece of spell paper. One-time use. Not a good investment. Unless, like me, you only *needed* to use it once.

"I think your idea is interesting, Leo," Sybilla said, "but I'm not a collector. I don't have a spare dragon scale lying around for us to use."

"No matter," I said, waving a dismissive hand. "We don't need something that can actually hold the curse for long right now. This is just the test." I had an idea where we could get an item like that when the time came, but it wasn't a very good idea, and Grimm was going to hate it, so I wasn't about to bring it up until the last possible minute. For now, I just needed to prove the curse could be moved at all, even if we didn't have anything strong enough to ensure it stayed put.

Which was how I found myself emptying the pockets of my sorcerer's coat and laying it at Grimm's feet. It was by no means a powerful object, but it was made with spider silk, which I thought was significantly magical enough for my purposes.

We'd come back down to the ground floor so that Grimm could cast. The furniture was still all pushed back from our unsuccessful attempt the day before, and he eyed my coat doubtfully.

"The counterspell tried to destroy you right along with the curse," he said, sounding very dubious about the whole thing. "How is this any different?"

"Because we're not trying to destroy it at all, just transplant it, like we moved the silver rot from soil to sunflower. All those little curse roots, wrapped around my mind and vital organs, they just need something new to cling to. *Then* we can destroy it. Once it's safely stored inside a chimera claw or whatever, instead of me, we can cast the counterspell without my insides being rearranged. It's very clever, if I do say so myself."

I picked up my bow with a flourish, pleased. This was much less risky than experimenting with Grandmagic. I didn't care that Sybilla looked skeptical, or that Grimm was reluctant. This was a solution I could control.

It didn't take me long to adapt the spellsong that we'd sung in the field for our purposes. I ran through the new words once or twice, then looked expectantly at Grimm, eager to get on with things.

He looked at me and said sternly, "Please tell me if this causes symptoms that are similar to the counterspell in any way. Preferably before you start bleeding from your ears this time." Then he began to sing.

Beaugard had been idly observing our preparations from a spot by Sybilla's feet, but as soon as the spellsong was cast, he rose onto his haunches, ears pricked, watching us with the same focus that the little monsters who'd listened to our message casting had. He whined, low in his throat, then he threw his head back and howled. Grimm's eyes widened in surprise, but his voice didn't falter. Beau's accompaniment, oddly in tune, lent a sharp and eerie quality to the spellsong that our other attempts had lacked. The hum of magic increased.

I watched the coat where it lay on the ground, but it was hard to tell if anything was happening. The curse wasn't visible, after all, unlike the silver rot. By the time Grimm finally stopped singing, my sorcerer's coat appeared just as it always had. Beau offered one last howl and then fell quiet as well.

Did I feel any different? I lowered my violin, scanning myself for signs of a change. Nothing had hurt while the spell was being cast, and nothing felt any different now. But it had already been clearly established that I was not the most reliable source when it came to parsing such things.

"Try telling me to do something," I suggested, but before I could even finish speaking, my coat fell to pieces in front of us.

It went fast, all the thread practically leaping out of its seams, followed by the unraveling of fabric, until every bit of black cloth (and every spell that had been woven into it) was completely ruined and lying in a heap on the floor. And then, just to top things off, the sad pile of scraps began to smoke. A little lick of flame appeared and quickly grew.

As soon as the fire caught, my body was suffused with a familiar warmth. I hadn't felt the curse leave, but I knew enough now to recognize the signs of its return, racing through my veins like liquid sunlight. I coughed, more from the fire in my chest than the one Sybilla and Grimm were currently stamping out on the floor.

Once it was out, the three of us looked at one another.

"It worked," I said. "I'm sure of it. And I didn't feel a thing until it came back. No pain like there was with the counterspell. Not even a pinprick."

"That's all well and good," Sybilla said, pursing her lips thoughtfully, "but what will you use for a vessel? You've just seen that it won't be held by anything so trivial as spider silk. Even if we sacrificed another coat to the cause, you wouldn't have time to cast the counterspell before it went up in smoke and the curse hopped back to you."

This brought us to my second idea. The bad one. This topic would have to be broached delicately. In fact, it would be best if I wasn't the one to bring it up at all.

I looked at Sybilla hopefully. "Are you certain you don't have anything hidden away? The Unquiet Wood is full of monsters, and you've lived here for years. Surely you have some sort of collection after all this time?"

"I don't go poking around in the trees," Sybilla said firmly. "I have a good sense of self-preservation, unlike *some* people, which is how I've managed to live here as long as I have. I stay within my tower or travel with Beau for protection."

"But you must at least have some idea where Grimm and I could find one."

"Not the foggiest. You can't expect the type of thing you're looking for to be found lying willy-nilly on the forest floor. It takes time and dedication to uncover the secrets and treasures hidden in these trees, as well as a good bit of skill. The two of you aren't—" Sybilla stopped and looked at me sharply. "Oh, you clever thing," she said, under her breath so that I was the only one to hear.

"We're not what?" I asked, all innocence.

"Foragers," Sybilla said. "The two of you are not foragers."

"No," I said, appearing to give this some thought. Then, very slowly, feigning reluctance, I said, "We do know some foragers though."

Grimm's posture grew absolutely rigid. "They are outlaws, not foragers."

"Come now, they can be both," I said, then winced at how this only made his expression grow darker. "They have a griffin feather, Grimm. Jayne said as much. That's exactly the sort of item that would be powerful enough to hold the curse. We need to try."

"They nearly killed us," he spat. "Are you really suggesting that they would hand over what you want because you, what? Ask nicely for it?"

"Not at all! We can pay them for it. Remember, they weren't trying to kill *me* at all. They needed me to write spells for them. We know what they want and can use it to make a deal. It's not so different from the trade you've made with Sybilla," I said, pleased with what I thought a quite apt comparison.

"It's entirely different." Grimm stood up. His frustration was a palpable thing, gathering in the air like a storm cloud and threatening to blot out the parlor's cheerful ambience. "These people broke their oaths to the Coterie. They stole from the Fount. If we make a deal with them, we're no better. Who knows what damage they might cause with the spells you could give them."

"Oh, spare me your moral grandstanding," I snapped, the edges of my own patience beginning to fray. "They're hiding in the woods foraging for scraps, not planning another heist. The outlaws didn't try to kidnap us because they're villainous masterminds. They did it because they were desperate. We have that in common, and we can use it to our advantage."

This was entirely the wrong thing to say, and I knew it as soon as the words left my mouth. It was too outrageous. Too self-serving. Too much of everything that had always made Grimm dislike me. I had expected the danger involved in my plan to be the biggest point of contention, but I had overlooked this more obvious barrier, the thing that always put us at odds: Grimm abhorred a rule breaker. He had principles. He saw the world in black and white, conveniently disdaining anything that fell into an area of gray.

Grimm tilted his chin up and stared down his nose at me, eyes cold. "You might be desperate enough to stoop to their level, but I am not. I will not be complicit in such a plan."

Before I could say anything else, he stormed out of the tower in a flurry of dark coat and offended dignity. The door slammed shut behind him.

As soon as he was gone, a hollow ache spread through my rib cage, pulsing in time with the beating of my heart.

I sighed and threw myself onto one of the sofas, staring gloomily at the shut door. "That went about as well as trying to give a cat a bath. How long do you think I should give him to brood before trying to talk him round?"

Sybilla sat down opposite me, folded her hands primly in her lap, and said, "I think you're being a little unfair, Leo."

"Me?" I said, outraged. "The curse is getting stronger by the hour. He hasn't been gone from this room a full minute yet and I already feel like a prize fish fighting against someone's line. And when he *is* in front of me, I'm not sure if I want to kiss him, or kill him, or just go someplace very quiet with him and ask if I could be allowed to pet his stupid, lovely hair. It's awful, Sybilla! Awful! And now I've come up with a brilliant solution to all our problems and he won't even pretend to consider it. *He's* the one being unfair."

If Sybilla was impressed in the slightest by my outburst, she didn't show it. "You should tell him the curse is getting stronger. How can you expect him to make the right decision when he doesn't have all the information?"

This was a very reasonable thing to point out. It was also not even a little bit what I wanted to hear. I shot Sybilla my most aggrieved look so she would know how betrayed I felt. Then, as she had probably known would happen, I got up and went after Grimm.

I expected to find him taking out his frustration by casting the rest of Sybilla's barrier, but instead the insistent tug of the curse led me around the eastern side of the tower, where I spotted him standing in a patch of sun, hands empty of spells. His expression was still thunderous and only grew more so as I approached.

I leaned my back against the sun-warmed stone of the tower beside Grimm and let him glower at me while I thought of what to say. It was rare that I needed such a pause, but I found that every persuasive argument I'd silently rehearsed on my way here had evaporated from my mind. The only thing left was Sybilla's voice in my mind saying, *You should tell him.*

Never mind, I decided. I didn't need rehearsal to argue with Grimm. I was naturally gifted in that arena.

"You wouldn't have to get your hands dirty, you know," I said, breaking the silence. "I would be the one writing the spells for them. It would be my crime; you just have to be... nearby."

Grimm rounded on me, eyes flashing. "How will that work, exactly, when you can barely remember a basic heating charm? There's no way your little plan works without me whispering the words you need in your ear, just like there's no way any of your plans so far could have functioned without me. But this is where I draw the line. I won't work with oath breakers."

The thought of Grimm whispering anything in my ear was mildly distracting, but the accusation that I needed him was too vexing for me to be diverted.

"I function just fine on my own," I snapped. "Or at least I did, until you cursed me. I don't think it's so terribly unreasonable that you learn to compromise for the sake of its removal. Why must you be so unyielding about this?"

"All I have done for weeks is yield!" Grimm did not shout, but there was something wild in his voice. As though his restraint was worn down to its last threads. We were within striking distance, I noted with a thrill, and Grimm's hands were already clenched into fists.

"I have gone along with every one of your ridiculous ideas, Loveage. I let you convince me to cross into the Wilderlands, even though I knew, *I knew* it would be dangerous. I thought hiring Jayne was a bad idea, but I went along with that too, and didn't even rub your face in it when she turned on us. Every day spent in this tower, indulging Sybilla's whims, has inched us closer to missing the trials, but I agreed to stay because *you* insisted she was our only chance at lifting the curse. But none of your plans have worked, Loveage! And this one is beyond my forbearance. I will not align myself with criminals. If that makes me unyielding, so be it."

"Poor Grimm," I sneered, pushing off the tower to stand in front of him, so that I could watch each of my words land. "How difficult it must have been for you, not being able to just follow the Fount's rules and instead having to follow me, with all my flaws. It makes sense why you want to join the Coterie—you'd much rather be told what to do, what to say, how to be good, rather than acknowledge that real life is full of imperfect decisions and mistakes with no lessons at the end of them. It's disappointing. I'd nearly forgotten how dull you can be."

Something flashed across Grimm's face. Some flicker of emotion other than anger. But it was gone too quickly to be named.

"I would rather be considered dull than reckless," he said.

"Well, I'd rather be considered reckless than spend the rest of my life cursed!"

"You're being overdramatic."

"I'm not!"

"You are. Why can't you just summon a speck of patience and come up with a different solution, rather than throw us into another impossible situation?"

"Because of this, you idiot!" I shouted, and then I took his face in my hands and kissed him.

I've often thought that kissing is a little like composing a spell. There are certain components that simply must be considered, and behind all of that, an unmistakable intent. But this was a different kind of magic altogether. The unthought-of, unlooked-for kind that swept over you in a rush, uncontrollable.

Grimm let out a muffled noise of surprise as our faces crowded together, and I had just enough presence of mind to catch the back of his head so it didn't hit the stone of the tower. My other hand twisted in his coat, holding on. I tilted my head and let our lips press unerringly together and thought, *There will be no recovering from this.*

My fingers slid down to rest on the back of Grimm's neck and he went completely still, except for the rabbit-fast pounding of his pulse under my thumb. It was too much for a first, I knew that, but we had never been anything but too much for each other. It was fitting then, that there was no poetry to the rough press of our mouths, just an outpouring of answers.

I drew back, resting my forehead against Grimm's, eyes screwed shut as I spoke.

"Do you know, I think this love spell is a little bit like being wounded, only spread out over days. Each morning I wake up and it's a little worse. It's happening so slowly that sometimes I forget and it doesn't even feel like a curse at all."

Dropping my hands, I moved back, putting a proper amount of space between us. Only then did I dare open my eyes.

Grimm looked stricken. As though I had stabbed him in the stomach instead of kissing him. His eyes were very dark.

"How long has it been like this?" he asked.

"Not long. I didn't lie to you before, you know. I really didn't notice to begin with. But it's getting worse. All of it. Every time you're out of sight now it feels like my nerves are on fire. I'm afraid it will be even worse by the time we're back at the Fount. That's why I wanted to go to the outlaws. I'm afraid that if we wait..." I was afraid that if we waited, I wouldn't want to fix this at all. That the last line of the curse would take effect and I would lose myself. "It will be too late," I finished.

Grimm was quiet, taking all of this in as he stared at the empty patch of grass between our feet. I wondered if I should apologize for the kiss, or if that would only make things worse.

"All right," Grimm said.

"All right, what?"

"We will get what we need for the spellsong."

"From the outlaws?" I asked, just to be certain.

Grimm nodded, looking deeply unhappy about it. Or perhaps just unhappy about everything that had happened in the past five minutes or so. "The curse cannot be allowed to worsen."

Something within me twinged, a discordant note. Between the thought of dealing with Jayne and risking my affection, Grimm would choose Jayne. It was hilarious, in the most unflattering sense, which was why my chest must have ached. From all the withheld laughter.

"Oh, Grimm," I said, curling my lips in a smile. "Who knew your mind would be so easily changed by a kiss? This is a method I obviously should have employed before."

"Your explanation changed my mind," Grimm said. "Not your—" He faltered.

"Mouth?" I suggested.

"Actions!" His face was pale as ever, but the tips of his ears were crimson. "If you'd just told me in the first place, there would have been no need to waste time with such dramatics."

"Ah, but you know me." I raised my hands, clasping them to my chest. "I'm a dramatic creature. I always find a way. And now that the air is clearer, hearts lightened, illusions shattered, et cetera, we can focus on what must be done without distraction. I feel better, don't you feel better?"

Grimm looked at me. The same searching look he'd turned on me before granting my wish for sleep. He sought to find hidden meaning to my words splashed across my face, but whatever he found there did not seem to provide any answers. "I feel tired," he said shortly. Then he turned his back on me and began to walk in the direction of the tower door. "Let's get this over with," I heard him mutter before he disappeared from sight.

CHAPTER TWENTY-SIX

Sybilla gave us paper from her stores and replaced my water-logged ink. She gave us food from her kitchen, and a sword that had previously hung as decoration in the bedroom I never slept in, and a bottle of wine to offer the outlaws. Because, as she said, "It's harder for someone to feel justified in killing you if you offer them a gift first."

I wasn't sure if this logic would work on Mathias (he didn't seem the type to be won over by hostess gifts), but wine wasn't something I ever refused. It went in my bag.

Sybilla also gave us Beaugard. Not to keep, of course, but because the wolf was the only one of us who knew where in the forest the outlaws made their home. She knelt down in front of Beau before we left, hands buried in the thick fur around his neck, and stared deeply into his eyes. I would have started to feel a little seasick, peering into those swirling silver depths, but Sybilla stayed like that for several minutes before getting to her feet and patting the wolf's head in a satisfied manner.

"Are you certain he'll know where to go?" I asked doubtfully.

"Beau and I understand each other," Sybilla said. "How do you think I told him to find you in the first place? Now, I know your pockets are already well stocked, but I have one more thing for each of you." She reached into her coat and drew out a sealed envelope, which she handed to Grimm. "This will be better than the standard nausea spells in a first aid kit. I wrote it specifically to quell the side effects of traveling with Beau, so you don't arrive at the outlaw camp as green as the trees."

Grimm looked faintly embarrassed but took the envelope. "Thank you."

Next, Sybilla retrieved a wrapped bundle that had been left sitting on one of the sofas and handed it to me. Upon unfolding the brown paper, I discovered a freshly pressed scriver's sash and a sorcerer's coat. It was only identifiable by the many pockets, for the fabric was a deep emerald green rather than the traditional black.

"I had this commissioned many years ago," Sybilla said, "when I thought green was my color. A serious lapse in judgment on my part, but it might as well be to someone's benefit. Go ahead, try it on."

I was doubtful that something meant to fit Sybilla's small stature would work for me, but in this I was proven delightfully wrong, for the coat shifted as soon as I swung it over my shoulders, lengthening to fit my longer torso and arms.

"I may have added a few of my own notions to the design," Sybilla said with a wink. "It suits you."

"Thank you," I told her sincerely. "I'll do my best not to destroy this one, I promise."

"Pshh, I'm not your keeper! What happens to you beyond this tower is no concern of mine."

"You'll miss me, admit it."

She looked at me archly. "Believe it or not, I have forms of entertainment other than you. There are doors in this tower you have yet to see, and they don't all lead to empty memories, or memories at all. If you ever decide to come back and visit, perhaps I will show them to you."

"I'd like that," I said, and found that it was true. Someday, I could see myself calling on the tower again for no reason other than Sybilla's company. I thought I should like to be here without the threat of the curse hanging over my head, free to explore the mysteries of the tower.

"Come now," Sybilla said, eyes twinkling. "Give me a kiss goodbye."

I leaned down and kissed her cheek. As I did, she whispered in my ear, "I hope someday to meet a version of Leovander Loveage who doesn't believe everyone else's well-being is dependent on what he denies himself. Come back to me, when that's the case, and we will craft magic to make the world weep with delight."

I drew back without replying, and Sybilla turned to Grimm. She shook his hand quite properly, but then, much to my surprise, she leaned forward and whispered something in his ear as well. I was intensely curious to know what was said, but Grimm's expression gave nothing away.

"Farewell to you both," Sybilla said, before ushering Beaugard forward to stand between us.

Beau tilted his head to look up at me, tongue lolling. For the first time I spared a moment to think about the fact that we were returning not just to the outlaws but to the forest itself, whose strangeness we had only scratched the surface of. The monsters out there were not all like Beau, happy to do our bidding.

"Changed your mind?" Grimm asked in a low voice.

Pushing my unease aside, I laid my hand firmly on Beau's furry head. "Of course not. This is our way forward, I'm certain of it."

I thought Grimm might say something else. It looked as though he wanted to. But then he bowed his head and rested his hand beside mine.

This was Grimm yielding, I thought, just as the world re-arranged itself.

The first thing to come back into being was the ever-present wan green glow of the forest.

We stood underneath the low-hanging boughs of sap trees, their drying needles scattered on the ground beneath our feet, quieting our steps. The air smelled like resin, familiar, but sweeter and sharper than the rosin in my pocket. To our left, the trees thinned enough to allow glimpses of patchy gray sky. To our right, the trees remained thick, but a faint path wound its way through them. It looked like someone had made a half-hearted effort to sweep needles back over the dirt, and this more than the path itself told me it was made by human feet.

"Good job, Beau," I said, and patted the wolf's head.

Beside me, Grimm reached hastily into his pocket for the envelope Sybilla had given him. He was not quick enough to avoid throwing up his breakfast behind the closest tree, but smoke rose from his hands soon after. By the time Grimm turned back around, the casting had taken effect, wiping away the misery from his face. He was only a little pale now, instead of outright sallow.

"If we're close, someone may have heard the sound of our arrival," he said. "We should be quick."

I stood still as Grimm cast a spell over my new coat to deflect attacks. This sort of magic was normally used over armor, not simple fabric, but when Grimm tossed a stone at me, it bounced off my sleeve without me feeling the impact. I doubted it would turn aside a blade, but it was better than nothing. Grimm cast the same spell over his own coat, then a different one over our swords to prevent them being taken from us by force. After that, he folded more spells and tucked them between the fingers of his left hand, ready to be used at an instant's notice.

Once all this was done, Grimm knelt down in front of Beau, who had sat back on his haunches to watch our preparations with interest.

"Time for you to go home," Grimm said.

The wolf whined, low in his throat. He lifted one giant paw and rested it briefly on Grimm's knee. Then there was one last *pop*, and we were alone. The forest seemed to press closer around us.

"Let's go," I said, and started for the path. Better we find the outlaw camp before I lost my nerve.

Grimm kept his sword drawn as we walked the path, but I left mine sheathed. My battle was to be fought with words, and if I did my job well, both the steel and the magic Grimm held would be unnecessary.

After about five minutes of walking, the trees around us shifted from the tall, rough-barked pines to a grove of red-leaved trees with dark gray trunks. Normally the sight of brightly colored branches would have been cheerful, but like most things in the Unquiet Wood, the effect was skewed somehow. The fluttering leaves were the scarlet of fresh blood, and the trees held on to them greedily, so that the ground we walked upon was undecorated except for ropy roots that buckled the soil here and there. The light beneath the branches washed everything in somber, uncanny mauve.

Grimm held up a hand to catch my attention, then pointed

his sword at a thin black line, running along the ground ahead of us, charred into the dirt.

A perimeter alarm.

I'd seen this spell before, during my time training with the Coterie. It would not stop anything passing through it, but its caster would hear a warning bell in their mind if anything—human, monster, or animal—crossed over the line.

Grimm frowned at the line of soot by his feet. "I would prefer to get one or two of them alone first, to explain ourselves."

"We could wait here all day for one of them to emerge," I whispered back. "Perhaps it's better to get this over with quickly. What do you say, Grimm?" I winked. "Shall we make an entrance?"

Grimm glanced up at the sliver of sky visible above us. It was already well into the day, and night fell quickly here. He took a moment to adjust the spells in his hand, moving one so that it was pinched ready between his thumb and forefinger. Then he nodded to me.

Heart in my throat, I plunged over the line.

Speed was more important than subtlety now, so we both began to run. Ahead of us, I heard the first shout of alarm, and Grimm, who had been keeping pace with me, lunged ahead, so that he was the one in front as we broke free of the trees and into a light-filled clearing.

A strange sight greeted us. The outlaws had made their camp up against a sheer rock face that rose up almost as high as the trees. Against that they had built a series of ramshackle platforms with ladders running up to them. Tents were pitched on these platforms, with makeshift plank bridges interconnecting them. Other signs of habitation were scattered around the clearing: a firepit with coals still glowing at its center, laundry hanging on a line strung between two platform supports, and (surprisingly) an upturned patch of earth that looked to be someone's attempt at the world's saddest garden.

I didn't have time to notice anything else before the outlaws came for us. There were at least three of them, and they'd clearly all stopped whatever they were doing the instant the alarm had been called in order to pick up the nearest sharp object.

Four of them, I amended, as an arrow came flying at us from one of the upper platforms.

Coterie members (even rogue ones) are not known for their lack of precision. The arrow was aimed at Grimm's chest and would have hit there, were it not for the already smoking spell in Grimm's hand. Instead of piercing his heart, the arrow bounced off the air directly in front of him and fell to the ground, harmless. But shielding spells were difficult to maintain.

"Hold your fire!" I flung my hands up to show the advancing outlaws I held no weapon. "We mean you no harm. We've come to talk to Jayne."

Another arrow bounced off our shield, and Grimm sucked in a sharp breath and began to cast out loud, a sure sign of strain. I looked up in time to catch sight of the archer, just a dark shape peeking out from one of the tents above. When I looked back down, two of the outlaws on the ground were a few feet away from us, swords drawn.

"Who are you?" the taller of the two asked. "How did you get here?" Her eyes were wide with alarm.

"We're looking for Jayne," I said again, then winced as another arrow hit the shield. Grimm gritted his teeth and spoke a little louder, the spell in his hand billowing black smoke.

"Please," I said desperately. "Call off your archer so we can talk. I've come to make a deal with Jayne. If I could just talk with her, I'm sure we can come to a mutually beneficial arrangement that doesn't involve us turning into pincushions, or you being on the receiving end of the other spells my friend here has tucked away in his hand."

Grimm held nothing but defensive spells, but *they* didn't need to know that.

"Also, we have wine!" I pulled the bottle Sybilla had given us out of my bag and then rolled it on the ground toward the outlaws, who looked at it with apparent confusion.

A fourth arrow rained down to poke another hole in Grimm's shield, so that didn't bode well for Sybilla's gift theory.

Without giving myself too much time to think about it, I stepped forward. If it was Mathias shooting (as I suspected), my red sash might make him pause—I was the one he and Jayne had wanted, after all—but before another arrow could be either loosed or held, someone broke through the trees on our right.

Sunlight flashed off golden hair and naked steel, a green cloak billowed, and then Jayne was shouting, "Hold!" She arrived in front of us slightly breathless, did a double take upon seeing Grimm and me, and said, "You're alive. I was certain the river claimed you."

Grimm chose that moment to let the first shield spell fall to ash and began casting the next one. His muttering in the old language continued behind me, comforting in its steadiness.

"Nearly." I glanced pointedly up to Mathias (for it was him), who had emerged from his hiding spot in one of the tents and stood at the edge of the platform looking down at us, expression stony. "This certainly didn't help matters." I shook back the sleeve of my coat to show Jayne my arm. The wound there had begun to heal during our time in the tower, but it would undoubtedly scar.

She had either enough grace or enough guile to look chagrined. "That was a mistake." Just as I had placed myself in front
of Grimm, Jayne angled herself so that the three outlaws on the
ground were behind her. Her sword was not raised, but her free
hand was in her pocket, almost certainly clutching a spell. "What
do you want, Leovander Loveage? For I don't think it's a coin-
cidence that our paths have crossed twice. We are not so easy to
find as all that."

Mathias was making his way down the ladder, crossbow
slung across his back. Somehow the thought of him coming
within speaking distance made me even more nervous than the
thought of him shooting at us from afar.

"The feather," I blurted, urgency making me blunt. "When
we first met, you said you were in possession of a griffin feather.
We have need of one. Do you still have it?"

"We might," Jayne said calmly, just as her brother reached
her side. "But why would we give such an item to you? Do you
have something to offer in return?" Jayne nudged the slightly
muddy bottle of wine with her boot tip. "Something *useful*."

I spread my arms wide, addressing not only Jayne but the
wary people at her back. "Myself. You said you wanted spells
written, well here I am, a scriver at your service. Give us what
we need, and in return I will scrive whatever magic you lack.
Provided it is not something that could be used to harm others," I added hastily. Grimm had been very clear on that point.
We would not supply the words to any spells that might be used
against the people of Miendor.

"I asked for your help before," Jayne said, hand still in her
pocket. "You threw yourself into the river rather than deal
with—what did you call us? Oh yes, thieves and oath breakers."

"Grimm's words, not mine," I said. "But I think he can be

forgiven, since at the time you were threatening his life. 'We don't need both of them,' wasn't that what your brother said?"

Mathias didn't so much as blink at the reminder, but Jayne's eyebrows shot upward. "You thought we were going to kill him?"

I hesitated. "At the time I did, yes. You must admit, the words had a distinct murdery feel to them."

Jayne took her hand from her pocket. I'd been right, she was holding a spell, but it wasn't smoking yet. She held it up for me to see. "It's a memory spell. We've had cause to use them a few times since setting up camp here, as a means of protection. We sent the other foragers who stumbled upon this place on their way none the wiser. *That* was what I was going to use on your friend." Jayne sighed and stuffed the spell away again. "I doubt it would work on either of you now, though. Memory spells are tricky to begin with, and you've had days to cement our encounter in your mind. How did you find our camp, anyway?"

"We had some help," I admitted. "From the sorcerer."

Jayne's eyes widened. "So you found her. And won her aid. Impressive. Yet you still came looking for us."

"The sorcerer isn't a forager. She couldn't give us everything we needed. Can you?"

Jayne didn't reply right away. We stood facing one another, and the only sound was Grimm's voice, little more than a hoarse whisper. The smoke around us was lesser than it had been before, as the strength of the spell faded. I tried to remember how many shield spells I had scrived and could not.

"We would need to agree on some strict terms," Jayne said eventually. "Not just for the exchange but what would happen after. We can't allow stories of our presence here to leak back into Miendor. But..."

"Jayne," Mathias said in a low voice, clearly unhappy with the direction this was going. "That feather is worth more than we could forage in a year."

"And ten times as difficult to sell without attracting notice," Jayne said, a touch of impatience creeping into her tone. "We need to be practical, Matt. It's not only up to me, of course, but I think we need the spells more than we need the coin."

She looked pointedly to the other members of the troop, who in turn exchanged glances with one another.

"I would like some spells for the garden," the man admitted. "There are charms that would keep pests away."

"Never mind your garden!" the tall woman said. "We need protection bubbles and alarm cantrips. Not to mention first aid spells, and enough heating charms to get us through the winter here without freezing."

These weren't at all the sorts of spells I'd been worried they might ask for, which was a relief. Even Grimm would have a hard time arguing that charms to keep tents warm or discourage pests were the sort of things that could be used for violence or grand larceny.

Jayne turned back to us, smiling slightly. "As you can see, our needs are varied, but we can supply a list. Write the spells we ask for, as well as a magical contract stating you won't speak a word of us after you cross back over the border, and the feather is yours."

At her side, Mathias briefly closed his eyes in defeat. When he opened them, his face wore an expression of long-suffering resignation. I wondered if, in every duo, there was one person more likely to plunge ahead, tugging the second in their wake like flotsam.

Jayne held out her hand, fingertips coming up short against the edge of our shield. "Do we have a deal?"

I glanced back and nodded to Grimm. He began to taper his casting off slowly, clearly reluctant to let the magic lapse, despite the strain. Once the smoke was fully cleared, I turned back around and took Jayne's hand without hesitation.

"I believe we do."

While Jayne disappeared into one of the tents to begin writing the spell list and Mathias glowered watchfully at us from a distance, the three remaining outlaws put away their weapons to fumble through introductions. The tall woman was Geraldine, and the short one with the round face was Camilla. The man so concerned about the garden was called Dodge. They seemed more nervous than unhappy with our presence, all uneasy silences and unreadable glances among themselves.

"A pleasure to meet you," I said, sweeping a half bow, as though we had met at a party, instead of while brandishing weapons at one another. "I am Leovander Loveage, and my traveling companion here is Sebastian Grimm." I looked around the camp with interest. "This is a very nice setup you've got."

Geraldine and Dodge looked a little suspicious of this, perhaps suspecting I was making fun of them, but Camilla brightened.

"We started building the platforms our first week here," she said, gesturing to the towering structure against the rocks. "The height doesn't keep all monsters away, of course, but it helps. They're interested in any scrap of unfamiliar magic, you see, and these tents have all sorts of charms woven into the fabric. At least with them up high, the beasties aren't as inclined to notice and come sniffing. Although, by now so many of the charms have worn off they might not care anymore. But we've got you to fix that!"

Camilla was the one to lead us up the rickety platform ladder to a tent. Staying the night hadn't been part of my original plan, but I couldn't see a way around it. The deal had been made, and I was quite certain Mathias wouldn't allow us out of his sight until we'd signed the contract ensuring our silence. There was an unsettling intensity to his gaze that made Grimm look positively cheerful by comparison, which was saying something.

Our tent was on the second level of platforms. It smelled a little musty ("Air freshening cantrips," Camilla muttered. "I'll have to make sure Jayne remembers to put those on the list.") and was clearly being used for storage, but there was enough room among the crates for me and Grimm to lay down our blankets. The ragged remains of whatever heating spell had been woven into the tent's fabric meant that the air was at least a little warmer, and a rather clever dimensional spell allowed both of us to stand upright while inside. The tent I'd been given while traveling with the Coterie the year before had been much the same, and it granted our strange surroundings a sense of familiarity.

"How did you get all of this up here?" I asked, nudging a crate with my boot.

"Pulley system," Camilla said promptly. "Mathias came up with it after Dodge nearly broke his neck trying to haul lumber for a bedframe up to his tent. We've come up with all sorts of ways to make living out here comfortable." She stopped and made a face. "Or at least we *were* fairly comfortable, until the heat spells on the tents started failing. Geraldine's started calling me a limpet on account of how close I cling at night, but I can't help it.

The blood just doesn't want to go to my fingers and toes when it gets cold. Oh! You're a musician?" Her eyes had lit up, fixed on my violin case.

"I am."

"It's been ever so long since we've had any music," she said wistfully. "Gerry has a lovely voice, and I used to have a penny whistle, but I think Dodge hid it somewhere. I miss..." Camilla let the words trail off, then looked back to us, flustered. "Never mind all that," she said quickly. "Find a place for your things and we can get back to the others. They probably have the fire going by now."

She looked expectantly at Grimm, who still held his pack.

"I will keep my things with me," he said.

He spoke without inflection, but the meaning was clear: He would not leave his belongings behind while we were among thieves.

Camilla's face fell. "Suit yourself," she said. "You can come down when you're ready."

She was nearly out of the tent when I called out, "Wait!"

I rifled through my pockets for quill and paper, then scribbled out a heating charm. I had to dig deep in my memory for a few words, but Grimm was glaring at me so hard I didn't dare ask him. I blew briefly on the wet ink and then handed the spell to Camilla.

"No doubt Jayne is asking for a stack of these," I said. "But no reason for you to suffer tonight."

A bit of the glow came back into her rounded cheeks. "Thank you," she said softly.

Once the tent flaps had closed behind her, I turned on Grimm.

"Must you conduct yourself in a way that entices people to

stab you in your sleep? I, the person who's sharing a tent with you, will be quite peeved if we're murdered simply because you couldn't be polite."

"We're not here to make friends," Grimm said sullenly.

"I'm not trying to make enemies either. If we're going to be stuck here for a day, we may as well try to be pleasant." I looked at Grimm, who stood scowling with one hand on the hilt of his sword and the other clenched at his side, and amended my words to "Civil, at the very least."

We ate around the fire that night, and if it was not a relaxed affair, at least most of the outlaws seemed to agree that it should not be entirely unfriendly either. The bottle of wine went a long way toward easing tensions, so maybe Sybilla hadn't been entirely wrong. By the time dusk faded into full night, we'd all settled into a wary sort of truce, except for Mathias and Grimm, who drank not a drop and sat on opposite sides of the fire wearing sour expressions, like twin bookends of disapproval.

Jayne had yet to emerge from her tent. I was beginning to wonder if I should have set a limit to the number of spells I was willing to scrive. How many spells was a feather worth, anyway? I hadn't thought to ask.

"Camilla says you play violin, Mr. Loveage," Geraldine said. She had a soft sort of voice, a little at odds with her towering frame.

"I do. Shall I fetch it? I'd be happy to play a few songs around the fire."

A flash of longing crossed Geraldine's face, but then she looked toward the tree line and shook her head. "Best not. It's better not to attract attention in the dark."

We had been spoiled by the magic of Sybilla's tower, forgetting that fear was an inherent part of nighttime in this place.

Now I was all too aware of how small a circle the firelight cast and the vast presence of the surrounding forest. The atmosphere grew tense and quiet once more. No one protested when Mathias said gruffly, "Put the fire out; we've let it burn longer than is wise already."

Jayne finally appeared as Dodge was escorting us back to our tent with a lantern. She carried with her a sizable stack of papers, which she offered to me.

"Your list. I wrote down the type of each spell required, as well as the quantity. I also took the privilege of outlining the terms of our contract, so you could begin writing that as well. And before you ask"—she reached into her pocket and withdrew something that glinted in the flickering light of the torch—"I thought you might like to see what your work is purchasing."

The feather lay across Jayne's palm, a marvel of delicately wrought gold.

"It's metal," I said, and my voice came out hushed.

"It transforms once shed," Jayne explained. "But you can always tell the difference between the real thing and any replicas. Look." She tilted the feather closer so I could make out the line of each individual barb. She was right, even a master would have trouble crafting something with this intricate level of detail. When I ran one finger along the feather's edge, I felt the faint thrum of magic.

Jayne slipped the feather back into her pocket. "It's yours upon delivery of spells and the signing of the contract."

I flipped through the papers she'd given me until I found the one detailing the parameters of our contract. Once signed, Grimm and I would not be able to tell anyone about Jayne and her troop, or their place of residence. In fact, the contract stated that none of our doings in the forest or related to the forest were to be spoken of.

I read it through, then looked over it again more carefully, giving Grimm a chance to finish reading over my shoulder.

"Very thorough," he said finally.

"I can't take any chances with the safety of my troop," Jayne said. "A good captain is always thorough."

"A good captain would not have led her people here in the first place," Grimm said.

Jayne's eyes widened in surprise and something like pain. A muscle in her jaw twitched.

"Well," she said in a brittle sort of voice. "We are none of us good all the time. Excuse me. The first watch tonight is mine."

It was fortunate we had only a few more planks to clamber across before we reached our tent, because Dodge looked tempted to leave us in the dark after that. He kept shooting murderous glances Grimm's way and muttered something unintelligible in reply when I bid him good night.

I waited until we'd ducked into our tent before punching Grimm on the shoulder. "What part of 'be civil' did you not understand? If someone's charmed your blankets to strangle you, I won't be at all surprised. Or sympathetic."

"And yet you're sympathetic to them?" Grimm asked, voice dangerously low.

The truth was, I did feel something remarkably like sympathy blooming in my chest. I'd expected a camp full of people like Mathias, but Camilla and the others didn't seem so bad. Just tired, and afraid. Yet it was impossible to forget Phade's limp, or that my brother's arm had been held in a sling the last time I saw him.

Scared people were capable of terrible things. I should know.

"Must we argue about this now?" I asked tiredly. "I know what they've done and you know what they've done, but we're here and we have a job to do. The sooner we get it finished, the sooner we can leave. Can we agree on that much, at least?"

It seemed we could. There was a small lantern in the tent that, when lit, cast enough light for us to look over Jayne's extensive list. I breathed a sigh of relief that all the Grandmagic spells she wanted were familiar to either Grimm or myself, so I would not have to explain that I could not compose my own. In fact, there were relatively few of them, with charms and cantrips making up the vast majority of the list. I found this perplexing until I remembered how the outlaws had earned their reputation—who knew how many powerful spells they had grabbed from the vault before they fled? They were able to stop monsters in their tracks but couldn't cast anything to keep themselves from freezing in winter.

In the end, there were only a few charms that neither of us could recall, but their purpose seemed straightforward.

"I can compose my own version easily enough," I said. "It will take more time, but not much. We should be able to get through the entire list tomorrow."

"All of them?" Grimm asked.

I waggled my eyebrows at Grimm suggestively. "Gracious, are you questioning my stamina? You needn't. I may be good for naught but writing frivolities, but I've a strong right hand."

"Glad to hear it," Grimm said dryly, but I noted with delight that his ears had turned decidedly pink.

"Most of these spells aren't even that taxing to scrive," I continued in a more serious tone. "I see now why my brother's friend was thinking of recruiting me during the trials. Everyone in the Coterie makes a fuss about Grandmagic, but when it comes right down to it, they mostly want charms to stop your socks getting wet or keep bugs out of your tent, and that's what I'm best at."

There was a long silence. Then Grimm said, "You had an offer of recruitment?"

I froze in the process of shuffling through the papers, cursing myself inwardly. "Ah, nothing official. I overheard something I shouldn't have at my father's party. Anyway, I'm fairly certain the scene I made that night changed his mind about my potential usefulness. Which is for the best."

"Is it?" Grimm asked skeptically. "You could be good at this, if you let yourself be."

I knew that. Of course I knew it. It's why I had made a fool of myself in front of that captain in the first place. It wasn't that I didn't want to say yes; I was just afraid of what would happen if I did.

"If there was no danger of me writing anything but charms, maybe you'd be right. But what happens when I get a little too cocky and compose something bigger than I meant to? In the heat of the moment, if I let myself get complacent, people could be hurt. You said it yourself, I'm reckless."

"With yourself," Grimm said. "Not with others. That town with the silver rot is certainly better off for you having been there. If it's harm that you're looking to avoid, you might consider that more people could suffer for your absence than some supposed bit of negligence you've yet to commit."

I couldn't think of anything to say in reply to that so I just sat there, blinking, wondering what this meant about how Grimm saw me. It felt very much like revisiting the judgment Grimm had laid upon me when I first told him I had no intention of joining the Coterie. Only this time, instead of resignation at my unwillingness, he was trying to peel aside some curtain long left closed.

I wished he wouldn't. It felt too much like kindness, which I wasn't equipped to handle. Not from Grimm.

Having said his piece, Grimm turned down the lantern and prepared to sleep. The tent was so crowded that our bedrolls lay scant inches apart, which I did my best to stop thinking about, with limited success.

I should have let us argue. It would have been better, I thought, to fall asleep with both of us fuming than to lie inches apart, trying not to imagine what it would be like to roll over and shatter that last bit of distance. Eventually I stopped trying altogether and let my thoughts do as they pleased, since the rest of me could not.

CHAPTER TWENTY-SEVEN

I awoke in the dark with a warm body pressed up against my left side and a hand covering my mouth.

"Please be quiet," Grimm whispered against my ear. "There is something outside the tent."

There were hardly any good options for what could be lurking outside at this time of night, but that wasn't the reason for my pounding heart. Sleep left me vulnerable, more apt to listen to the steady flow of magic under my skin, and every part of me wanted to lean into Grimm. I wanted to bury my face in the crook of his neck and inhale. I wanted to press my lips to the junction of throat and jaw and feel his pulse stutter. If I just let myself—

I licked Grimm's palm. It was both a relief and a disappointment when he jerked his hand away.

"Please behave," he said sternly, which did nothing to help matters and, in fact, illuminated rather more of my own inner psyche than I was comfortable being aware of.

Grimm wiped his hand on the front of my shirt and then moved away, which was what I had wanted and was also the worst thing to have ever happened. I did my best to blink both sleep and longing from my eyes before following him to crouch by the door of the tent.

Carefully, Grimm began to undo the ties holding it shut.

"Don't open it!" I whispered. The magic on the tent was faded, but it still provided some protection against the creatures of the forest.

"I think it's one of *them*," Grimm whispered back. "The outlaws. I heard footsteps." He finished untying the door, and we both leaned forward to peer through the sliver of parted fabric.

Sitting on the walkway leading to our tent was a dark shape. Nighttime rendered most features unrecognizable, but the crossbow he held was easy enough to place.

Mathias was outside our tent.

He sat propped against the railing, still and watchful. His crossbow was not pointing at anything, only resting by his side, but that was enough to make a shiver run down my spine. Whatever the reason he was here, I was willing to bet it wasn't in our best interest. Perhaps he was laying breadcrumbs to lead the monsters to our door.

I tried to lean forward for a better look, but Grimm put a hand on my shoulder to stop me just as the faint brush of boots over wood sounded.

Someone else was approaching our platform.

Grimm reached into his pocket and drew out several spells. Was this how it would be? Had the outlaws pretended welcome only to ambush us in the night? But when the second figure appeared, they sat down beside Mathias without even glancing our way.

"I had first watch tonight, not you."

Jayne's voice was faint but recognizable. She said something else, and Mathias's voice rumbled low in response. I couldn't make out a word of it.

Frustrated, I turned to Grimm. "I want to hear what they're

saying," I murmured, before leaning in close to hum a spellsong in his ear.

I had not used this spell since I was very young, listening at keyholes, but the tune came back to me quickly. There weren't words, just a melody for the magic to cling to. It was all I dared to cast as a child. If I took advantage of the situation slightly by drawing the last notes out longer than necessary, just so I could linger with my lips nearly brushing the curved shell of Grimm's ear... well, no one was to know but me. And perhaps Grimm, who looked at me a moment before beginning to cast. I was grateful it was too dark to interpret his expression.

He hummed, and what little sound the spellsong made was quickly consumed by magic.

There was a beat, then everything around us became loud. The sounds of the forest, each call of a night bird or whisper of wind through the trees. The rustle of Grimm's and my clothing. The unsettling creak of the platform we were on. It was enough to make you want to clap your hands over your ears, but Mathias's and Jayne's voices were there in the midst of it all, and with a bit of effort I was able to focus on them.

"There are ways around a contract, you know that," Mathias was saying. "And the Loveage boy likely has the right connections to find those ways. You know who his father is."

"Yes, I know," Jayne said. "But in order to do that, they would have to admit to making a deal with us in the first place, signing the contract of their own free will. I can't imagine that's something they'll be eager to do. It would be a black mark against them." She hesitated. "Besides, it's worth the risk. We need those spells, Matt."

"I know. But inviting them into our camp..."

"Who invited them? Not me. But they're here now, and I think they mean to cooperate."

"You're too trusting."

Jayne chuckled softly. "And you're too quick to think ill of people. You worried about the foragers who found us too, and look, nothing has come of it. The memory spells held. The contract will hold too. This will be the same."

Mathias was quiet for a long time before saying, "Yes." The single word was heavier than I'd known a human voice could sound. "This will be the same."

Jayne persuaded him to abandon his vigil soon after that. Grimm and I watched them go before securing the door and returning to our blankets.

I stared at the peaked roof of our tent, waiting for the listening spell to wear off. Then I said, "I'm thinking that we shouldn't turn our backs on that one. What about you?"

"I wasn't planning to turn my back on any of them. But yes, I won't be surprised if Mathias makes trouble for us."

Grimm's words proved true in short order.

We rose early the next morning, not wanting to waste valuable time. After clambering down the platform, we discovered the outlaws grouped around the fire, carrying on a conversation that ceased as soon as our arrival was noted.

"Are we interrupting something?" I asked.

"No," Jayne said, at the same time as Mathias growled, "Yes."

The siblings looked at each other. I sensed that a wordless yet furious conversation was taking place. Jayne was the first to look away, biting her lip.

"We were discussing our foraging routes for the day," Mathias said. He looked pointedly at Grimm. "You'll be coming with us."

"He most definitely will *not*." The words felt like they'd been pulled from me, an involuntary protest. There was no way

I could be apart from Grimm that long now. Even the threat of such separation was enough to make my insides twinge with phantom pain. I shuddered to think what sort of state I would be in with him miles away.

Mathias looked unimpressed by my fervor. "He will. There are only five of us, and someone will have to remain behind to watch over you while you're scriving. I don't fancy one of us being outnumbered."

"Then you'll just have to leave two people behind to soothe your worries."

"It's harvest season in the woods too," Camilla explained. "Two people guarding you is two fewer sets of hands for our labors. Two sets of eyes that we don't have guarding our backs."

"Just so," Mathias said. "And you're not in a position to be making demands. This is our camp. Our rules."

"That may be true, but if you take Grimm, you won't get any spells." I smiled apologetically, except I didn't feel apologetic about it at all. "I did try to tell you before, during our discussion on the riverbank, but I'm an absolutely terrible scriver. Spells run right through my head. Grimm, on the other hand, has a fantastic memory. So, unless one of you is capable of reciting the words of every spell on the list you gave me, he will be staying here."

Mathias squinted at me. "You're lying."

"I promise you I'm not. I really won't be able to function without him." I was being perfectly honest, if not entirely truthful.

"Dodge and I will stay with them," Jayne said, and held up a hand when Mathias opened his mouth to protest. "I fought off a snapbark last week, Matt; please don't insult me by implying I couldn't handle these two. One day with a few less hands will be worth what we're getting."

For all that they were a band of ragtag outlaws hiding in the woods, Jayne still spoke like a Coterie captain, and her crew responded as thus. Even Mathias let the issue drop with only a somewhat threatening final look in our direction.

I thought this was more for show than anything else. Mathias didn't actually fear what we would do while in their camp—he was worried about what would happen once we were allowed to *leave*. A part of me couldn't help but think that taking Grimm foraging would have been the perfect opportunity for Mathias to ensure he never got a chance to push against the bounds of our contract. I didn't think the other outlaws would help him, but Mathias was sneaky, and the forest was dangerous. All sorts of accidents and tragedies took place under the cover of those leaves.

The same idea seemed to have occurred to Grimm, for he pulled me aside and said, "We should get started as soon as possible. I'd like to be gone before the others return to camp."

I heartily agreed. And so, it was with little fanfare that Grimm and I sat ourselves down to begin our work. An empty crate became my desk, placed by the fire to ward off the day's brisk air. I took more care than usual rolling up my sleeves, so that I would not have to waste time rewriting smudged words. Grimm, in addition to reciting the spells I could not recall, was in charge of whisking away the spells as they were completed, replacing them with blank paper.

In Sybilla's tower, my attention had wavered constantly. But now, with our clock winding down, I was uncommonly focused. The promise of the feather being ours soon was like having the biggest, brightest carrot dangled in front of my usual donkey brain, allowing me to put my head down and plow through spell after spell without distraction. I was aware of things in the camp moving around us, of Mathias leaving with Camilla and Geraldine, of the steady sound of Jayne's axe as she chopped more wood for the fire, of Dodge, watching us surreptitiously from the garden, but all of that was distant compared to the sound of Grimm's voice and the sight of the words in front of me.

It was well into the afternoon when my hand began to ache enough that I called for a break. The rest of me ached a little too. Not the pain I felt when casting, but in the same way my muscles protested after I spent too long sparring with Agnes. Like I'd stretched myself. When Dodge showed up with food, I found myself ravenously hungry, as though I'd been running for miles instead of writing.

I was halfway through my plate before I noticed Dodge lingering. He was a tall man, but almost painfully thin. He didn't seem to know what to do with his limbs when he wasn't holding a sword or enacting some sort of task, and he looked awkward as he stood there, watching me.

"Something you need?"

"Yes," he said, looking relieved to have been asked. "There's a spell I would like added to the list."

"Something you didn't want to ask Jayne for?"

Dodge shook his head. "Something she would never ask for herself." From under his arm, he took a black bundle, shaking it open to reveal the tattered remains of a sorcerer's coat. The shape of it was familiar, as were the many pockets, but the dark fabric was marred by several slashes that nearly ripped the coat in two. The thin band of gold braid running around the collar and along the shoulders marked this garment as belonging to a captain.

I had wondered why Jayne was the only outlaw not wearing a sorcerer's coat. Here was my answer.

Dodge held the coat out to me, jaw set at a determined angle. "She said mending spells cost too much to be justified, but I know she misses wearing it."

I hesitated. Mending spells were, indeed, costly. Not quite Grandmagic, but fickle, specific work nonetheless. They had to be written with exactly what needed mending in mind, which meant that almost no two mending spells could be the same. I still had half the list to get through, and the coat was very damaged. When I held it, it didn't have the same weight that my own coat did. It would take me precious time to weave this back into a functional garment.

Dodge shifted back and forth on his feet and then said, all in a rush, "I heard what you said about her." He was looking at Grimm. "But she's not to blame for what happened. Jayne was—is—a good captain. Do you even know why we went to the library vaults in the first place? Do you know what we stole?"

Grimm looked back at him and said slowly, "I heard you stole many things. One of them nearly being my mentor's life."

Dodge's whole face seemed to fold in upon itself for a moment. Then, with visible effort, he collected himself and said, "Phade wasn't meant to be there. They surprised Mathias."

Grimm looked on the edge of saying something sharp in response, but I spoke first. "I heard you were looking for Titus's healing spell."

"That's right." Dodge pointed to the coat I held. "That happened when the Coterie sent our troop to refresh the spells on a portion of the barrier not too far from here. It's a common assignment. We could have cast those spells in our sleep, almost. But we didn't realize how far the magic in that section of the barrier had atrophied, and before we could finish the job, three monsters broke through. They killed our scriver, Mandin, and mangled Jayne so badly it was a miracle we got her back to the city alive."

I looked at the coat again, trying to imagine what the body that had worn it looked like after such an attack. All those loose threads and jagged edges didn't paint a pretty picture.

"The doctors told us there was nothing they could do. She was cut up too badly. Her insides all in pieces. But Mathias wasn't having it. He didn't ask us to come with him, you understand—he knew we had our own families outside the Coterie to think about. But we did anyway. We'd already lost one member of our troop; we were all willing to do anything not to lose another. And those spells were just sitting there!" Dodge's voice turned pleading, begging us to understand. "We asked first, but the Citadel said no, the spells in the library were being used for research. Years and years and no one has ever been able to do anything with them. They were meant to help people, but they were just gathering dust on a shelf! I'm not proud someone got hurt, but I'm also not sorry we took that spell to heal Jayne. Or the rest, to help us survive out here.

"She didn't have to come here with us, you know, after. She didn't do anything wrong, but when we had to run, she came with us. She's a good captain."

Dodge tilted his chin up, daring us to disagree.

I looked at the coat again. Despite its state of ruin, someone had still washed and pressed it, taken care of it even though they didn't expect it to be worn again.

"I'll add it to the list," I said.

Dodge's shoulders slumped a little. "Thank you."

He left after that, returning to his garden to pull up the frost-bitten remains of his stunted plants in hopes that their next year in this place would be better. And the one after that. And the next. Looking at him, I could finally parse the desperate gleam I'd noticed in Jayne's eyes when we first met, and the reason she had dared to lure us into the woods after: She was trying to make a home for the people who had loved her enough to throw theirs away.

"This changes how you view them, doesn't it?" Grimm asked.

"Maybe," I admitted. "Does it not for you?"

Grimm's lips settled into a thin line, but I knew him well enough by now to recognize this was the expression he wore when he was feeling stubborn rather than truly sure of something. "It shouldn't. They acted desperately and selfishly."

"I think perhaps it is not so uncommon, to be selfish in the face of a loved one's pain." I looked down at my own hands as I spoke, rather than watching Grimm's face. I could still *feel* it when he understood my meaning. That subtle shift as he sat a little bit straighter.

I waited for him to argue. To say that it was still wrong. Because it was, I knew that. Plenty of people had died while Titus's spell sat on that shelf. The only thing that made Jayne different was that Mathias had refused to accept her fate. He had thought he could do better. I knew that urge.

It didn't make me like Mathias, but I thought I understood him a little more. If you'd already traded your whole life for one thing, it made sense you would be protective of it. That's what Mathias was, unreasonably protective of this place and these people, as though he could stop bad things happening to them ever again by lashing out at any threat, real or perceived.

Grimm was still quiet, so I picked up my pen and a fresh piece of paper. There were many items on the list that should come before this one, but the coat was right there, and I couldn't drag my attention away from it now. The neat split of it, nearly all the way through. It would only distract me if I tried to return to the list without fixing this first.

I'd never had reason to write mending spells before. I had sent many items away for someone else to fix and replaced many others without thought of the cost. But some things weren't so easy to replace. As I wrote my first mending spell, I thought of how sometimes you wanted to make something right for a person without them asking, and what that meant.

CHAPTER TWENTY-EIGHT

The shadows of the trees were growing long in the golden light of late afternoon by the time we finished the last spell on our list. I had hoped to be done sooner, leaving plenty of time to put distance between ourselves and the camp before dark, but figuring out how to write a mending spell took even longer than I'd thought it would, and by the end of the process, I'd decided it was nearly criminal that the Fount didn't teach practical household spells. I likely wouldn't have paid attention even if they did, but Grimm would have, and then he could have given me tips.

At least Mathias hadn't returned yet. Our luck had held in that regard.

The spells were stacked and laid out for Jayne's approval. It was an impressive array, including heating charms, barrier spells, alarm cantrips, a nifty charm to purify water, various wards to protect the camp, and so many first aid spells that I lost count. There was even something they hadn't thought to ask for—a spell meant to amend the rocky soil of Dodge's garden. Grimm had recited it to me without comment, but I knew very well that it hadn't been on the list.

The coat and mending spell had been given back to Dodge for him to cast and gift to Jayne whenever he felt the time was right.

"Well done," Jayne said approvingly, once she had finished inspecting each pile. "I don't think I've ever seen anyone copy so many spells in a single afternoon." She raised an eyebrow at me. "Not such a terrible scriver after all."

"The contract is finished too," I said, handing that over as well. "We'll be happy to sign as soon as we have the feather."

"Of course." Jayne reached into her pocket and drew out the same delicately beautiful feather she'd shown us before. It gleamed gold in the light. She looked down at it for a moment, apparently hesitating, and my heart sank. Then Jayne reached into her pocket again and withdrew a second feather.

She pressed both of them into my hand.

"Matt would curse me for a fool, but at least I'm a fair fool. You've written us a fortune in magic. It's worth more than the cost of a single feather, and these things are hard to move anyway. No one in the smaller towns we trade with can afford them, and we dare not risk going into the city just yet. So here you go. Consider it both payment and apology."

The second feather had a bronze sheen but was just as lovely as its mate. They sat in my palm, surprisingly heavy for their size.

"Thank you," I said, oddly touched by the gesture, even knowing it came partially from guilt.

Grimm and I signed the contract with little fanfare and offered up our thumbs for Jayne to prick with her silver casting knife. Then, with both our blood smeared on the contract, she began casting.

Smoke crawled down my throat, and a tingling sensation tightened my vocal cords as the magic took effect. The feeling faded almost as soon as Jayne was finished casting, but I knew it wasn't gone entirely. Agnes and I had cast a contract on each other once—a silly thing meant to keep some secret, the importance of which had long since faded from memory. I did, however, remember how quickly my throat closed upon the words when we tested the effectiveness of our work. The same would happen to me and Grimm if we ever tried to speak a word of our time in this camp or the forest to anyone but each other or the outlaws themselves. Their secrets were safe with us.

"It will be dark soon," Jayne noted. "You're more than welcome to stay another night."

"The offer is appreciated," I said, "but we need to get back to the Fount before the harvest break is over, and we're already cutting things a little close." This was a convenient excuse to leave quickly. It was also true. The promise I had made to Grimm was stretched to its very limit.

"Ah yes, it's time for the trials. I remember." Jayne looked wistful. She shook her head a little and said, "It feels like a different life now. You both must be very anxious to get back to it. Well, if you're certain, I'll see you off."

We gathered our scant possessions and bid Dodge farewell before walking with Jayne into the woods. She moved assuredly, glancing back every now and again to make sure Grimm and I were following close in her footsteps. It was very much like the day we'd first ventured into the trees, only this time we'd only walked for ten or fifteen minutes before Jayne stopped and gestured to a faint path, winding through the ferns on our left.

"This is where I leave you. You said time is of the essence, and this path will take you back to the border much quicker than any other. Speed is sometimes a trade-off in this place, but you've been here long enough to get a feel for the dangers. Stick to the path and remember what I taught you." She looked each of us over and smiled. "Your trials will likely feel easy after your sojourn here. I have no doubt you will both find a place in exemplary troops."

The automatic refusal was on the tip of my tongue, but somehow it stuck there. Grimm was the one who responded instead.

"Thank you, Captain," he said simply.

Jayne went very still, then bowed her head in acknowledgment. "Good luck to you both," she murmured, before turning away and disappearing into the trees, with barely a whisper of sound to mark her leaving.

Once I was quite certain she was gone, I reached for the feathers in my pocket again—an instinctive reaction. Sorcerers' coats were spelled against thievery, and I was certain the one Sybilla gave me was no exception, but I couldn't resist the urge to make sure they were still there. They were, of course. Even in the dull light the metal feathers were brilliant, resting against my palm.

"Two chances," I said softly.

"We can't cast a spellsong out here," Grimm reminded.

"I know." Tempting as it was to rid myself of the curse immediately, it wouldn't do to draw the attention of whatever monsters were nearby with a song. "Here. For safekeeping."

I handed one feather to Grimm and slipped the other one back in my pocket.

Grimm looked at the bronzed feather in his palm, then back at me. "As soon as we're past the barrier," he promised, before stowing it away.

As we began to walk down the path Jayne had shown us, Grimm said, "Perhaps waiting is for the best. We'll still have to travel back to Luxe together after it's cast, but this leg of the journey will be more pleasant for you, at least."

"What do you mean?"

"Just that things will be different. With the curse gone."

I looked at Grimm, nonplussed. "So, what, you think that as soon as the curse is gone, I'm going to go from not wanting to be parted to not being able to stand the sight of you in the blink of an eye?"

"Isn't that how it was before?"

"Well, yes," I spluttered, even though that wasn't exactly right. The only thing I'd never been able to stand was Grimm's indifference. "Look, it's not as though I won't remember what happened. I've been here the entire time, Grimm. Me, not just the curse."

"There's really no telling how much the curse has altered your perceptions and actions recently," Grimm said. "We won't know until it's gone."

It bothered me. To think that he was crediting everything I had done over the past few weeks, good and bad, to a spell. As though he didn't know me, nor I him. It made me angry, in fact, that no speck of goodwill was allowed to be my own.

I stopped walking. Grimm did not realize for several more steps, and by the time he'd turned round, I'd already dropped my bag and begun pulling paper and quill from my pockets.

"What are you doing?"

"I'm proving a point," I said, shrugging my violin case off my shoulder so I could use it as a desk.

Grimm's brow furrowed. "Can't this wait? It will be dark soon."

"No, it can't wait because apparently you think I'm just some sort of—of mindless curse puppet! Which is, quite frankly, insulting considering the amount of time I've spent resisting getting my strings jerked by this thing. No, don't argue, just be quiet and let me work."

Aside from one short exasperated sigh, Grimm did just that.

This spell didn't take long. I'd spent quite a bit of time writing one that worked on a similar principle very recently, after all, and this version was more personal and therefore easier for me to scrive. I was intimately familiar with the item I wanted to mend, how it had once looked and felt, and how I wanted it to look now.

When it was finished, I blew the ink dry and handed the spell to Grimm. "Cast this."

"Loveage—"

"Just cast it. It will mend your sash."

Grimm's expression, which had been inching closer and closer toward irritation while he waited, slowly melted into confusion. His hand automatically flew to rest on his sash, which was tied in such a way that only a glimpse of the rough stitching that held it together showed.

"Hurry up," I said. "It will be dark soon."

Grimm stared at me a moment longer, a measuring sort of look. Then he untied his sash and laid it on the ground.

The indigo fabric was badly wrinkled, and with it laid out flat, it was clear that Grimm's repairs had suffered during our time in the forest. The stitches holding the pieces together were strained, and the fraying edges underneath showed—little tufts of silk coming undone.

I watched as Grimm read the spell over a few times silently. The telltale smoke began to pour through his fingertips.

On the ground before us, the sash quivered. Threads began to reach for one another, drawing closer and closer. The repair stitches that were no longer needed unpicked themselves and drifted away, while any loose threads of embroidery drew themselves just a little tighter, a little stronger than they had been.

It was fascinating to watch—something making itself right before your very eyes.

When the smoke cleared, Grimm leaned down and picked the sash up. He ran a finger over the faint scar in the fabric, a darker strain of blue that ran through it like a vein.

"Our sashes are meant to tell a story, right?" I said. "So, I hope you look at that mark and remember that *I'm* the one who fixed this for you, not the curse. And that will be just as true a few days from now when it's gone."

Grimm stared and stared at me. I'd surprised him. I could tell because, for an instant, his eyes flashed with the same astonishment I'd glimpsed after kissing him. Then he looked away and began to tie the sash back around his waist.

"I'll remember," he said.

The path back to Miendor was barely more than a line in the dirt for us to follow. It wove through the trees and undergrowth, growing neither wider nor fainter, simply continuing. Grimm set his eyes on the ground, making sure we didn't lose the trail and that our feet didn't come down on anything unexpected, while I set my sights on the trees around and above us.

We'd slept in this place, woken among its inhabitants, been surrounded by it for days now. A sense of familiarity had smuggled itself into my senses at some point, mixed in with the wariness.

I've heard it said that familiarity breeds complacency.

Grimm raised his hand for us to halt when the light began to fade. "An extra hour or two in the morning will be safer than pressing on now."

I nodded my agreement. All the scriving I'd done had caught up with me, and my limbs were heavy with the need to sleep. Even the thought of monsters lurking on the other side of our protective bubble wasn't enough to make the idea of lying down unappealing.

We began looking for a spot clear enough of bracken for us to comfortably spend the night as the light took on an even deeper greenish-gray cast—the Unquiet Wood's version of dusk.

"What about there?" Grimm said, pointing ahead to where a giant tree bordered our path. Its roots formed a nest of sorts, cozy to look at but probably a nightmare to rest your back against. I opened my mouth to say just this and then went utterly still.

It was as though Grimm had bidden me not to move, but no command had passed his lips. I was simply frozen midstride, mouth parted upon the words I'd been about to speak. My eyes were the only thing that could move.

"Loveage?" Grimm said, looking at me questioningly.

The fact that my lungs and heart were still working suggested that whatever had overcome me was only effective against my outsides. With great effort, I was able to relax my frozen vocal cords enough to emit a strangled sound of distress.

Grimm's eyes narrowed, and his hand went to his sword—and then paused there. And paused, and paused.

We stood looking at each other in the gathering gloom. I smelled smoke on the air. Not the comforting warmth of a campfire but the telltale metallic tang of magic.

"That's the second time this spell has been wasted on you," a voice said.

I immediately tried to look over my shoulder, but my neck remained locked in place. No matter. I recognized Mathias's voice perfectly well without being able to see him.

Footsteps sounded behind me. I had no choice but to stare straight ahead and listen to him come nearer, finally stopping right at my back. The closeness made my blood run cold. I would have shivered if my muscles allowed it, but this was the same magic that had rendered the wood kraken motionless—there was no question of its hold over me.

Grimm's eyes widened minutely in a warning I could not heed, right before cold steel pricked the back of my neck and everything went numb. Before, my limbs had been frozen, but I'd at least been able to feel them. Count each toe and each useless finger, locked in place. Now I couldn't feel anything.

Briefly, I wondered if Mathias had severed something vital in my neck and this lack of sensation was my body shutting down piece by piece. Then I remembered the mushrooms Jayne had stopped to gather.

We make them into an elixir to coat our weapons with, she'd said.

It was right about then that everything went dark.

CHAPTER TWENTY-NINE

I spent an indeterminable amount of time trapped in the dim space between unconsciousness and waking life—a feverish place that I disliked intensely. Occasionally shapes wavered in front of me, or I felt myself being moved, but I could do nothing about it. My eyelids remained gummily closed, my limbs felt either absent or extraordinarily heavy, and I bounced between awareness and black emptiness like a child's ball.

When I was finally able to break through this haze, I found myself lying on the forest floor in near darkness. A scuffling noise came from my right, but I could not move to look at it; the after-effects of whatever Mathias had dosed me with were too strong. My mouth was very dry and my stomach churned.

With all the speed of a snail, I finally turned my head enough to look around. The sound I'd heard came from Mathias, crouched next to me and tapping his dagger rhythmically against my boot. It was hard to make out much of anything else with my senses so befuddled, but I tried anyway, squinting into the forest's gloom and hoping for some sign of Grimm. I found none.

The tapping against my boot stopped as Mathias noticed my movement.

"Good, you're awake." He shifted, and now the dagger was

at my throat. "You have something I want. Return the feather, quickly, so we can be done with this."

"Where's Grimm?" I croaked. "If you've done something to him..." My voice trailed away. Any threat I made would be meaningless. My limbs were limp as a dead fish. And if Grimm was already...gone, there was no bit of violence that would make it right.

"I haven't," Mathias said flatly. "Some things are still distasteful to me."

I closed my eyes briefly in relief. When I looked at Mathias again, I forced my voice to remain steady and scornful. "You shrink from outright murder, yet not from kidnapping or drugging. Forgive me, but the lines of morality you draw in the sand are less than comforting."

"They're not meant to be. I've done many things I didn't want to do, and will yet. Just because I don't have the stomach to kill you doesn't mean I'll let you carry our secrets back to Miendor. The forest will take care of you."

"We signed the contract!" I protested. "We couldn't spill your secrets even if we wanted to. You let the foragers who found you go with just a memory spell; don't you think a contract marked with blood is more binding?"

Mathias only looked at me.

"Oh," I breathed. "You didn't let them leave either, did you?"

Mathias's head bowed, but the hand holding the dagger didn't waver. "They'd seen our camp, just as you have, and memory and contract spells can be undone. Not easily, maybe, but I'm sure the right scriver could find a way. I remember your name, Leovander Loveage. I knew your brother too. Not well, but we served a few missions together. He was very green then. Very talkative. Very proud of you, his younger brother, who he said was the most creative scriver he'd ever known. It made an impression on me. Such heartfelt sibling loyalty."

Damn Rainer, I thought despairingly. Damn his unfaltering good opinion of me. Better I had told him the truth a long time ago.

"I'm a terrible scriver," I said, knowing it wouldn't make a difference.

Mathias looked down at me with eyes that were both like and so unlike his sister's.

"Jayne would trust you, but I can't. If it's your lives or ours, I choose ours. I'll keep making this choice every time, so the others don't have to."

"She wouldn't want you to do this," I whispered.

"No," Mathias agreed. "That's why I don't tell her. Now, give me that feather back."

"Or what?"

The dagger pressed closer against my neck. I swallowed against it involuntarily and felt the bite of metal, then the warm trickle of blood running down to collect in the hollow of my throat. The pain was bright, almost grounding.

"That feather could feed us for a year, once we figure out how to sell it," Mathias said. "Or it could help us purchase new lives somewhere else, once the rest of them accept there will never be a place for us in Miendor again. I'm not leaving it behind to keep your corpse company."

"Very sensible. But I am under no obligation to make this easy for you," I said, very aware of how each word caused my throat to bob against the blade. "You know as well as I do how difficult it is to steal from a sorcerer's coat. Everything in my pockets will be just as much mine in death as in life. You won't get your hands on that feather."

My defiance was met with a blank stare. Had I thought Grimm expressionless once? I'd been wrong. There was life in his eyes. Warmth, even, if you knew what to look for. Mathias was the one whose face was cold, deadened. The annoyed twitch of his mouth seemed to come more from habit than any true feeling.

I was surprised when the dagger left my throat. Even more so when Mathias grabbed me under the arms and hauled my still limp body a few feet forward.

"Look," he said.

The ground dropped away steeply in front of me. Below was a small valley. No trees grew there, but in the center was a grassy rise dotted with luminescent night flowers. They were just starting to open, and the glow of their petals was enough to send glimmering reflections dancing across the water collected in a dip at the bottom of that small hillock. There was also enough light for me to see Grimm in the process of hauling himself out of that shallow trough, dripping and muddy.

He was half out of the water, still obviously under the influence of the same sedative that kept me so pliant in Mathias's grip. Grimm's hands sank into the grass, using it to pull himself laboriously up the hill. The process was neither dignified nor graceful.

Mathias held me up long enough to witness this, then let me slump over again. Hands free, he reached for the crossbow slung across his back. Carefully, silently, he loaded an arrow and pointed it down into the valley. At Grimm.

"Give me the feather, or I will shoot him."

I tried to shrug, found my shoulders weren't capable of that yet, and so was forced to speak. "You don't intend for him to live anyway."

Mathias's eyebrows raised. "That's very different than watching someone you love die, knowing you could have stopped it."

Ah.

There it was. The demoralizing icing on top of this disastrous cake of a day. Week. Month.

Mathias *knew*. Oh, not the whole complicated mess, but the core of it. Maybe all the outlaws knew. Maybe my caring for Grimm was written so clearly on my face at this point that anyone could have spotted it. I had jumped in front of an arrow for him, after all. I had stood there in their camp that morning and refused to let them take Grimm from my sight.

There was nothing I could say. Mathias cocked his head expectantly and looked down at me, waiting.

What else could I do?

With painful slowness, I reached into my pocket. My hand felt more like the idea of a hand than anything of use, but eventually I got my fingers to close around something cold and metallic. If by some miracle we escaped whatever trap Mathias had laid for us, there was another feather in Grimm's possession, but it still cost me something to throw this one at Mathias's feet. I let out a helpless breath when he lowered his crossbow to pick it up.

He inspected the feather carefully before tucking it away. Then he said, "I would have made the same choice," before casually rolling me over the lip of the valley.

It was fortunate the slope he pushed me down was relatively soft. There were no rocks to bump my head against and only a few blunt roots. Still, it was not a comfortable journey to the bottom, with my arms and legs flailing every which way and my senses scrambling more thoroughly than an egg. My violin case was still tied to my back, and it left new bruises each time I rolled over on top of it, digging painfully into my spine.

I landed at the bottom with a splash in blessedly shallow water. Perhaps it was the shock of cold, but when I moved to sit up, my muscles seemed to respond a little faster. Much good it did me now.

"Loveage?" Grimm squinted down the hill in my direction.

"Yes, just me," I answered. Half-wiggling and half-crawling, I splashed through the water until I reached the same rise Grimm had dragged himself up. The luminescent flowers I'd noted from up above were opening further now, casting everything in bluish-white light. It made it easy to see how steep the walls of the valley were. I could not spot Mathias.

My legs were wobbly as those of a newborn colt, but eventually I was able to stumble up the hill. Grimm was standing, too, when I reached him, though he leaned on his sword as though it were a cane. He looked me over and said, "You're bleeding."

"A scratch." I ran the back of my hand over the nick on my throat, and it came away red. "We have bigger problems. What is this place?"

"Don't know." Grimm looked around uneasily. I turned so that my back was to his and we could view our surroundings in a somewhat protected state.

At first glance, the valley seemed...well, it was actually quite lovely. Much more idyllic than any part of the forest I'd seen so far. The grass underneath our feet was soft and brilliant green, and the air down here seemed warmer by several degrees. The water I'd landed in, though shallow, was fresh rather than stagnant, a tiny contained stream that flowed round and round the hill we stood on. The glowing flowers around us made the air smell faintly sweet, like the first blooms of spring.

"This is alarmingly pleasant," I said. "But..."

But I didn't feel like we should be there. And not just because I doubted that Mathias had thrown us down into the valley to sit in the grass and braid flowers into each other's hair. One never felt truly alone inside the Unquiet Wood, but standing in the valley was akin to standing in the circle of trees around Sybilla's tower or walking into the middle of the outlaw camp.

"This place," Grimm said slowly. "It feels inhabited."

That was it. This valley felt owned, and not by us. We were unwilling trespassers.

I looked closer at the steep walls beyond the flowers' glow. There, off to my right, I discovered a patch of darkness that was not simply shadow. It was—

"A cave," I said, nudging Grimm's arm to get his attention.

Now that I'd seen it, there was no ignoring the yawning emptiness. It stretched to cover a space many times the width of my own arm span. I couldn't have touched the top of it even if I clambered onto Grimm's shoulders and reached.

Everything in the valley seemed subtly angled toward the cave, like a teardrop waiting to fall into its mouth.

"Over there," Grimm said, voice quiet. He pointed to the ground at the base of the cave, where specks of white dotted the grass at the edge of the water. At first glance they looked like pale stones, but the urgent note in Grimm's voice prompted me to look again.

Bones. They were bones, scattered all along the opening of the cave.

I swallowed hard, arms prickling with goose bumps even though the air was warm against my skin.

"Those foragers who discovered the outlaw camp, Mathias

found a way to get rid of them." I glanced over my shoulder at Grimm. "He said the forest would take care of us."

Grimm's eyes stayed fixed on the cave a moment longer, as though he were afraid to look away. "We need to get out of here." He reached into a pocket and drew out a piece of paper. It was a lightfoot charm, part of the stash we'd readied before entering the outlaw camp.

Without any prompting, I grabbed hold of Grimm's wrist so the spell would cover me, too, and held tight as the paper went up in smoke. Within seconds my limbs began to feel buoyant instead of ungainly. When Grimm nodded, we both jumped.

The spell carried us off the hill, toward the lip of the valley. We rose up and up, until we could nearly see over the rim—and then we crashed into a wall. That's what it felt like, anyway. Even though the air above us appeared perfectly clear of impediments, we had hit something, and hard. The force of our collision sent us careening back toward the ground. The fall tore us apart, and we each tumbled down the hill a little way from each other. I lay there, gasping, feeling the tingle of unfamiliar magic crawl across my skin.

"I think there's a lid on this place," I said once my breath had returned.

Grimm looked up at the deceptively empty air above us. "Mathias's doing?"

"I don't think so." The magic we'd touched didn't have the same flavor as a sorcerer-written spell. It blended with our surroundings too well, sinking into the thrum of the forest. I looked over at the cave again.

Something looked back at me.

A great golden eye, its pupil black and slitted. Then it blinked and was gone.

"Grimm! There's something—" That was all I had time to say before the black curtain of darkness inside the cave began to shift and the golden eye I had seen blinked open again. And then a second one. And another. Another. Seven giant golden eyes scattered across one giant face, moving out of the darkness toward us.

CHAPTER THIRTY

Grimm was the first to move. He scrambled to his feet and caught my arm.

"To the top of the hill," he said, and then pulled me along with him when I didn't move. I couldn't look away from the thing that had come out of the cave.

The monster was *massive*. It took up my whole field of vision, seeming to rise up above us as it emerged, even though we now stood at the highest point of the valley. It walked on all fours, like a bear, and was covered in rough-looking gray fur that hung off it in clumps and wisps. A few shocking white pieces of bone could be glimpsed in the tangled mass, like twigs might be woven into a nest. Vines curled down over its sides to brush along the ground, seemingly sprouting from someplace on the creature's back, too high up for me to see. Moss grew thick between the toes of its great paws, and its head was wide and wreathed in spikes of bark, like a crown. The monster's seven eyes were all different sizes, scattered unevenly above a wide, grinning mouth full of blunt teeth.

When the monster took a step, the whole valley quivered.

"Draw your sword, Loveage," Grimm said.

"And do what?" I asked incredulously. "Stab it? I may as well be armed with a needle for all the good that would do."

The thing hadn't even started up the hill toward us and yet it was nearly at eye level. The best I could hope to reach was a leg, and those were all covered with fur so thick that I imagined trying to cut through it would be similar to the time I'd tried to cut my own hair with a blunt pair of scissors.

My heart was pounding, rabbit fast. "I need time! I need time to come up with something. A spell, an idea, anything. I just need time; can you get me that?" I turned to look desperately at Grimm and found him staring not at the monster but at me, sword held loose in his hand like he'd forgotten it was there at all. His eyes were wide and far more helpless than I'd known Grimm could look.

"Do something!" I shouted, and he turned away, back to the monster, seeming to snap out of whatever daze had come over him. He reached into a pocket and pulled out a spell.

The paper began to smoke immediately, and magic shivered through the air as it took effect. Then the monster's eyes flashed, and Grimm swore at the same time as I felt the spell die.

I'd never heard him do that before. I wished I were in a better mood to appreciate it.

"What happened?"

"It ate my spell," Grimm said unhappily.

The monster cocked its head at us and blinked its eyes. Not all at once, but one after another, a wave of golden eyes opening and closing. There was something catlike about its attention.

I wondered if the monster had toyed with the foragers before licking their bones clean.

Here was the forest, come to take care of us.

This monster didn't seem inclined to move quickly (perhaps because it knew we had no way of escaping), but due to the size of its steps, it was already halfway up the hill we stood on. I was struck with an absurd urge to call out for it to stop. To plead for mercy. I wanted to tell the monster it could have me, but please let Grimm go because it was my fault he was here in the first place. I don't know why, but in my panicked state I thought that the forest had a sense of justice and might listen to this type of reasoning if only I could explain. But I didn't know how to bargain with a monster. What did it want? What could I give except my flesh? What words could I possibly use that a monster would listen to?

These are rhetorical questions, you understand. I didn't expect for them to be answered, by the monster, or the forest, or even my own panicked mind, searching for a solution. But funnily enough, I found I did have an answer to one of them: Monsters liked to listen to music.

When the monster took another step, my lips parted and I began to sing. The message spell we had sent Sybilla was the first thing that came to mind, because I had been desperate to talk with someone then too. I did not truly have the power to sustain such a spell, but I threaded what little I could into the casting of it and sang the words in the old language I most wanted the monster to hear.

Please, I sang. *Please listen. Please don't harm us, oh creature of the woods. Let me sing for you.*

My voice broke a little on the last note, and I winced, but when I looked up, the monster had paused its slow march up the hill. All seven of its eyes were open and alight with interest as it stared down at me, listening.

I was so surprised it actually worked that my voice trailed away, but it didn't matter because Grimm was there to fill the silence. He sang the same lines I had, only this time it was a true casting, with all the power of a fully trained caster. He poured magic into the melody until it rang out through the valley, and the monster—

The monster didn't move except to tilt its head to the other side, watching us through slitted eyes.

"Keep going," I said, unstrapping my violin case from my back.

Grimm sang the same line three times while I readied myself hastily. Tuning in front of an audience is always slightly nerve-racking, but it is exponentially worse when you aren't sure if the audience is about to lose its patience and eat you. Each minute adjustment seemed to me to take an age, but the monster didn't appear to care. It lowered itself down onto the hill so that its enormous chin rested right in front of us.

Finally, I nodded to Grimm, raised my bow, and began to play.

To truly explain the spell we cast would be to explain both music and magic, and neither of those things can ever be fully understood. All I know is that there are some moments when the two are allowed to overlap, and that's what happened for Grimm and me on that hill. I laid a tune before him and he followed. I scrived and he cast, but it happened all at once. Perfect harmony with only a monster there to witness it. Our captive audience.

It was a strange and wilder song than any I had composed before. I do not think it was the sort of spell that could ever be replicated.

Despite everything, the danger, the curse, all of it, listening to Grimm's voice still sent a thrill of pure happiness through me. The spell was meant to help us communicate with the monster, but it allowed us to speak to each other too, in a way. I knew him, for a moment, and felt known in return. A connection born of necessity, but beautiful all the same.

The monster closed its eyes and began to purr.

Who knows how long it could have gone on like that. Perhaps I would have played until my fingers bled and Grimm would have sung until his voice gave out and then the monster would have eaten us anyway. But that is not what happened.

Instead, when the monster began to purr, Grimm turned to look at me in a sort of astonished elation, and I grinned back at him, flush with victory—just as Grimm's voice faltered and his eyes narrowed on something behind me. I only had an instant to register that something had changed before Grimm leapt forward and wrapped his arms around me.

My violin screeched as he swung us around. Then everything went quiet. Over Grimm's shoulder I glimpsed Mathias, standing on the rim of the valley, back from wherever he'd been hiding and watching.

He lowered his crossbow.

And then, slowly, Grimm's arms dropped from around me, and he fell to his knees. The arrow in his back stuck out at an awkward angle, dark and wrong looking. Wrong because it had been meant for me. Mathias had thought he knew the forest best, yet I had found a way to speak to it. So he had decided to dirty his hands after all.

I dropped my violin on the grass and sank down beside Grimm. Beneath his coat was a spreading scarlet stain. The head of the arrow pierced through his shirt just below his collarbone. "Grimm," I said, breathless. My hands were raised, but I was afraid to touch.

Grimm took a shuddering breath. Then another. He opened his mouth, and one pained note fell from his lips.

"Don't," I said harshly. "No more singing now."

Hearing this, the monster's golden eyes opened. It raised

its chin and looked at us curiously, taking in Grimm's slumped form. Then it raised its eyes to where Mathias stood.

The monster growled, low in its throat. It was not a happy sound. It was the sound of a creature who had been deprived of something and, like a toddler with a lost toy or a cat with an escaped mouse, was unhappy with this change in circumstance.

Mathias took a step back. Then another. Then he turned and fled into the trees.

The monster gathered its limbs underneath itself and sprang. Whatever magic that kept Grimm and me from escaping did not bother it. The creature soared through the air and landed neatly on the lip of the valley in one graceful leap, then it disappeared into the trees.

Three breaths later, there was a scream.

I stopped paying attention after that because Grimm fell forward onto his hands, which made the arrow sticking out of his back all the harder to ignore.

"You should run," Grimm said. His voice was only a little raspier than usual, even though there was blood dripping down onto the grass. "Get out of here before it comes back."

"Ridiculous," I said numbly. "There's no place to run."

"The cave," Grimm said. "There might be another way out through there."

"Then we work quickly. I'm going to break off the arrow shaft so I can move you easier. And then we'll go through the cave together."

Grimm raised his head a little to look at me. Then he looked down at the tip of the bolt pointing through his chest and said, in a resigned sort of voice, "All right."

I did it as gently as possible, which was not that gently at all. I didn't know what I was doing. Maybe I made it worse. It was already pretty bad, but I was doing my best to ignore that fact. When I snapped the arrow off, there was no exclamation. No scream to split the night. This was Grimm, after all. Instead, there was just a small sound of pain, quickly aborted as he bit his lip and bowed his head.

"Sorry," I said. My hands were steady, but every part of my insides trembled. My thoughts were all shaken up inside my skull, and it made it hard to think. I moved to pull Grimm to his feet. "Come on. Slowly now."

We did go slowly, with many stops and starts. By the time we got to the bottom of the hill, my own shirt was sticky with Grimm's blood. By the time we made it to the cave mouth, his legs gave out beneath him.

"Can't do it," he said, and now I could hear the hopelessness in his voice. And the pain.

"First aid spells," I muttered, plunging my hands into my pockets. "If we cast a few, maybe the bleeding will stop long enough for us to get out." That wasn't how first aid spells worked, and I knew it. They would cleanse the wound, but they would do nothing for the blood pouring out of it or the piece of arrow stuck inside. Still, I found the spell paper in my pocket and pressed it into Grimm's limp hand.

"I can't," he said again.

"You're the most powerful caster I know," I snapped. "And the most stubborn. You're not unconscious yet, so just cast the spell. Or else I'll do it myself."

The threat worked. Grimm's lips began to move, a whisper of a sound as the paper went up in smoke. And then it was done and he was still lying there with a horrid, gaping hole in his chest, only a little weaker than before because I'd made him cast and, oh, it was going to happen again.

I had gotten it wrong. I'd thought I was protecting Grimm by making him cast, by making him go to the outlaws, by making him come to the forest in the first place. I had avoided Grandmagic because that felt safer than giving myself permission to try and fail. But the worst had happened anyway, and in fact it had very little to do with me at all. Maybe it never had. Now, when it was too late for him to cast it, I would have thrown aside all my carefully held precautions and tried to write the grandest magic possible—something big enough to heal Grimm's wound and stop the gentle seep of blood through his shirt, leaving him whole once more.

Instead, all I could do was take off the pretty green sorcerer's coat Sybilla had given me and press it against Grimm's shoulder. Then I let my knees buckle and slumped onto the ground next to him. The ground was rocky here, and a little damp from the water nearby. The mouth of the cave yawned behind us, beckoning.

"You should keep going," Grimm said. "I'd rather you weren't here for this anyway. You, of all people."

He meant he didn't want me here to watch him dying. That made sense. I had no bedside manner to speak of. He was the one in pain, and yet, selfishly, I was the one who wanted to cry.

"Too bad," I said. "I'm not leaving."

Grimm sighed. "It will come back."

"Yes, and then I suppose we will die together, and won't that just be a fitting end to this whole disaster. The two of us, dying side by side and wishing we were with anyone else." Except I didn't really. Grimm had to know that. It would break my heart to watch him die, and it didn't even matter if the curse was what made it hurt. The pain felt real, just as the love did. I was helpless to stop it.

"At least Mathias is dead too," Grimm said, so unexpectedly that I couldn't help but laugh.

"You're such a bastard. I've been trying to tell everyone that for years and they didn't believe me, but you are. It's actually delightful. Come on, now, let's move just a little bit. No, don't make that face at me. If we're going to die, we might as well paint a fitting tableau, rather than sitting in this puddle. That's it, slowly."

I kept babbling as I helped Grimm move just a little bit farther. We settled against the cave opening, where I could prop him up in a way that didn't press against his wound too badly. I sat down next to him and let him lean into my shoulder. Neither of us said anything about it. I kept talking, because there was nothing else to do, and I didn't want to listen to the sound of Grimm's breath becoming more labored.

"Have I ever told you that turning your hair pink is one of my most cherished memories?" I said. And, "My toes are freezing. If you were feeling just a little more chipper, I'd make you cast my clothes-warming spell. You turned your nose up at it before, but it would come in handy right about now." I rambled about everything that came to mind. Spoke every frivolous word I could think of until all that was left were truths I didn't normally utter.

Grimm was very still at my side. I nudged him with my shoulder, just for the relief of watching his eyes flicker open.

"Grimm. Hey, Grimm."

"Mm?"

"I never told you what I wanted to do after the Fount."

"You told me many things, each of them more unfitting than the last."

"Those were just ideas. They weren't things I wanted. They weren't real."

"What's real, then?"

"Sahnt. The house I grew up in. Where my mother grew up before me. I haven't been there in many years, and I always thought that, once I was finished with the Fount, I could go home. I want that. Someplace to keep all my instruments and drag Agnes to when she's been working too hard. Maybe my brother would visit. You could come too, if you want. You could teach me how to plant flowers like the ones you grow at home. I don't know what else I'll do there—get bored, probably, because you were right, I get bored very easily. But it will be mine."

Grimm tilted his head to look up at me. "Starflowers," he said.

"What?"

"I'll help you plant starflowers. They're hardy. Even you would have trouble killing them."

I huffed out a broken laugh. "That sounds nice."

Oh, how I loved him. So much so that it was like a living thing, growing through every crack in me. Too hardy to kill.

A little while after that the monster came back.

Beside me, Grimm did not move or make a sound. When I looked down, his eyes were closed. His shirt was a crimson blanket. I felt for the pulse in his wrist and found it fluttering still, but he did not stir when I called his name.

The monster sat at the top of the hill, licking its claws.

"Will you come for us now?" I called up to it, suddenly angry. "Will you end this?"

Two of the monster's eyes blinked at me, but otherwise it paid me no mind.

I shifted Grimm gently so that he was leaning against the cave wall rather than me, and moved around to kneel in front of him. His face was nearly as pale as his hair, and I—

My chest felt like it was caving in. There were spells capable of leveling whole buildings, I knew. I'd watched them in action once or twice and remembered the sight now. That inward collapse with only rubble left behind. A devastation.

Amid all of that, a single thought stood clear of the wreckage: I did not want to watch another person I loved die in front of me. Not without trying to stop it. Even if that meant breaking the only rule I'd ever followed.

I got to my feet and walked back through the water, up the hill to where the monster waited. It watched me approach with curious eyes but did nothing. In fact, when I finally reached the place I'd dropped my violin, its mouth seemed to stretch into a wider smile.

I picked the instrument up, turned my back on that blood-stained grin, and returned to Grimm. Then I began to play.

The music sounded lonely without words, but that was fitting. I was all alone, no one to scrive for, no one to bear the burden of casting. Whatever payment the spell demanded, it would have to come from me. Whatever the magic wanted, I would give, if only I could have what I asked for in return. I couldn't run from this, otherwise what would have been the point of it all?

Here is my bargain, I offered, speaking to the magic as though it might whisper something back into the unquiet of my own mind. *I shall scrive a spell like no other, and you will use it to knit his flesh back together. To make whole what has been torn asunder. And in return, you can take what you like. I accept the cost, only give me this.*

Then I began to cast.

Instantly, I felt the sharp bite of resistance. *You are not meant for this*, the pain reminded. *Dig your teeth in further and there will be no coming back.* This was no cantrip meant to summon butterflies, nor even a charm like the propulsion spell I'd dared cast. It was well beyond the invisible line I'd toed so often but never dared to cross. Now I teetered on the edge, and each note I played pushed me a little further forward.

I kept going, eyes fixed on Grimm. I did not think of the words to Titus's spell, could not have remembered them if I tried, though mine was asking for the same thing.

My chest began to tighten, as though in the grip of a vise. My heart beat faster in warning. Instead of listening, I focused on keeping my bow steady and played on, feeding more and more into the spellsong.

On the hill, the monster leaned forward, watching intently. Distantly, I noticed shapes moving around the lip of the valley, and more stirring deeper within the cave, but I did not stop playing. The monsters could listen. I was beyond fearing their interest.

On the ground, Grimm sucked in a harsh breath. The remains of the arrow burst through his chest and fell, bloodied, onto the cave stones. Then, like torn threads knitting themselves back together, the wound in his chest began to close. Slowly, so slowly.

Too slowly.

My heartbeat was frantic now. Something dripped down my face, and I tasted copper in my mouth. Pressure built in my head, greater and greater, until I was certain one more note would kill me.

Just when my vision began to flicker, I heard something—a low thrumming that was a feeling as much as a sound, vibrating up from the ground through my boots. I didn't dare look away from Grimm, but I knew where the sound came from nonetheless: the monster.

The monster was singing.

The casting was still mine, but its weight didn't rest solely on me. The monster's voice wove a strange harmony that I leaned on readily, watching with hungry eyes as the hole in Grimm's chest made itself smaller.

The monster's harmony grew louder and louder, until it seemed made up of many voices, rather than one, and the rising wave lent strength to my trembling arms. Like I'd been sipping from a thimble and now found myself swimming in a lake, water all round. I was able to continue playing for another minute, and another after that, until Grimm's skin was smooth and unbroken. Once his chest rose and fell in a steady fashion, I finally allowed the spell to end, finishing with a flourish.

As the last notes faded, I swayed on my feet and looked up.

Hundreds of eyes blinked back at me. There was the grinning, many-eyed monster, blinking at me from its place on the hill, but beyond that were more. They sat crowded on the lip of the valley, looking down, and perched up in the tree branches high above. When I turned to my left, I discovered more eyes glowing in the dark of the cave. They were everywhere, drawn by the spellsong. It was all their voices I'd heard, carrying me to the finish. Now they sat silently, watching. Waiting.

Moving delicately, so as not to fall over, I swept them a bow. "Thank you," I said. "You've been a great crowd."

Those were the last words I spoke for quite some time.

CHAPTER THIRTY-ONE

I will tell the next bit as it was told to me, since I was not in a fit state to make observations of my own. It's a good story—though Grimm's narrative flair is distinctly lacking—mysterious in all the right ways.

He awoke on the edge of the forest at dawn, right next to the spot we had first crossed the barrier. Both of our swords were missing. My violin, however, had been placed lovingly atop my chest.

Grimm said I looked like a corpse laid out and waiting for funeral rites to be cast, but I choose to believe I cut a more romantic figure than that. ("You didn't. There were flies feasting on the blood that had poured out of your nose. Your hands were folded over the violin. I was certain you were dead.")

Anyway, in the pale first light of day, Grimm spent a few moments racked with grief over my untimely death before he realized that I was, in fact, still breathing. A little. Then in a feat of strength born of true concern ("I still had several lightfoot spells in my pocket. It really wasn't that difficult."), he carried me and my violin all the way back to the town where we'd first met Jayne.

There was a great uproar once Grimm arrived in town. Since we were returning heroes, a place for my recovery was immediately offered up, and the best doctor in town was called in to see to me ("He's the only doctor in town, but I guess he did his best."), whereupon it was discovered I was suffering from such severe spell exhaustion that it truly was a wonder I *wasn't* a corpse. No one knew exactly what had happened, of course, because I stayed quite unconscious for a long while, unable to be moved. I'm told that Grimm didn't leave my side. ("We were staying in that same loft above the bar, Loveage. My bed was right next to yours. Where was I supposed to sleep?")

During that time, the trials took place.

We both missed them.

And then I woke up.

Have you ever had your insides scraped out, mashed with a fork, and then put back in place? That's certainly what it felt like had happened when I woke up. From my pinkie toes to the hair follicles on my head, everything hurt.

"Dear me, no thank you," I muttered, and forced myself back asleep.

My second foray into consciousness lasted slightly longer. I blinked my eyes open and croaked for water, at which point Grimm did a very poor job of tipping a glass of water down my throat. I would have mocked him for it if only I was slightly more coherent. As it was, I lay down with my front soaking wet and promptly fell back asleep.

It continued on like this for a while. Until, eventually, one day, I opened my eyes and was actually able to focus on the ceiling beams above me. They were vaguely familiar, but the setting still struck me as wrong. There weren't enough trees. I was meant to be in the Unquiet Wood, not someplace with a roof, lying underneath a threadbare patchwork quilt.

Everything came flooding back to me. Mathias's ambush. The monster. The arrow in Grimm's back. I sat up quickly and then immediately regretted it and sank back down onto the pillows with a groan.

"It's not recommended you move just yet," Grimm said. "But you probably know that now."

He was sitting in a chair to my right. After a moment or two passed and I was still awake, he got up and poured me a glass of water from the pitcher next to my bed. This time I was able to drink it by myself, though my hands trembled. When I gave it back to him, I noticed that the nails on each of my fingers were black as pitch. My left hand was the same.

"How did we get here?" I asked.

Grimm told me.

"Huh," I said. "I'm sorry about the trials. I really did think we'd be back in time."

"It doesn't matter," Grimm said, brushing the issue aside with uncustomary impatience. He was watching me intently. "What happened, Loveage? When I woke, you were half-dead and I... I didn't have a scratch on me. What did you do?"

I studied my ruined nails and the blanket covering my knees instead of answering right away. The events of the valley had a dreamlike quality to them. Had it all really happened like that? It felt a little too strange, even for someplace like the Unquiet Wood. But it did make for a good story, so that's how I told it to Grimm. Like it was a story that happened to someone else.

I thought he might comment on the fact that I had written a

successful healing spell. Or perhaps the bit where I claimed the monsters sang along with me to cast it. But when I was finished, Grimm looked at me and said, "You scrived Grandmagic?"

"Yes."

"And it worked."

"Obviously."

For a moment I thought he might say something else. Something congratulatory perhaps. But then Grimm's brows drew together in a familiar expression of dismay. "You *cast* it."

I smiled at him wryly. "It's uncharitable for you to look so angry, Grimm. After all, I saved your life."

"Nearly at the cost of your own."

"Hardly," I scoffed. "I'll admit I overextended myself a little, but it worked out in the end."

"Who do you think you're fooling?" he snapped. "You've been insensible for five days. You can't sit up straight, even now. The doctor said he'd never seen such a severe case of magical depletion and—" Grimm stopped abruptly midsentence and looked at me. "Thank you. For what you did."

"Saving your life," I prompted.

Grimm sighed. "Fine. Yes. That."

"It seemed only right, since I'm fairly certain that arrow was meant for me. Which reminds me, what on earth prompted you to get in the way?"

"You got in the way of an arrow for me. Before."

"Yes, but I was compelled to do so. Love spell, remember? What's your excuse?"

"I just reacted. Didn't really think about it."

"How impulsive of you. You've spent too much time around me."

"Yes," Grimm said with feeling. "I have."

"Oh!" I sat up a little straighter against my pillows. "The feather! Mathias took mine, but he didn't know about the other. I imagine it's been a bit of a chore for you, sticking close while I was asleep. We can cast the spell now."

I expected Grimm to protest that I was too weak for any casting. In fact, I was rather counting on it. It wasn't that I didn't want to be free, but I didn't know how it would feel. Our proximity was familiar by this point, and who else was going to hand me glasses of water during my convalescence? If the comfort I gained from having Grimm there with me was a lie, I didn't want to know it just yet. But this was a selfish thought. I at least had to offer. It wasn't just my freedom at stake.

"There's no need," Grimm said. "The curse is gone."

"What do you mean?" I asked, certain I had misheard.

"I removed it while you were asleep. I thought you wouldn't want to wait. Was I wrong to do so?"

"No, I just thought—"

I thought I would have noticed. I stared at Grimm's face and tried to make sense of how it made me feel. But I was too tired and sore to make much sense of anything at all. Besides, the curse was sneaky. It had hidden itself from me before.

"Where's the feather? I want to make sure."

Grimm looked away. "After I removed the curse, I cast Sybilla's counterspell on it. It was destroyed, feather and all."

I frowned. "You're sure?" Casting the counterspell while I was unconscious seemed uncommonly reckless of him, and he wasn't meeting my eyes. What had happened while I slept?

"The curse is well and truly gone," Grimm said firmly.

"We need to test it." It wasn't that I didn't trust him, but there was only one way I would truly believe the curse was destroyed. "Tell me to do something."

Grimm sighed and finally looked me in the eye. "Stand up, Loveage."

Nothing. There was no buzz of insistence when he spoke. No burst of joy at the thought of carrying out the action. I did, however, take great pleasure in answering.

"*No*," I said, then laughed aloud. "It really worked. We're free of each other."

"Yes," Grimm agreed. "We really are. That being the case, I think I'm going to go for a walk. The doctor asked me to fetch him once you were awake."

He got to his feet and headed for the stairs. The farther away he walked, the more certain I was there would be a pull, that strange discomfort I'd grown almost used to. But the restlessness was gone. Grimm was halfway down the stairs before I called out to him. He climbed back up again to peer over the railing at me.

"If the curse was gone, why didn't you go back for the trials?" I asked.

Grimm hesitated before answering. "Someone once told me that any sorcerer worth their salt could find placement without parading themselves around like a prize stallion. I don't think I would have been worth anything much at all if I left for Luxe before you woke up."

I felt it again, that little flutter kick in my chest, so faint I wasn't sure if it was real or simply habit. Echoes of the curse making themselves felt, like a phantom limb. It was so confusing that I became distracted trying to untangle what was real and what was remembered, and by the time I had decided to save such serious contemplation for another time, Grimm was gone.

We stayed in the loft above the bar awhile longer so I could rest on the advice of the best ("Only.") doctor in town. On the second day after I woke up, Phade arrived.

Grimm had written to them while I was still unconscious, but apparently even Grimm's word that my unexcused absence from the Fount was a result of near death (and not just me being my usual self) was not quite good enough for the Fount's academic board. Phade had been sent to *observe my convalescence.* A prospect that made shivers of dismay roll down my poor, abused spine.

The only good part of this was that they did not come alone. Agnes, blessedly familiar and beloved Agnes, came with them. Officially she was there to take notes for Phade while they assessed my condition and listened to the story Grimm and I had concocted about our chance encounter with a monster that had snuck through the barrier. She did this with a very dedicated air and only a few raised eyebrows at the parts in our tale where the truth grew most thin. But as soon as Phade and Grimm allowed us a moment alone, Agnes dropped her veil of professionalism and launched herself to sit on the end of my bed. Her hand sought mine and clasped it tightly.

"Your story is shit, I hope you know," Agnes said, voice rough. "The only reason the two of you are getting away with this—whatever *this* is—is because Phade has a soft spot for Grimm. And because anyone can tell by looking at you that the part where you almost died is true." She stopped and drew in a strange hiccuping breath, fingers going even tighter around my own. "Magic preserve us, Leo. *You almost died.* What actually happened out there?"

I opened my mouth to tell her, but I couldn't. My throat closed in on the words. We had made the outlaws a promise, and our contract with them held.

Agnes did not appreciate being left in the dark. She tried a myriad of ways to get me to reveal what happened, until my own frustration was almost equal to her own, and Mathias's certainty that I would find a way to break the contract began to seem less paranoid. But I was in no shape to give thought to such things just yet, and so the secrets remained.

"Is this some weird curse thing?" Agnes asked me eventually. "Has Grimm told you not to speak? Because if he has, I will—"

"Nothing like that," I said hurriedly. "The curse is gone."

"What? How?" Agnes's eyes widened comically behind her spectacles. "Don't tell me the sorcerer was *real!*"

But the contract had been very specific: *None* of our doings in the forest were to be spoken of, and that included Sybilla. My throat clenched up again at the mere thought of speaking her name. All I could do was smile apologetically as Agnes groaned in frustration. That story belonged to me and Grimm alone.

"My turn for questions," I said, before the lack of answers could become too heavy between us. "Tell me about the trials. How did you do?"

Agnes finally smiled. "Let's just say this," she said, sounding immensely satisfied. "Even if Grimm *had* been there, he would have had a hard time topping the number of offers I received."

"I'm glad," I said, even though I felt an unaccustomed twinge on Grimm's behalf over opportunities lost.

Agnes and Phade didn't stay long. The Fount was back in session, but I was not ready to make the journey back with them just yet, so Grimm and I lingered in the town until I could stand without seeing black spots. Even once I was cleared to travel, it was under very strict orders that I not tax myself by riding, and so Grimm used two of my remaining rings to buy the most comfortable carriage anyone in town was willing to sell to us. It was an ancient coach that required two horses to pull it and smelled strongly of goat for some reason, but at least there was plenty of room inside for me to nap as Grimm drove us back to Luxe.

I'd become quite fond of naps since our return from the forest. Even though I'd slept for five days straight, my body didn't seem to think that was sufficient, and I'd developed a habit of falling asleep at the drop of a hat. Midconversation. Sitting at the bar. In the bath.

There were a few other signs of my overextension. Or, as Grimm liked to refer to my adventures in casting, "consequences of poor decision-making."

My eyes had changed. They were a much paler blue than they'd been before, which I noticed once my hands stopped trembling enough for me to request a mirror for shaving. I'd also lost a tooth. It was toward the back of my mouth, thankfully, but it was definitely gone. And then there were my nails, which I was inclined to think were permanently blackened.

"You're lucky it wasn't worse," Grimm was fond of reminding me.

"Lucky I charmed a monster into being my backup singer, you mean," I replied smugly. "Do you think it was old seven-eyes who carried us back to the barrier, or one of my other admirers?"

Grimm said nothing to that. He'd said very little at all lately.

I had plenty of time to ponder the mystery of our deliverance, alone in the coach. I'd managed to smuggle a bottle of wine in under Grimm's nose, but truthfully the jostling didn't mix all that well with alcohol, so I spent most of my time sleeping or staring out the windows, remembering everything that had happened to us inside the Unquiet Wood. There was one thing in particular that I spent quite a bit of time thinking about. A question that had been poking and prodding at me ever since I awoke.

By midday, I'd had enough of thinking about it by myself. I wanted an answer, and I wanted it before we were back in the Fount. I banged my fist against the wall until the carriage rolled to a stop. Then I grabbed my violin from its case, opened the door, and walked around to look up at Grimm.

"You once said you were willing to risk the danger of casting Grandmagic written by me. Is that still true?"

Grimm's eyes settled on the violin in my hand. "You want to write a Grandmagic spellsong."

I nodded. "I need to know if what happened in the woods was just a fluke. I don't think it was. Everything in my heart says that something was rearranged by what happened that day, but I have to know for sure."

"All right," Grimm said, simple as that.

"I could be wrong," I warned. "This spell might set your hair on fire or fling you twenty feet in the air."

"I've healed from worse," Grimm said mildly, before getting down from the coach.

We walked a little way away from the road, just to be safe. The sun hung high and bright in the sky. Probably one of the last truly warm days of the season.

"When was the last time you cast a rain spell, Grimm?" I asked.

He looked at me, eyes dark. "You know the answer to that."

I nodded, then tucked my violin snugly beneath my chin and said, "Well, I suppose this will be a second chance for the both of us, then."

I'd been thinking of what words to use as we drove, and they came to my lips easily now. The tune they went with was lilting and bright. This was not a day for storms; rather it called for downpours. Here and then gone, leaving the world clean.

Grimm listened to the song once before beginning to sing. There was no hesitation in his voice. If there was fear, it belonged to me, waiting, *waiting* for the song to end and to see what would happen.

Lightning did not strike anyone down.

No bones were broken.

No one died.

All that happened was that clouds began to roll in, swift and dark. I barely had time to put my violin safely away before they burst over us in a shower of rain and we stood there, getting drenched. Grimm held up a hand and let the water collect and run over his palm.

"I'd like to keep doing this," I said abruptly. "Writing spell-songs, I mean. If you'll keep casting them, that is."

Grimm's hand fell. I had become fairly adept at reading his face over the past few weeks, but it was hard for me to make sense of his expression now. I thought it almost looked angry, but I genuinely couldn't find anything offensive in what I'd said.

"We're free of each other now. You said so yourself. Why would you want to change that?"

I did remember saying something along those lines, but I'd meant it in a different way than it sounded on Grimm's lips, harsh and final.

"That doesn't mean we're not still . . ." The word *friends* was on the tip of my tongue, but I suddenly doubted that was what he would want to hear.

"Still what?"

"Partners," I blurted out. "In Duality class. We still need to work together there for the remainder of the year. And we're good at this, are we not?"

Grimm's eyebrows rose a fraction. "Are you saying you're going to give me something to work with besides cosmetic charms and cantrips that call insects?"

I closed my eyes and tipped my face up into the rain. A part of me was still waiting for it to go terribly wrong. But even though my heart pounded, it wasn't entirely from terror.

I scrubbed a hand over my face and turned to Grimm. "I can't promise to never slip a charm or cantrip into the mix, but I'm trying to branch out. And I think..." I held up my own hand and let the water pool there. I had done that. "I think I want this."

Grimm looked at me sharply. "Want what?"

"The same thing you do. To be a part of things. To better them, somehow. Isn't that strange?" I grinned at him. "All our years of opposition, and yet we both want the same thing, in the end."

"You've changed your mind about joining the Coterie?"

"I'm considering it," I admitted. "I healed you, Grimm. I'm not sure I can write something like that again, but I have to at least try." I needed to learn more. I needed experience and practice writing the sort of magic I'd avoided for so long. And I really did *want* it. I could admit that now. I'd denied myself the Coterie the same way I'd denied myself Grandmagic, because I thought I wasn't fit for such things.

Now I wasn't so sure.

I let the rainwater run from my hand and said lightly, "Maybe I'll finish fifth tier and get myself recruited into the most illustrious Coterie troop I can find. Make a name for myself by writing the grandest spells you can imagine and become exactly the sort of sorcerer everyone's always telling me to be."

Grimm shook his head, expression sober. "You have a rebel heart, Leovander Loveage. You will never be anyone but yourself."

Somehow, this did not feel like the condemnation it once might have been. It almost sounded like praise, though Grimm did ruin the effect slightly by adding, "Besides, you'll need to work very hard to get recruited by *any* troops now that we've missed the trials."

"I can put in effort when properly motivated. And I like a challenge. What do you say, Grimm?" I asked, feeling oddly nervous. "Would you like a little help on your quest to change the Coterie from the inside? You know how much I love disrupting things."

Grimm's silver hair was plastered against his forehead and cheeks. He had to blink water from his eyes when he looked at me. "Are you sure that's what you really want? You told me before that you wished to leave when you were done with the Fount. To go to your mother's estate."

"You remember that?" I'd thought Grimm was nearly insensible while I babbled in his ear.

He nodded. "I remember."

"Well," I said. "It's not that I don't still want that too, but . . . things change, don't they?"

I meant me. I meant the rain pouring down on us and where it came from. I meant Grimm a little bit, breaking rules and standing there beside me.

"I suppose they do," he agreed quietly.

We walked back to the carriage after that, both of us soaked through. The rain was already beginning to taper off, sun peeking through the clouds. I climbed up onto the bench next to Grimm rather than going to sit inside.

"You should rest," Grimm said.

"I will," I told him. "In a little while." Inside the coach was safe and warm, but I wanted to catch the last of the raindrops as they fell.

I wanted to look down the road and see where I was headed.

The story continues in...

Book TWO of the
Wildersongs

Acknowledgments

The idea for this book came to me a long time ago, but I didn't begin writing it in earnest until March of 2020. In many ways it was a time of great isolation, yet I never felt alone during the process of bringing *Sorcery and Small Magics* to life. There are a host of people I have to thank for that.

I am forever grateful to my wonderful agent, Allegra Martschenko. Thanks for your unwavering enthusiasm and guidance, and for letting me freak out with you so I can pretend to be cool with everyone else.

Many thanks to my incredible editors, Brit Hvide and Emily Byron, for championing this quietly whimsical, stubborn slow burn of a book. It's been a dream come true. Thanks also to Angela Man, Tiana Coven, Lisa Marie Pompilio, Alexis Kuzma, and the rest of the fantastic team at Orbit, without whom none of this would be possible.

I was fortunate enough to have a handful of early readers and friends who helped me tremendously along the way. Shout-out to Cate Baumer and Chandra Fisher, who told me it was ready when I most needed to hear it. To Kat Hillis, for being Leo and Grimm's biggest fan and keeping me writing even when I would have rather been watching dramas. To Danielle Murray, whose keen observations swept in at the perfect moment. To the whole crew of lovely folks who make up my Fork Fam, for being an endless source of both wisdom and hilarity. And extra thanks and appreciation to Hayley Stone, Lee O'Brien, and Karen McCoy, my faithful companions and sounding boards throughout the drafting process. This story would not be what it is today without your help.

Thank you to my family, who I feel so lucky to have in my corner, now and always. My dad, who has always cheered for every accomplishment, big and small. Joe, whose voice is closest to my own, and who therefore understands what I'm trying to say best of all. Tori, for every bit of fierce enthusiasm and for bringing me cake and flowers. And Archie, who does not help me write at all but is my favorite distraction.

To Dustin (WTFID?), for being by my side through every up and down and listening to me read not one but two versions of this book aloud: Thanks for loving and supporting my frenzied book brain. Let's plant flowers together forever.

And to my mom, who taught me to love stories by reading so many aloud to me: You introduced me to countless magical worlds and you made *our* world magical too. I love you. I miss you. I think you would like the stories I'm telling.

extras

orbit

meet the author

Maiga Doocy

MAIGA DOOCY lives in a house where the people are out-numbered by cats, has a serious tea habit, and loves sad songs. She likes to write stories that are full of bittersweet longing and as much unexplainable magic as she can get away with. *Sorcery and Small Magics* is her debut novel.

Find out more about Maiga Doocy and other Orbit authors by registering for the free monthly newsletter at orbitbooks.net.

if you enjoyed
SORCERY AND SMALL MAGICS

look out for

THE HONEY WITCH

by

Sydney J. Shields

The Honey Witch of Innisfree can never find true love. That is her curse to bear. But when a young woman who doesn't believe in magic arrives on her island, sparks fly, in this deliciously sweet debut novel of magic, hope, and love overcoming all.

Marigold Claude has always preferred the company of meadow spirits to the suitors who've tried to woo her. So when her grandmother whisks her away to the tiny isle of Innisfree with an offer to train her as the next Honey Witch, she accepts immediately. But her newfound magic and independence come with a price: No one can fall in love with the Honey Witch.

Then Lottie Burke, a notoriously grumpy skeptic, shows up on her doorstep, and Marigold can't resist the challenge to prove to her that magic is real—even at the risk of losing her home and her heart.

Part One

It is the spring of 1831, and Althea Murr celebrates her hundredth birthday alone.

She sits beneath the wisteria tree, her orange cat curled in her lap. The bee-loud glade sings for her, a song worthy of the one hundred years she has lived.

A century of honey, earth, stone, and sky.

Of blood, venom, blooms, and ash.

She thinks of everything that was, and everything that could have been.

The stars peek through the twilit sky, asking her to make a wish, but she has none.

She has no wants, no needs, and no wishes that could be granted in the short time that she has left.

The springtime buds that decorate the earth remind her of childhood when she wanted to grow up to be a flower. She had told her mother, "One day, I will be a rose. And I will plant myself somewhere so beautiful that I will never want to leave."

Her mother laughed. "And what if someone wants to pluck you?"

"That is what the thorns are for," she said.

Since then, she has bloomed, she has thorned, and now she is happily withered. So, instead of granting her a wish, the spirits send her a message. From the sky descends a crow, an omen, a warning—she knows that death is near.

And thus, she has much to do.

Chapter One

Saying no—even thirteen times—is not enough to avoid tonight's ball. On this unfortunately hot spring day, Marigold Claude is trapped between her mother and younger sister, Aster, in a too-tight dress, in a too-small carriage. It's her sister's dress from last season, for Marigold refuses to go to the modiste to get fitted for a new one; an afternoon of being measured and pulled and poked is an absolute nightmare. Her blond hair is pulled up tightly so that her brows can barely move and her eyes look wide with surprise. Her father and her younger brother, Frankie, sit across from them, likely feeling quite lucky to have the luxury of wearing trousers instead of endlessly ruffled dresses. A bead of sweat snakes down the back of her neck, prompting her to open her fan. It's as if the more she moves, the larger the dress becomes. With every flap of her fan, the ruffles expand into a fluffy lavender haze. She is almost sure that she is suffocating, though death by silk might be preferable to the evening ahead.

This ball is the first event since her twenty-first birthday, so now she has a few months to marry before she is deemed an old and insufferable hag. The ride is far too short for her liking, as with any ride to another Bardshire estate. The opulent village was a gift from the prince regent himself; it is the home of favored artists from all over the world, including painters like Marigold's father. Sir Kentworth, a notable composer, is hosting tonight's event as an opportunity to share his latest works. Though the occasion is more of a way to hold people hostage for the duration of the music, and force them to pretend to enjoy it.

The carriage door flies open upon arrival, the wind stinging Marigold's eyes, and she is the last to exit. Under different circumstances, she would have feigned illness so she did not have to attend, but her younger siblings are an integral part of the program this evening, and Frankie requires her support to manage his nerves before his performance. He's been practicing for weeks, but the melodies of Sir Kentworth's music are so odd that even Frankie—a gifted violinist who has been playing since his hands were big enough to hold the instrument—can hardly manage the tune. Aster will sing Sir Kentworth's latest aria, even though the notes scrape the very top of her range. Since their last rehearsal, Aster has been placed on vocal rest and openly hated every minute, her dramatic body language expressing her frustration in lieu of words. That rehearsal was the first time Marigold saw the twins struggle to use their talents, making her feel slightly better about having none of her own. She's spent her entire life simply waiting for some hidden talent to make itself known. So far, nothing has manifested, meaning she has only the potential to be a wife, and even that is slipping by her with every passing day. Her back is still pressed firmly against the carriage bench. If she remains perfectly still, her family may somehow forget to usher her inside, allowing her to escape the event altogether.

There are countless things she would rather be doing. On a night like this, when the blue moon is full and bursting with light like summer fruit, she wants nothing more than to bathe in the moon water that now floods the riverbanks. She wants to sing poorly with no judgment, wearing nothing but the night sky. And like all nights that are graced by a full moon, she has a secret meeting planned for midnight.

"Marigold, dear, come along," her mother, Lady Claude, calls.

Dammit, she thinks. *Escape attempt number one has failed.* She huffs as she slides out of the carriage, declining the proffered hand of the footman at her side. Her feet hit the ground with an impressive thud.

"Do try to find someone's company at least mildly enjoyable tonight," Lady Claude pleads. "You're not getting any younger, you know."

She adjusts her corset as much as she can without breaking a rib and says, "I do not want any company other than my own, and I do not intend on staying a moment longer than required."

Her mother has long tried (and failed) to turn Marigold into a proper Bardshire lady. The woman has introduced her to nearly every person even remotely close to her in age, hoping that someone will convince her that love is a worthy pursuit. So far, they've all been bores. Well, all except one—George Tennyson—but Marigold will not speak of him. He will most certainly be here tonight, and like always, they will avoid each other like the plague. Their courtship was a nightmare, but there is great wisdom to be found in heartbreak. Call it intuition, call it hope, or delusion, but Marigold knows she is not meant to live a life like that of her mother.

Rain whispers in the twilight, waiting for the perfect moment to fall. Dark clouds swirl in the distance, reaching for the maroon sun. This oppressive heat and the black-tinged sky remind her of a summer, almost fifteen years ago now. The summer they'd stopped visiting the only place in the world where she felt normal—her grandmother's cottage.

She'd always loved visiting Innisfree as a child. It was like a postcard, with fields of thick, soft clover to run through, gnarled trees to climb, and wild honeybees to watch tumble lazily over the wildflowers. And best of all, there was her grandmother. Althea was a strange woman, speaking in riddles and rhymes and sharing folktales that made little sense, but it didn't matter. Marigold didn't need the right words to understand that she and her grandmother were the same in whatever they were. She closes her eyes tightly, trying to remember the last summer she'd visited, but it's fuzzy with age.

She had made a friend—a boy her age who was dangerously curious and ferociously bright. He would come in the morning with his mother, and as the ladies sipped their tea, he and Marigold would run among the wildflowers together. She thinks of him often, dreaming of their mud-stained hands intertwined, though she does not remember his name. After what happened that day, she doesn't know if he survived.

She remembers the cottage window—always open, always sunny. Most of the time it could have been a painting, the world behind the glass as vivid as soft pastels. That day, she and her friend were told to stay inside. They snacked on honeycomb and pressed their sticky cheeks to the window, searching for faces in the clouds until the storm consumed the sky and turned the world gray. Her grandmother had run outside and disappeared into the heart of the storm, and the boy tried to grab her hand before he disappeared from her side. She remembers her mother's cold fingers pulling on her wrist, but everything else is blurry and dark.

For years, she has been asking her mother what happened. What was the gray that swallowed the sky? And what happened to the boy who tried to hold on to her hand? Her questions have gone unanswered, and they have never returned to her grandmother's cottage. She still questions if any of these memories are real. But her mother's hand bears the beginnings of a white scar peeking out from a lace glove. The truth is there, hidden in that old wound.

The other attendees spill out of their carriages in all their regalia. They stand tall and taut like they are being carried along by invisible string. Just before they walk inside, her father pulls her into an embrace and whispers in her ear, "Come home before the sun rises, and do not tell a soul about where you are running off to."

He winks, and Marigold smiles. Her father has always been kind enough to aid in her escape by distracting her mother at the right moment.

"I never do," she assures him. It's already too easy for people to make fun of a talentless lady trapped in Bardshire. She and everyone else know that she is not a normal woman. She sometimes wonders if she is even human, often feeling a stronger kinship with mud and rain and roots. Every day, she does her absolute best to play a part—a loving daughter, a supportive sister, a lady of marital quality. But in her heart, she is a creature hidden beneath soft skin and pretty ribbons, and she knows that her grandmother is, too. These are the wild women who run barefoot through the meadow, who teach new songs to the birds, who howl at the moon together. Wild women are their own kind of magic.

She is standing in between her twin siblings when Aster, stunning with her deep blue dress against her pale white skin, is immediately approached by handsome gentlemen. Aster was not meant to come out to society until Marigold, as the oldest, was married. After a time—really, after George—Marigold abandoned all interest in marriage, and the sisters convinced their parents to allow Aster to make her debut early. It was a most unconventional decision, one followed by cruel whispers throughout Bardshire at Marigold's expense, but she has lost the energy for bitterness. She tried love, once. It didn't work, and it is not worth the risk of trying again with someone new. Now Aster is the jewel of the Claude family, and Marigold is simply resigned.

Frankie clings to her side, his hands clammy with pre-performance nerves. She flares her fan and waves it in front of his face, calming the redness in his cheeks.

"Thank you, Mari," he says with a shaky voice. She hands him a handkerchief to dry off his sweaty palms.

"You're going to be fine, Frankie. You always are."

He scoffs. "This music is nearly impossible. It was not written for human hands."

"Well, we'll get back at him next time when you have fewer eyes on you," she says with a wink. She and Frankie have always found some way to playfully disrupt events. Snapping a violin string so Frankie won't have to play. Pretending to see a snake in the middle of the dance floor. Stealing an entire tray of cake and eating it in the garden. Anything to escape the self-aggrandizing conversations. She leads Frankie through the crowd while noting the tables lined with sweets and expertly calculates how much she'll be able to eat without any snide remarks. She can probably get away with three—the rest, she'll have to sneak between songs.

The dance floor has been freshly decorated with chalk drawings of new spring flora. The art perfectly matches the floral arrangements throughout the ballroom. Decor of such elaborate design is not common, but Sir Kentworth is known for his flair, and he is exceptionally detail-oriented. His signature style shows in his music as well, though his latest works are growing increasingly baroque, as are his decorations. As they stroll toward the banquet table, Marigold catches the eye of her mother, who is leading a handsome young man toward her. She tries to increase her pace, but the crowd around her is impenetrable. In a matter of seconds, she's trapped in the presence of her mother and the young man while Frankie leaves her alone, set on taking all the good desserts.

Lovely. My freedom is thwarted, once again.

As she turns away from her brother, she flashes a vulgar gesture at him behind her back. Her mother places a hand on each of their shoulders.

"Marigold, this is Thomas Notley," her mother says. She knows this name—Sir Notley was the architect who designed the remodels of the Bardshire estates after they were purchased from the landed gentry. The man in front of her is the famed architect's grandson. They have seen each other many times, across many rooms, but this is their first proper introduction.

Her mother looks up at Mr. Notley. "And this is my beautiful daughter, Marigold Claude."

"It is an honor to be introduced to you, Miss Claude." His smile is bright and earnest as he takes her hand and kisses it. His cropped hair allows the sharpness of his facial features to be fully admired, while his warm brown skin glows in the yellow light of the ballroom. He is extremely handsome, but like Marigold, he is plagued with a very poor reputation as a dancer. It is likely that not many people will be fighting to add his name to their dance card, despite his good looks.

"The pleasure is mine," she replies with a clenched jaw. It is embarrassing enough to be her age with no prospects or talents, but her mother makes it so much worse with these desperate matchmaking attempts.

"Well, I'll leave you two to dance," her mother says as she pushes them slightly closer together and disappears into the crowd. Marigold glares in the direction that her mother left. Normally, she at least gets one bite of something before she takes to the ballroom floor. "Mr. Notley," she says, "I know not what my mother said to you, but please do not feel obligated to dance with me. I should warn you I have no rhythm."

"Nor do I. My talents are better suited for sitting behind a desk and drawing architectural plans," he says with a smile.

"Then who knows what disaster will take place if we take to the floor together? It may become dangerous for all others involved."

"I disagree, Miss Claude. I believe we'll make a perfect pair."

She often has trouble filling up her dance card, and she must get out of this place as quickly as possible, so she devises a plan to make this work in her favor. Softening her demeanor, she looks up at him through her thick lashes. "All right then, Mr. Notley. Would it be too bold of me to request that you have all my dances tonight?"

He looks stunned, but then a pleased smile inches across his face. This proposition is perfect—she doesn't have to wait for anyone else to ask for a dance or feign interest in multiple stuffy artists all night long. If she can hurry through the obligations of the evening with this gentleman, she'll be able to leave with plenty of time for her own nightly plans. Now, if she can simply pretend to have a good time long enough to get through her dance card...

"I would be honored. Shall we make our way to the floor?"

She pauses, for she absolutely requires a scone while they are still warm and fresh.

"Might we get refreshments first? We have a lot of dancing ahead of us," she says sweetly, and he obliges as he leads them to the table. The luxurious scents of ginger, cinnamon, and cardamom grow stronger as they approach.

"I am guessing you are a fan of sweets?" he says with a bewildered laugh.

She nods as the excitement falls from her face, replaced by embarrassment. "Eating sweets is perhaps my only talent."

"I was not teasing. Please forgive me if it felt as if I were. I am known to have a sweet tooth as well. Shall we select our favorites and share them with each other?" he says politely, and his idea is delightful—less dancing, more eating. The pair find themselves stuffing each other's faces with scones and marmalades and other small nameless cakes that are too tempting to ignore. She removes her glove with her teeth and picks up a small square of honey cake. The white icing is covered in a thick layer of warm honey that drips onto its sides, so it must be eaten quickly.

"Open," she commands, and he almost cannot stop smiling long enough to allow her to feed him, but he does, and she drops the cake into his mouth before taking her fingers to her lips and sucking off the dripping honey.

"That is fantastic," he says with a full mouth, and she laughs as she nods in agreement.

"People always overlook the honey cake because it's messy and impossible to eat with gloves. But that never stops me. I refuse to walk past a tray of honey cakes without tasting them. They have always been my favorite, and the only part of these events that I actually enjoy," she says as she takes another and pops it into her mouth, savoring the sweet golden liquid that coats her lips.

orbit

Follow us:

📘 **/orbitbooksUS**

𝕏 **/orbitbooks**

▶ **/orbitbooks**

Join our mailing list
to receive alerts on our
latest releases and deals.

orbitbooks.net

Enter our monthly
giveaway for the chance
to win some epic prizes.

orbitloot.com